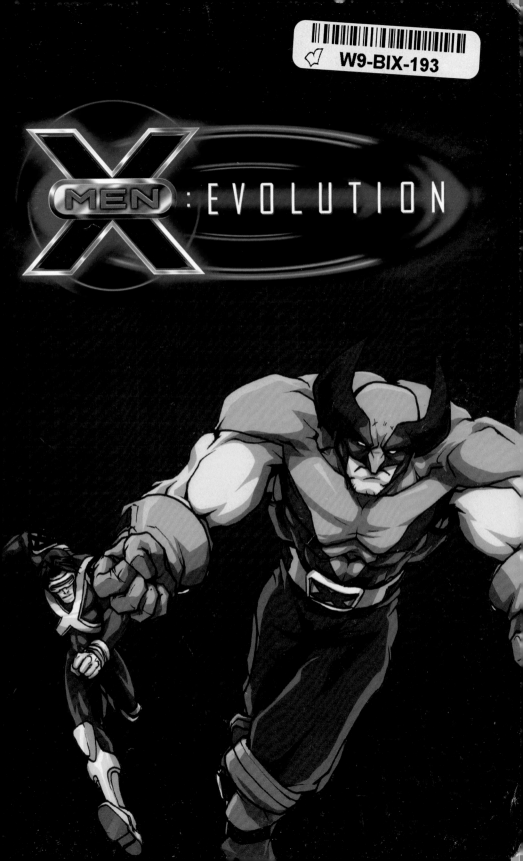

X-MEN: EVOLUTION

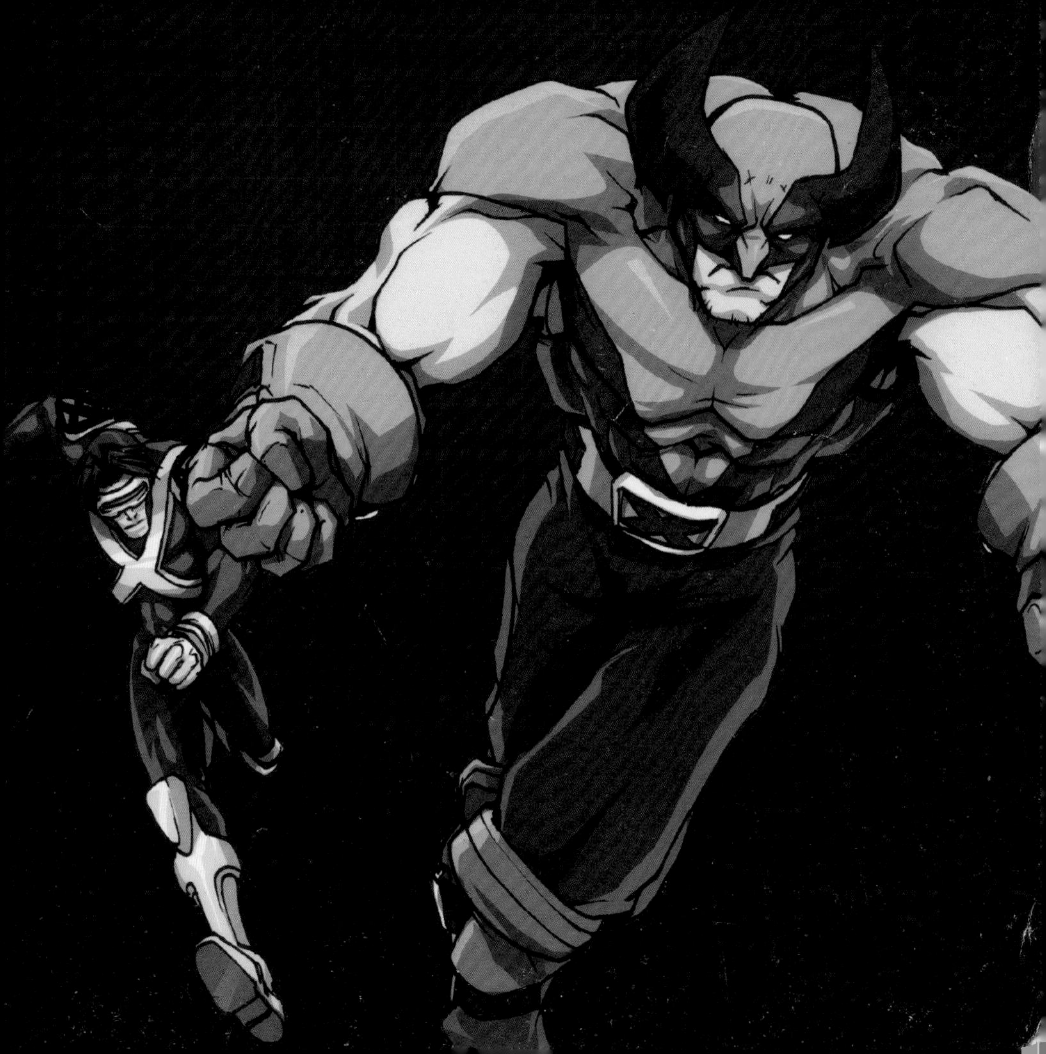

X-MEN CREATED BY STAN LEE & JACK KIRBY

COLLECTION EDITOR **JENNIFER GRÜNWALD** · ASSISTANT EDITOR **DANIEL KIRCHHOFFER**

ASSISTANT MANAGING EDITOR **MAIA LOY** · ASSISTANT MANAGING EDITOR **LISA MONTALBANO**

ASSOCIATE MANAGER, DIGITAL ASSETS **JOE HOCHSTEIN** · VP PRODUCTION & SPECIAL PROJECTS **JEFF YOUNGQUIST**

BOOK DESIGN **JAY BOWEN** · SVP PRINT, SALES & MARKETING **DAVID GABRIEL**

EDITOR IN CHIEF **C.B. CEBULSKI**

SPECIAL THANKS TO **JESS HARROLD**

X-MEN: EVOLUTION. Contains material originally published in magazine form as X-MEN: EVOLUTION (2001) #1-9. First printing 2020. ISBN 978-1-302-92776-9. Published by MARVEL WORLDWIDE, INC., a subsidiary of MARVEL ENTERTAINMENT, LLC. OFFICE OF PUBLICATION: 1290 Avenue of the Americas, New York, NY 10104. © 2020 MARVEL No similarity between any of the names, characters, persons, and/or institutions in this magazine with those of any living or dead person or institution is intended, and any such similarity which may exist is purely coincidental. **Printed in Canada.** KEVIN FEIGE, Chief Creative Officer; DAN BUCKLEY, President, Marvel Entertainment; JOE QUESADA, EVP & Creative Director; DAVID BOGART, Associate Publisher & SVP of Talent Affairs; TOM BREVOORT, VP, Executive Editor; NICK LOWE, Executive Editor, VP of Content, Digital Publishing; DAVID GABRIEL, VP of Print & Digital Publishing; JEFF YOUNGQUIST, VP of Production & Special Projects; ALEX MORALES, Director of Publishing Operations; DAN EDINGTON, Managing Editor; RICKEY PURDIN, Director of Talent Relations; JENNIFER GRÜNWALD, Senior Editor, Special Projects; SUSAN CRESPI, Production Manager; STAN LEE, Chairman Emeritus. For information regarding advertising in Marvel Comics or on Marvel.com, please contact Vit DeBellis, Custom Solutions & Integrated Advertising Manager, at vdebellis@marvel.com. For Marvel subscription inquiries, please call 888-511-5480.

OLUTION

X-MEN: EVOLUTION #1-8

DEVIN GRAYSON
WRITER

UDON STUDIOS with LONG VO, CHARLES PARK & SAKA of STUDIO XD
ARTISTS & COLORISTS

UDON STUDIOS with LONG VO, CHARLES PARK
& SAKA of STUDIO XD (#1, #4-5 & #7-8);
UDON STUDIOS with LONG VO of STUDIO XD (#2);
UDON STUDIOS with LONG VO & CHARLES PARK of STUDIO XD (#3);
AND KIA ASAMIYA & STUDIOTRON (#6)
COVER ART

X-MEN: EVOLUTION #9

JAY FAERBER
WRITER

J.J. KIRBY
ARTIST

CHRIS WALKER
COLORIST

J.J. KIRBY & CHRIS WALKER

COVER ART

SHARPEFONT's RANDY GENTILE
LETTERER

BRIAN SMITH & C.B. CEBULSKI
ASSOCIATE EDITORS

RALPH MACCHIO
EDITOR

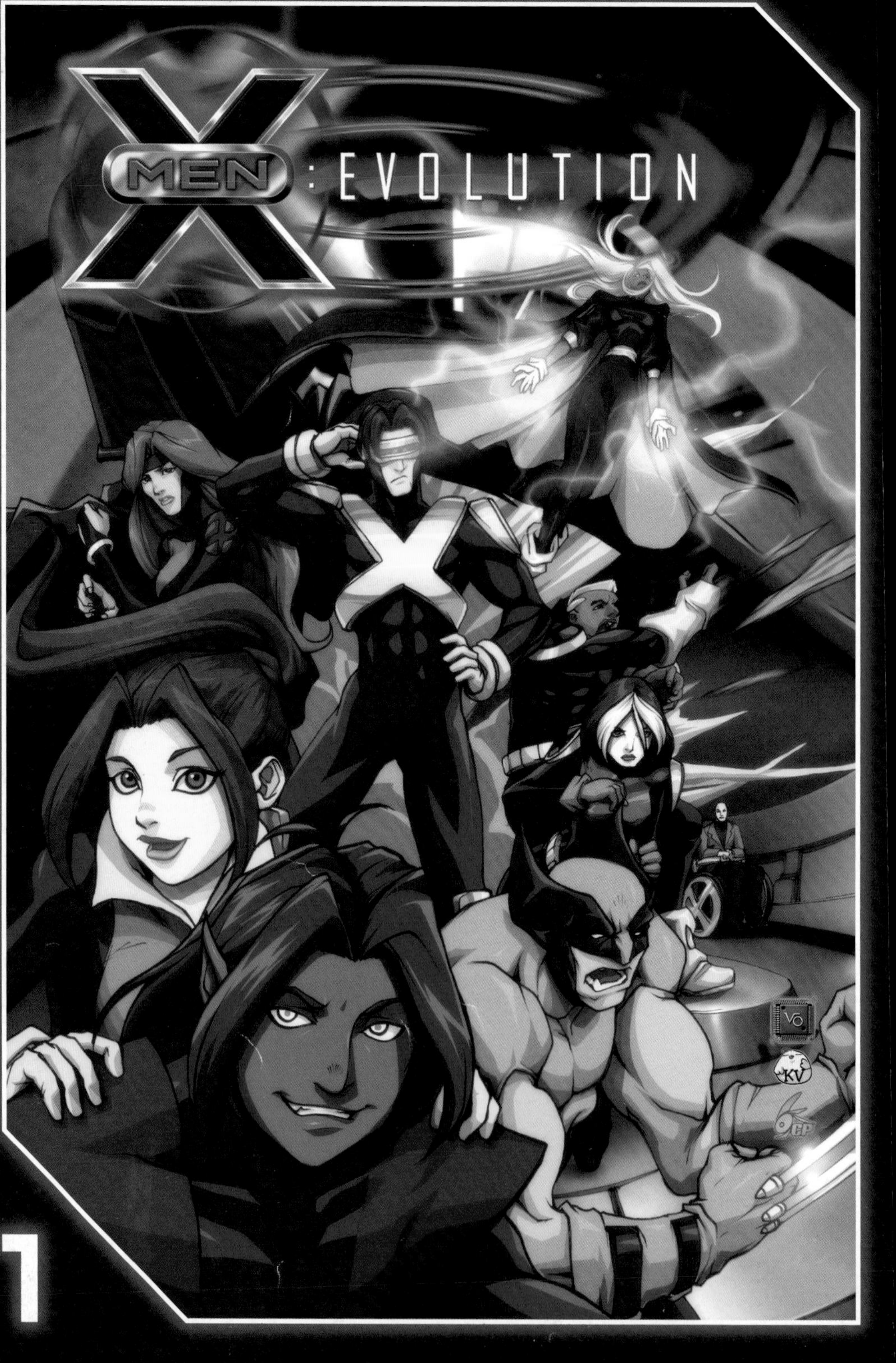
X
MEN
: EVOLUTION

1

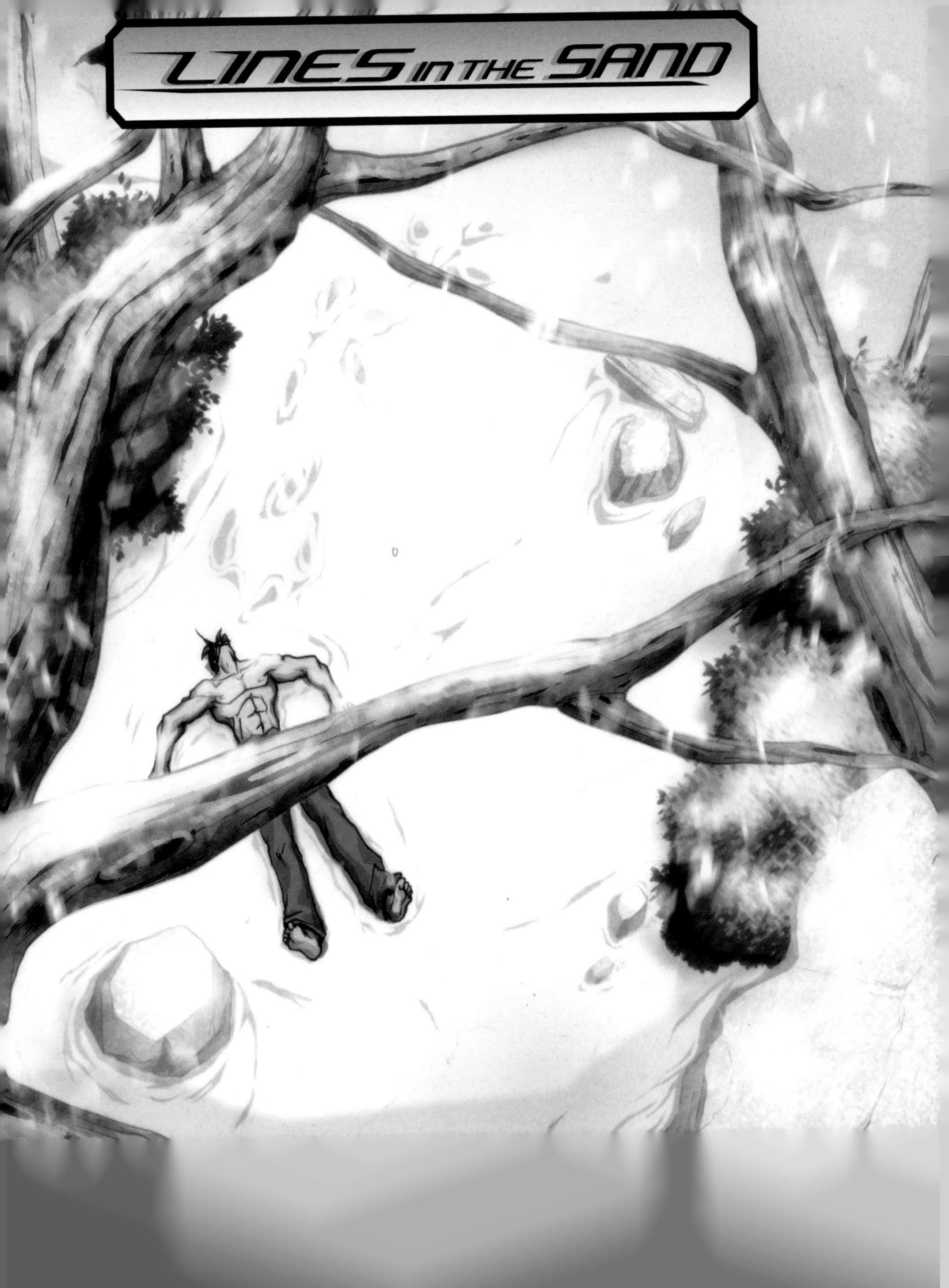
LINES IN THE SAND

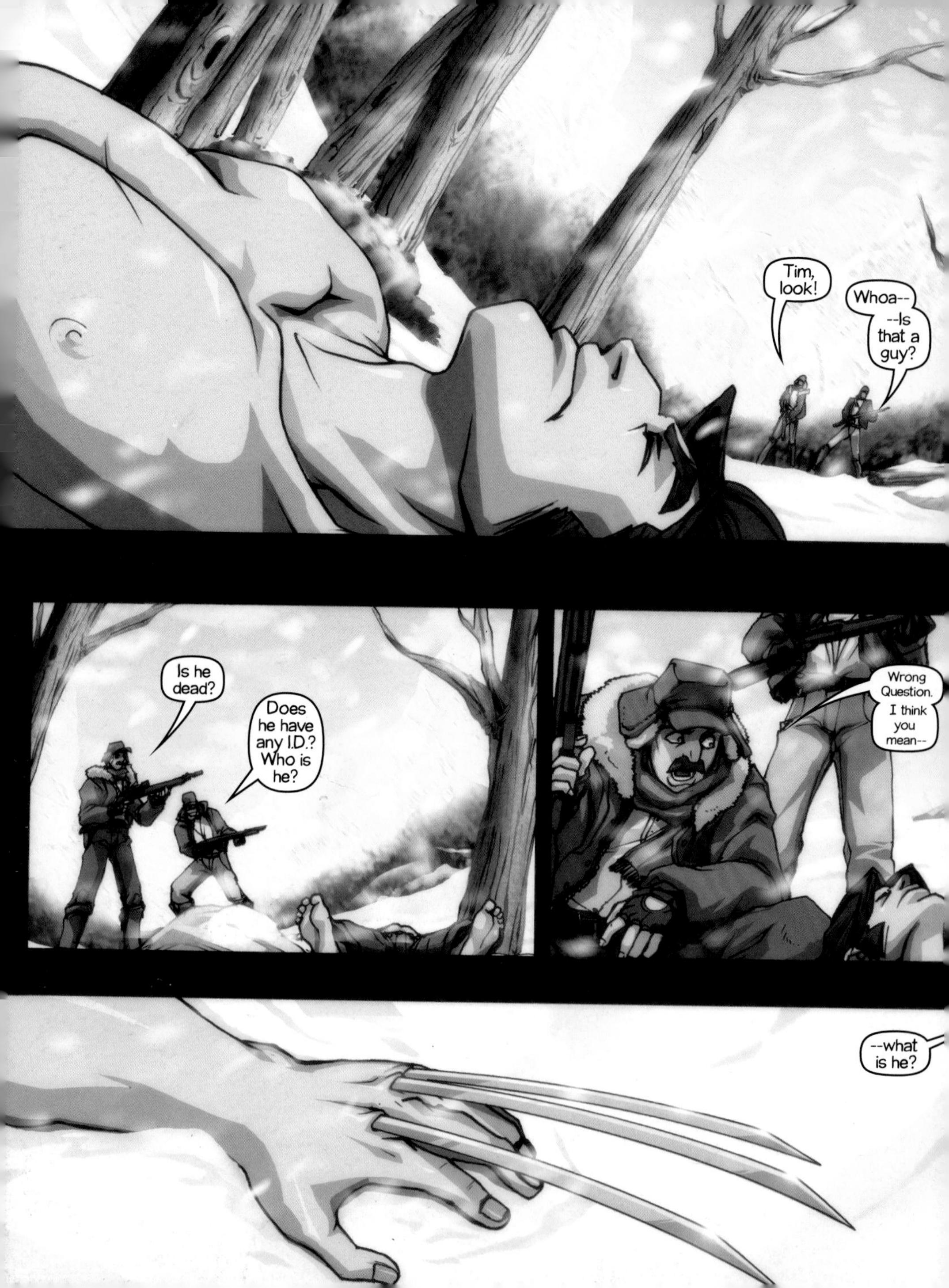
Tim, look!
Whoa--
--Is that a guy?
Is he dead?
Does he have any I.D.? Who is he?
Wrong Question. I think you mean--
--what is he?

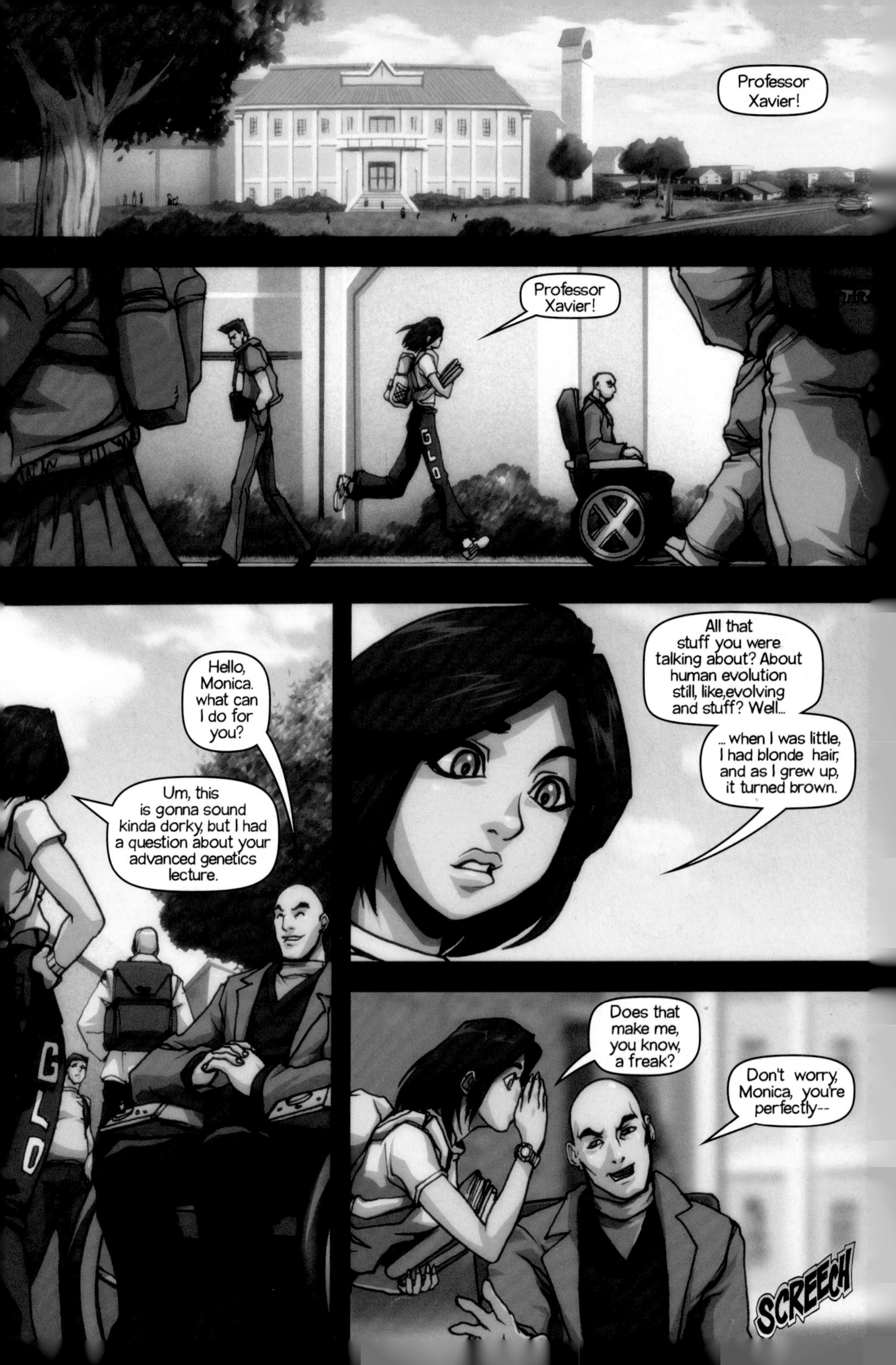
Professor Xavier!
Professor Xavier!
Hello, Monica. what can I do for you?
Um, this is gonna sound kinda dorky, but I had a question about your advanced genetics lecture.
All that stuff you were talking about? About human evolution still, like,evolving and stuff? Well...
... when I was little, I had blonde hair, and as I grew up, it turned brown.
Does that make me, you know, a freak?
Don't worry, Monica, you're perfectly--
SCREECH

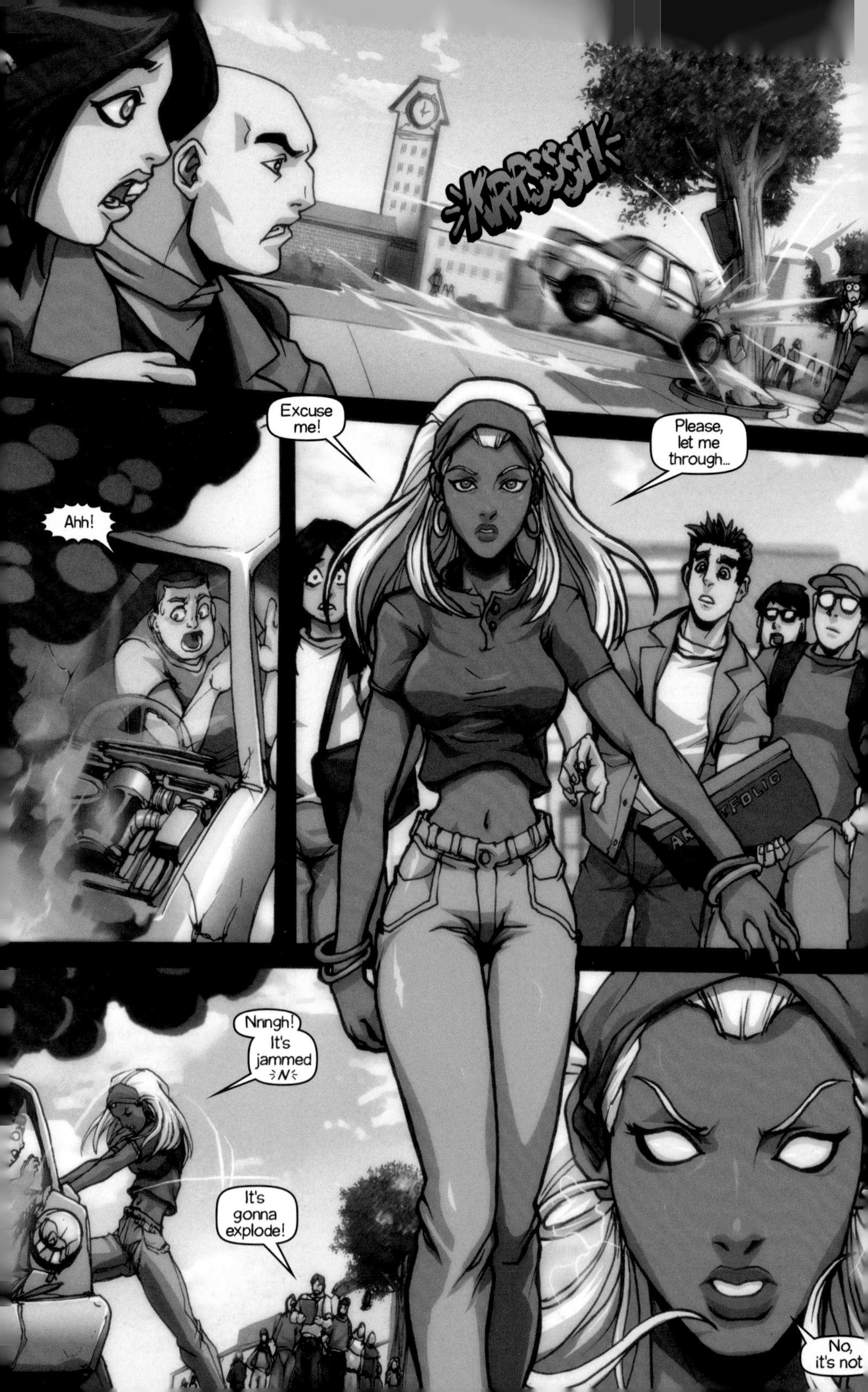

KRRSSSH
Excuse me!
Please, let me through...
Ahh!
Nnngh! It's jammed
N
It's gonna explode!
No, it's not

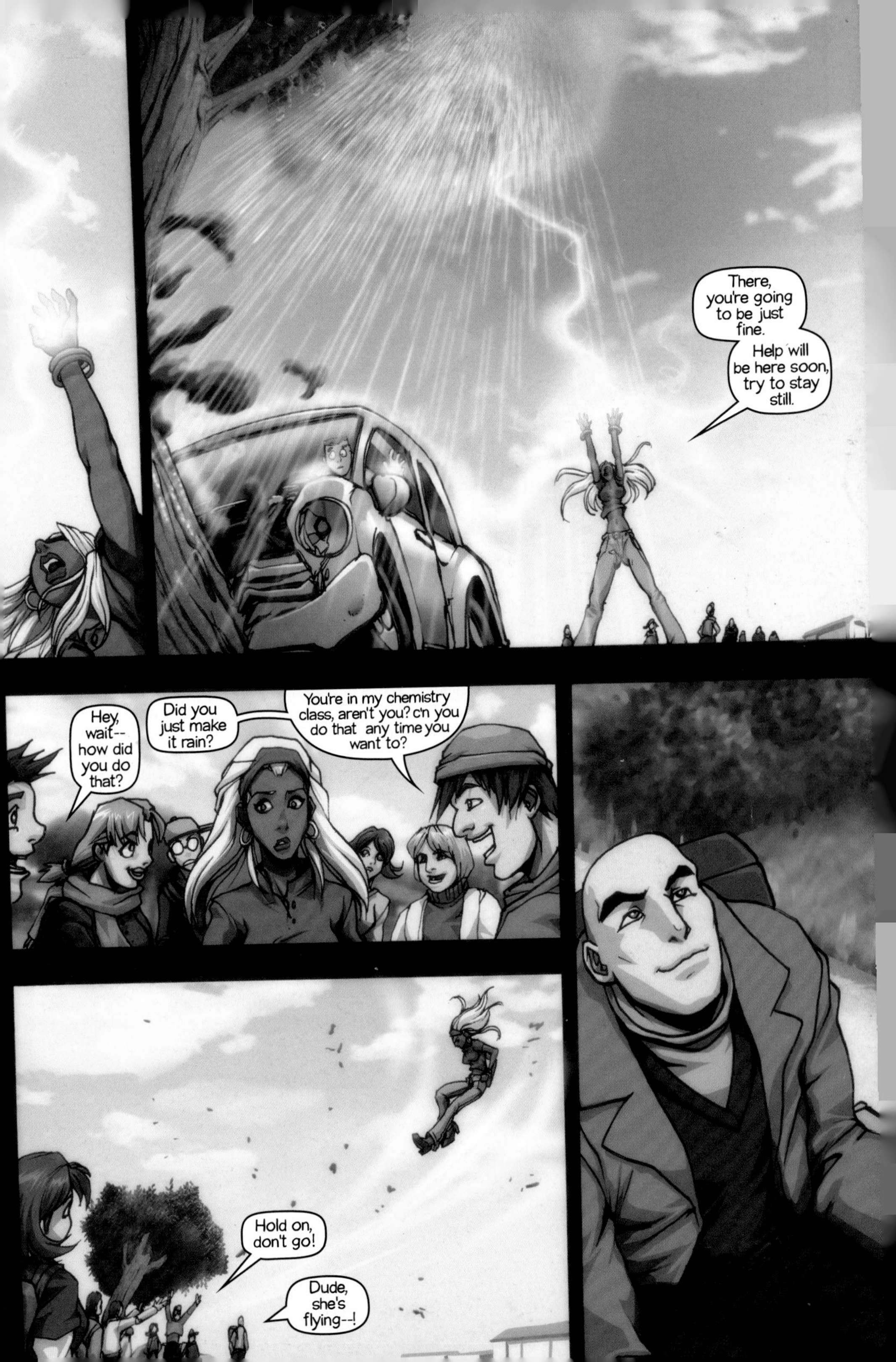
There, you're going to be just fine.
Help will be here soon, try to stay still.
Hey, wait-- how did you do that?
Did you just make it rain?
You're in my chemistry class, aren't you? c'n you do that any time you want to?
Hold on, don't go!
Dude, she's flying--!

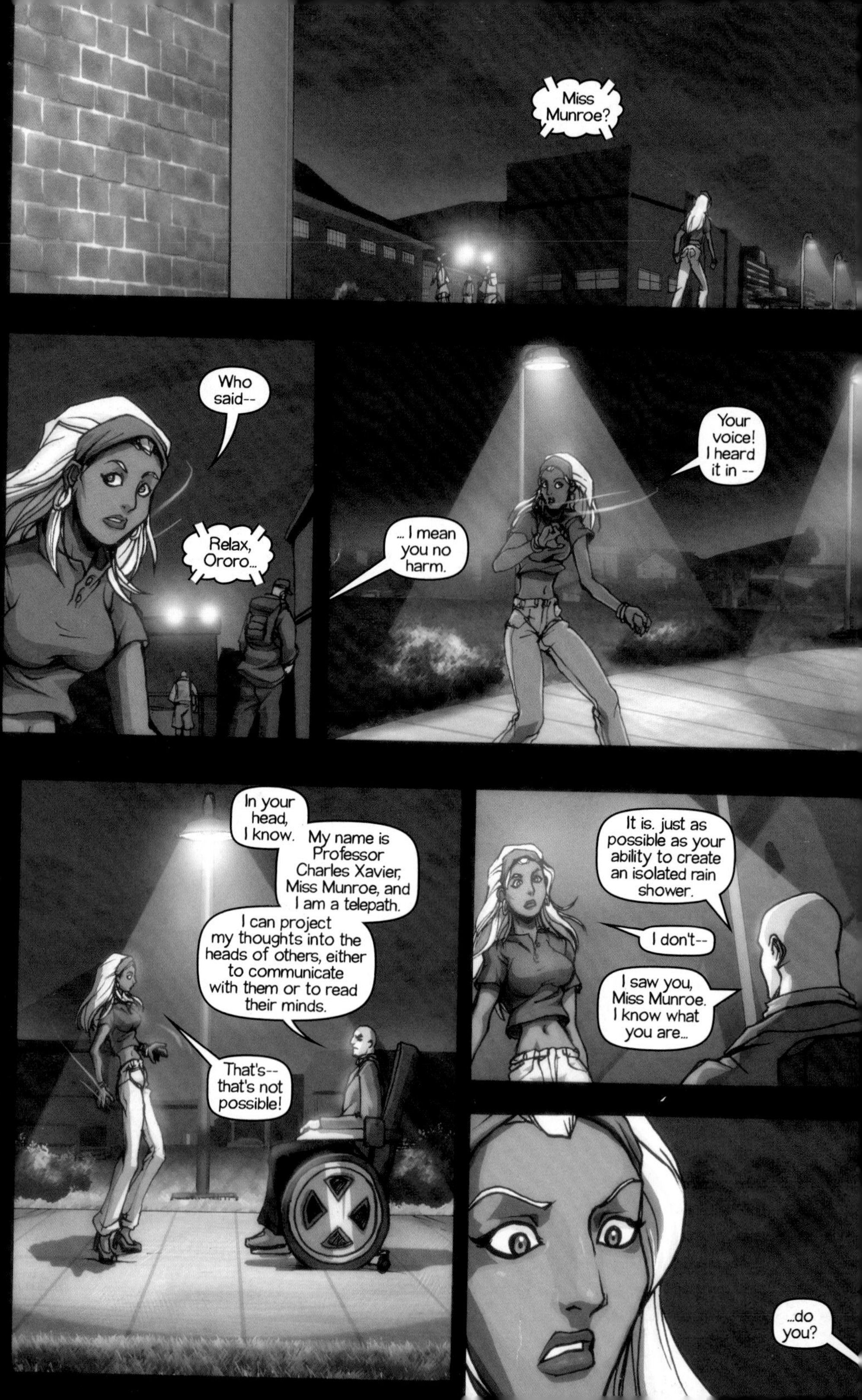
Miss Munroe?
Who said--
Relax, Ororo...
Your voice! I heard it in --
... I mean you no harm.
In your head, I know.
My name is Professor Charles Xavier, Miss Munroe, and I am a telepath.
I can project my thoughts into the heads of others, either to communicate with them or to read their minds.
That's-- that's not possible!
It is. just as possible as your ability to create an isolated rain shower.
I don't--
I saw you, Miss Munroe. I know what you are...
...do you?

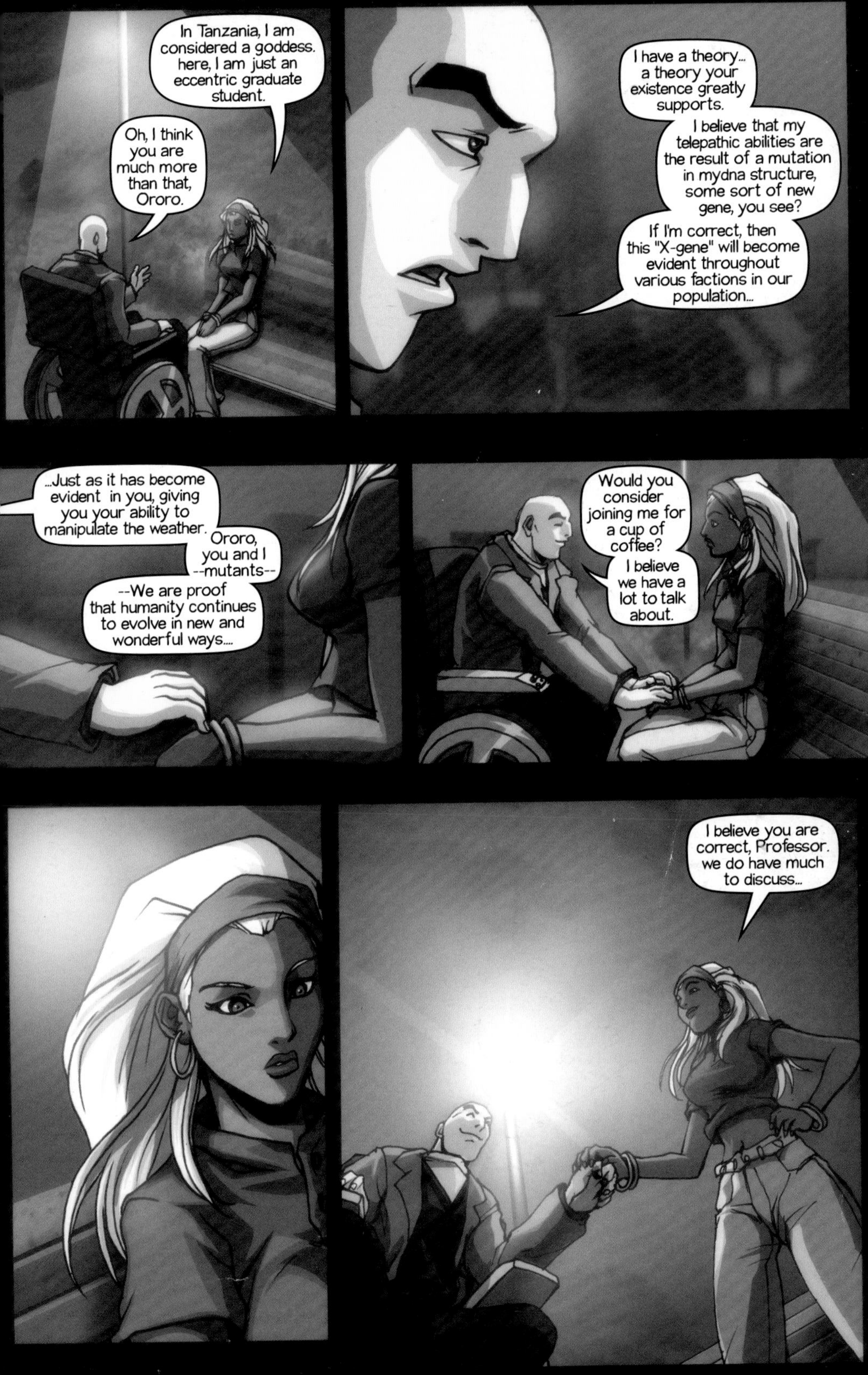
In Tanzania, I am considered a goddess. here, I am just an eccentric graduate student.
Oh, I think you are much more than that, Ororo.
I have a theory... a theory your existence greatly supports.
I believe that my telepathic abilities are the result of a mutation in mydna structure, some sort of new gene, you see?
If I'm correct, then this "X-gene" will become evident throughout various factions in our population...
...Just as it has become evident in you, giving you your ability to manipulate the weather.
Ororo, you and I --mutants--
--We are proof that humanity continues to evolve in new and wonderful ways....
Would you consider joining me for a cup of coffee?
I believe we have a lot to talk about.
I believe you are correct, Professor. we do have much to discuss...

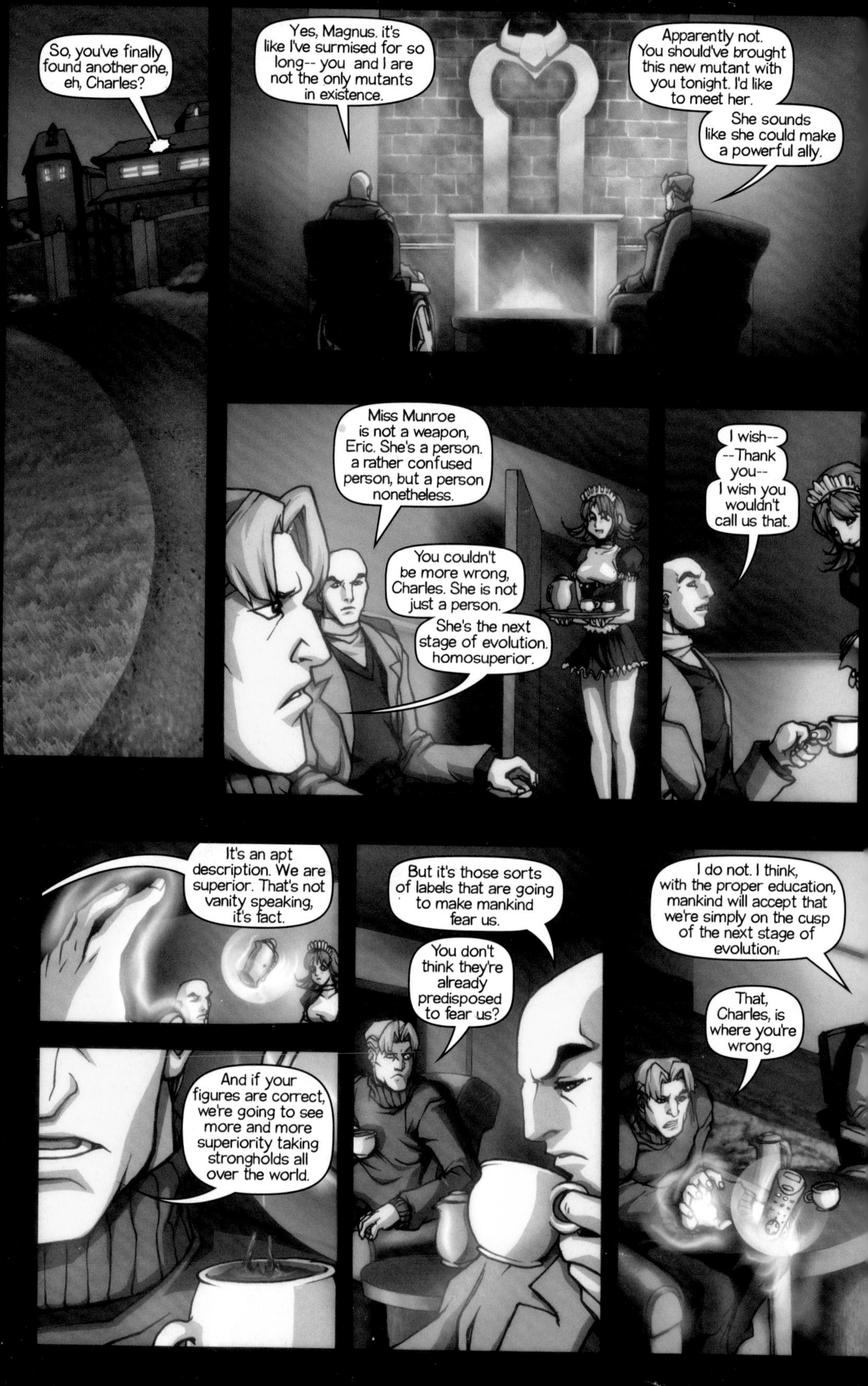

So, you've finally found another one, eh, Charles?
Yes, Magnus. it's like I've surmised for so long-- you and I are not the only mutants in existence.
Apparently not. You should've brought this new mutant with you tonight. I'd like to meet her.
She sounds like she could make a powerful ally.
Miss Munroe is not a weapon, Eric. She's a person. a rather confused person, but a person nonetheless.
You couldn't be more wrong, Charles. She is not just a person.
She's the next stage of evolution. homosuperior.
I wish--
--Thank you--
I wish you wouldn't call us that.
It's an apt description. We are superior. That's not vanity speaking, it's fact.
And if your figures are correct, we're going to see more and more superiority taking strongholds all over the world.
But it's those sorts of labels that are going to make mankind fear us.
You don't think they're already predisposed to fear us?
I do not. I think, with the proper education, mankind will accept that we're simply on the cusp of the next stage of evolution.
That, Charles, is where you're wrong.

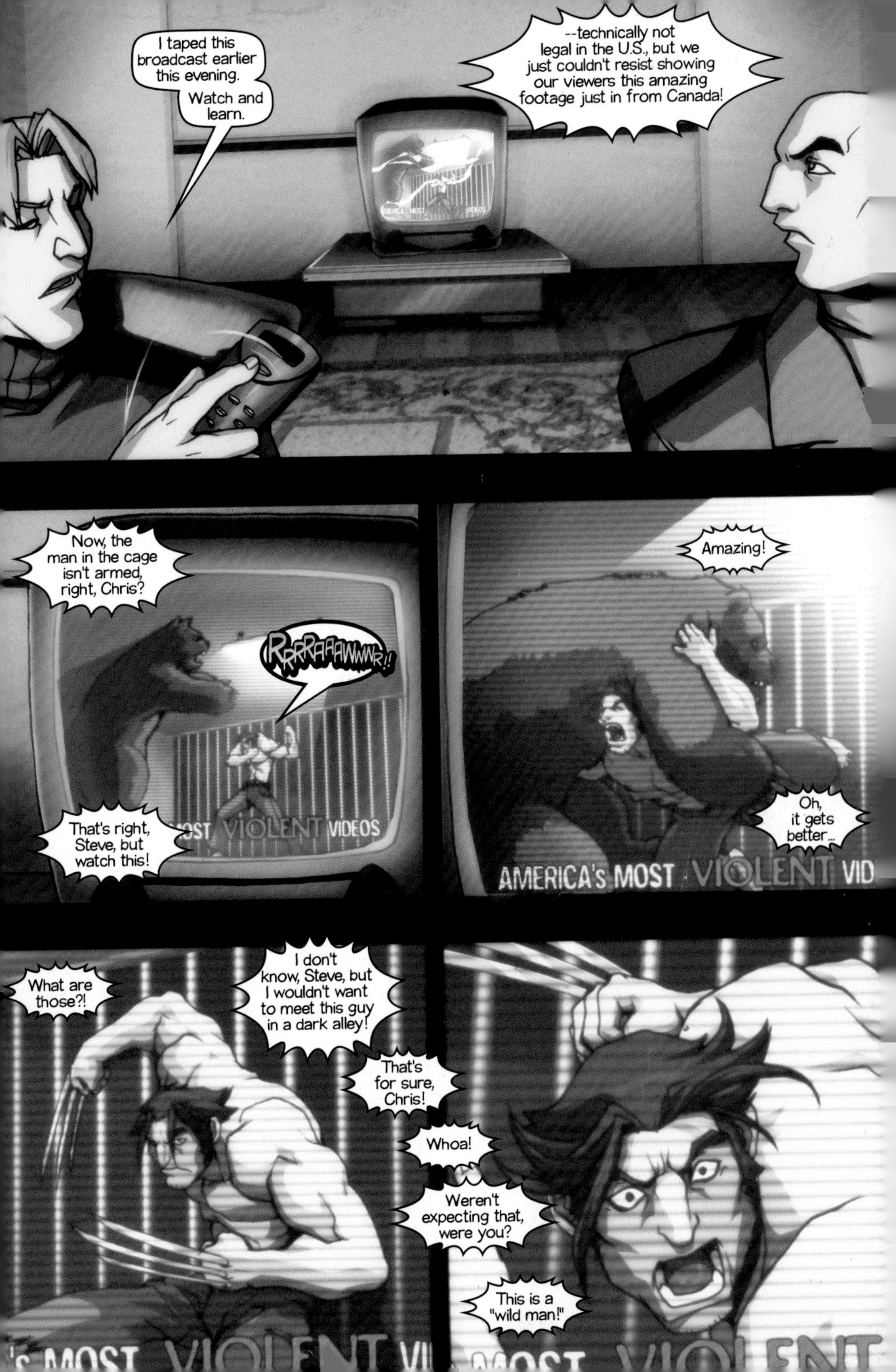
I taped this broadcast earlier this evening.
Watch and learn.
--technically not legal in the U.S., but we just couldn't resist showing our viewers this amazing footage just in from Canada!
AMERICA'S MOST VIDEOS
Now, the man in the cage isn't armed, right, Chris?
RRRRAAAWWWR!!
MOST VIOLENT VIDEOS
That's right, Steve, but watch this!
Amazing!
Oh, it gets better...
AMERICA's MOST VIOLENT VID
What are those?!
I don't know, Steve, but I wouldn't want to meet this guy in a dark alley!
That's for sure, Chris!
Whoa!
Weren't expecting that, were you?
This is a "wild man!"

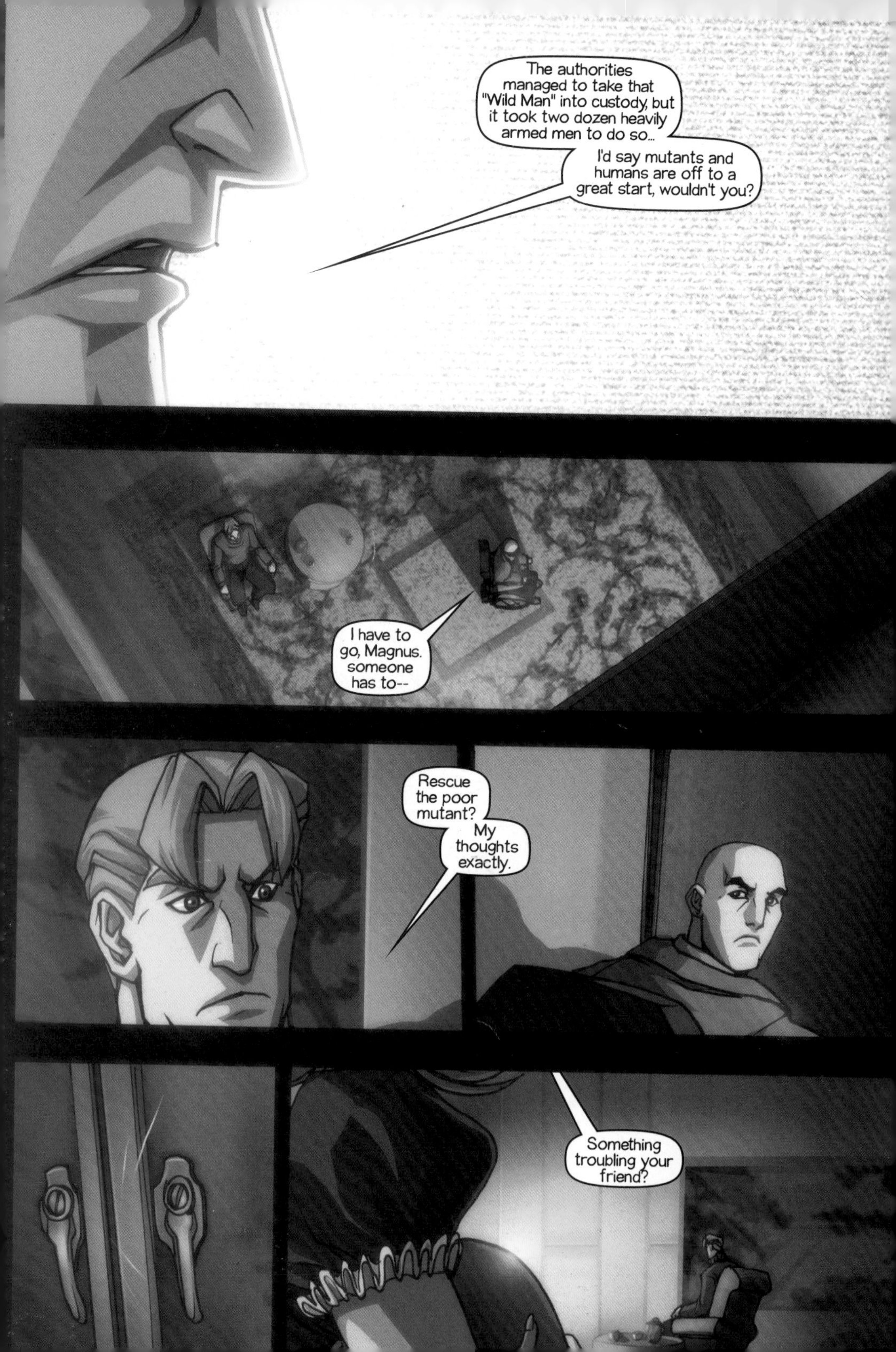
The authorities managed to take that "Wild Man" into custody, but it took two dozen heavily armed men to do so...
I'd say mutants and humans are off to a great start, wouldn't you?
I have to go, Magnus. someone has to--
Rescue the poor mutant?
My thoughts exactly.
Something troubling your friend?

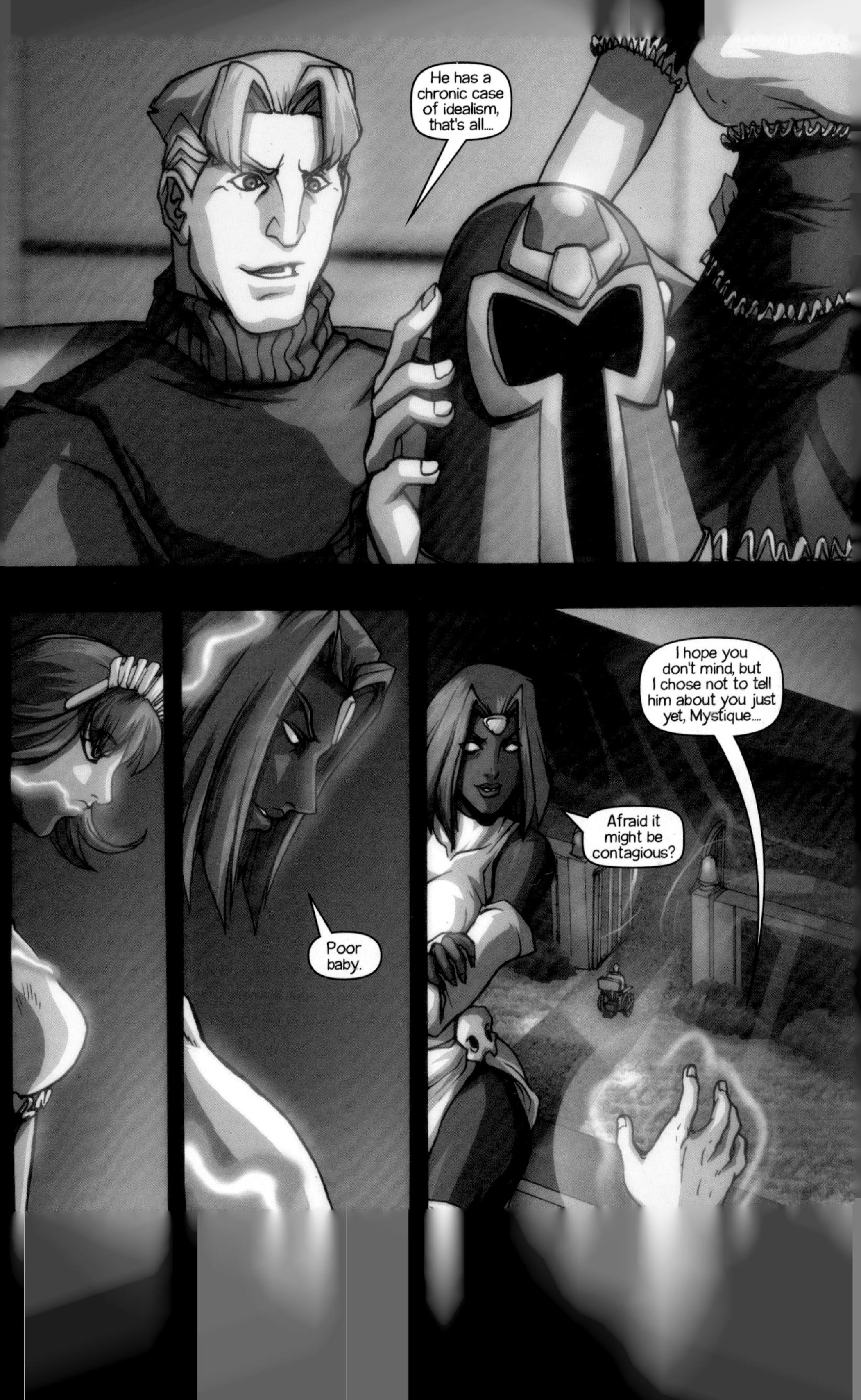
He has a chronic case of idealism, that's all....
Poor baby.
I hope you don't mind, but I chose not to tell him about you just yet, Mystique....
Afraid it might be contagious?

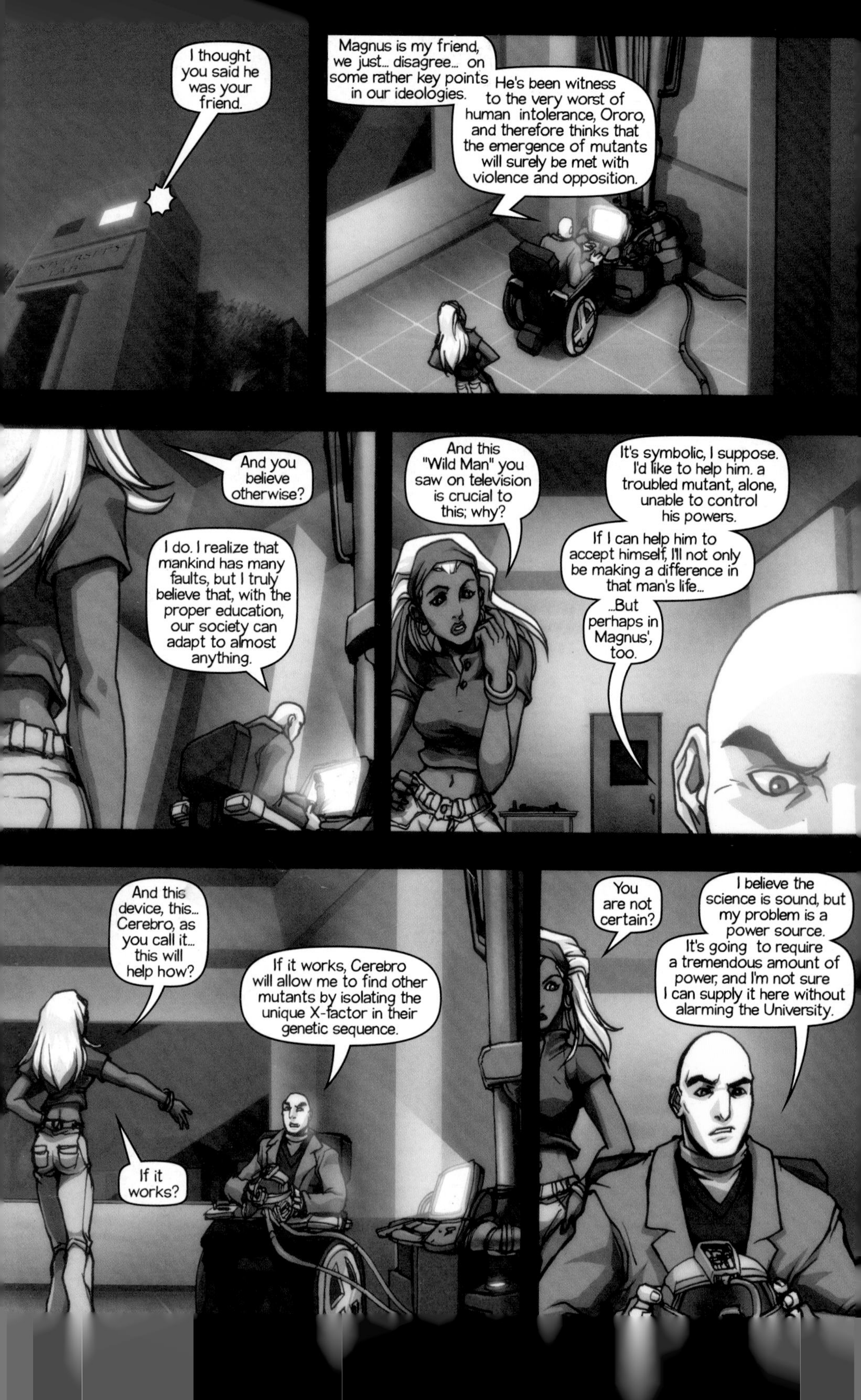

I thought you said he was your friend.
Magnus is my friend, we just... disagree... on some rather key points in our ideologies.
He's been witness to the very worst of human intolerance, Ororo, and therefore thinks that the emergence of mutants will surely be met with violence and opposition.
And you believe otherwise?
I do. I realize that mankind has many faults, but I truly believe that, with the proper education, our society can adapt to almost anything.
And this "Wild Man" you saw on television is crucial to this; why?
It's symbolic, I suppose. I'd like to help him. a troubled mutant, alone, unable to control his powers.
If I can help him to accept himself, I'll not only be making a difference in that man's life...
...But perhaps in Magnus', too.
And this device, this... Cerebro, as you call it... this will help how?
If it works, Cerebro will allow me to find other mutants by isolating the unique X-factor in their genetic sequence.
If it works?
You are not certain?
I believe the science is sound, but my problem is a power source. It's going to require a tremendous amount of power, and I'm not sure I can supply it here without alarming the University.

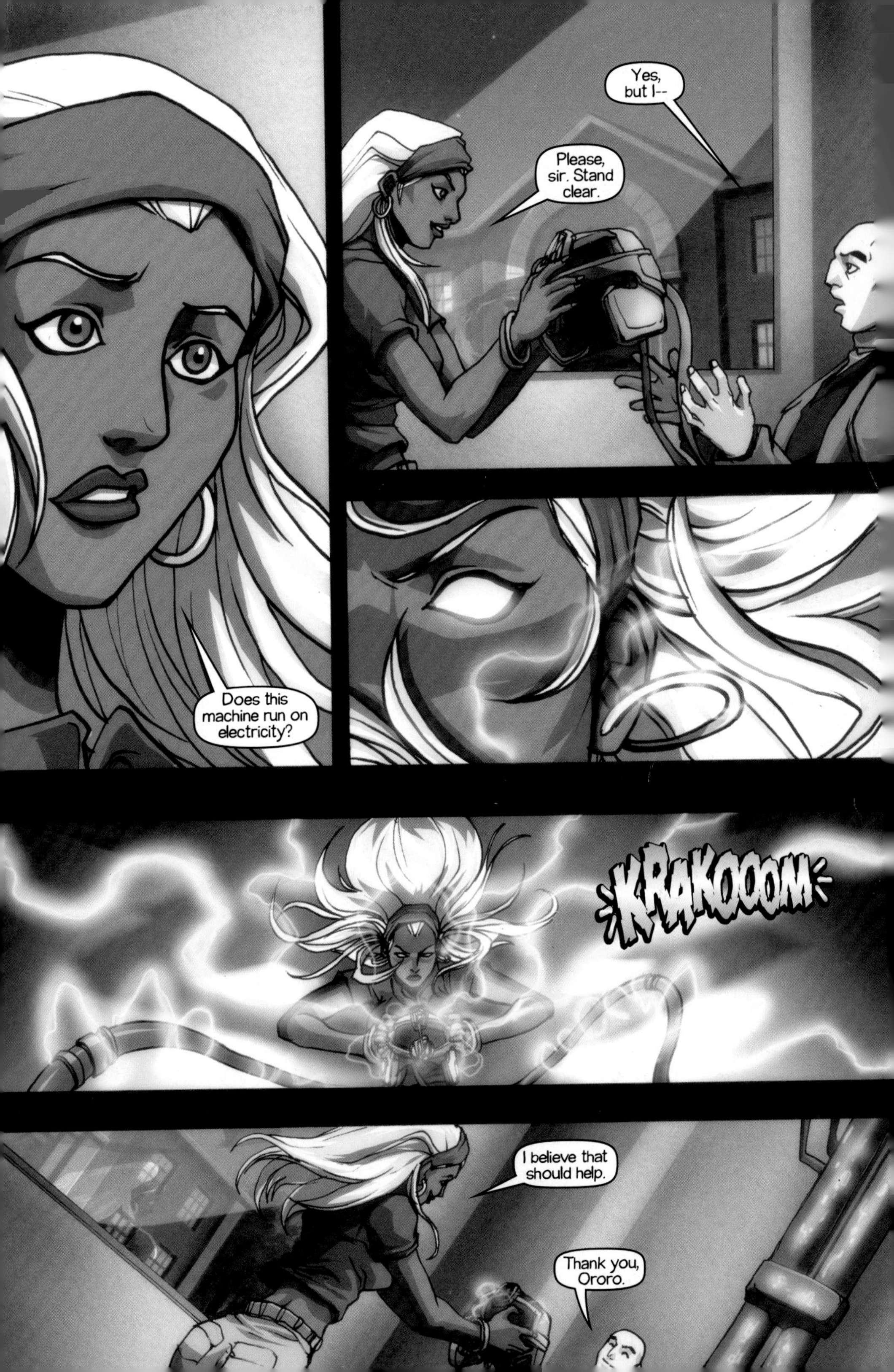
Does this machine run on electricity?
Yes, but I--
Please, sir. Stand clear.
KRAKOOOM
I believe that should help.
Thank you, Ororo.

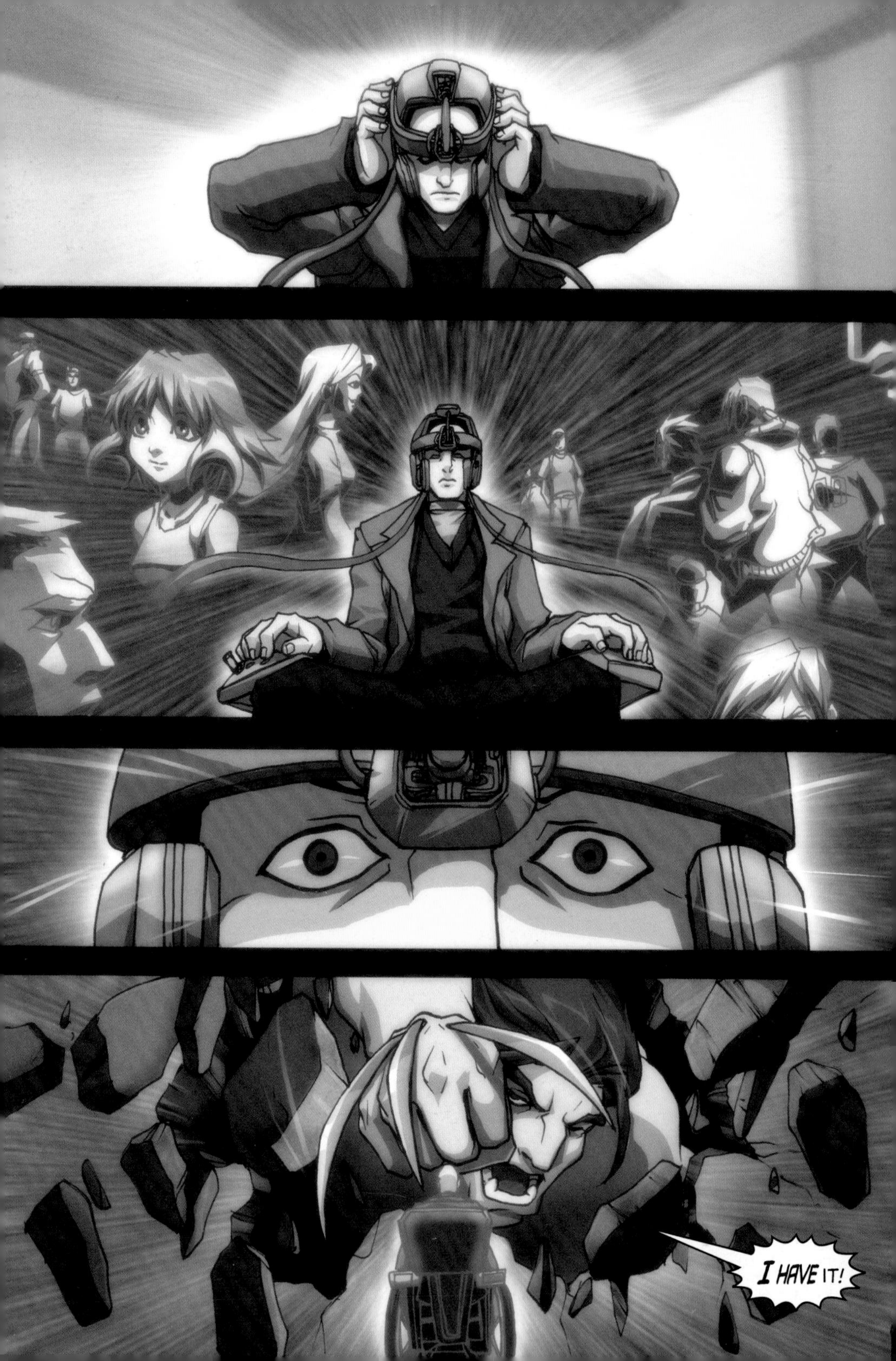
I HAVE IT!

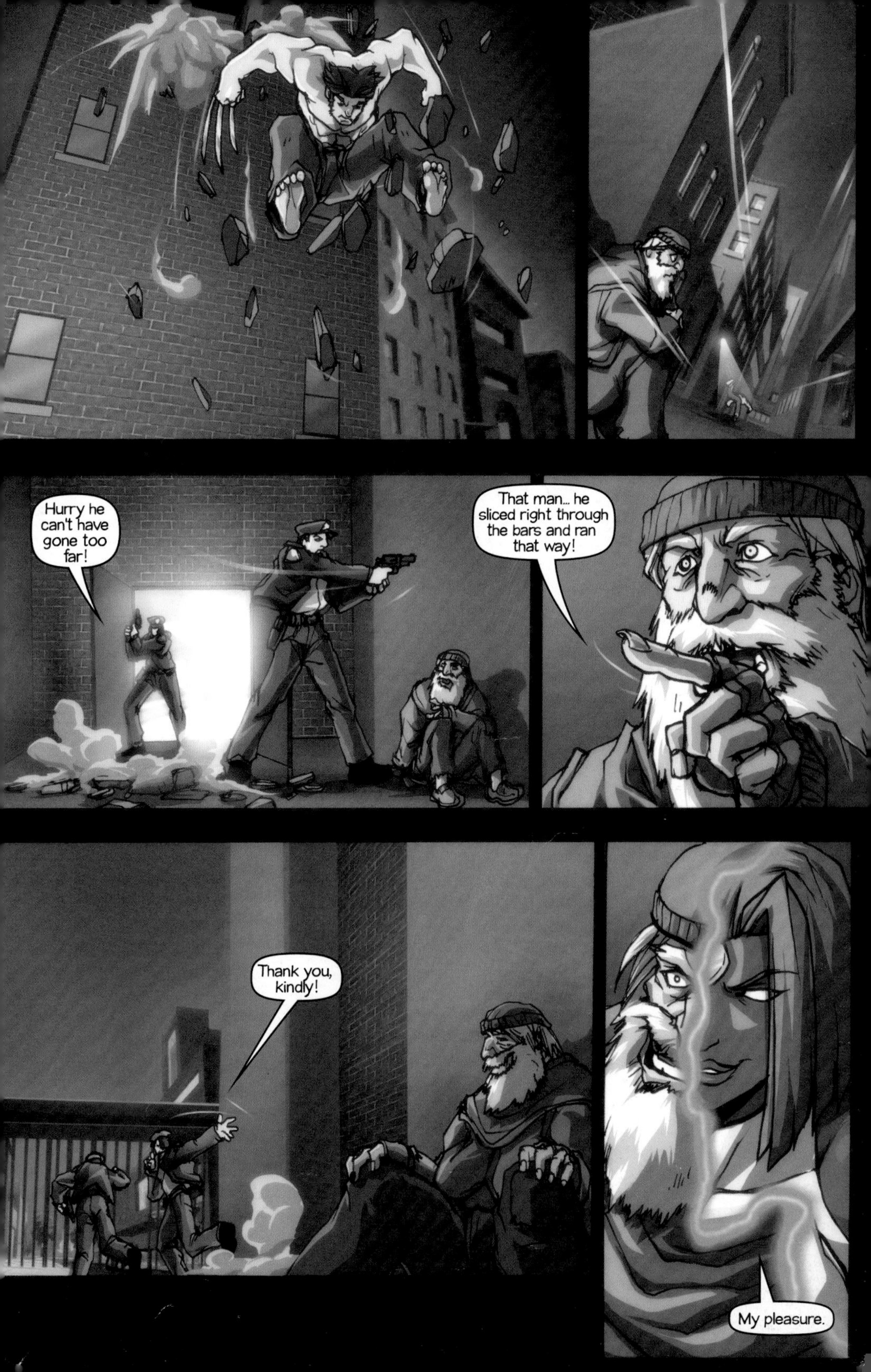
Hurry he can't have gone too far!
That man... he sliced right through the bars and ran that way!
Thank you, kindly!
My pleasure.

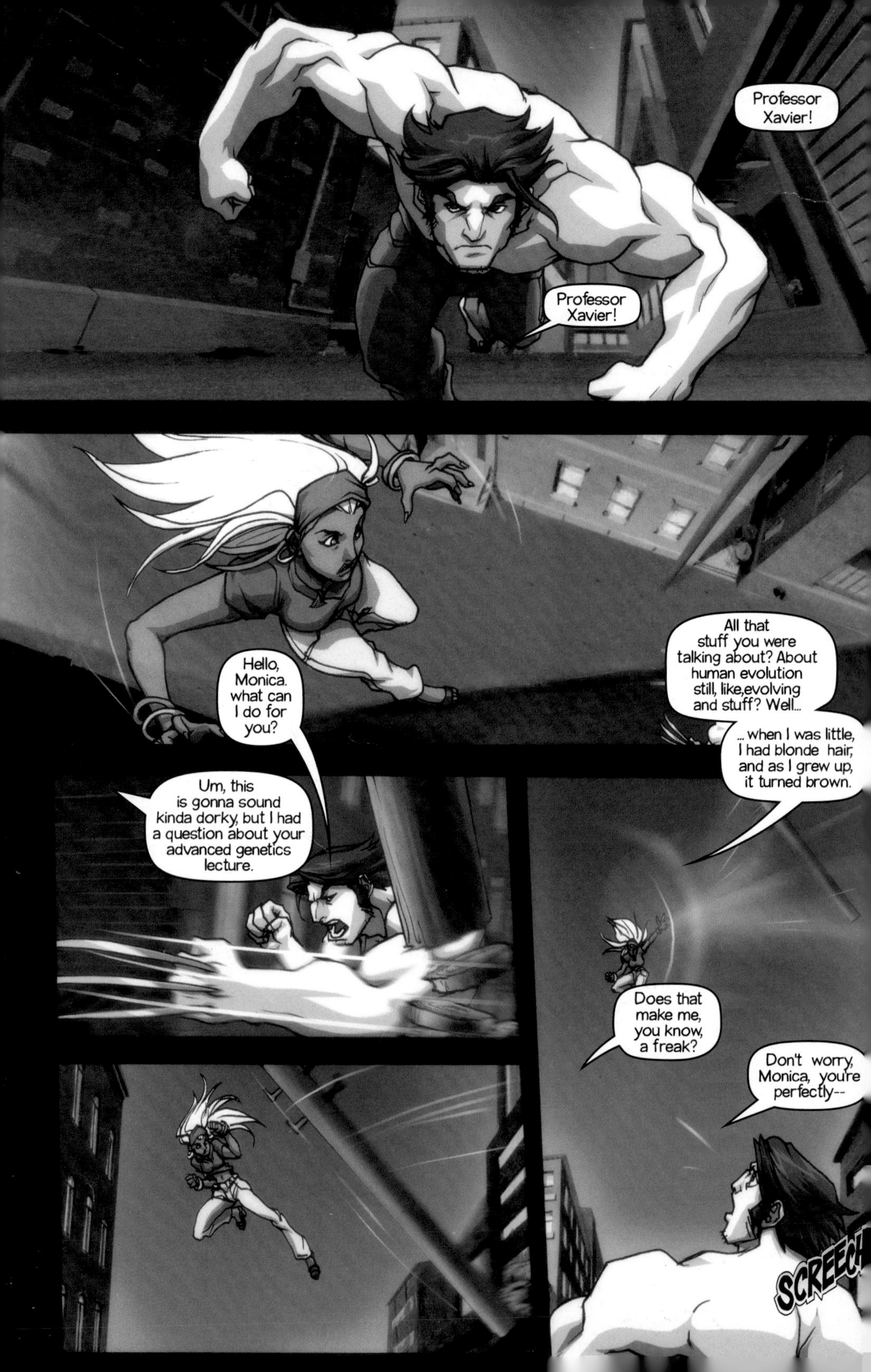
Professor Xavier!
Professor Xavier!
Hello, Monica. what can I do for you?
Um, this is gonna sound kinda dorky, but I had a question about your advanced genetics lecture.
All that stuff you were talking about? About human evolution still, like,evolving and stuff? Well...
... when I was little, I had blonde hair, and as I grew up, it turned brown.
Does that make me, you know, a freak?
Don't worry, Monica, you're perfectly--
SCREECH

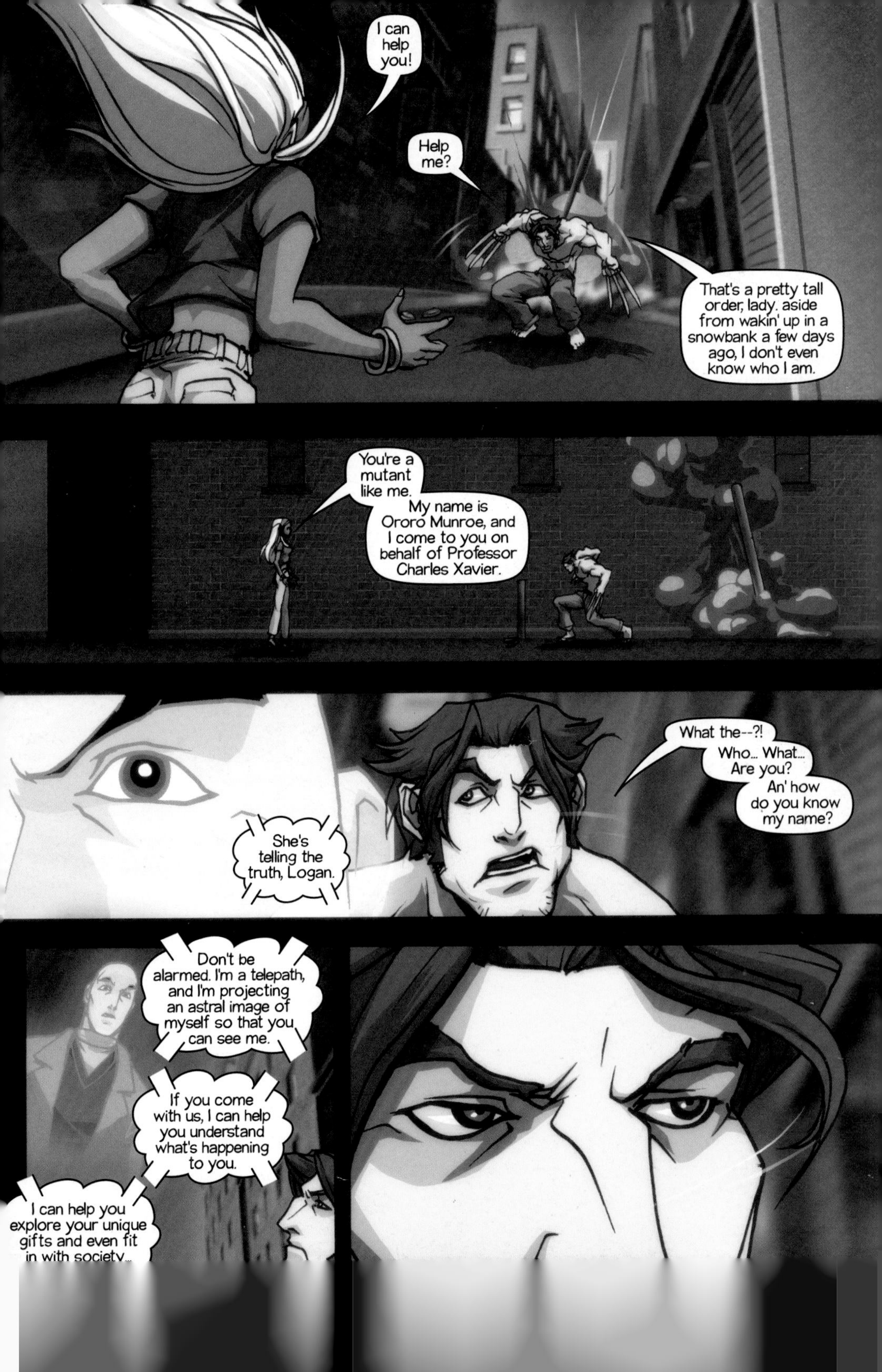
I can help you!
Help me?
That's a pretty tall order, lady. aside from wakin' up in a snowbank a few days ago, I don't even know who I am.
You're a mutant like me.
My name is Ororo Munroe, and I come to you on behalf of Professor Charles Xavier.
What the--?!
Who... What... Are you?
An' how do you know my name?
She's telling the truth, Logan.
Don't be alarmed. I'm a telepath, and I'm projecting an astral image of myself so that you can see me.
If you come with us, I can help you understand what's happening to you.
I can help you explore your unique gifts and even fit in with society...

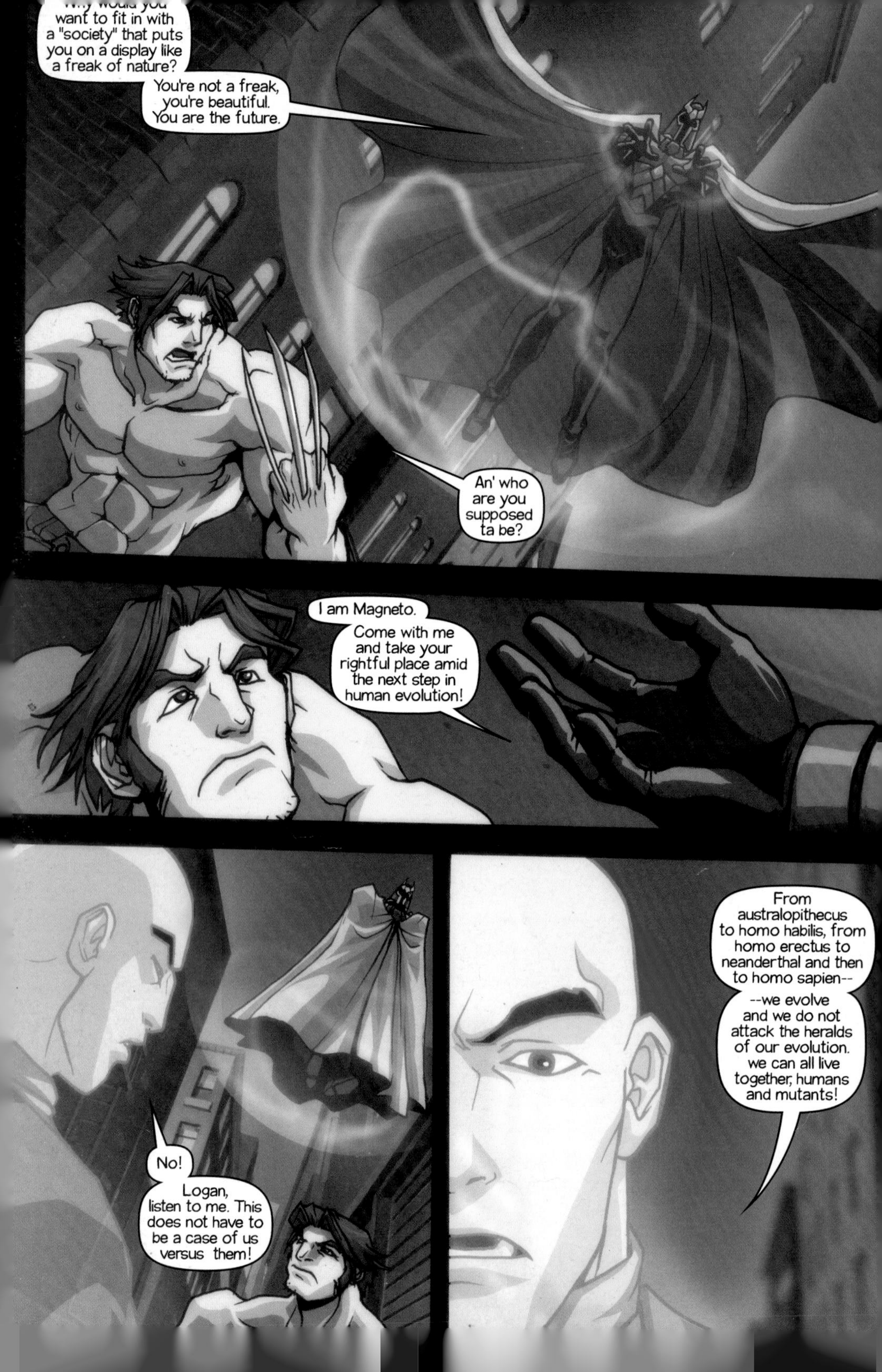
want to fit in with a "society" that puts you on a display like a freak of nature?
You're not a freak, you're beautiful. You are the future.
An' who are you supposed ta be?
I am Magneto.
Come with me and take your rightful place amid the next step in human evolution!
No!
Logan, listen to me. This does not have to be a case of us versus them!
From australopithecus to homo habilis, from homo erectus to neanderthal and then to homo sapien--
--we evolve and we do not attack the heralds of our evolution. we can all live together, humans and mutants!

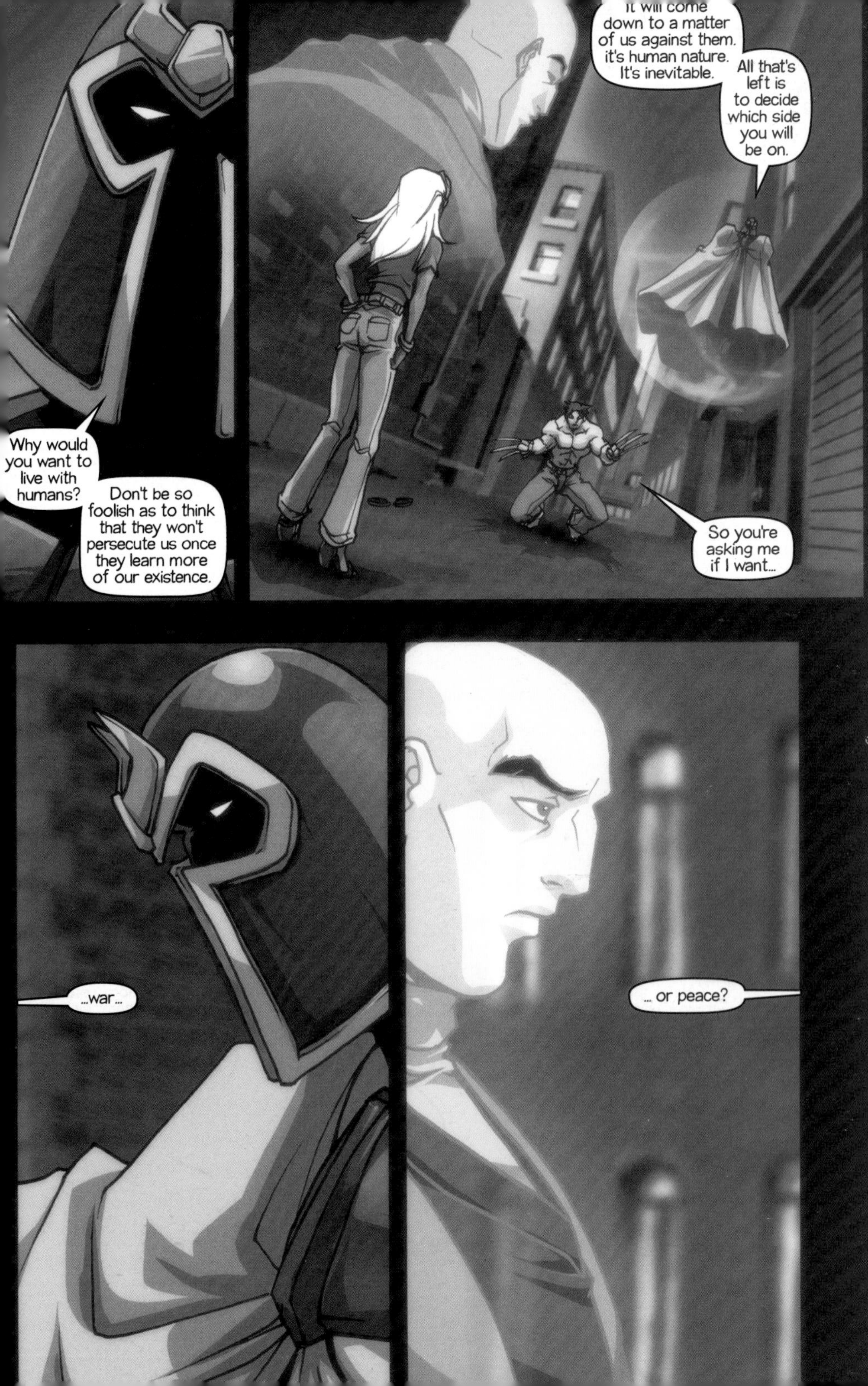
Why would you want to live with humans?
Don't be so foolish as to think that they won't persecute us once they learn more of our existence.
It will come down to a matter of us against them. it's human nature. It's inevitable.
All that's left is to decide which side you will be on.
So you're asking me if I want...
...war...
... or peace?

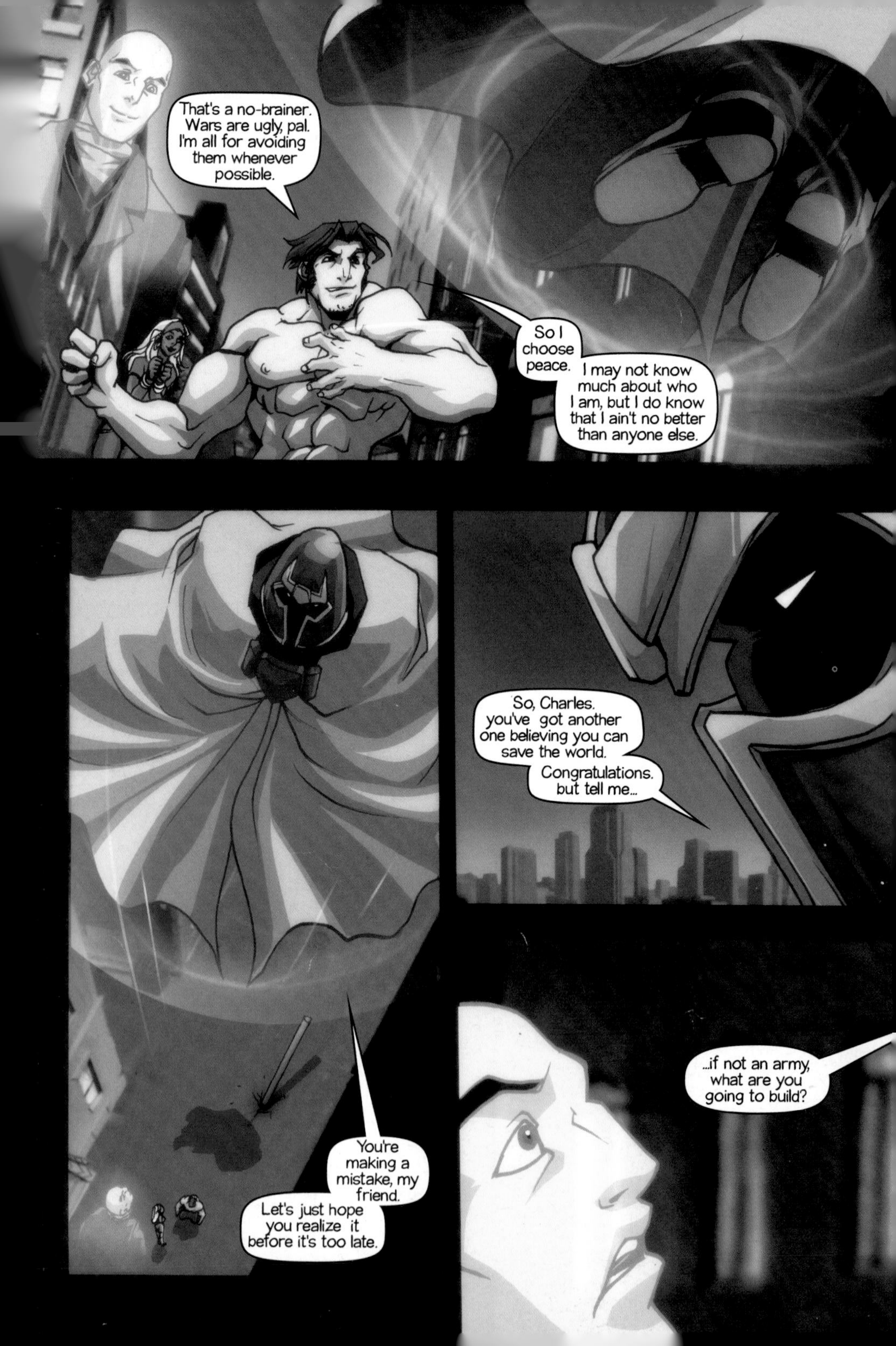
That's a no-brainer. Wars are ugly, pal. I'm all for avoiding them whenever possible.
So I choose peace.
I may not know much about who I am, but I do know that I ain't no better than anyone else.
So, Charles. you've got another one believing you can save the world.
Congratulations. but tell me...
...if not an army, what are you going to build?
You're making a mistake, my friend.
Let's just hope you realize it before it's too late.

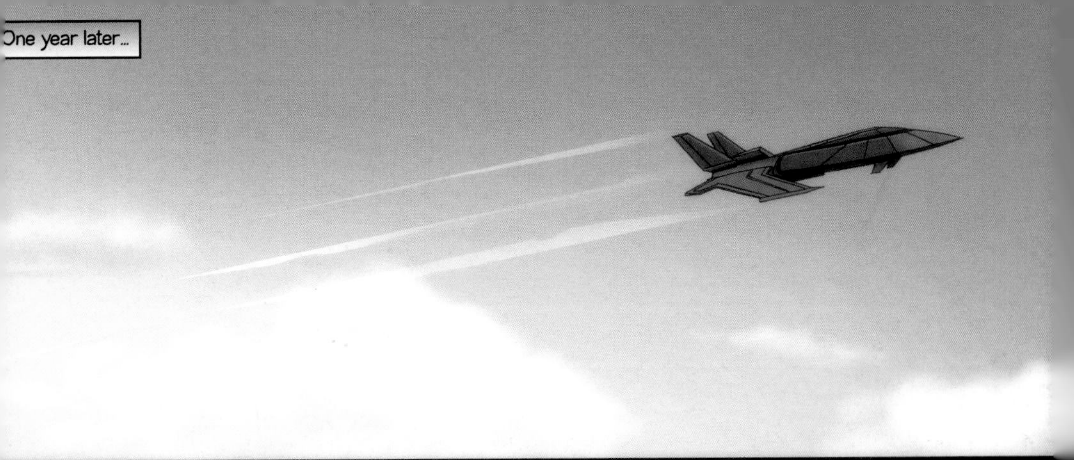
One year later...

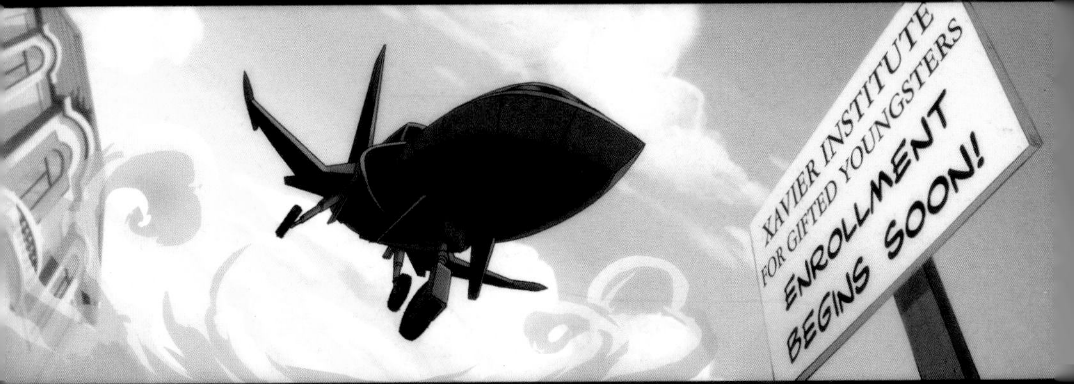
XAVIER INSTITUTE
FOR GIFTED YOUNGSTERS
ENROLLMENT
BEGINS SOON!

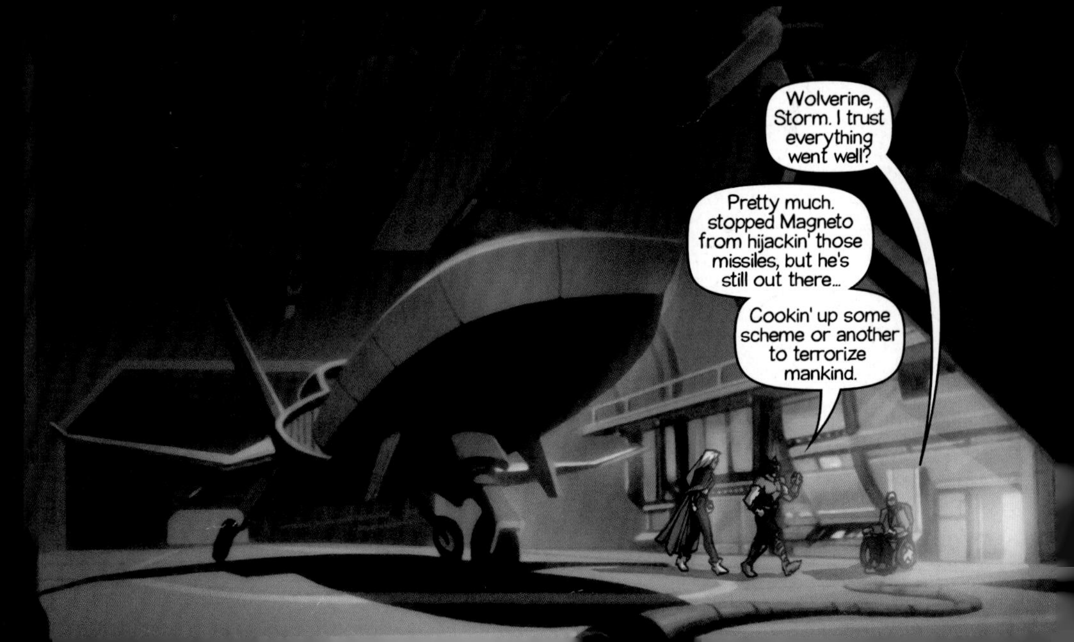
Wolverine, Storm. I trust everything went well?
Pretty much. stopped Magneto from hijackin' those missiles, but he's still out there...
Cookin' up some scheme or another to terrorize mankind.

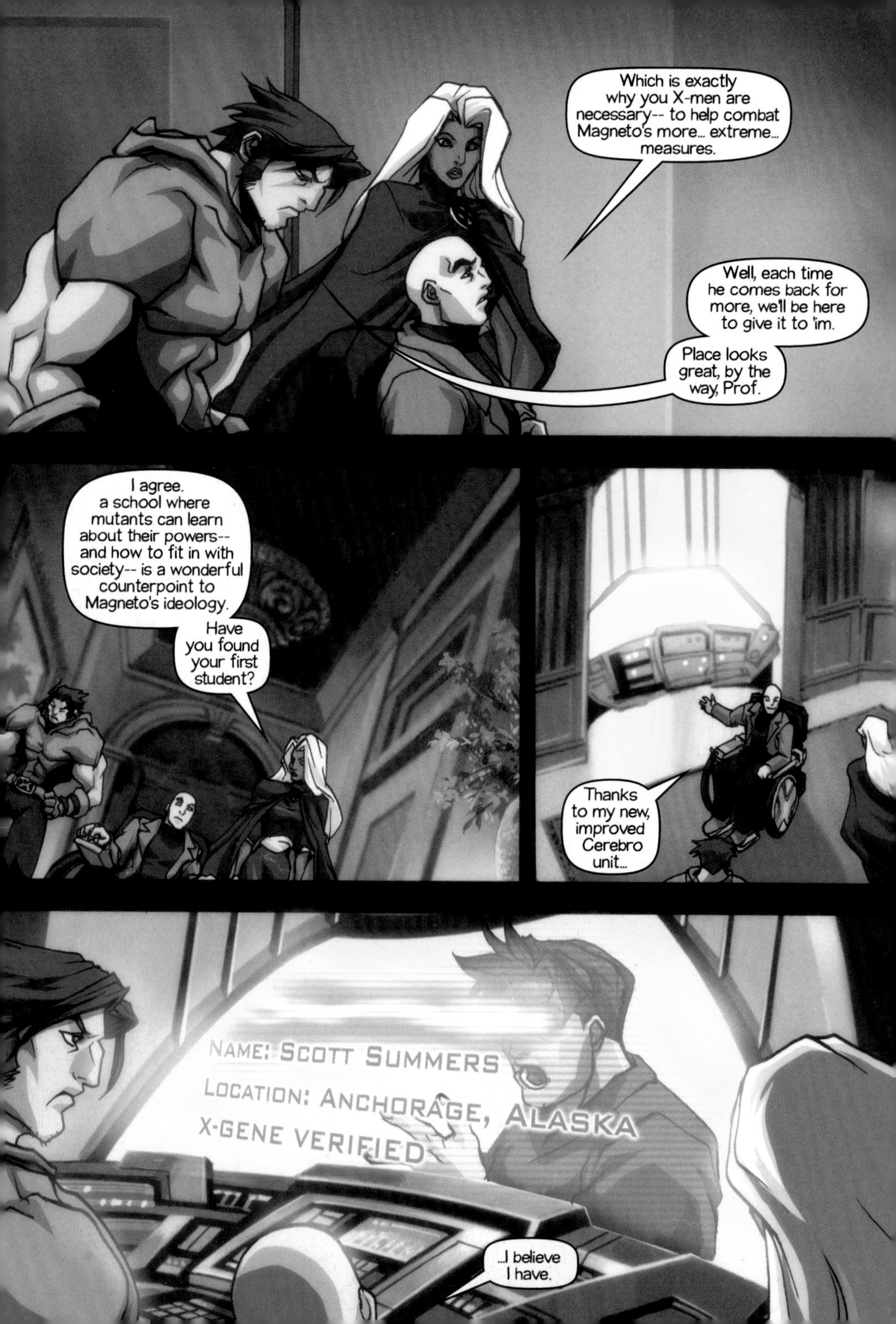

Which is exactly why you X-men are necessary-- to help combat Magneto's more... extreme... measures.
Well, each time he comes back for more, we'll be here to give it to 'im.
Place looks great, by the way, Prof.
I agree. a school where mutants can learn about their powers-- and how to fit in with society-- is a wonderful counterpoint to Magneto's ideology.
Have you found your first student?
Thanks to my new, improved Cerebro unit...
NAME: SCOTT SUMMERS
LOCATION: ANCHORAGE, ALASKA
X-GENE VERIFIED
...I believe I have.

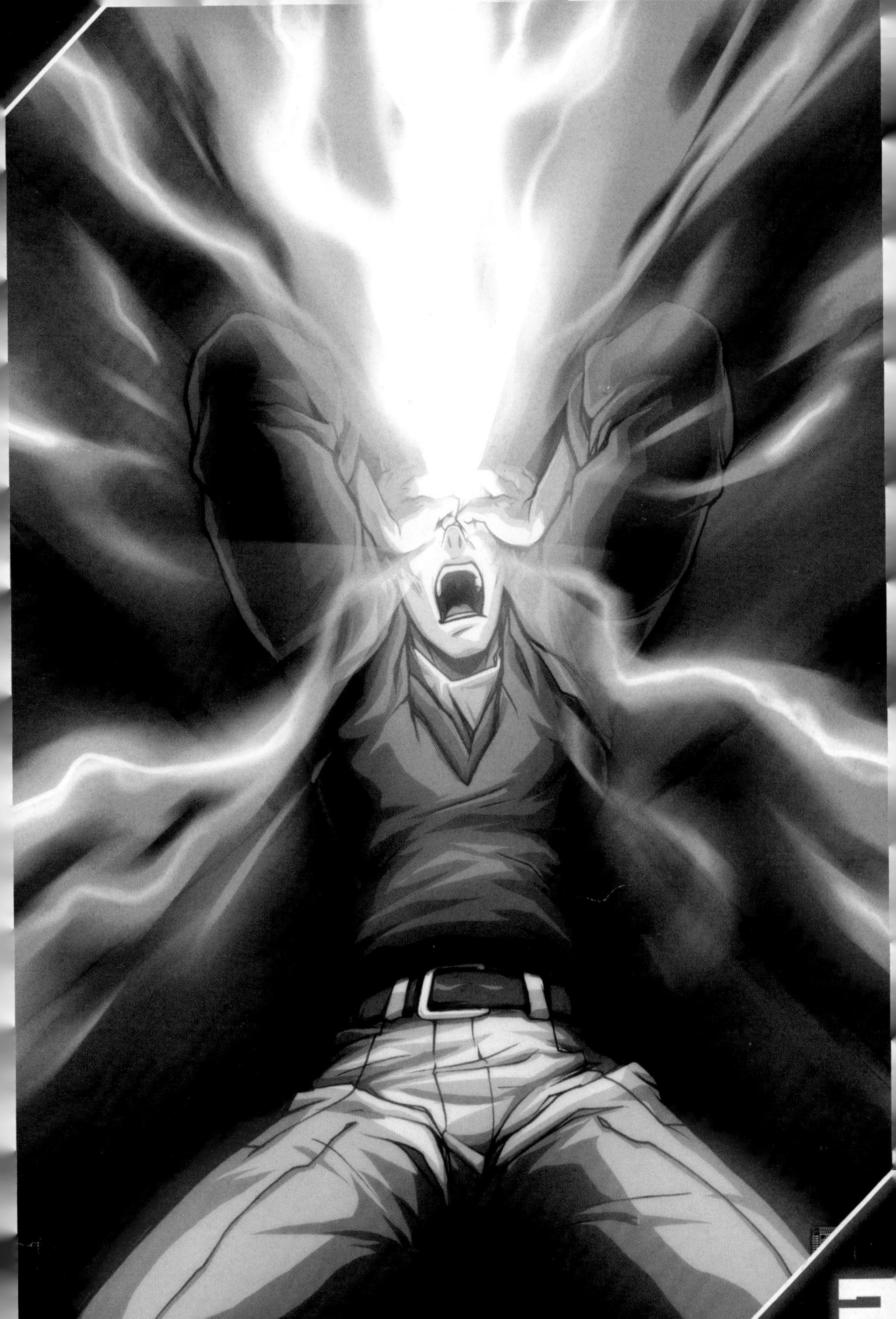

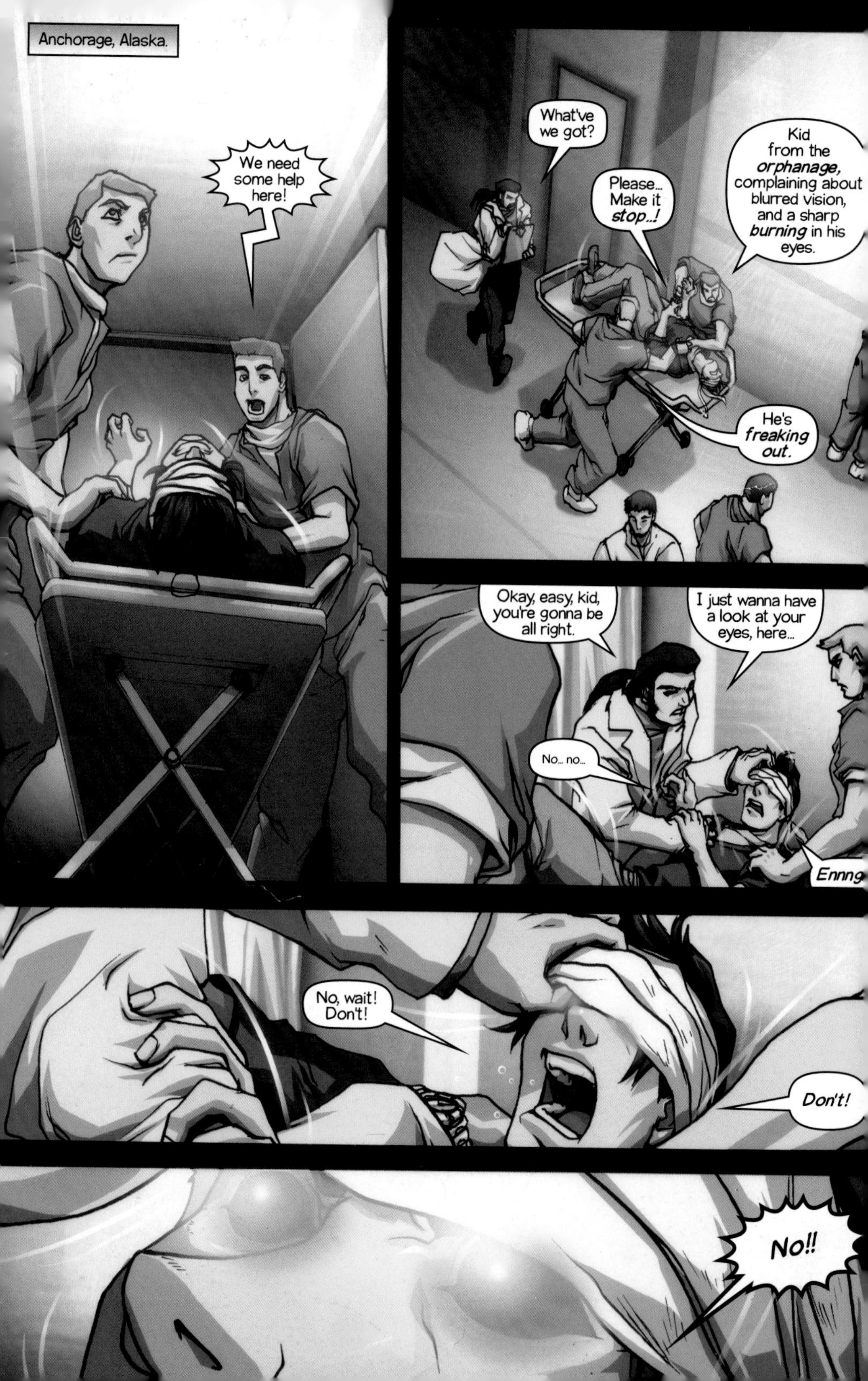
Anchorage, Alaska.
We need some help here!
What've we got?
Please... Make it *stop...!*
Kid from the *orphanage,* complaining about blurred vision, and a sharp *burning* in his eyes.
He's *freaking out.*
Okay, easy, kid, you're gonna be all right.
I just wanna have a look at your eyes, here...
No... no...
Ennng
No, wait! Don't!
Don't!
No!!

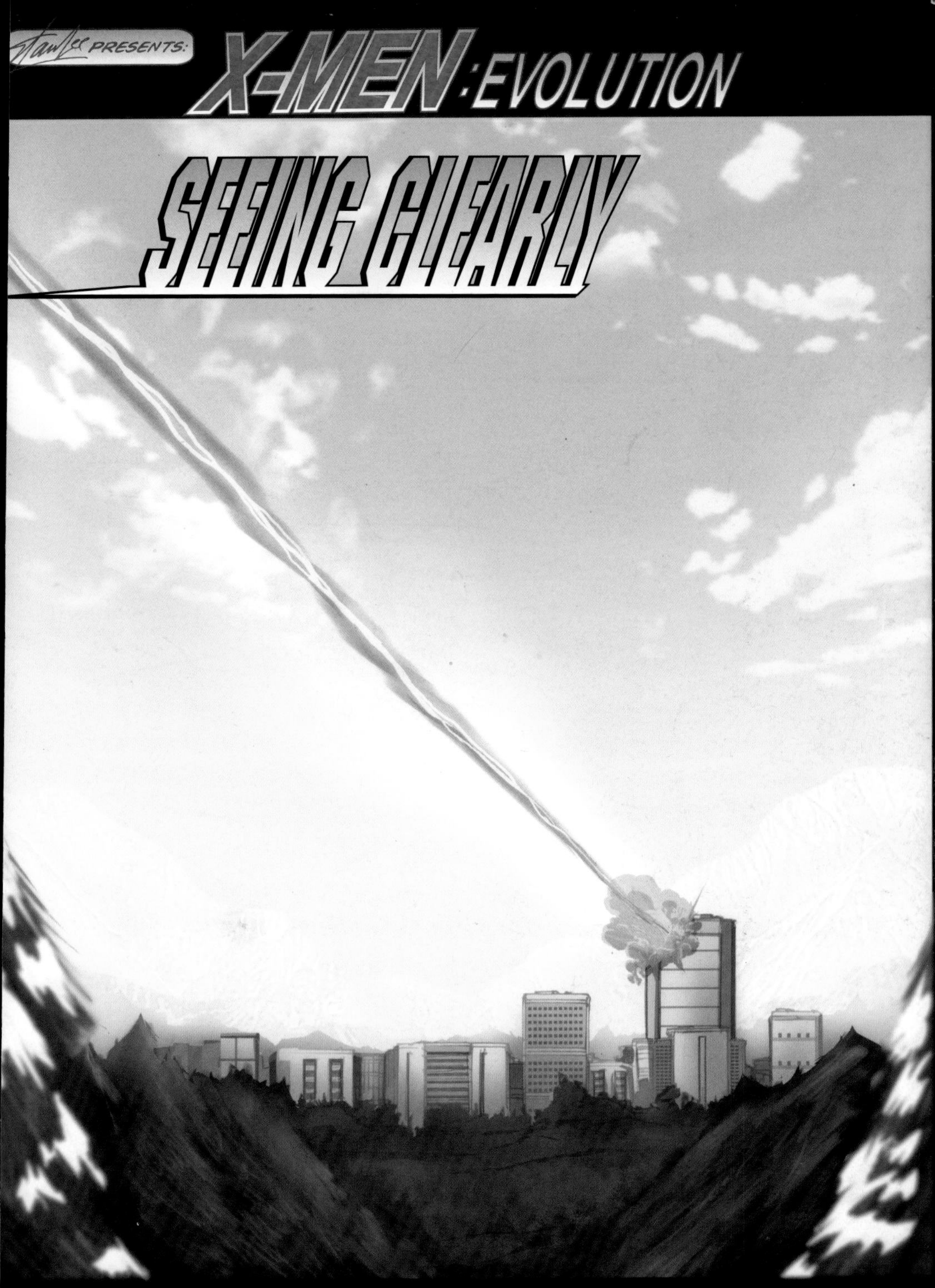

STAN LEE PRESENTS:
X-MEN: EVOLUTION
SEEING CLEARLY

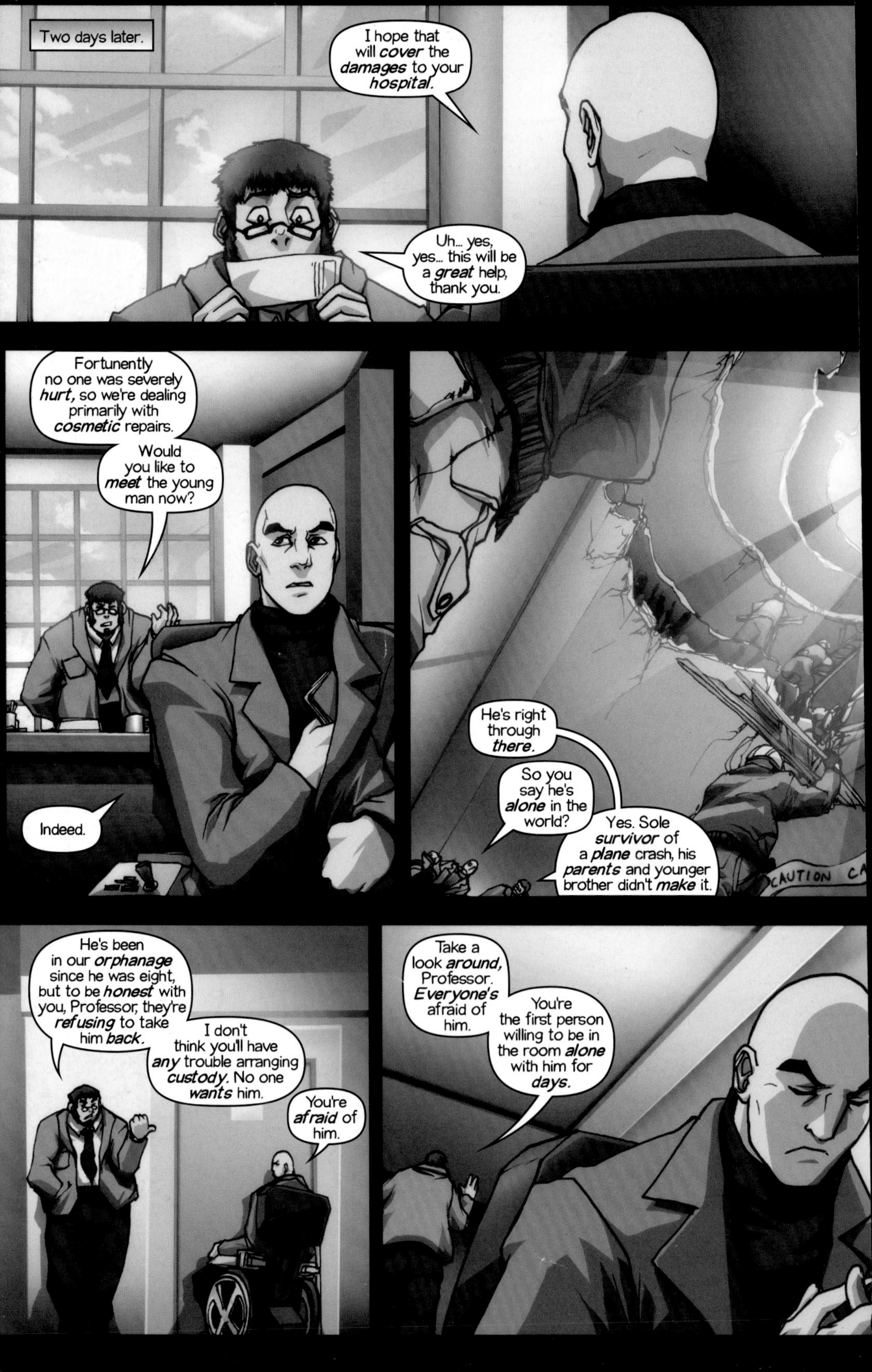
Two days later.
I hope that will cover the damages to your hospital.
Uh... yes, yes... this will be a great help, thank you.
Fortunently no one was severely hurt, so we're dealing primarily with cosmetic repairs.
Would you like to meet the young man now?
Indeed.
He's right through there.
So you say he's alone in the world?
Yes. Sole survivor of a plane crash, his parents and younger brother didn't make it.
CAUTION CA
He's been in our orphanage since he was eight, but to be honest with you, Professor, they're refusing to take him back.
I don't think you'll have any trouble arranging custody. No one wants him.
You're afraid of him.
Take a look around, Professor. Everyone's afraid of him.
You're the first person willing to be in the room alone with him for days.

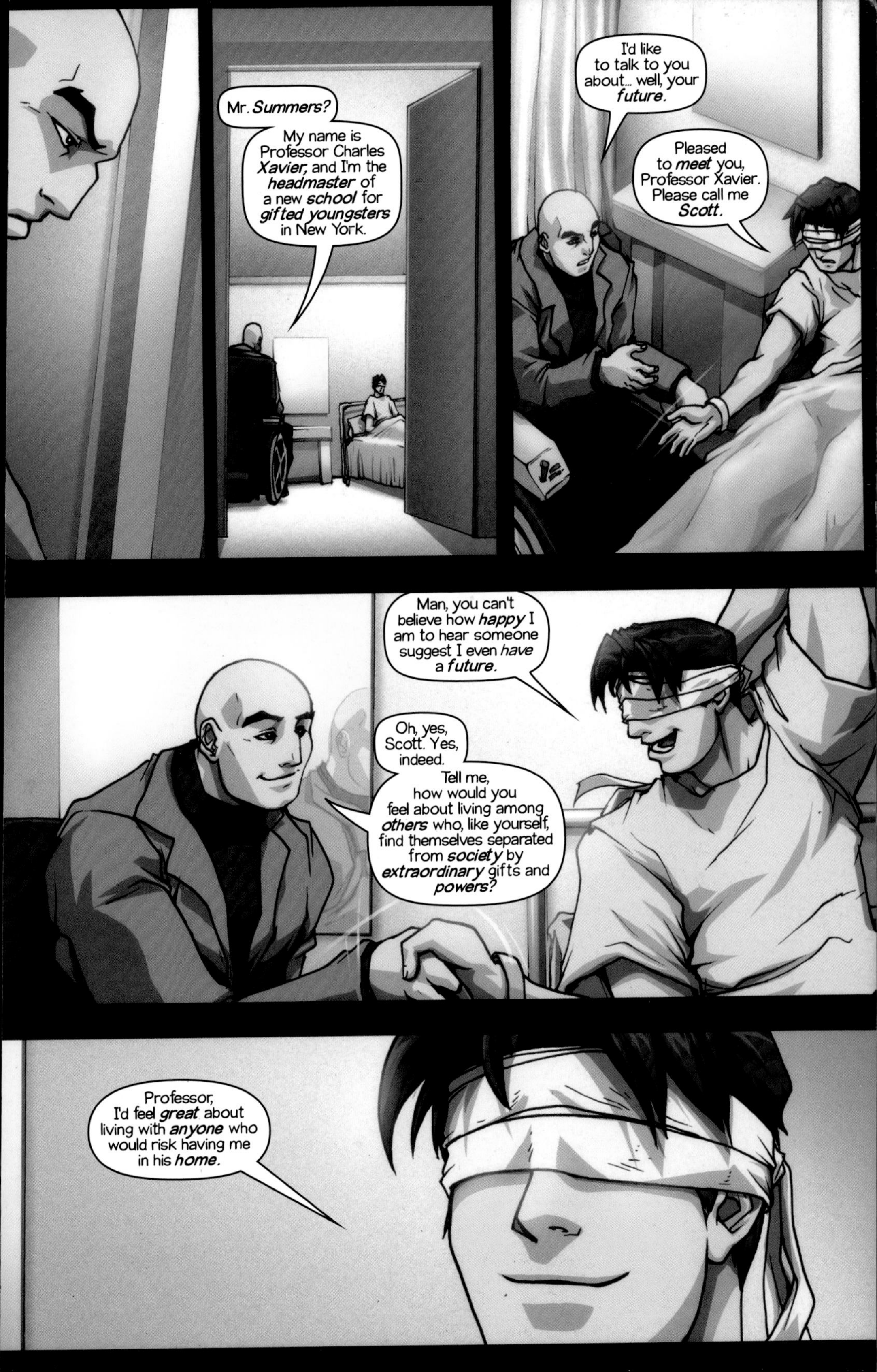
Mr. Summers?
My name is Professor Charles Xavier, and I'm the headmaster of a new school for gifted youngsters in New York.
I'd like to talk to you about... well, your future.
Pleased to meet you, Professor Xavier. Please call me Scott.
Man, you can't believe how happy I am to hear someone suggest I even have a future.
Oh, yes, Scott. Yes, indeed.
Tell me, how would you feel about living among others who, like yourself, find themselves separated from society by extraordinary gifts and powers?
Professor, I'd feel great about living with anyone who would risk having me in his home.

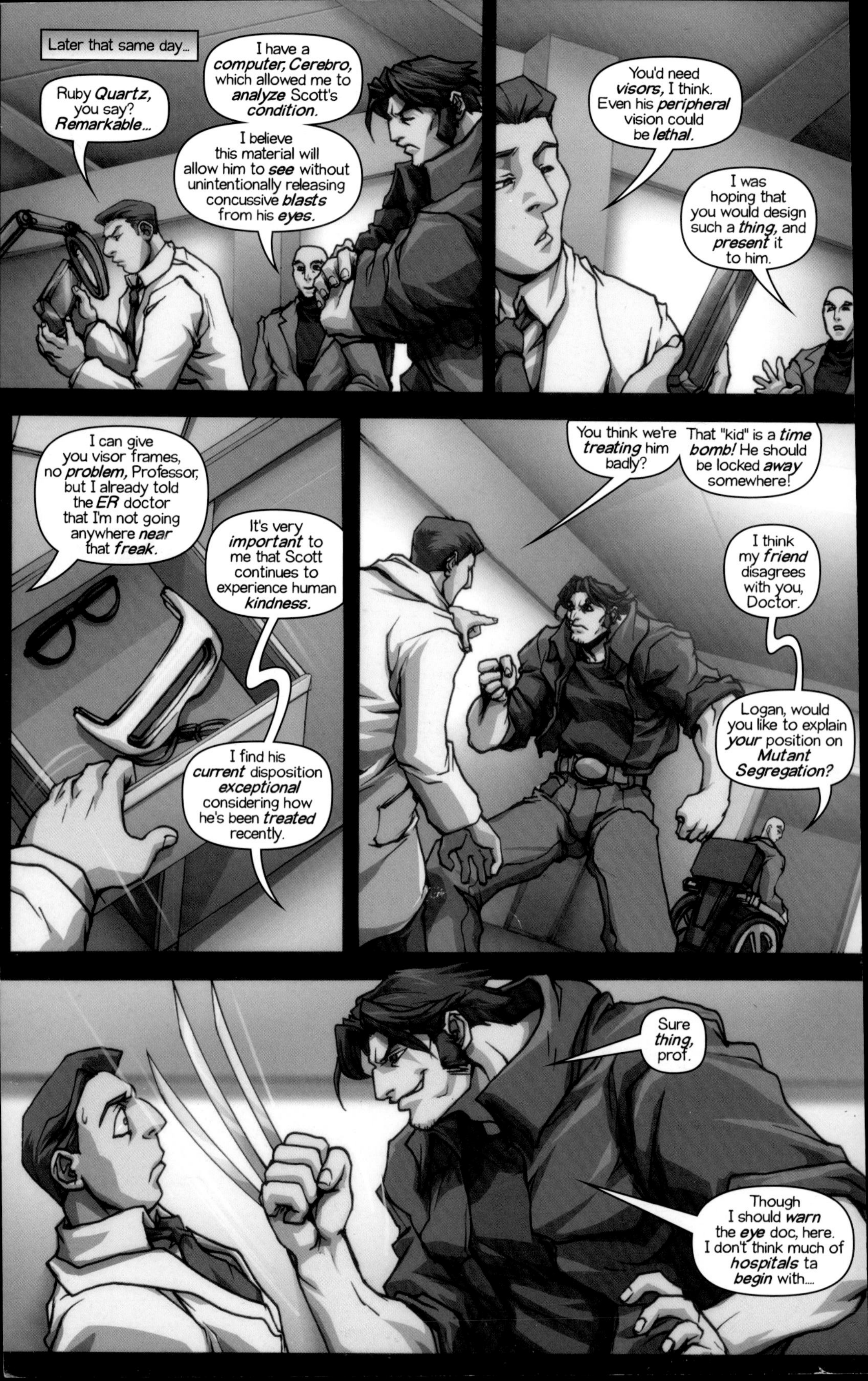
Later that same day...
Ruby Quartz, you say? Remarkable...
I have a computer, Cerebro, which allowed me to analyze Scott's condition.
I believe this material will allow him to see without unintentionally releasing concussive blasts from his eyes.
You'd need visors, I think. Even his peripheral vision could be lethal.
I was hoping that you would design such a thing, and present it to him.
I can give you visor frames, no problem, Professor, but I already told the ER doctor that I'm not going anywhere near that freak.
It's very important to me that Scott continues to experience human kindness.
I find his current disposition exceptional considering how he's been treated recently.
You think we're treating him badly?
That "kid" is a time bomb! He should be locked away somewhere!
I think my friend disagrees with you, Doctor.
Logan, would you like to explain your position on Mutant Segregation?
Sure thing, prof.
Though I should warn the eye doc, here. I don't think much of hospitals ta begin with....

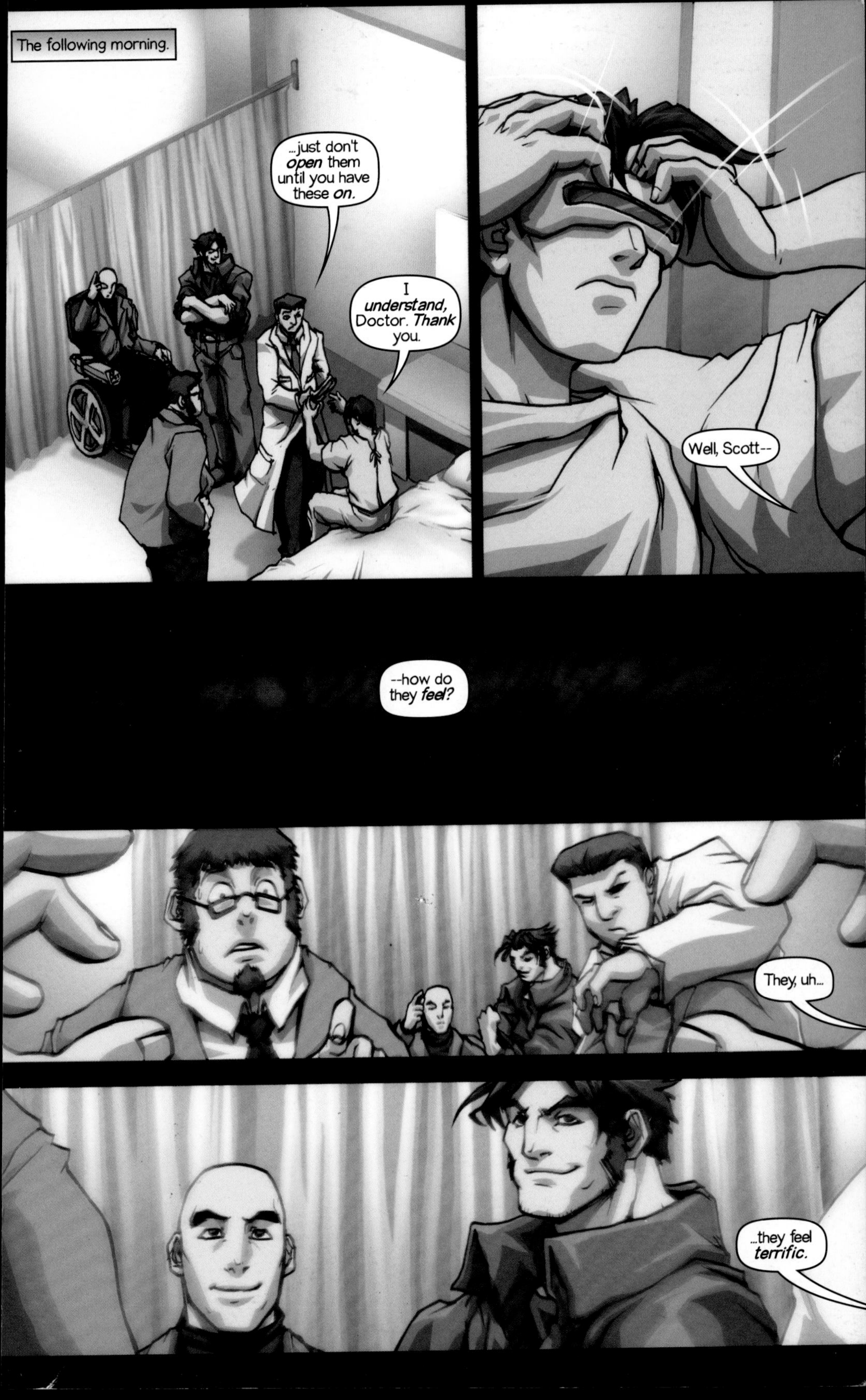
The following morning.
...just don't *open* them until you have these *on.*
I *understand,* Doctor. *Thank* you.
Well, Scott--
--how do they *feel?*
They, uh...
...they feel *terrific.*

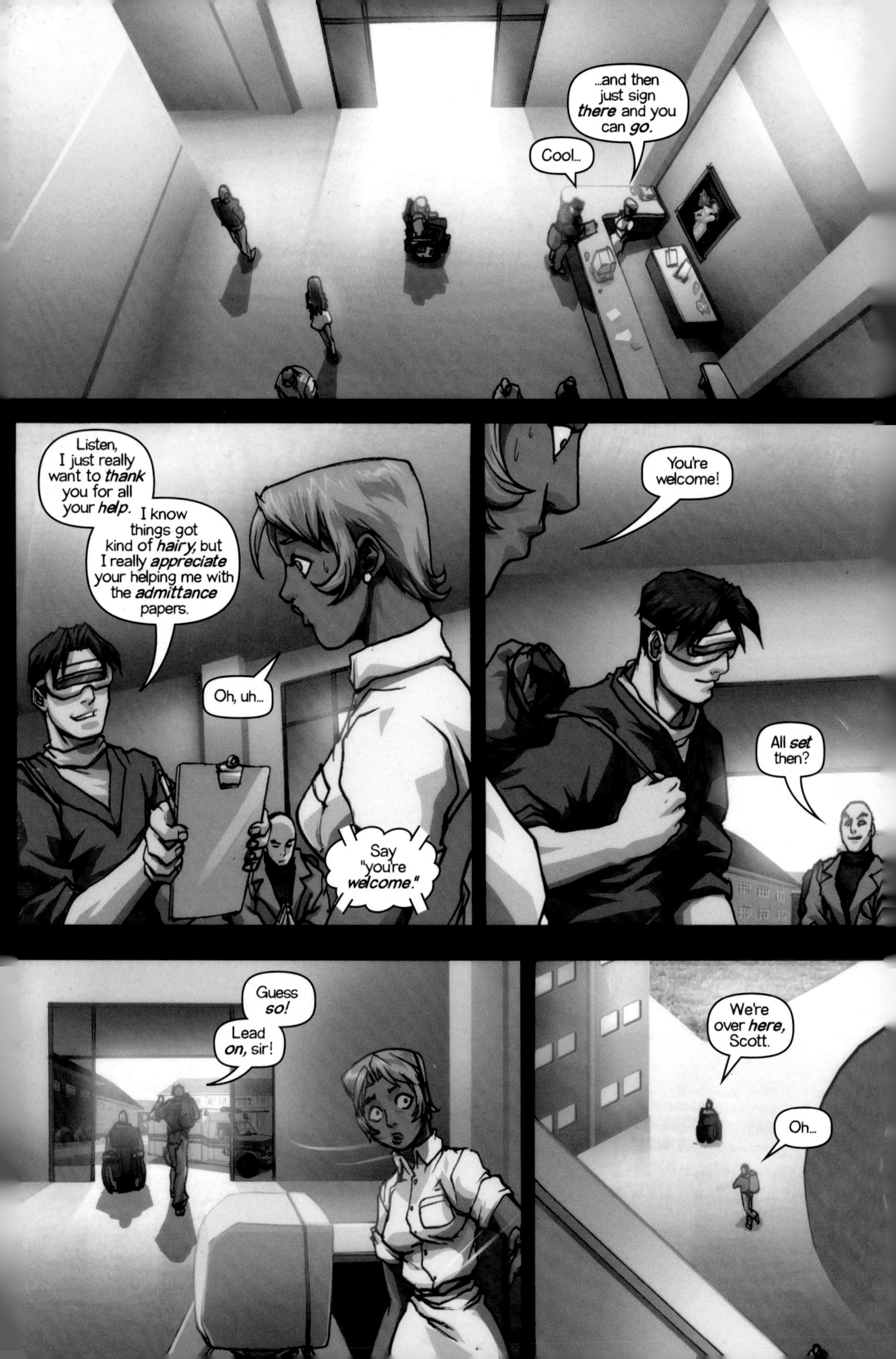

...and then just sign *there* and you can *go.*
Cool...
Listen, I just really want to *thank* you for all your *help.*
I know things got kind of *hairy,* but I really *appreciate* your helping me with the *admittance* papers.
Oh, uh...
Say "you're *welcome.*"
You're welcome!
All *set* then?
Guess *so!*
Lead *on,* sir!
We're over *here,* Scott.
Oh...

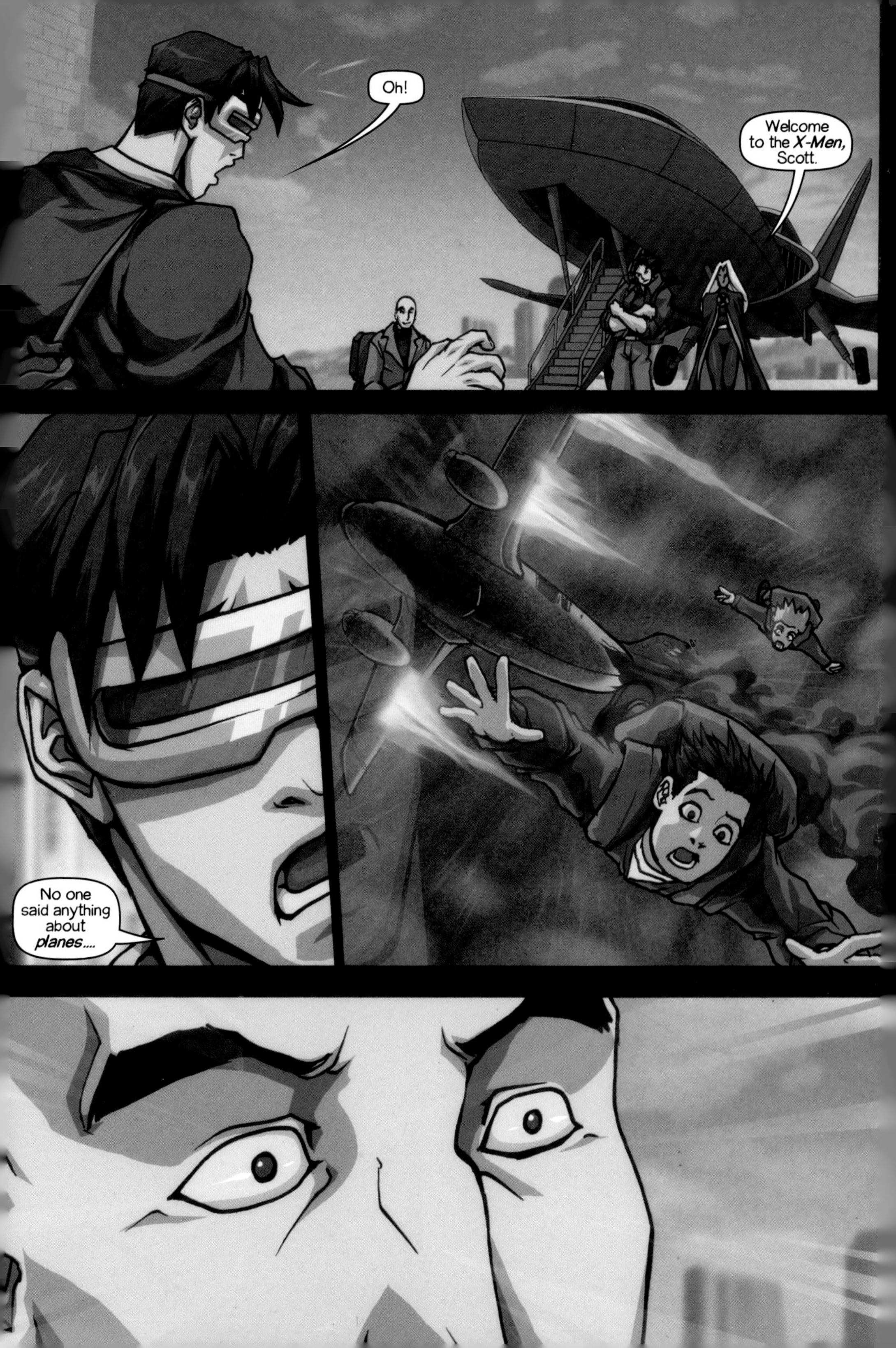
Oh!
Welcome to the *X-Men,* Scott.
No one said anything about *planes....*

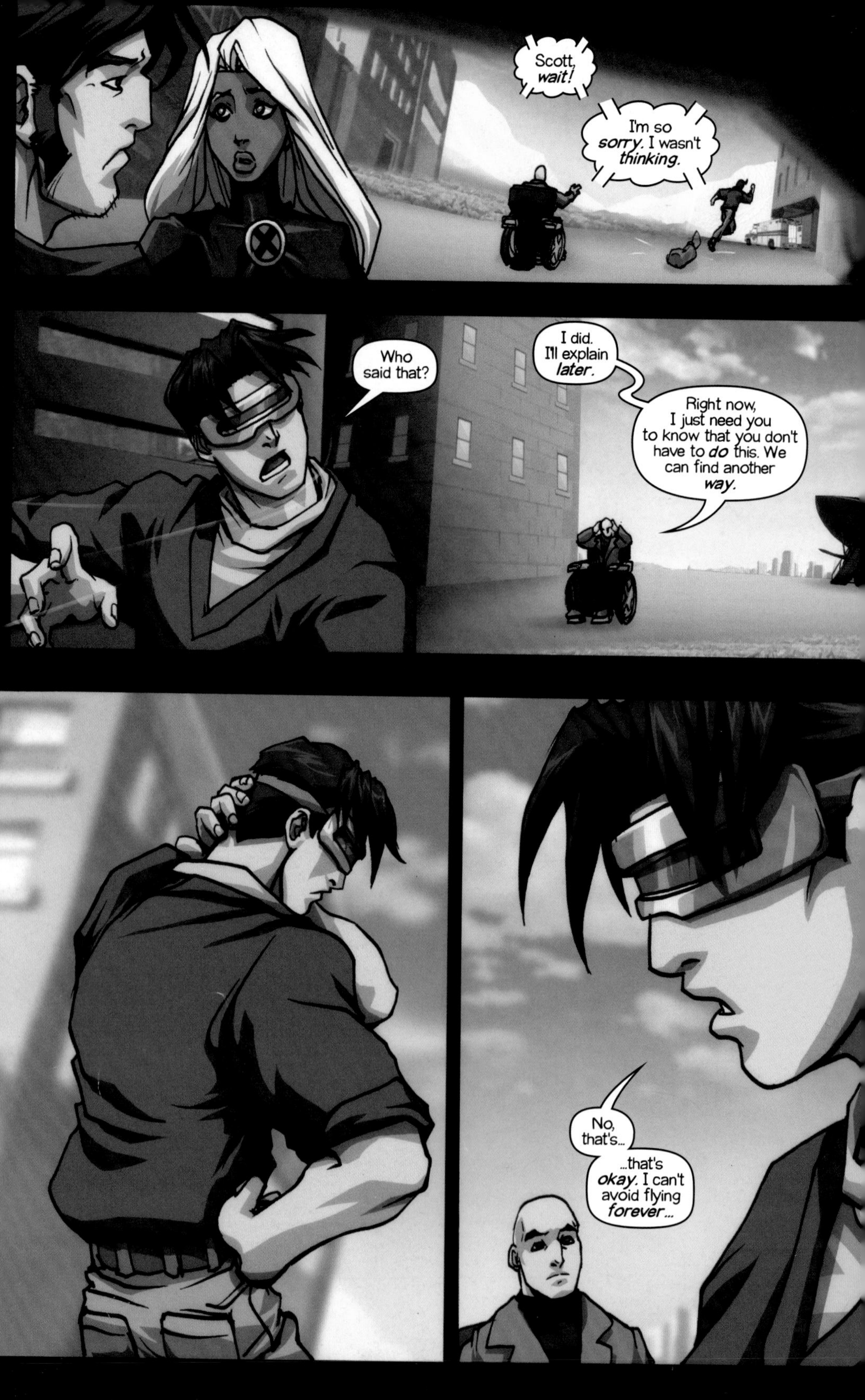
Scott, *wait!*
I'm so *sorry.* I wasn't *thinking.*
Who said that?
I did. I'll explain *later.*
Right now, I just need you to know that you don't have to *do* this. We can find another *way.*
No, that's...
...that's *okay.* I can't avoid flying *forever...*

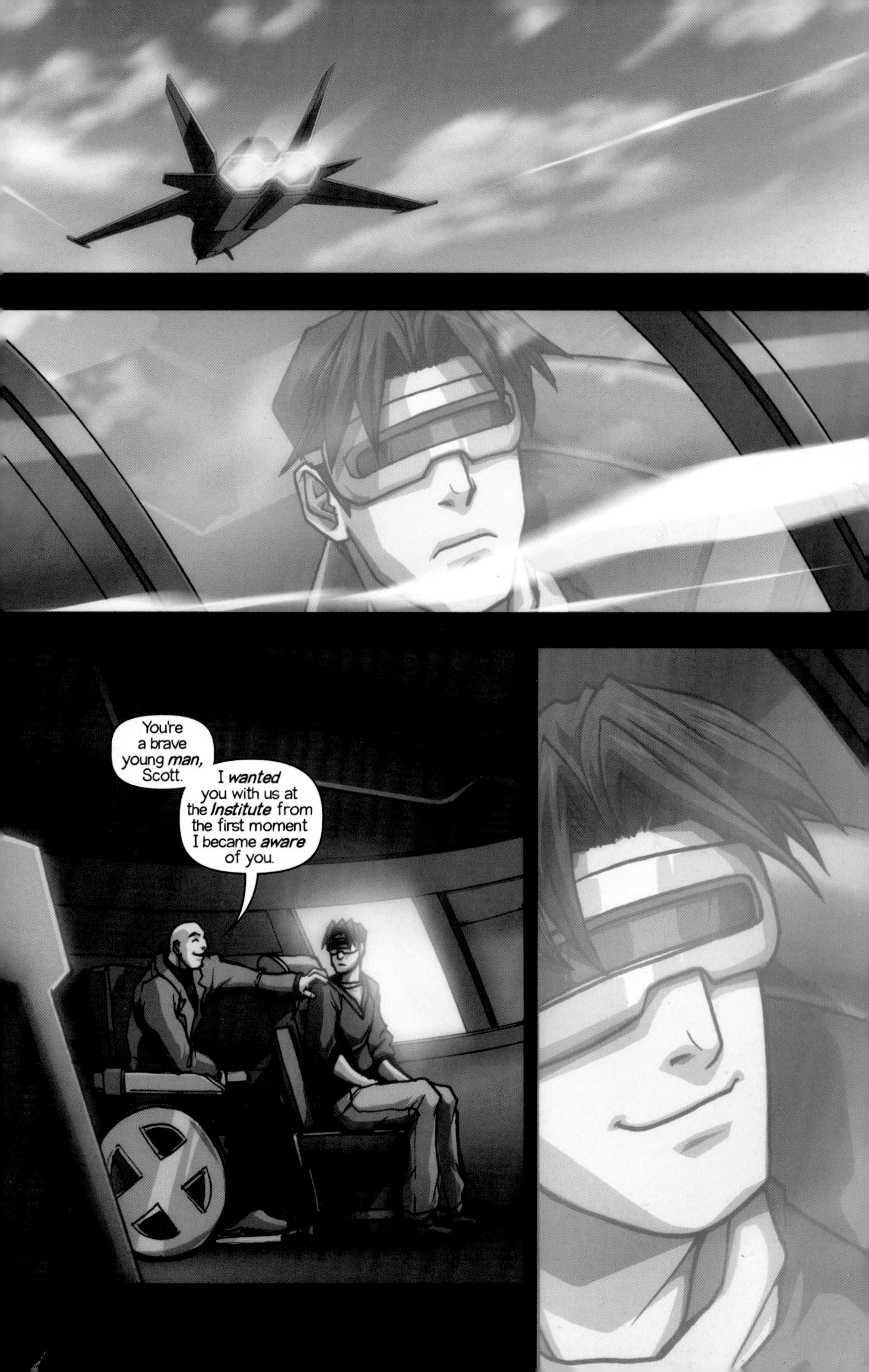
You're a brave young *man,* Scott.
I *wanted* you with us at the *Institute* from the first moment I became *aware* of you.

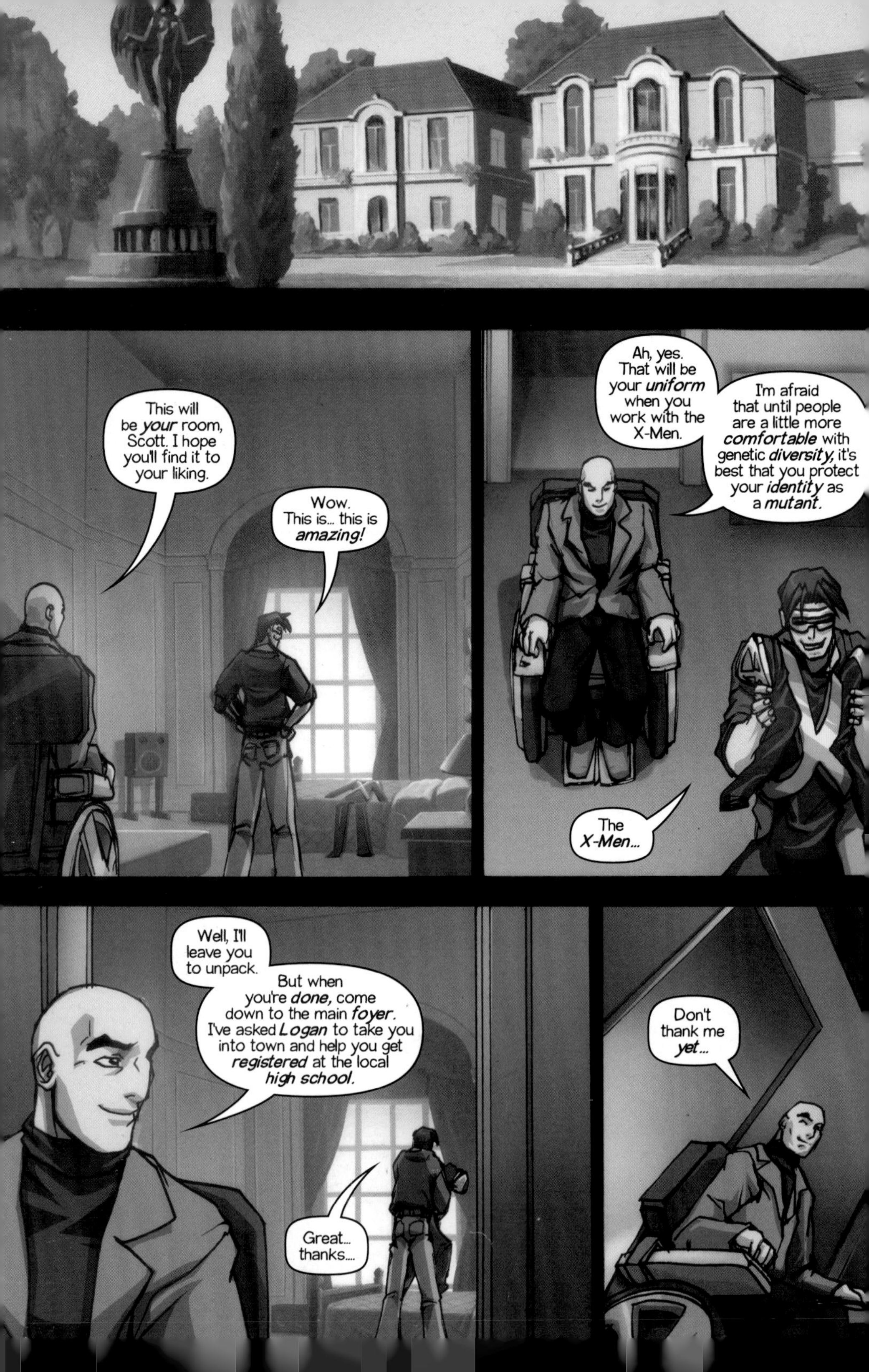
This will be your room, Scott. I hope you'll find it to your liking.
Wow. This is... this is amazing!
Ah, yes. That will be your uniform when you work with the X-Men.
I'm afraid that until people are a little more comfortable with genetic diversity, it's best that you protect your identity as a mutant.
The X-Men...
Well, I'll leave you to unpack.
But when you're done, come down to the main foyer. I've asked Logan to take you into town and help you get registered at the local high school.
Great... thanks....
Don't thank me yet...

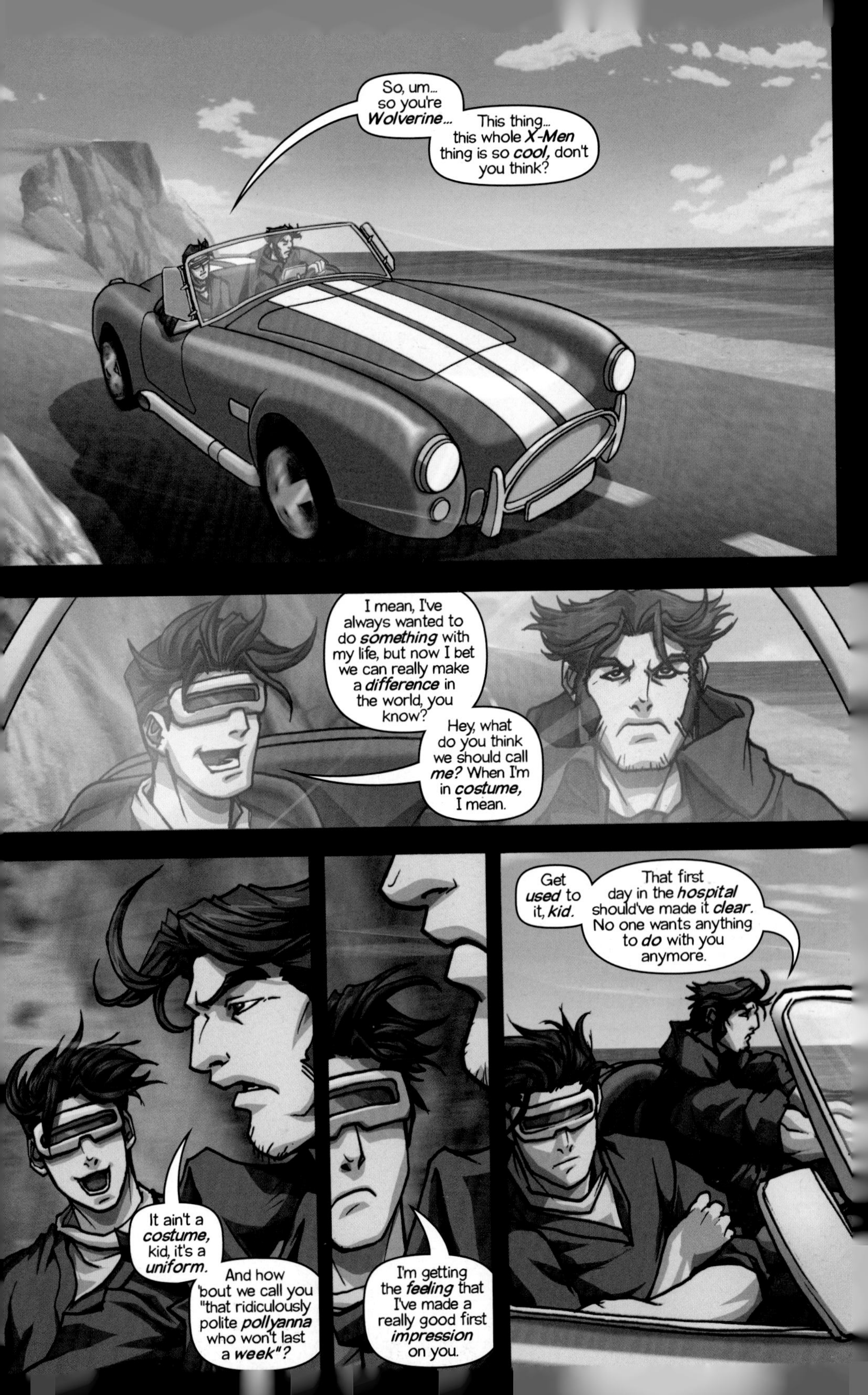
So, um... so you're Wolverine...
This thing... this whole X-Men thing is so cool, don't you think?
I mean, I've always wanted to do something with my life, but now I bet we can really make a difference in the world, you know?
Hey, what do you think we should call me? When I'm in costume, I mean.
It ain't a costume, kid, it's a uniform.
And how 'bout we call you "that ridiculously polite pollyanna who won't last a week"?
I'm getting the feeling that I've made a really good first impression on you.
Get used to it, kid.
That first day in the hospital should've made it clear. No one wants anything to do with you anymore.

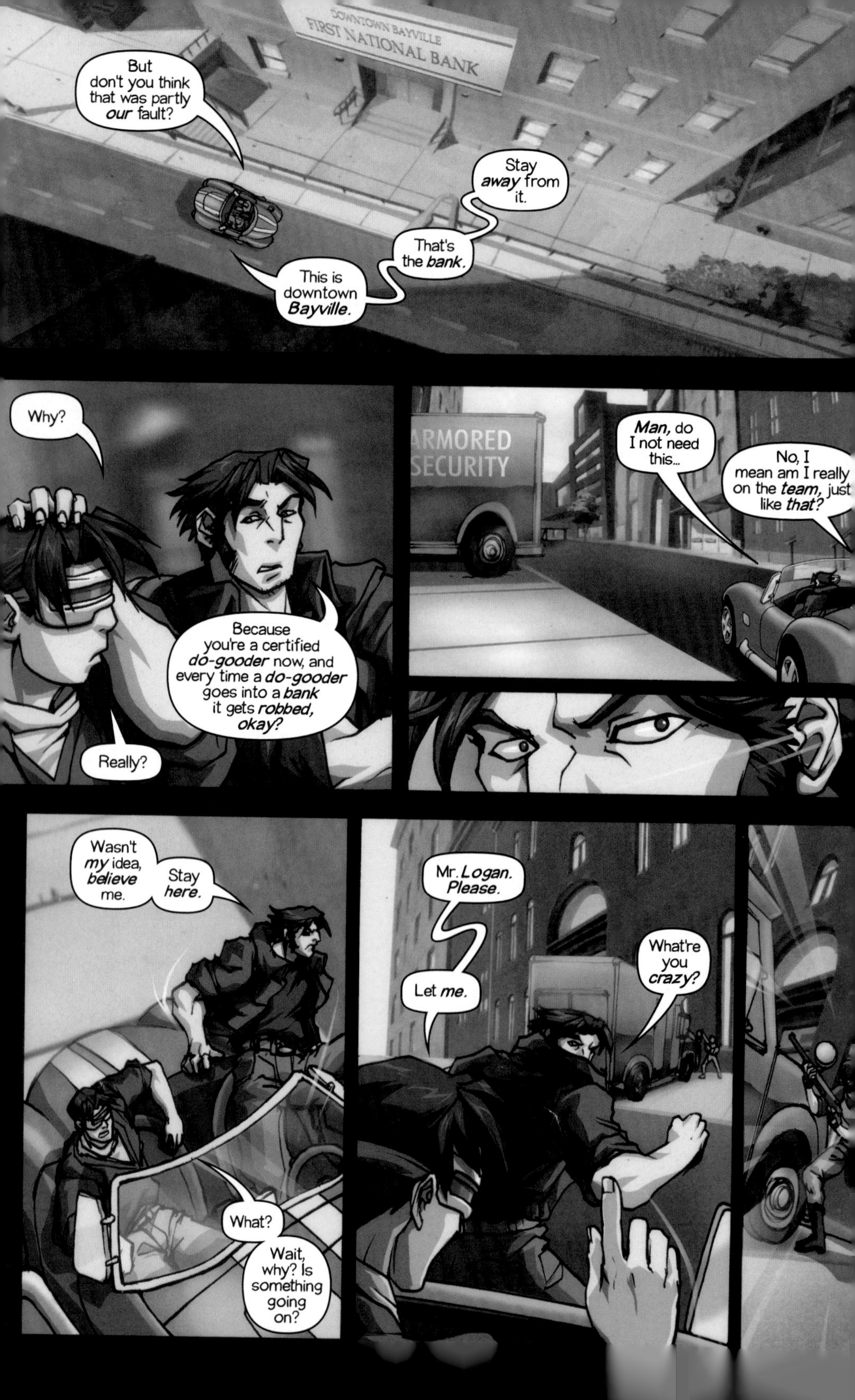

DOWNTOWN BAYVILLE FIRST NATIONAL BANK
But don't you think that was partly *our* fault?
This is downtown *Bayville.*
That's the *bank.*
Stay *away* from it.
Why?
Because you're a certified *do-gooder* now, and every time a *do-gooder* goes into a *bank* it gets *robbed, okay?*
Really?
ARMORED SECURITY
Man, do I not need this...
No, I mean am I really on the *team,* just like *that?*
Wasn't *my* idea, *believe* me.
Stay *here.*
What?
Wait, why? Is something going on?
Mr. *Logan. Please.*
Let *me.*
What're you *crazy?*

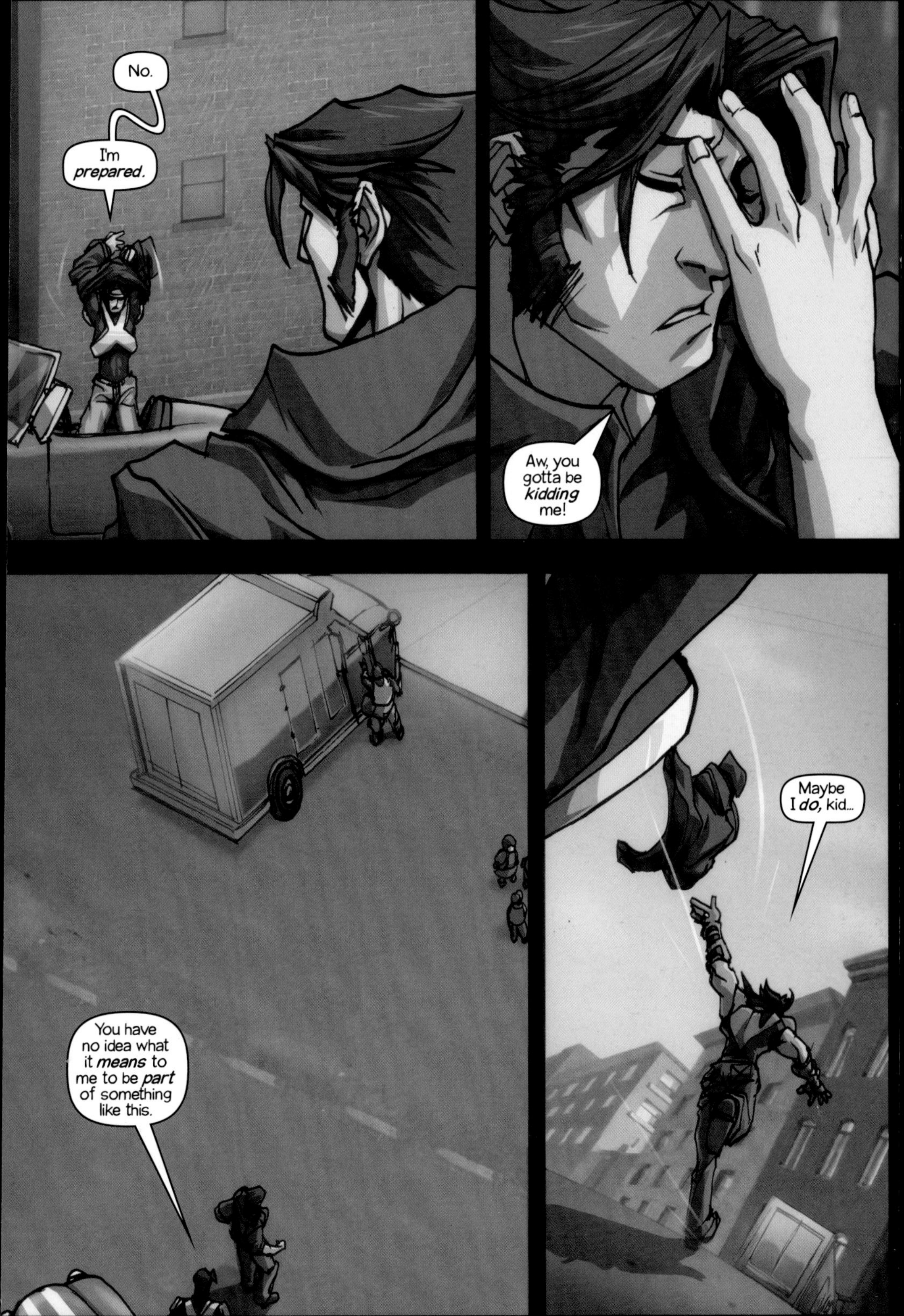
No.
I'm *prepared.*
Aw, you gotta be *kidding* me!
You have no idea what it *means* to me to be *part* of something like this.
Maybe I *do,* kid...

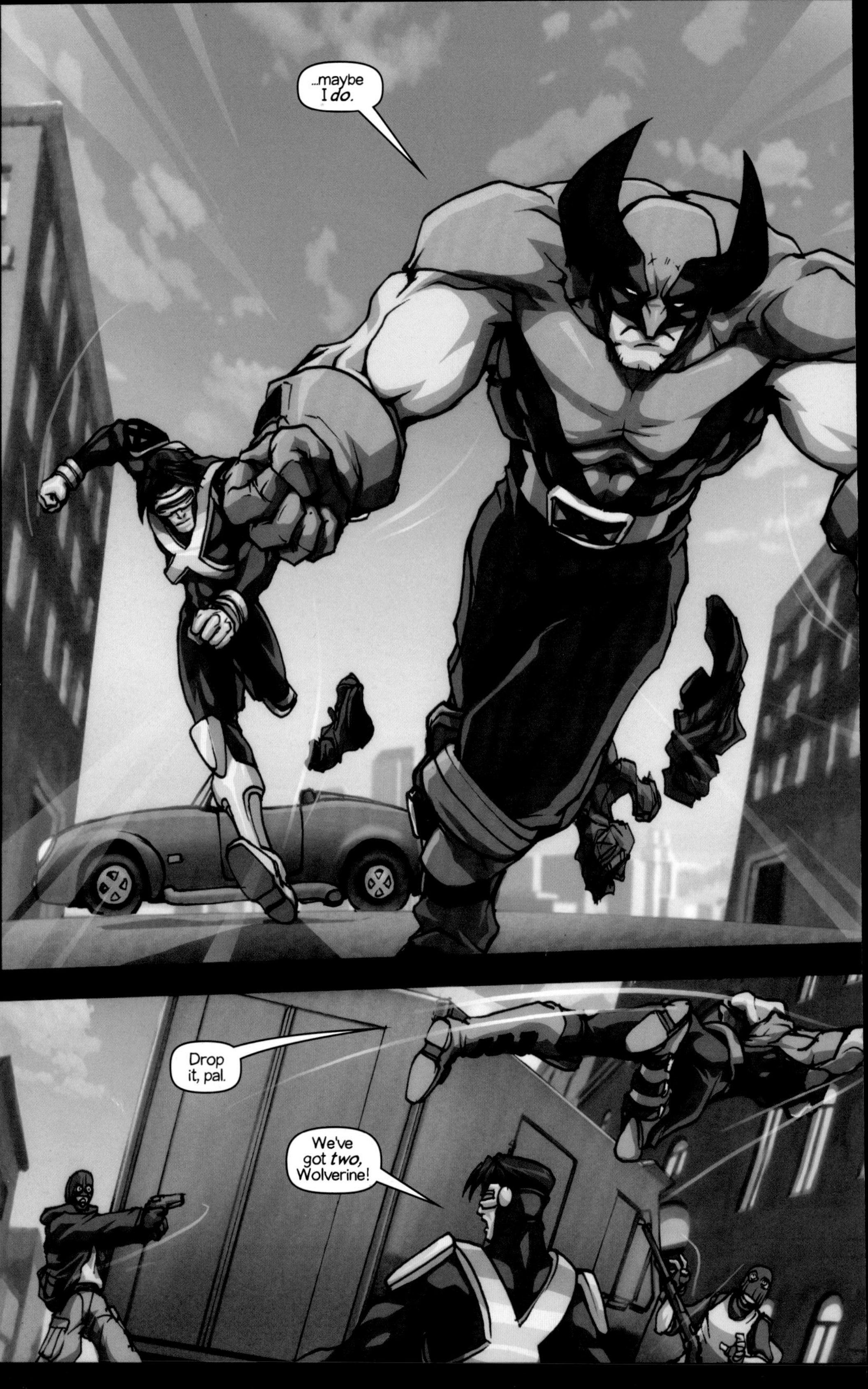
...maybe I *do.*
Drop it, pal.
We've got *two,* Wolverine!

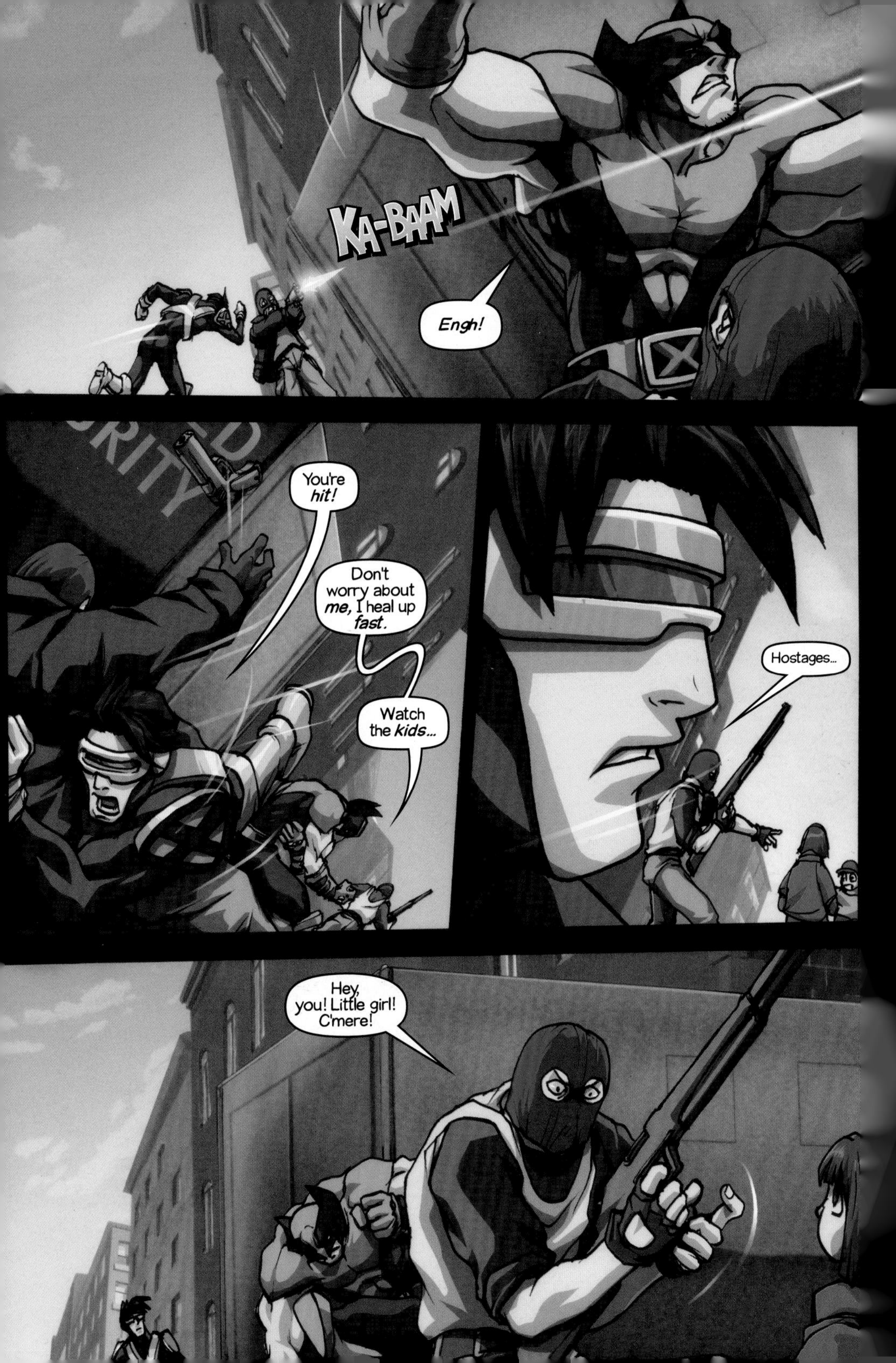

KA-BAAM
Engh!
You're *hit!*
Don't worry about *me,* I heal up *fast.*
Watch the *kids...*
Hostages...
Hey, you! Little girl! C'mere!

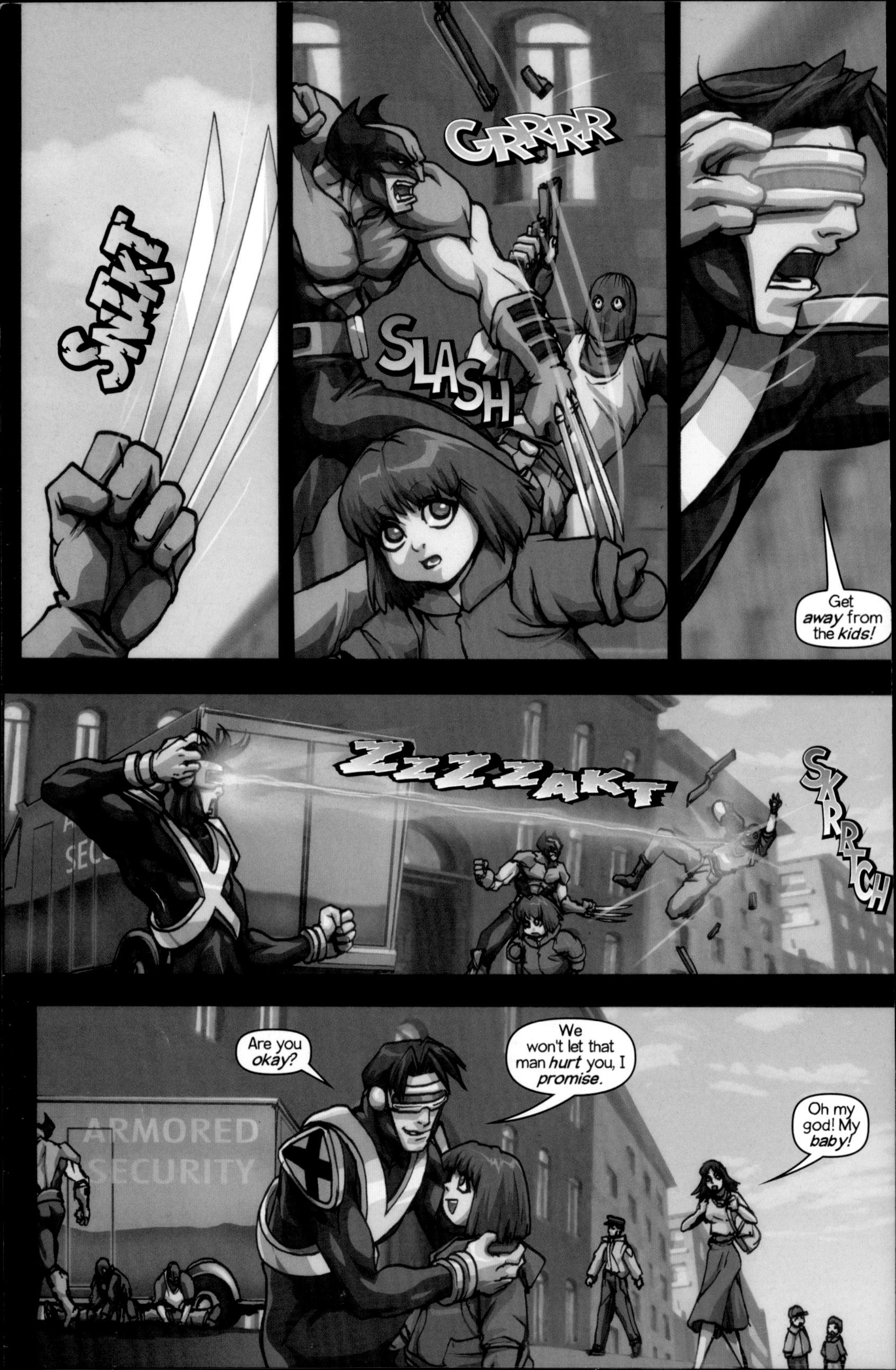
SNIKT
GRRRR
SLASH
Get away from the kids!
ZZZZZAKT
SKRRTCH
ARMORED SECURITY
Are you okay?
We won't let that man hurt you, I promise.
Oh my god! My baby!

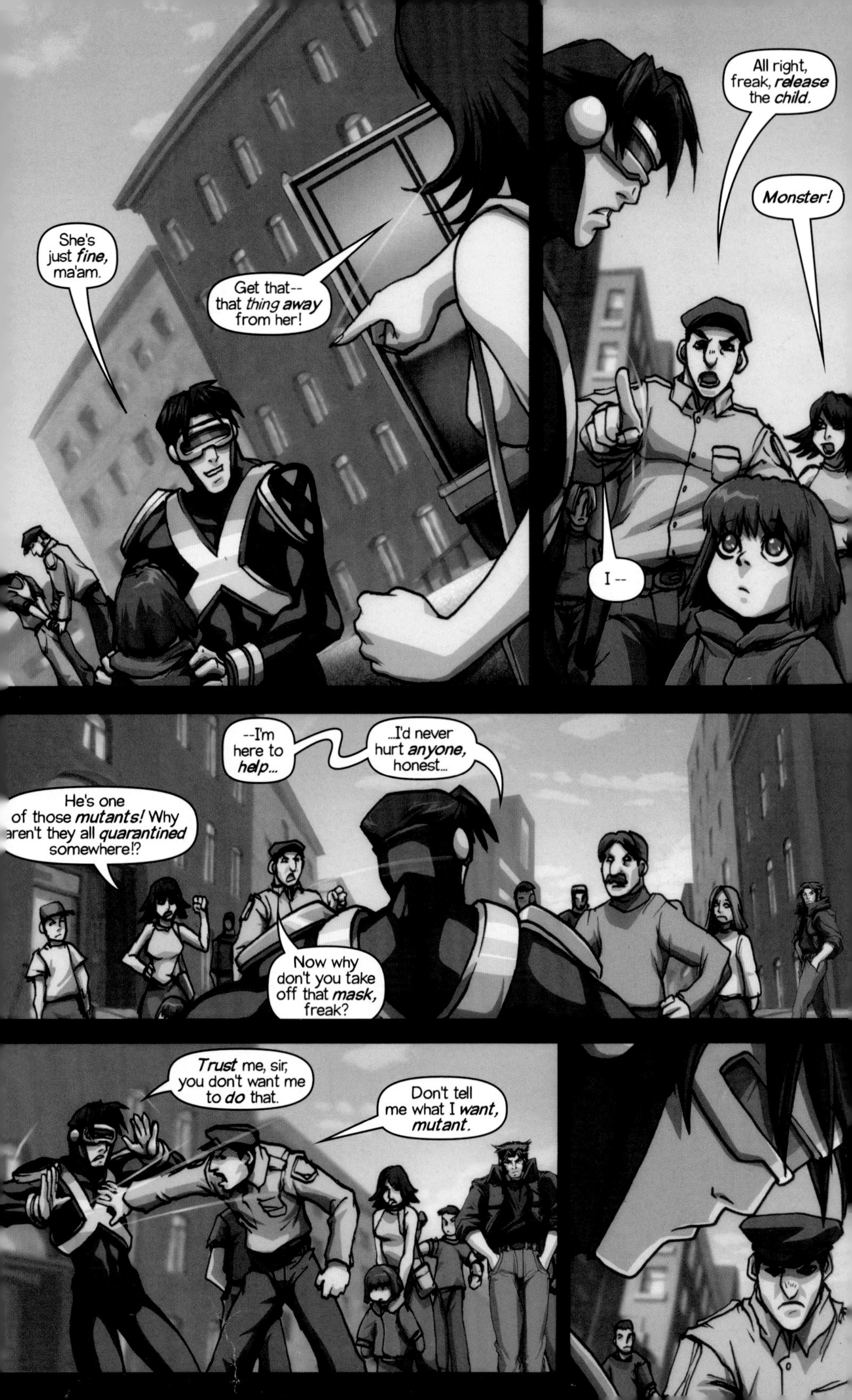

She's just fine, ma'am.
Get that-- that thing away from her!
All right, freak, release the child.
Monster!
I --
--I'm here to help...
...I'd never hurt anyone, honest...
He's one of those mutants! Why aren't they all quarantined somewhere!?
Now why don't you take off that mask, freak?
Trust me, sir, you don't want me to do that.
Don't tell me what I want, mutant.

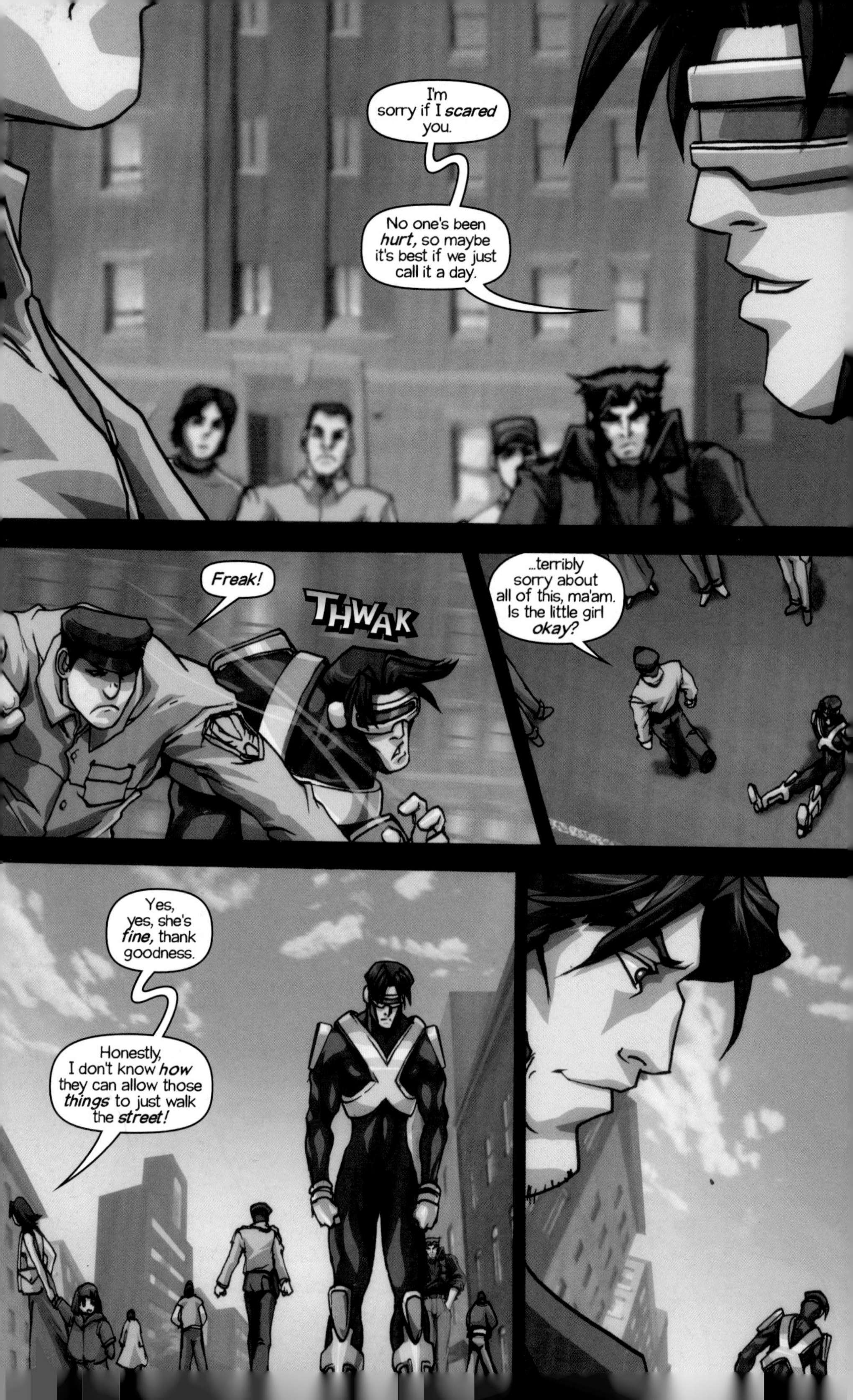
I'm sorry if I *scared* you.
No one's been *hurt,* so maybe it's best if we just call it a day.
Freak!
THWAK
...terribly sorry about all of this, ma'am. Is the little girl *okay?*
Yes, yes, she's *fine,* thank goodness.
Honestly, I don't know *how* they can allow those *things* to just walk the *street!*

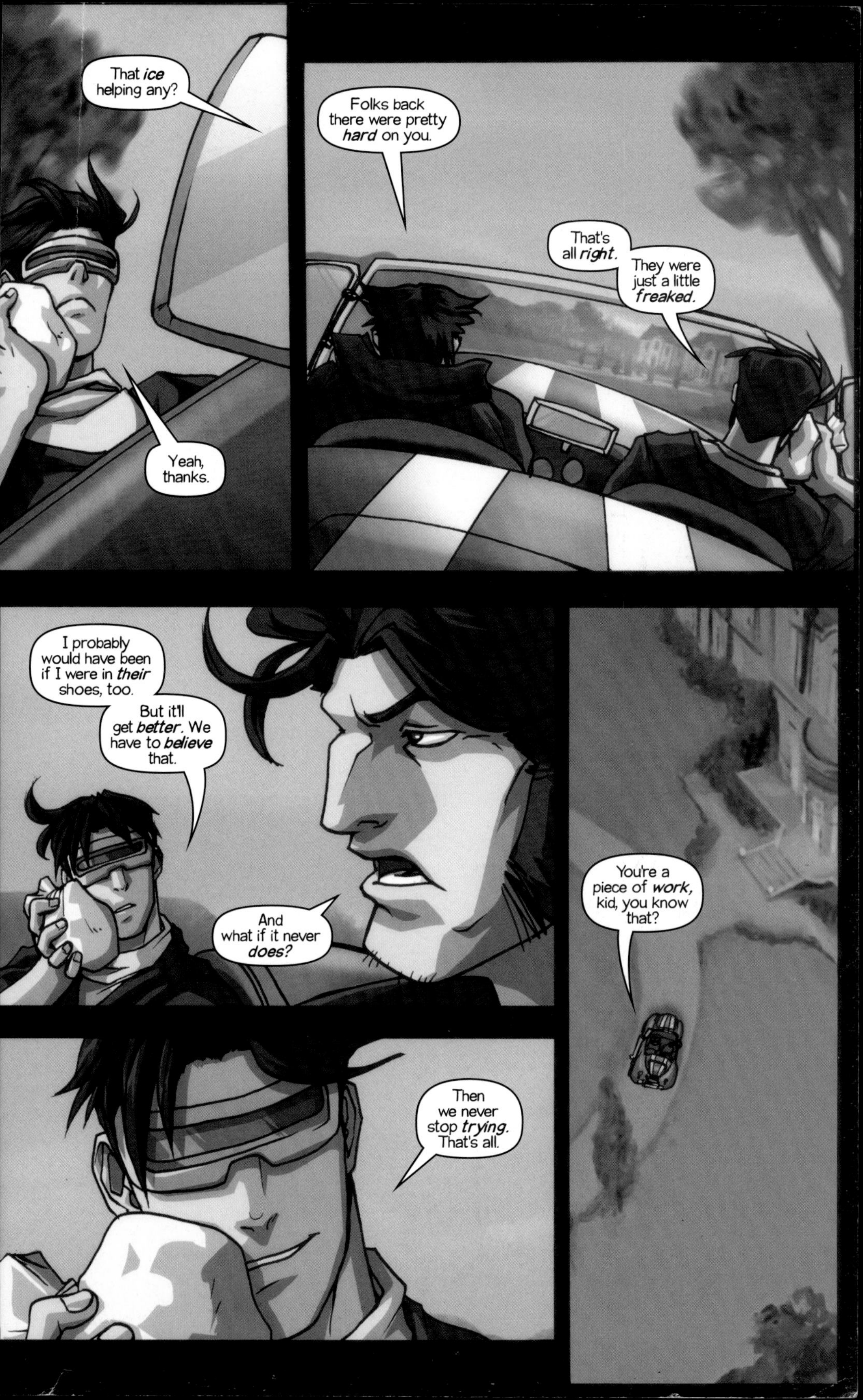
That *ice* helping any?
Yeah, thanks.
Folks back there were pretty *hard* on you.
That's all *right.*
They were just a little *freaked.*
I probably would have been if I were in *their* shoes, too.
But it'll get *better.* We have to *believe* that.
And what if it never *does?*
Then we never stop *trying.* That's all.
You're a piece of *work,* kid, you know that?

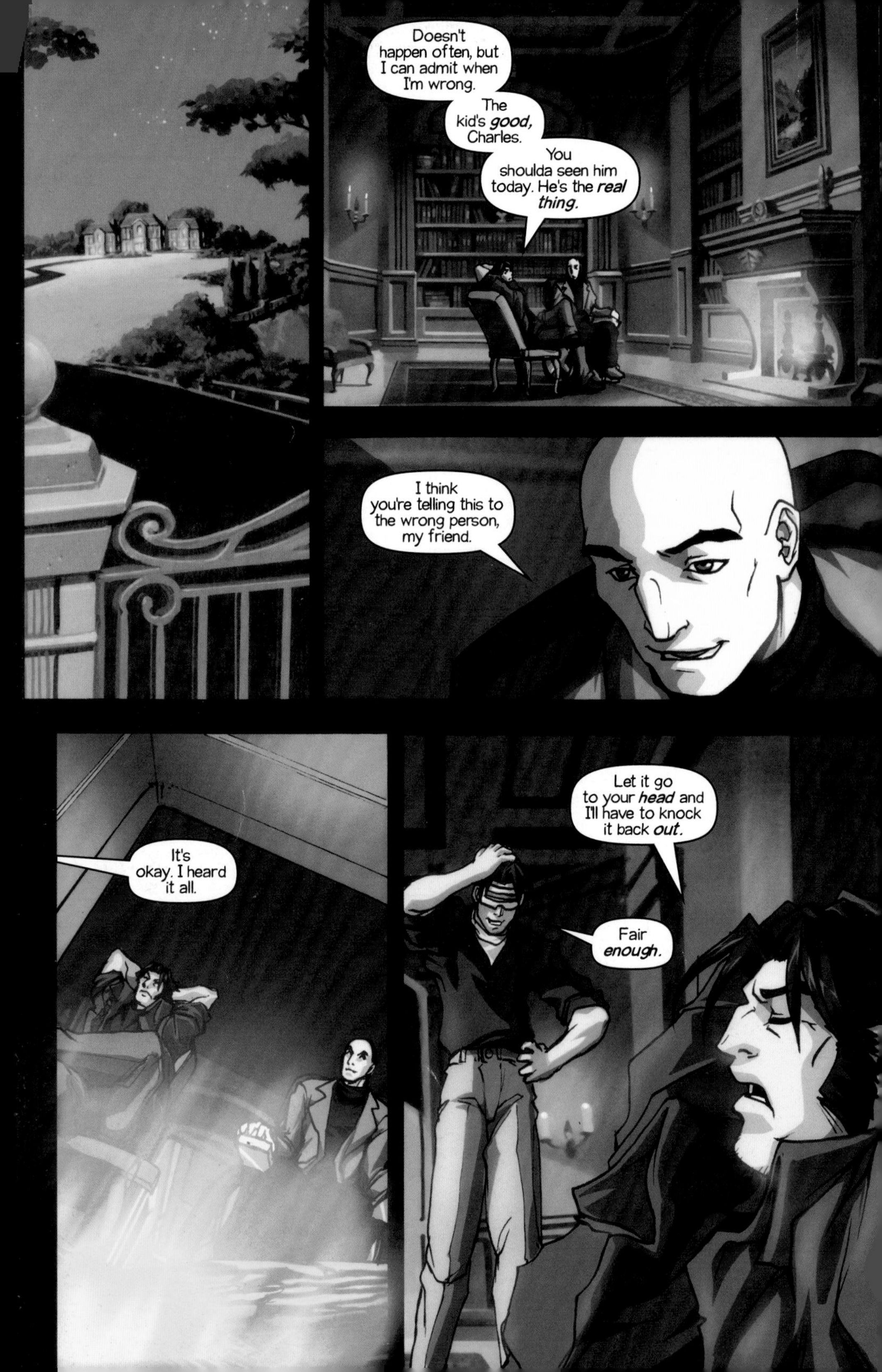

Doesn't happen often, but I can admit when I'm wrong.
The kid's *good,* Charles.
You shoulda seen him today. He's the *real thing.*
I think you're telling this to the wrong person, my friend.
It's okay. I heard it all.
Let it go to your *head* and I'll have to knock it back *out.*
Fair *enough.*

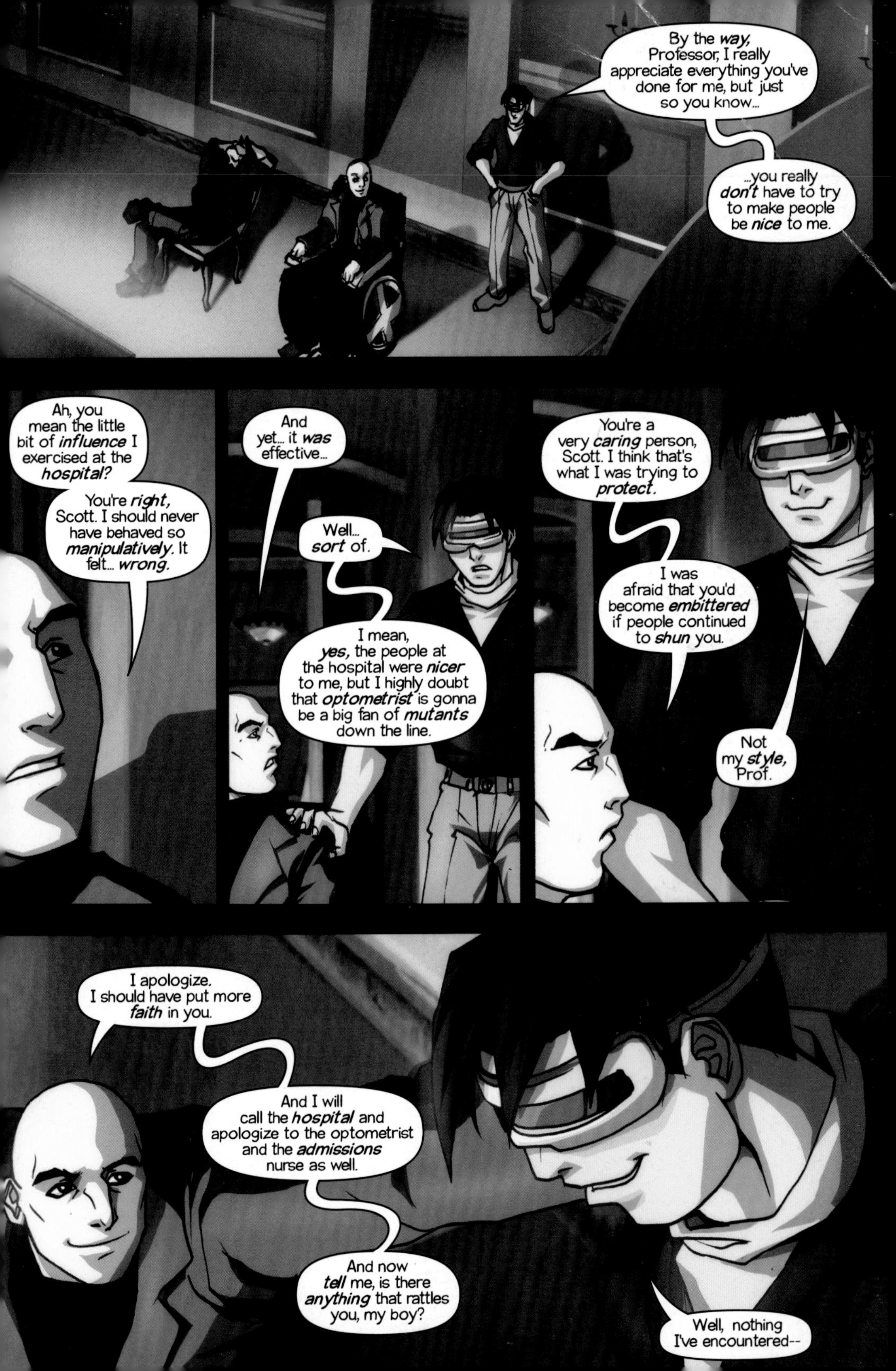
By the way, Professor, I really appreciate everything you've done for me, but just so you know...
...you really don't have to try to make people be nice to me.
Ah, you mean the little bit of influence I exercised at the hospital?
You're right, Scott. I should never have behaved so manipulatively. It felt... wrong.
And yet... it was effective...
Well... sort of.
I mean, yes, the people at the hospital were nicer to me, but I highly doubt that optometrist is gonna be a big fan of mutants down the line.
You're a very caring person, Scott. I think that's what I was trying to protect.
I was afraid that you'd become embittered if people continued to shun you.
Not my style, Prof.
I apologize. I should have put more faith in you.
And I will call the hospital and apologize to the optometrist and the admissions nurse as well.
And now tell me, is there anything that rattles you, my boy?
Well, nothing I've encountered--

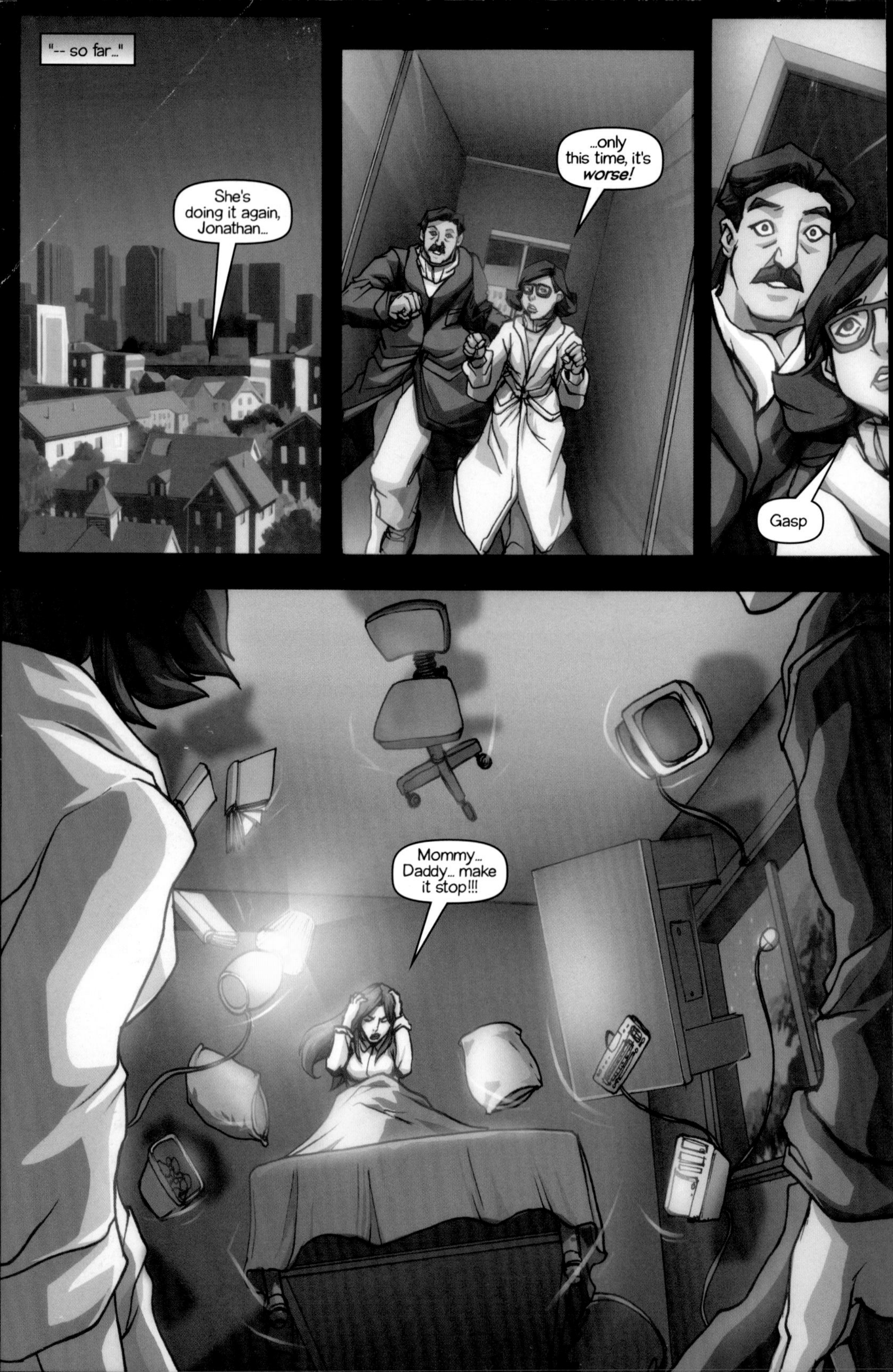
"-- so far..."
She's doing it again, Jonathan...
...only this time, it's *worse!*
Gasp
Mommy... Daddy... make it stop!!!

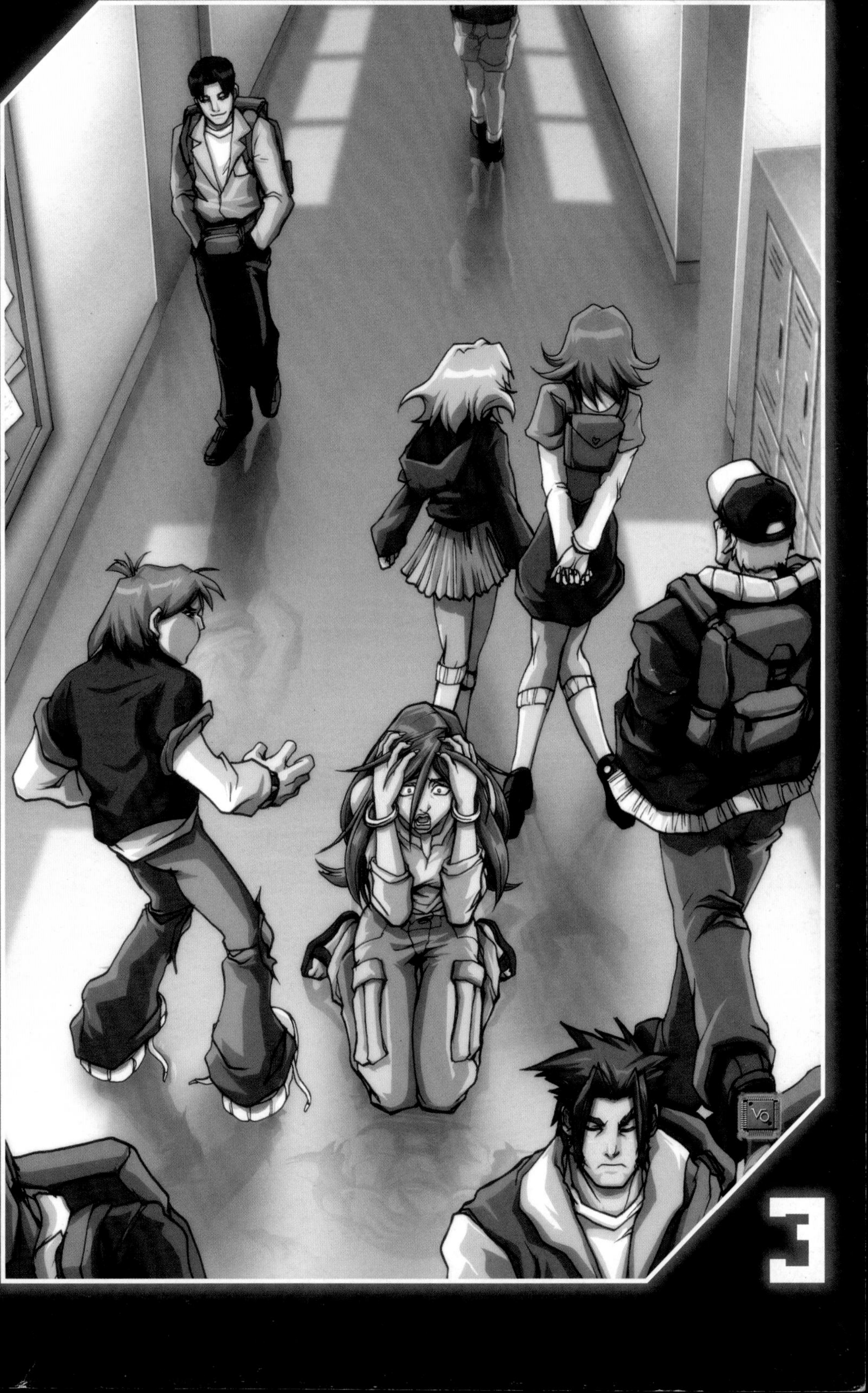

3

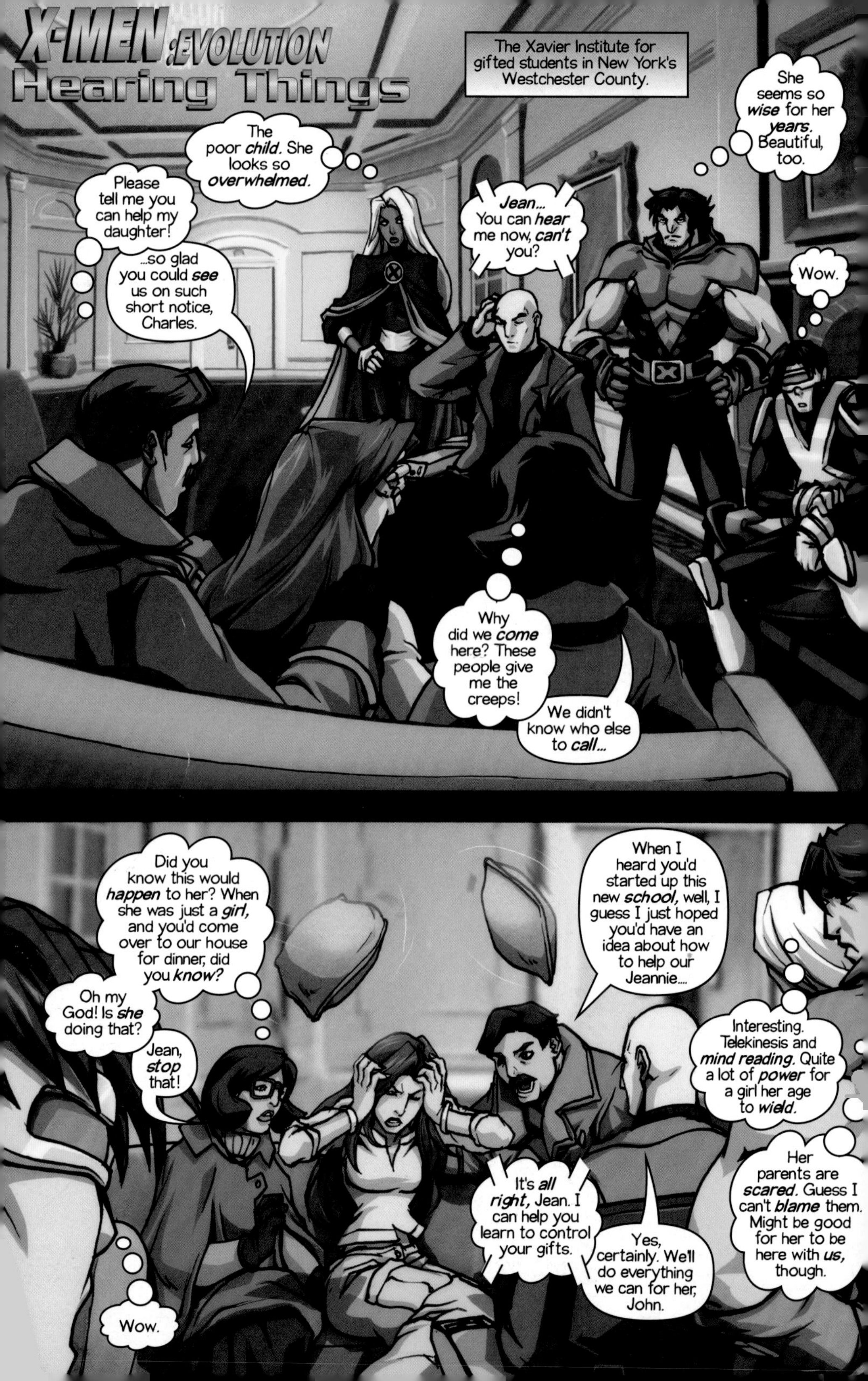
X-MEN: EVOLUTION
Hearing Things
The Xavier Institute for gifted students in New York's Westchester County.
Please tell me you can help my daughter!
The poor child. She looks so overwhelmed.
...so glad you could see us on such short notice, Charles.
Jean... You can hear me now, can't you?
She seems so wise for her years. Beautiful, too.
Wow.
Why did we come here? These people give me the creeps!
We didn't know who else to call...
Did you know this would happen to her? When she was just a girl, and you'd come over to our house for dinner, did you know?
When I heard you'd started up this new school, well, I guess I just hoped you'd have an idea about how to help our Jeannie....
Oh my God! Is she doing that?
Jean, stop that!
Interesting. Telekinesis and mind reading. Quite a lot of power for a girl her age to wield.
It's all right, Jean. I can help you learn to control your gifts.
Yes, certainly. We'll do everything we can for her, John.
Her parents are scared. Guess I can't blame them. Might be good for her to be here with us, though.
Wow.

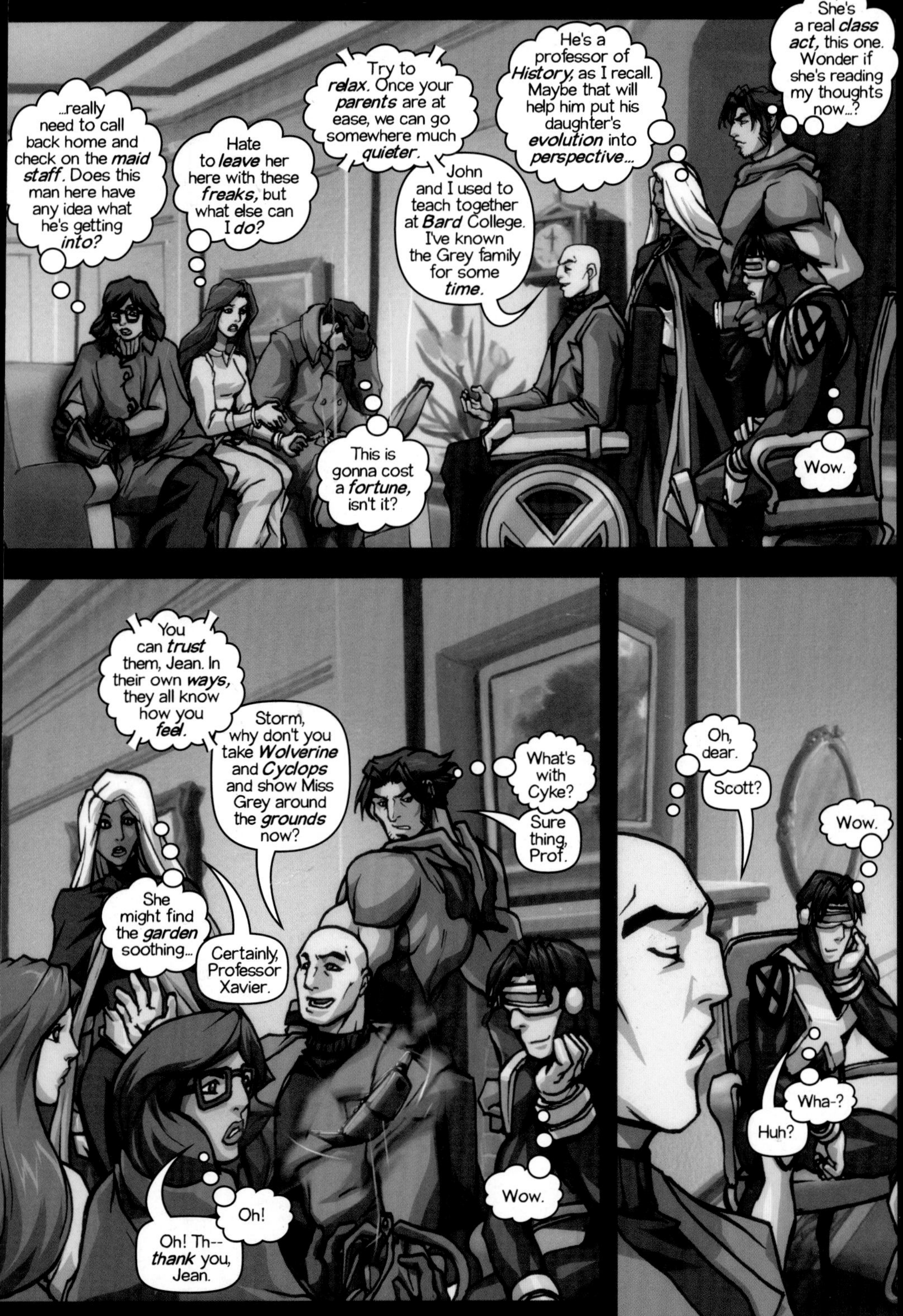
...really need to call back home and check on the maid staff. Does this man here have any idea what he's getting into?
Hate to leave her here with these freaks, but what else can I do?
Try to relax. Once your parents are at ease, we can go somewhere much quieter.
John and I used to teach together at Bard College. I've known the Grey family for some time.
This is gonna cost a fortune, isn't it?
He's a professor of History, as I recall. Maybe that will help him put his daughter's evolution into perspective...
She's a real class act, this one. Wonder if she's reading my thoughts now...?
Wow.
You can trust them, Jean. In their own ways, they all know how you feel.
Storm, why don't you take Wolverine and Cyclops and show Miss Grey around the grounds now?
What's with Cyke?
Sure thing, Prof.
She might find the garden soothing...
Certainly, Professor Xavier.
Oh!
Oh! Th--thank you, Jean.
Wow.
Oh, dear.
Scott?
Wow.
Wha-?
Huh?

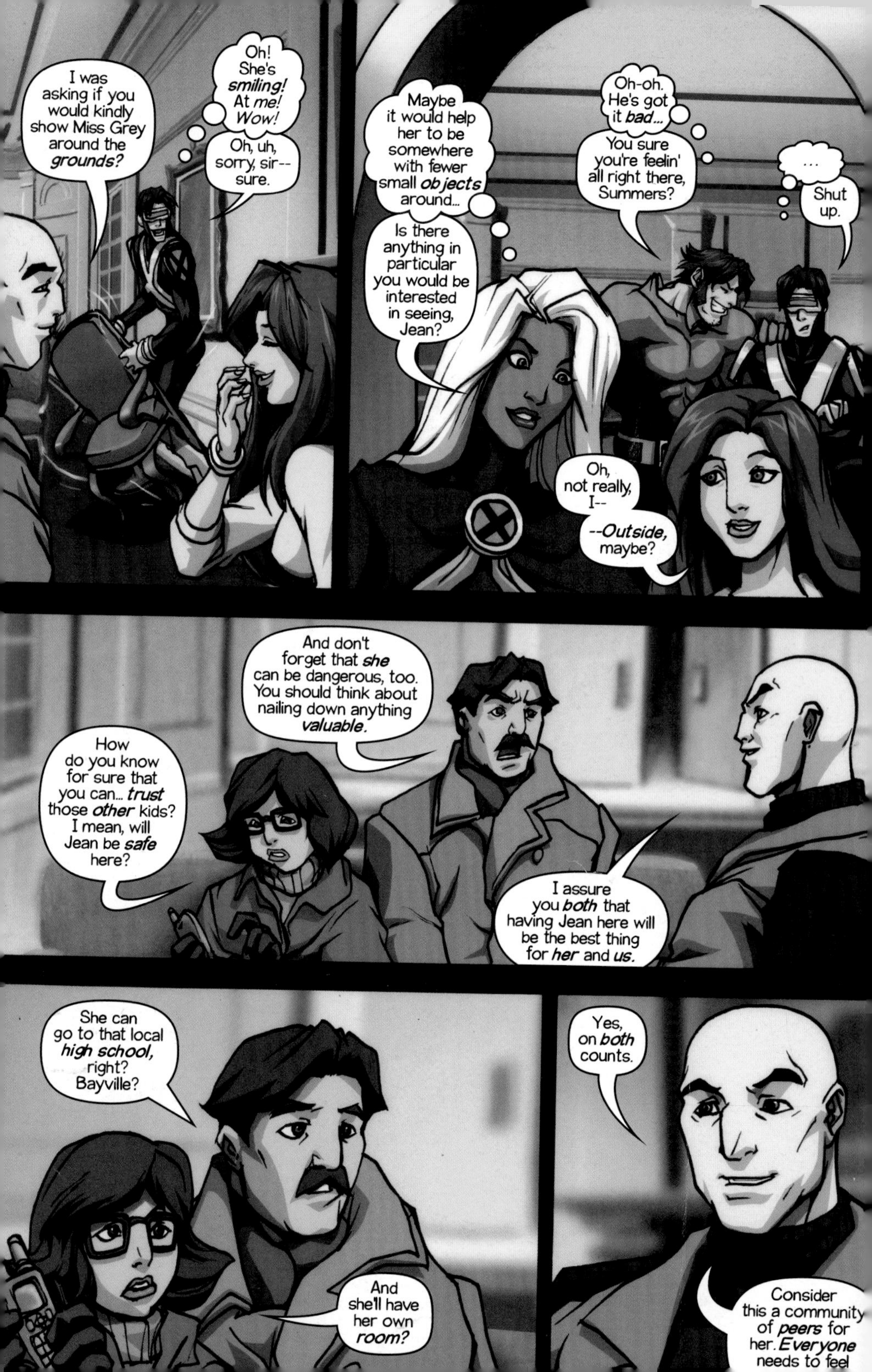
I was asking if you would kindly show Miss Grey around the grounds?
Oh! She's smiling! At me! Wow!
Oh, uh, sorry, sir-- sure.
Maybe it would help her to be somewhere with fewer small objects around...
Is there anything in particular you would be interested in seeing, Jean?
Oh-oh. He's got it bad...
You sure you're feelin' all right there, Summers?
...
Shut up.
Oh, not really, I--
--Outside, maybe?
And don't forget that she can be dangerous, too. You should think about nailing down anything valuable.
How do you know for sure that you can... trust those other kids? I mean, will Jean be safe here?
I assure you both that having Jean here will be the best thing for her and us.
She can go to that local high school, right? Bayville?
And she'll have her own room?
Yes, on both counts.
Consider this a community of peers for her. Everyone needs to feel

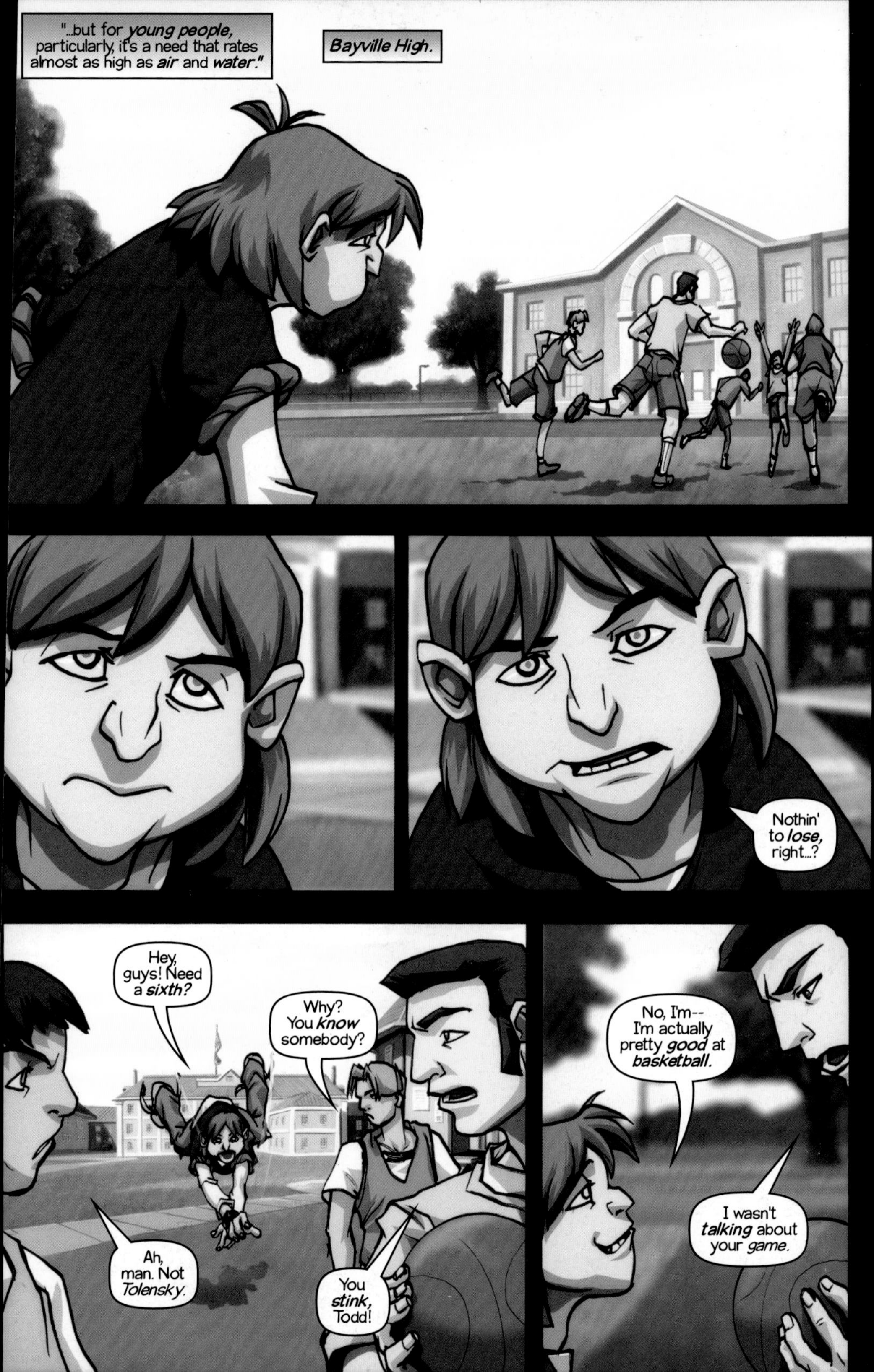
"...but for *young people,* particularly, it's a need that rates almost as high as *air* and *water.*"
Bayville High.
Nothin' to *lose,* right...?
Hey, guys! Need a *sixth?*
Ah, man. Not *Tolensky.*
Why? You *know* somebody?
You *stink,* Todd!
No, I'm-- I'm actually pretty *good* at *basketball.*
I wasn't *talking* about your *game.*

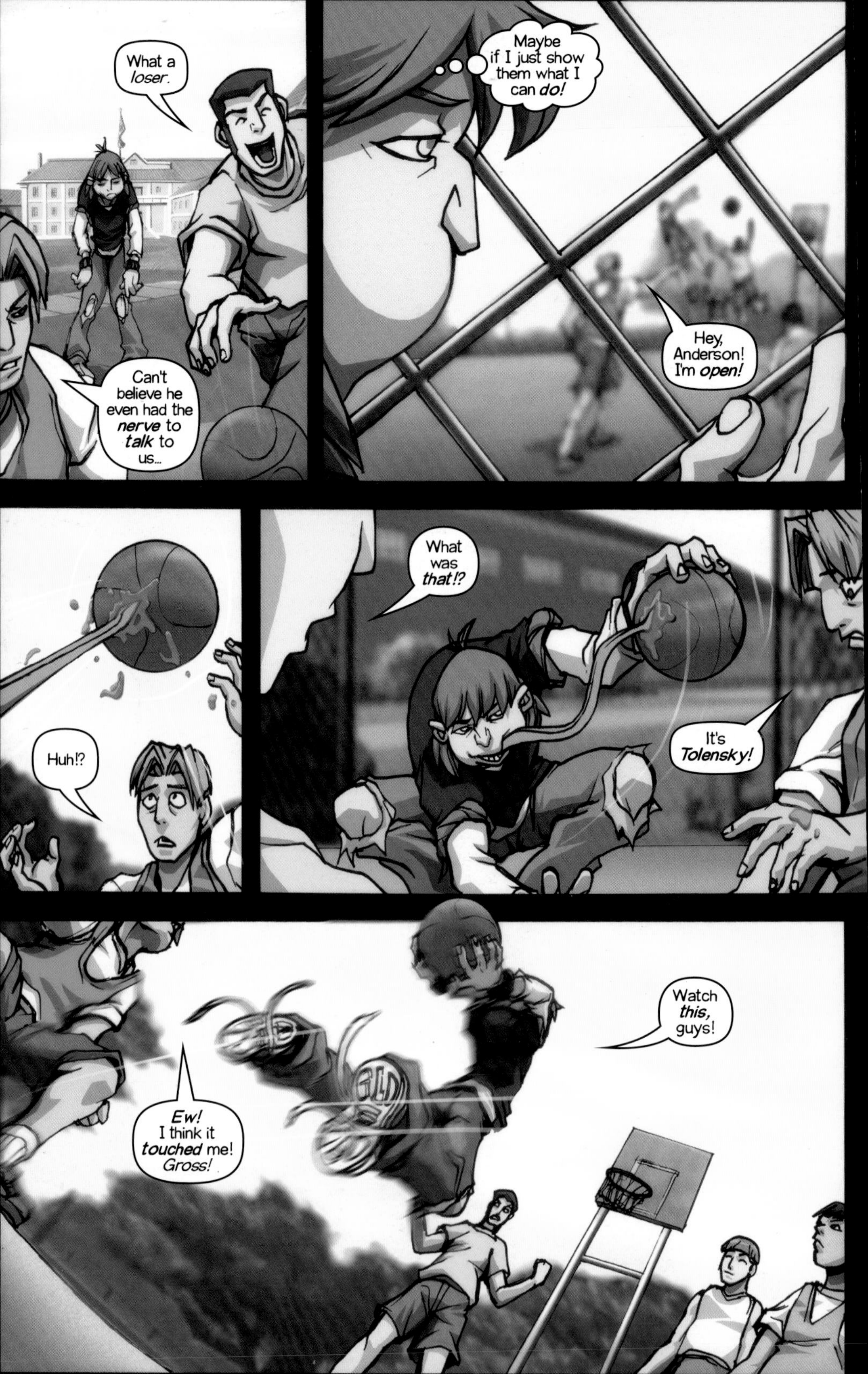
What a *loser*.
Can't believe he even had the ***nerve*** to ***talk*** to us...
Maybe if I just show them what I can ***do!***
Hey, Anderson! I'm ***open!***
Huh!?
What was ***that!?***
It's ***Tolensky!***
Watch ***this,*** guys!
Ew! I think it ***touched*** me! *Gross!*

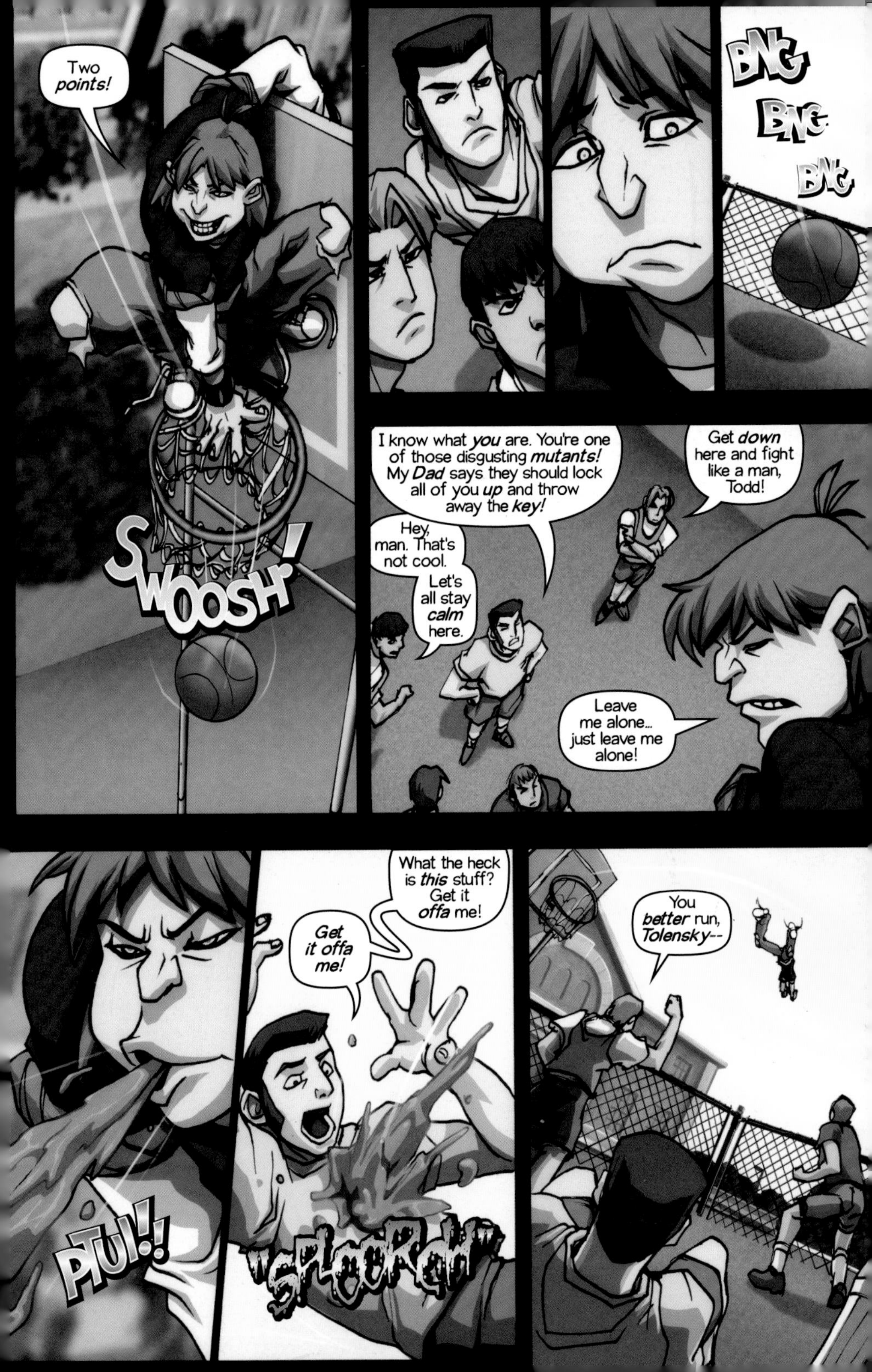
Two points!
SWOOSH!
BNG
BNG
BNG
I know what you are. You're one of those disgusting mutants! My Dad says they should lock all of you up and throw away the key!
Get down here and fight like a man, Todd!
Hey, man. That's not cool.
Let's all stay calm here.
Leave me alone... just leave me alone!
PTUI!!
What the heck is this stuff? Get it offa me!
Get it offa me!
SPLOORCH
You better run, Tolensky--

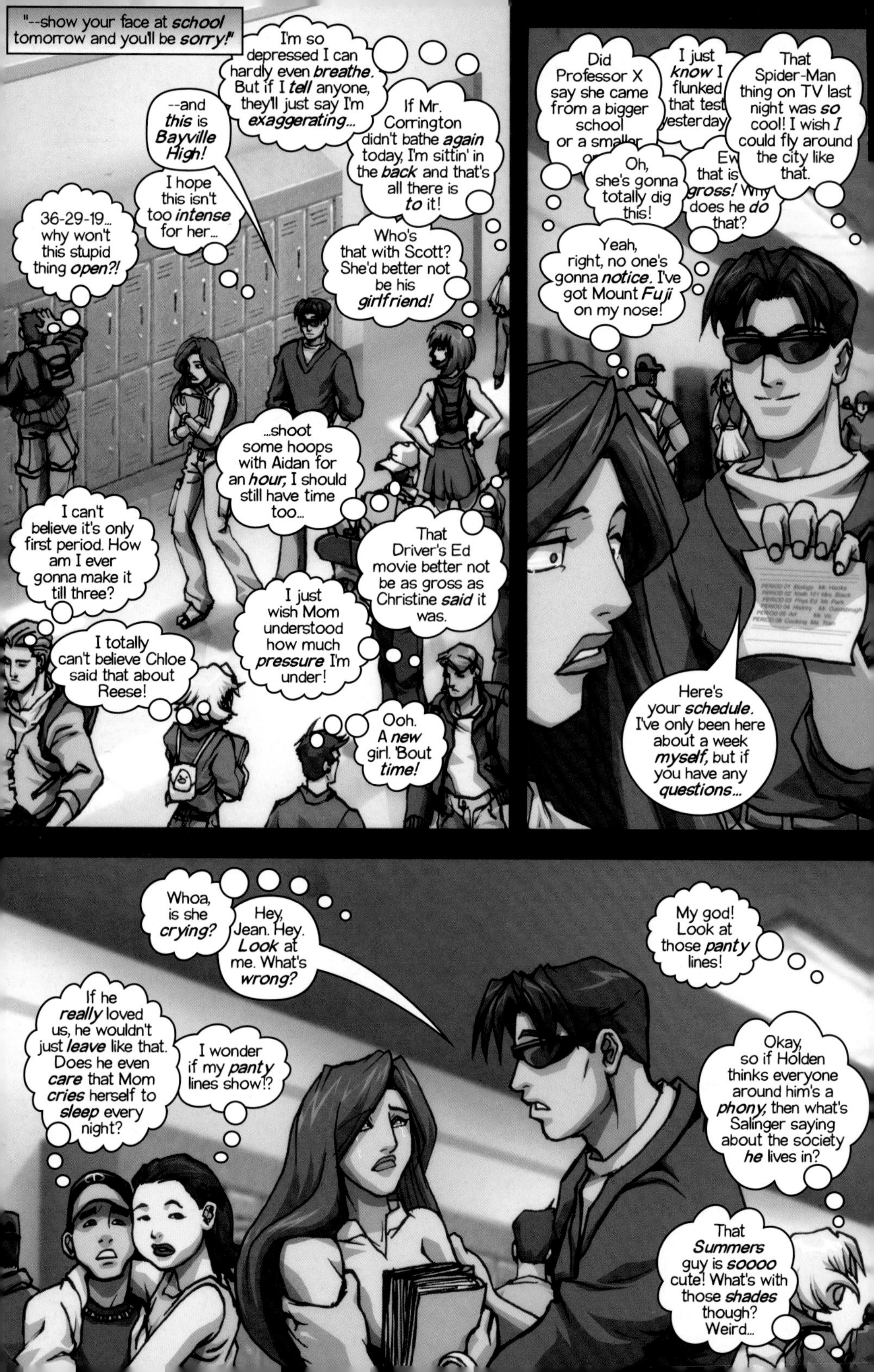
"--show your face at *school* tomorrow and you'll be *sorry!*"
I'm so depressed I can hardly even *breathe.* But if I *tell* anyone, they'll just say I'm *exaggerating...*
--and *this* is *Bayville High!*
If Mr. Corrington didn't bathe *again* today, I'm sittin' in the *back* and that's all there is *to* it!
I hope this isn't too *intense* for her...
36-29-19... why won't this stupid thing *open?!*
Who's that with Scott? She'd better not be his *girlfriend!*
...shoot some hoops with Aidan for an *hour,* I should still have time too...
I can't believe it's only first period. How am I ever gonna make it till three?
That Driver's Ed movie better not be as gross as Christine *said* it was.
I just wish Mom understood how much *pressure* I'm under!
I totally can't believe Chloe said that about Reese!
Ooh. A *new* girl. 'Bout *time!*
Did Professor X say she came from a bigger school or a smaller
I just *know* I flunked that test yesterday
That Spider-Man thing on TV last night was *so* cool! I wish *I* could fly around the city like that.
Oh, she's gonna totally dig this!
Ew that is *gross!* Why does he *do* that?
Yeah, right, no one's gonna *notice.* I've got Mount *Fuji* on my nose!
Here's your *schedule.* I've only been here about a week *myself,* but if you have any *questions...*
Whoa, is she *crying?*
Hey, Jean. Hey. *Look* at me. What's *wrong?*
My god! Look at those *panty* lines!
If he *really* loved us, he wouldn't just *leave* like that. Does he even *care* that Mom *cries* herself to *sleep* every night?
I wonder if my *panty* lines show!?
Okay, so if Holden thinks everyone around him's a *phony,* then what's Salinger saying about the society *he* lives in?
That *Summers* guy is *soooo* cute! What's with those *shades* though? Weird...

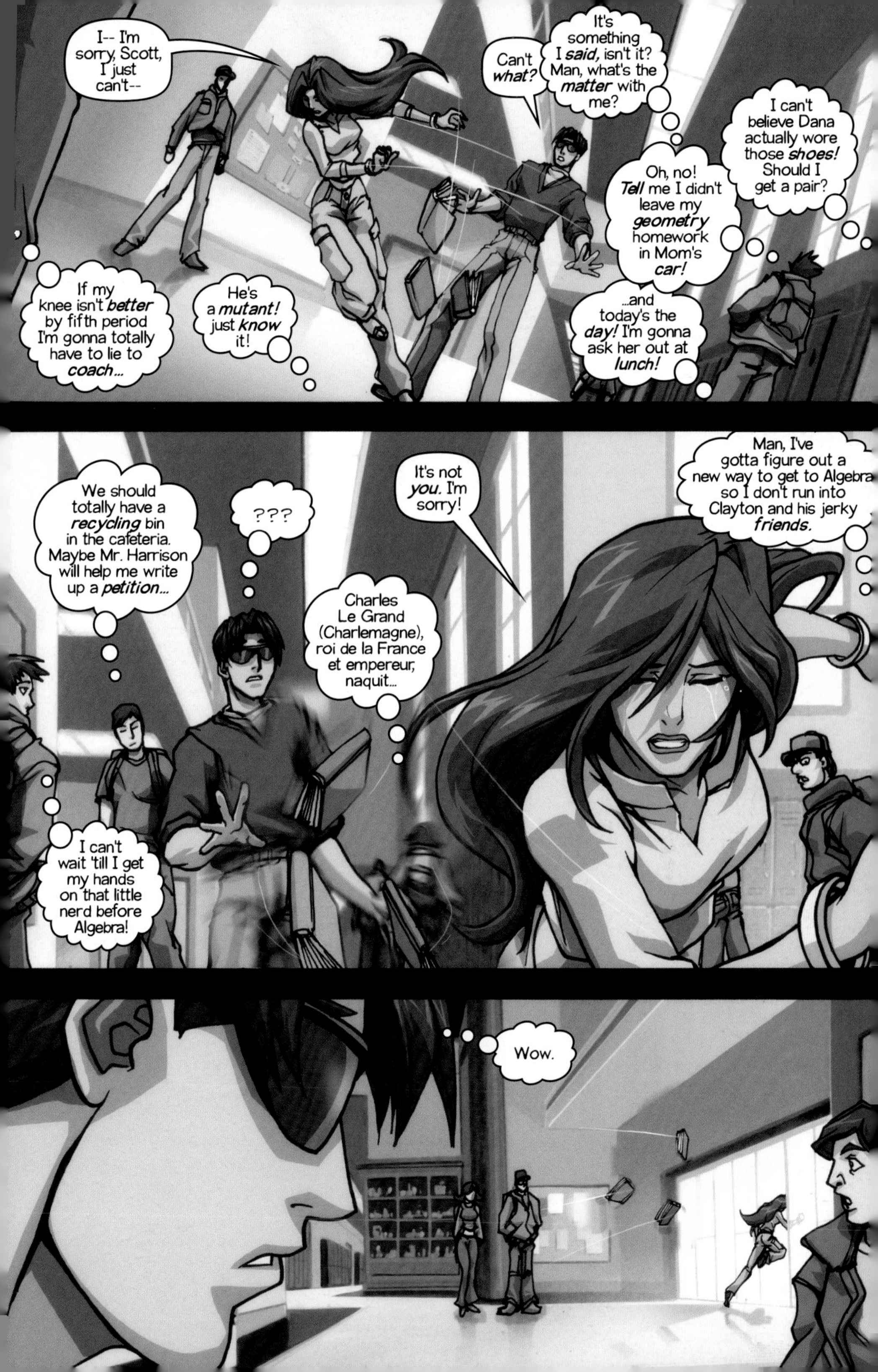
I-- I'm sorry, Scott, I just can't--
Can't *what?*
It's something I *said,* isn't it? Man, what's the *matter* with me?
I can't believe Dana actually wore those *shoes!* Should I get a pair?
Oh, no! *Tell* me I didn't leave my *geometry* homework in Mom's *car!*
If my knee isn't *better* by fifth period I'm gonna totally have to lie to *coach...*
He's a *mutant!* just *know* it!
...and today's the *day!* I'm gonna ask her out at *lunch!*
We should totally have a *recycling* bin in the cafeteria. Maybe Mr. Harrison will help me write up a *petition...*
???
It's not *you.* I'm sorry!
Man, I've gotta figure out a new way to get to Algebra so I don't run into Clayton and his jerky *friends.*
Charles Le Grand (Charlemagne), roi de la France et empereur, naquit...
I can't wait 'till I get my hands on that little nerd before Algebra!
Wow.

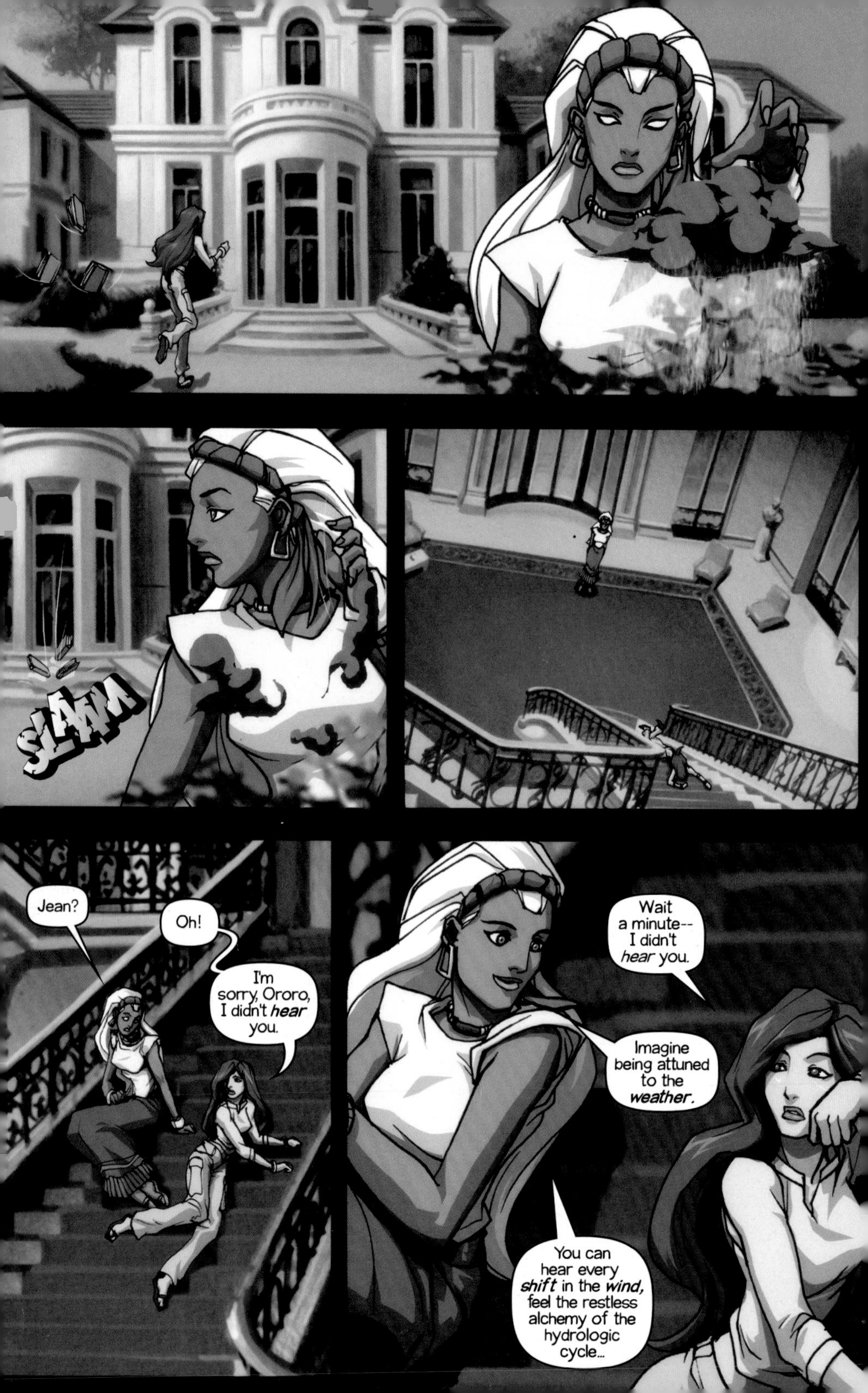
SLAM
Jean?
Oh!
I'm sorry, Ororo, I didn't *hear* you.
Wait a minute-- I didn't *hear* you.
Imagine being attuned to the *weather.*
You can hear every *shift* in the *wind,* feel the restless alchemy of the hydrologic cycle...

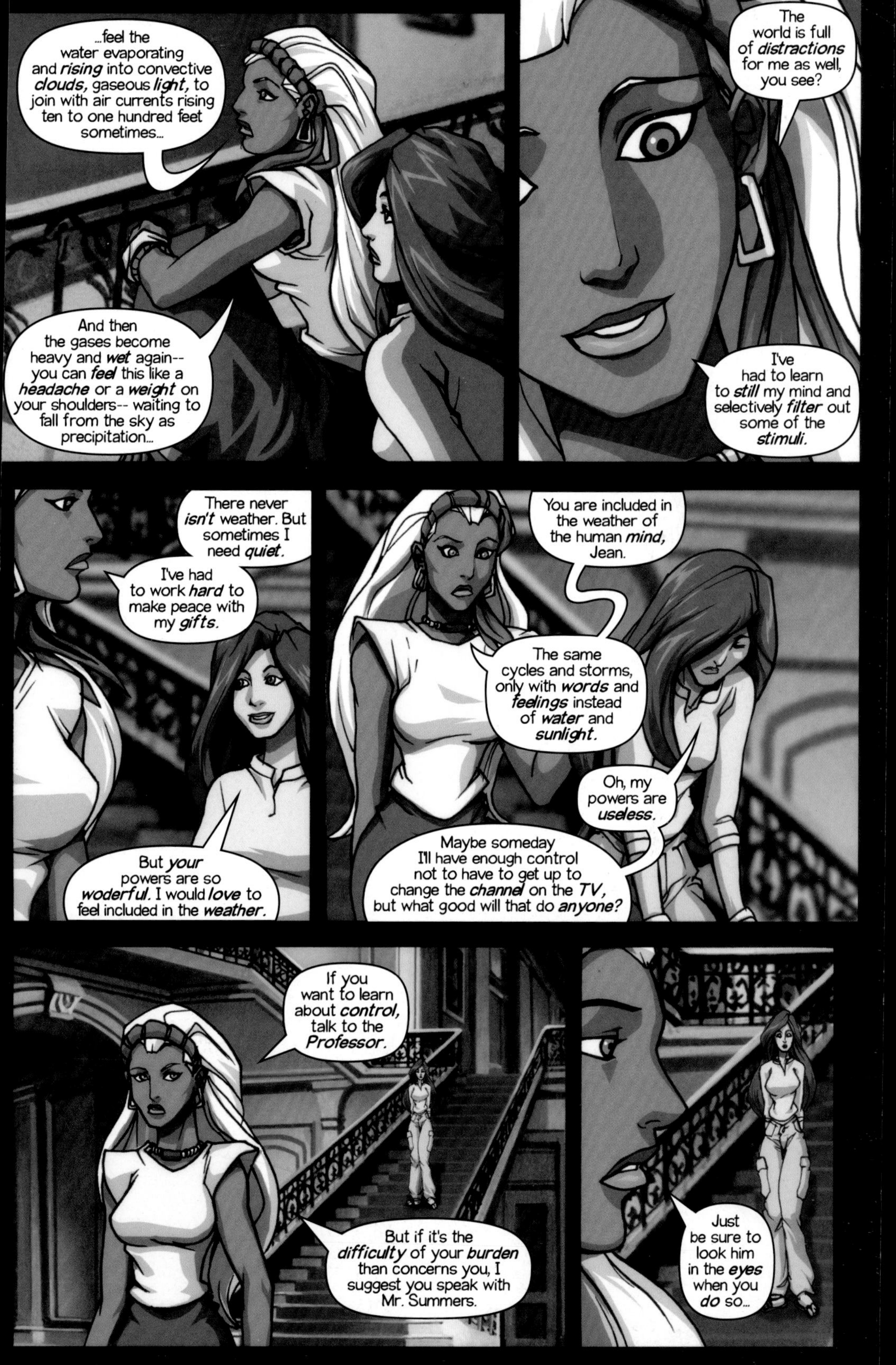
...feel the water evaporating and rising into convective clouds, gaseous light, to join with air currents rising ten to one hundred feet sometimes...
And then the gases become heavy and wet again-- you can feel this like a headache or a weight on your shoulders-- waiting to fall from the sky as precipitation...
The world is full of distractions for me as well, you see?
I've had to learn to still my mind and selectively filter out some of the stimuli.
There never isn't weather. But sometimes I need quiet.
I've had to work hard to make peace with my gifts.
But your powers are so woderful. I would love to feel included in the weather.
You are included in the weather of the human mind, Jean.
The same cycles and storms, only with words and feelings instead of water and sunlight.
Oh, my powers are useless.
Maybe someday I'll have enough control not to have to get up to change the channel on the TV, but what good will that do anyone?
If you want to learn about control, talk to the Professor.
But if it's the difficulty of your burden than concerns you, I suggest you speak with Mr. Summers.
Just be sure to look him in the eyes when you do so...

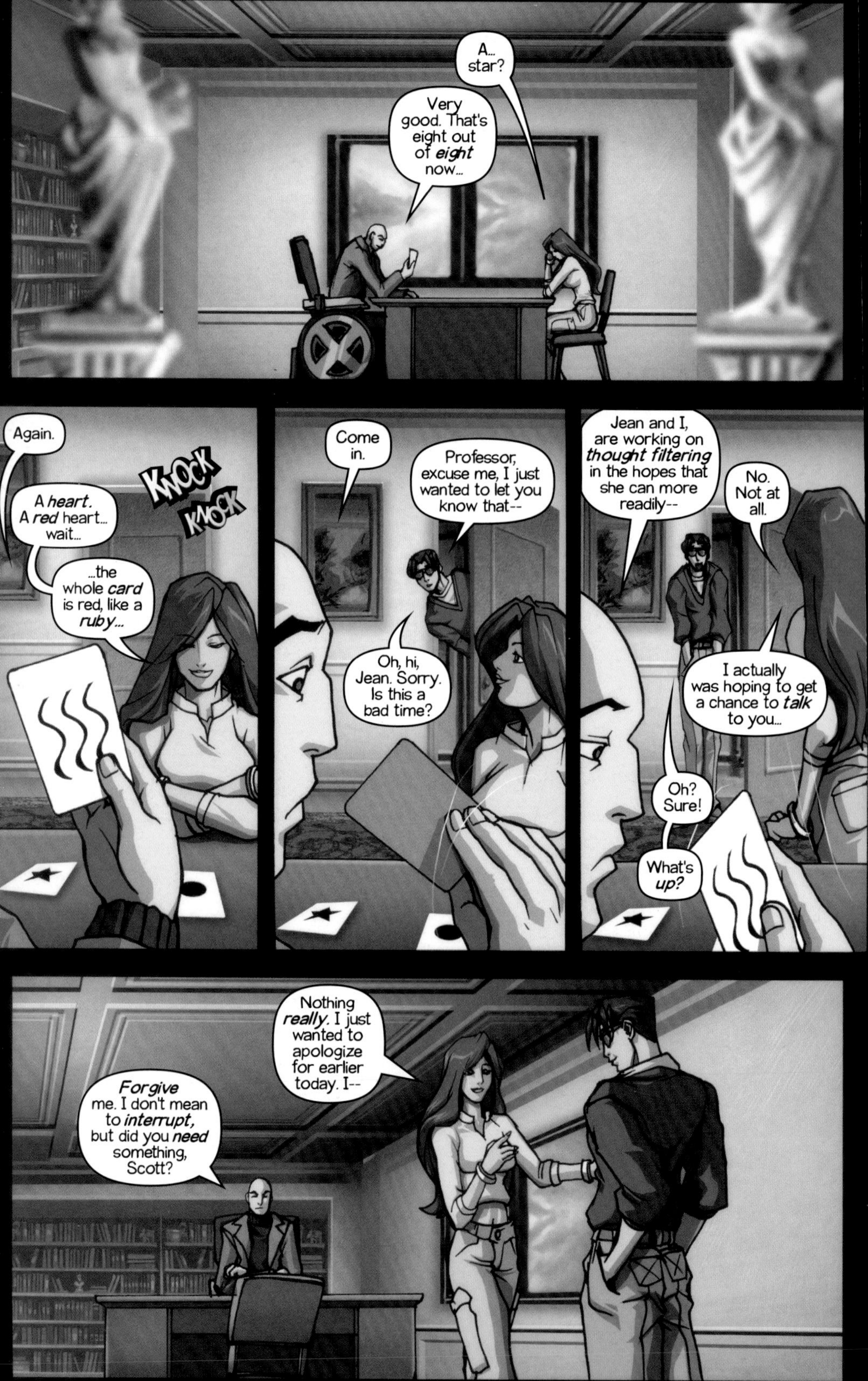
A... star?
Very good. That's eight out of *eight* now...
Again.
A *heart.* A *red* heart... wait...
KNOCK KNOCK
...the whole *card* is red, like a *ruby...*
Come in.
Professor, excuse me, I just wanted to let you know that--
Oh, hi, Jean. Sorry. Is this a bad time?
Jean and I, are working on *thought filtering* in the hopes that she can more readily--
No. Not at all.
I actually was hoping to get a chance to *talk* to you...
Oh? Sure!
What's *up?*
Nothing *really.* I just wanted to apologize for earlier today. I--
Forgive me. I don't mean to *interrupt,* but did you *need* something, Scott?

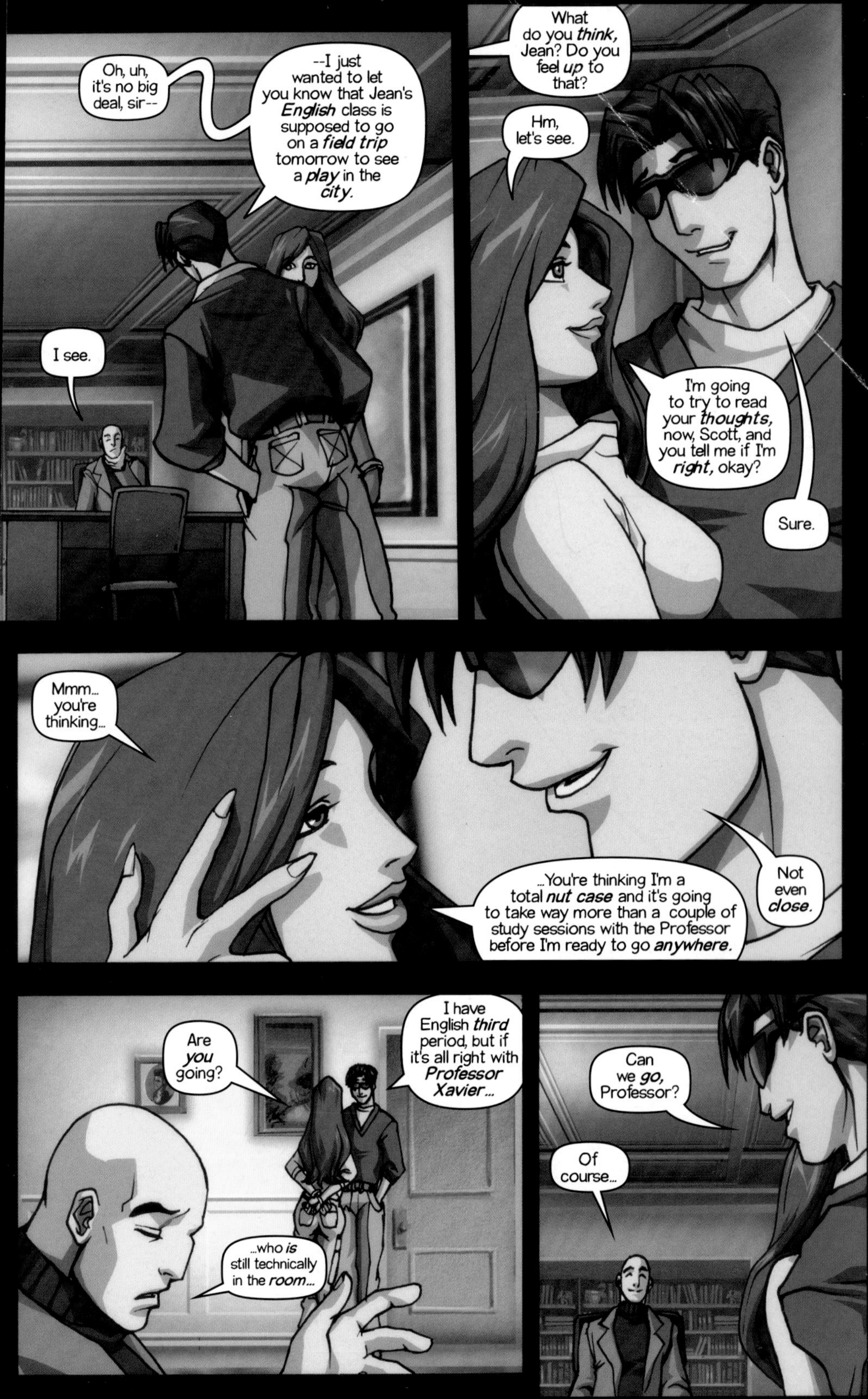
Oh, uh, it's no big deal, sir--
--I just wanted to let you know that Jean's *English* class is supposed to go on a *field trip* tomorrow to see a *play* in the *city.*
I see.
What do you *think,* Jean? Do you feel *up* to that?
Hm, let's see.
I'm going to try to read your *thoughts,* now, Scott, and you tell me if I'm *right,* okay?
Sure.
Mmm... you're thinking...
...You're thinking I'm a total *nut case* and it's going to take way more than a couple of study sessions with the Professor before I'm ready to go *anywhere.*
Not even *close.*
Are *you* going?
I have English *third* period, but if it's all right with *Professor Xavier...*
...who *is* still technically in the *room...*
Can we *go,* Professor?
Of course...

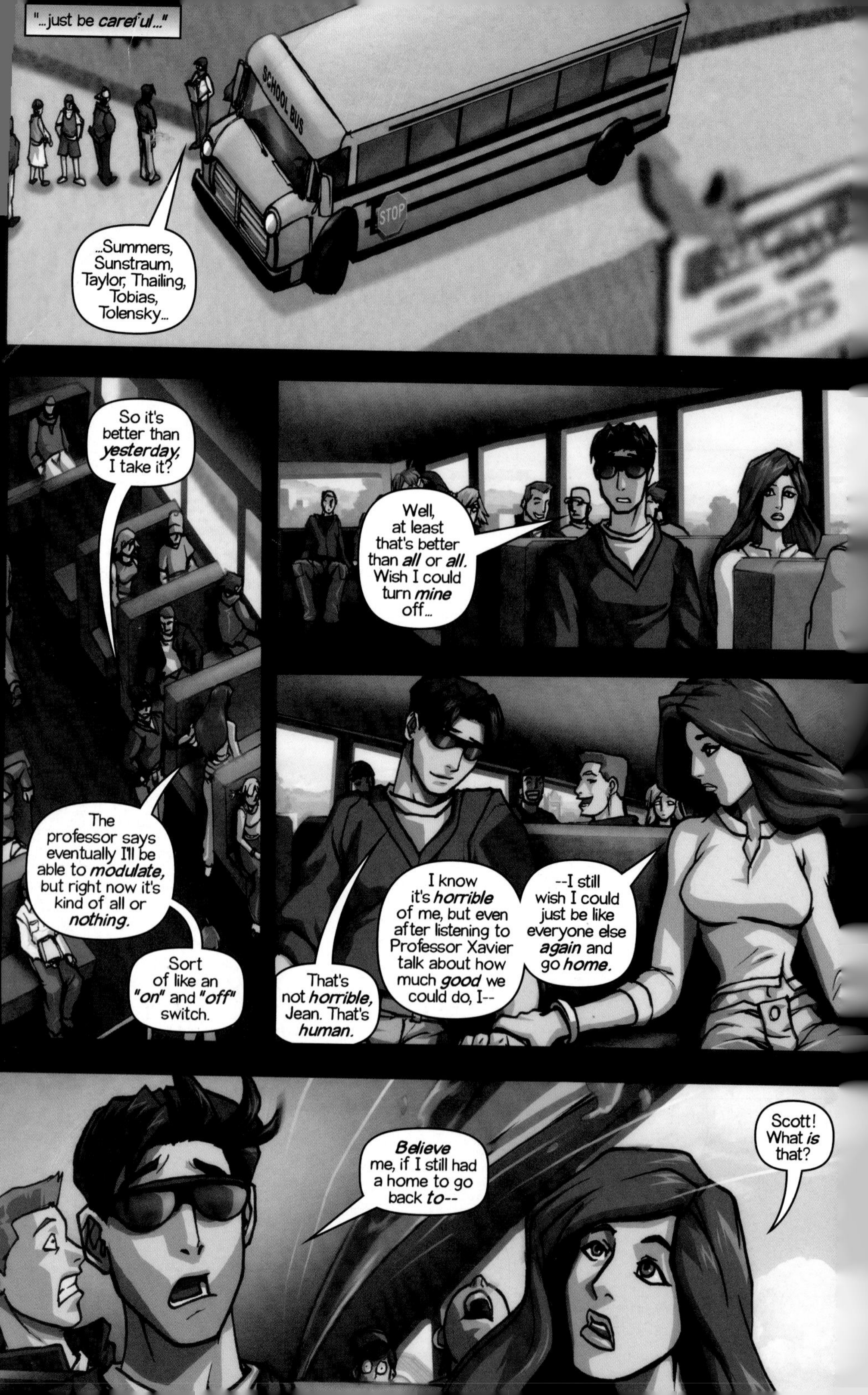
"...just be careful..."
...Summers, Sunstraum, Taylor, Thailing, Tobias, Tolensky...
SCHOOL BUS
STOP
So it's better than *yesterday,* I take it?
Well, at least that's better than *all* or *all.* Wish I could turn *mine* off...
The professor says eventually I'll be able to *modulate,* but right now it's kind of all or *nothing.*
Sort of like an *"on"* and *"off"* switch.
I know it's *horrible* of me, but even after listening to Professor Xavier talk about how much *good* we could do, I--
--I still wish I could just be like everyone else *again* and go *home.*
That's not *horrible,* Jean. That's *human.*
Believe me, if I still had a home to go back *to*--
Scott! What *is* that?

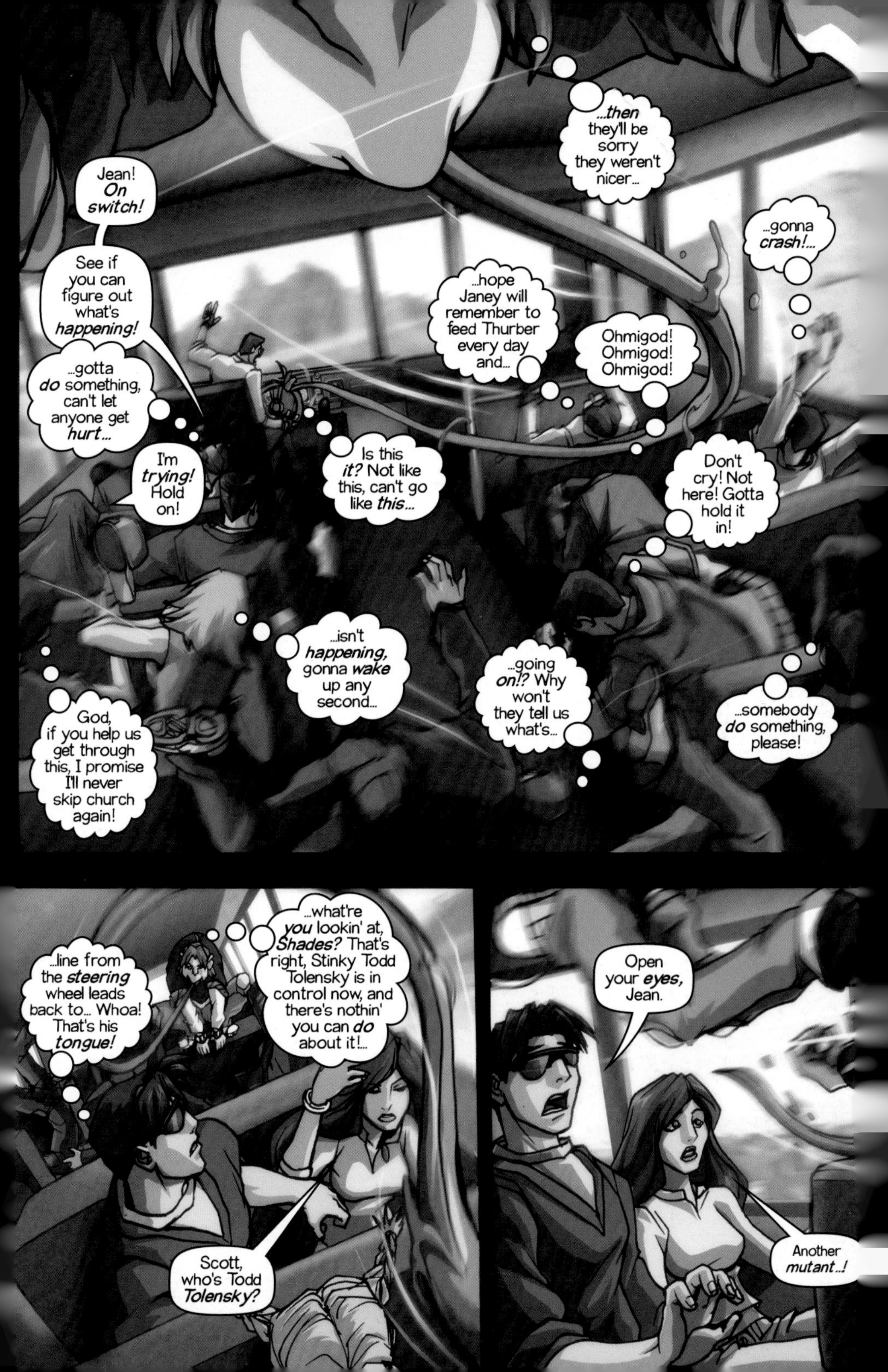

Jean! *On switch!*
See if you can figure out what's *happening!*
...*then* they'll be sorry they weren't nicer...
...gonna *crash!*...
...hope Janey will remember to feed Thurber every day and...
Ohmigod! Ohmigod! Ohmigod!
...gotta *do* something, can't let anyone get *hurt*...
I'm *trying!* Hold on!
Is this *it?* Not like this, can't go like *this*...
Don't cry! Not here! Gotta hold it in!
God, if you help us get through this, I promise I'll never skip church again!
...isn't *happening,* gonna *wake* up any second...
...going *on!?* Why won't they tell us what's...
...somebody *do* something, please!
...line from the *steering* wheel leads back to... Whoa! That's his *tongue!*
...what're *you* lookin' at, *Shades?* That's right, Stinky Todd Tolensky is in control now, and there's nothin' you can *do* about it!...
Scott, who's Todd *Tolensky?*
Open your *eyes,* Jean.
Another *mutant*...!

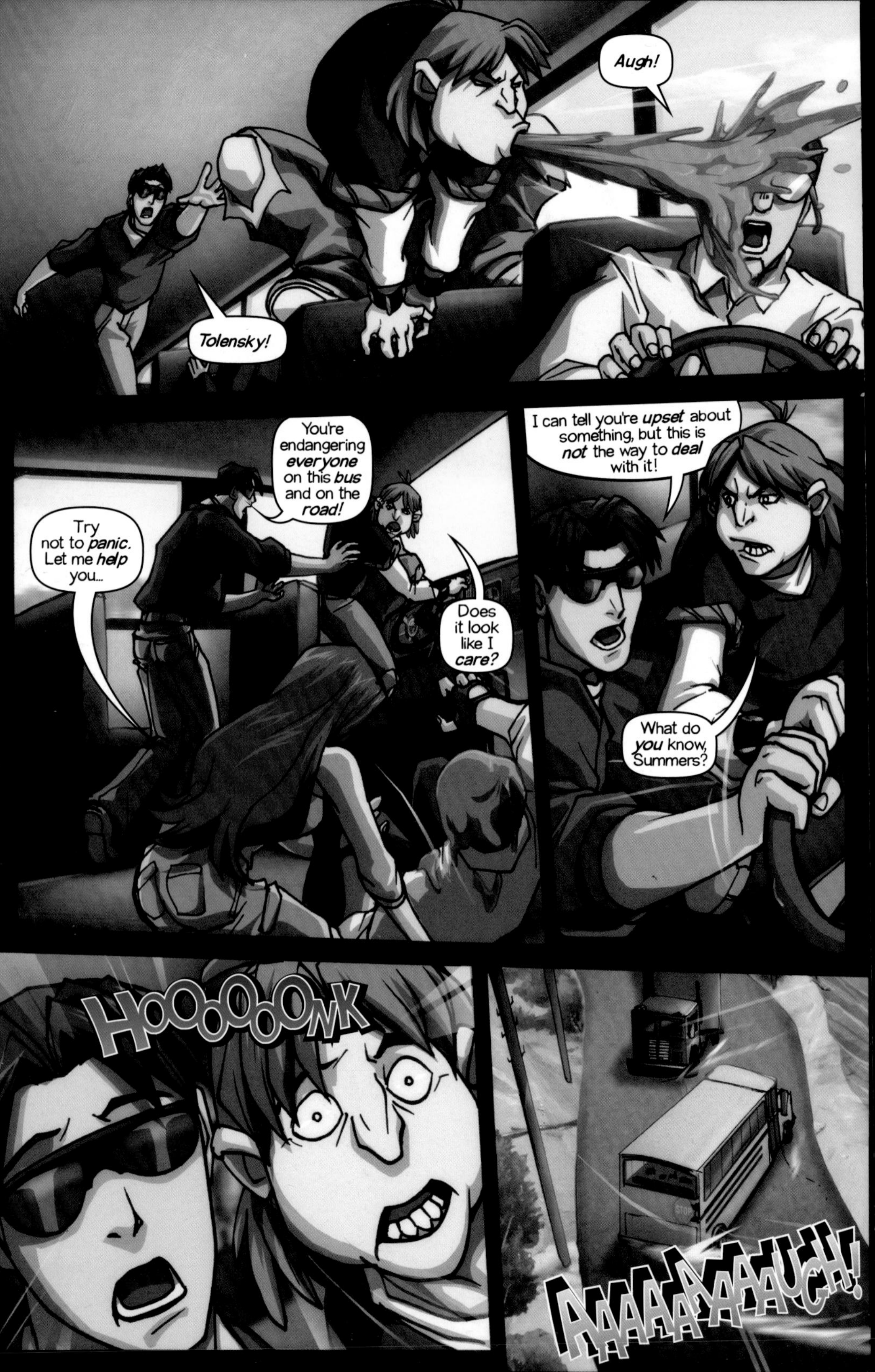
Augh!
Tolensky!
You're endangering *everyone* on this *bus* and on the *road!*
Try not to *panic.* Let me *help* you...
Does it look like I *care?*
I can tell you're *upset* about something, but this is *not* the way to *deal* with it!
What do *you* know, Summers?
HOOOOOONK
AAAAAAAAAUGH!

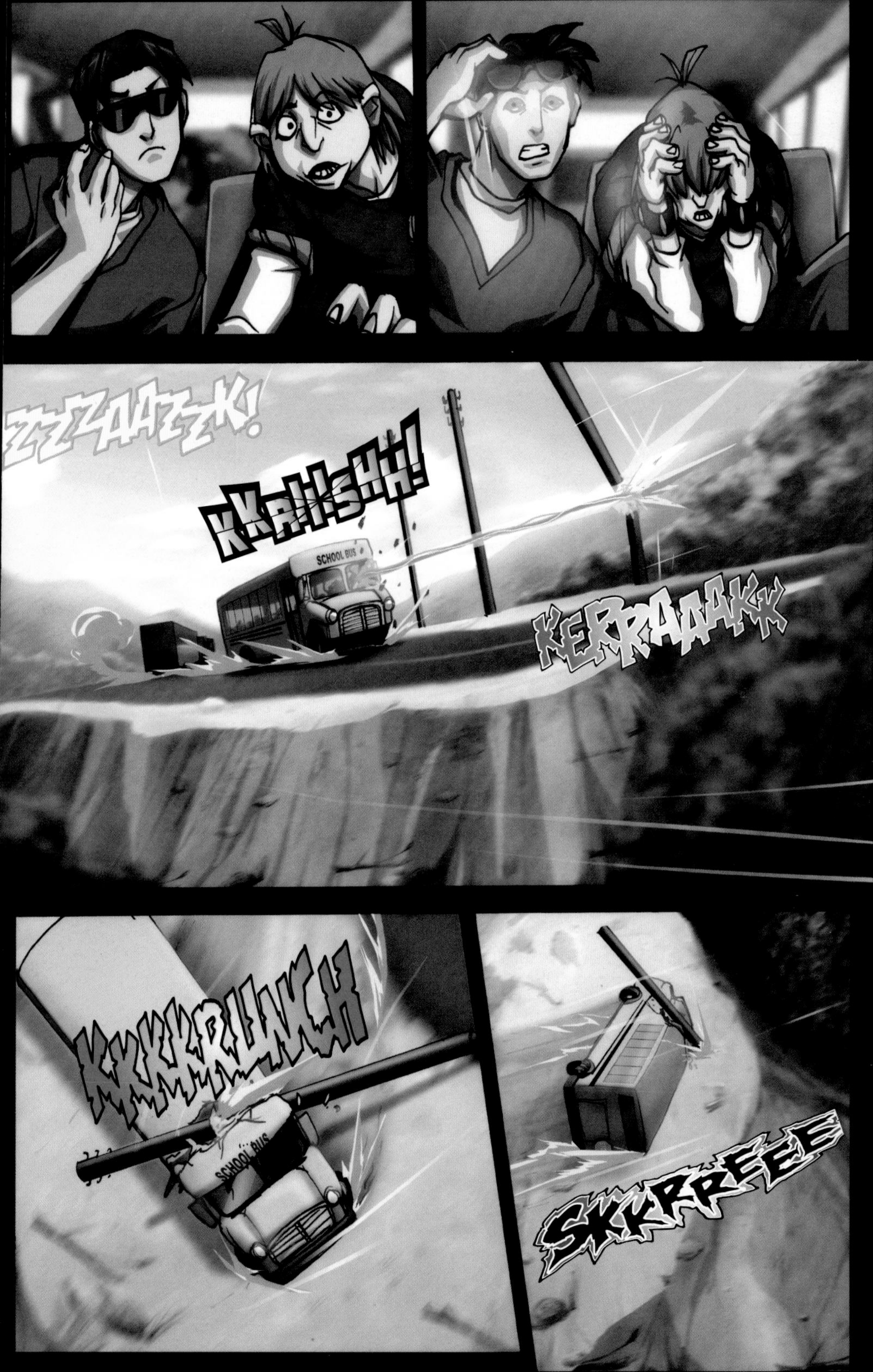
ZZZAAAZZK!
KKRIISHH!
SCHOOL BUS
KERRAAAKK
KKKRUNCH
SCHOOL BUS
SKKREEE

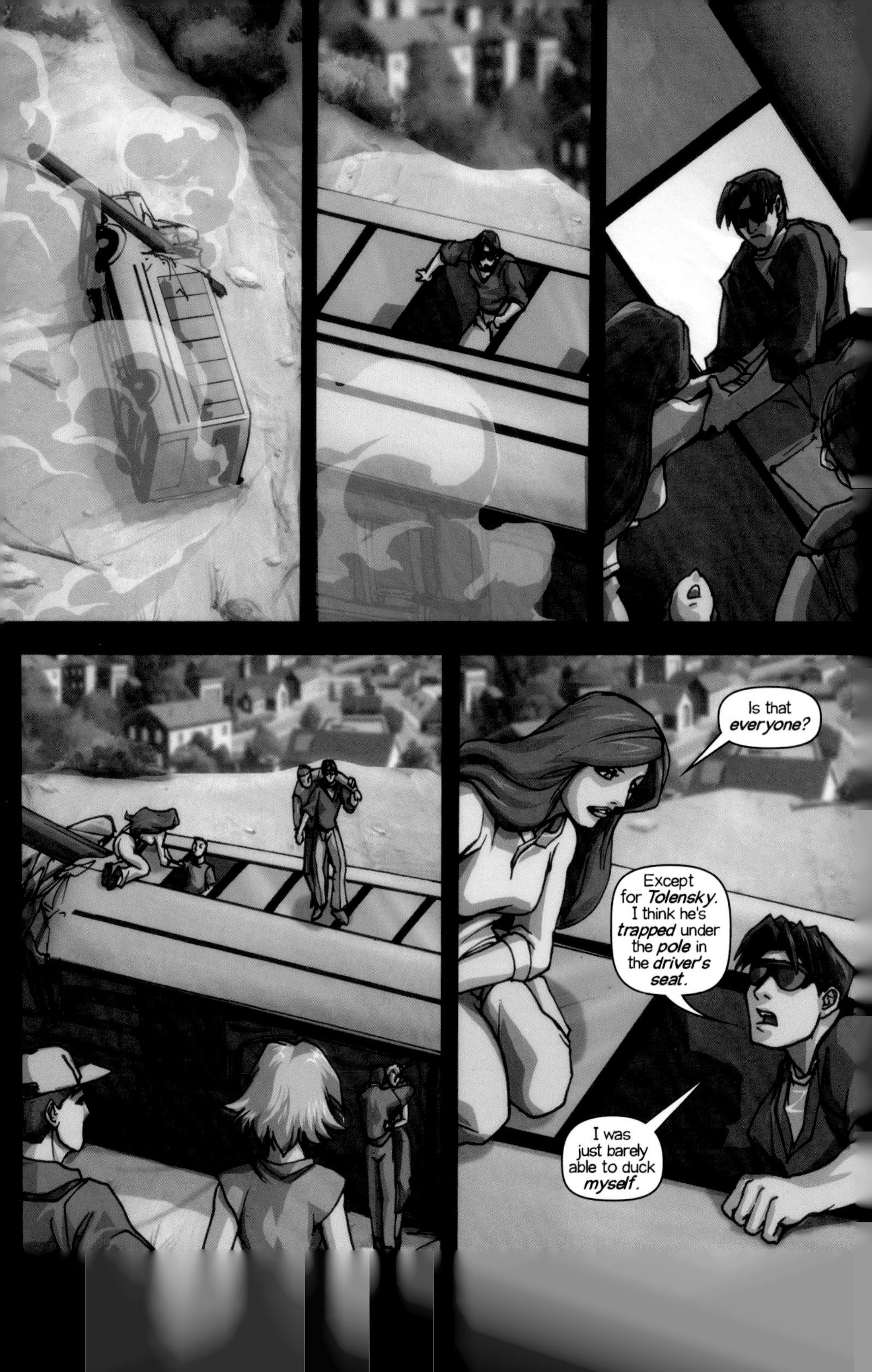
Is that *everyone?*
Except for *Tolensky.* I think he's *trapped* under the *pole* in the *driver's seat.*
I was just barely able to duck *myself.*

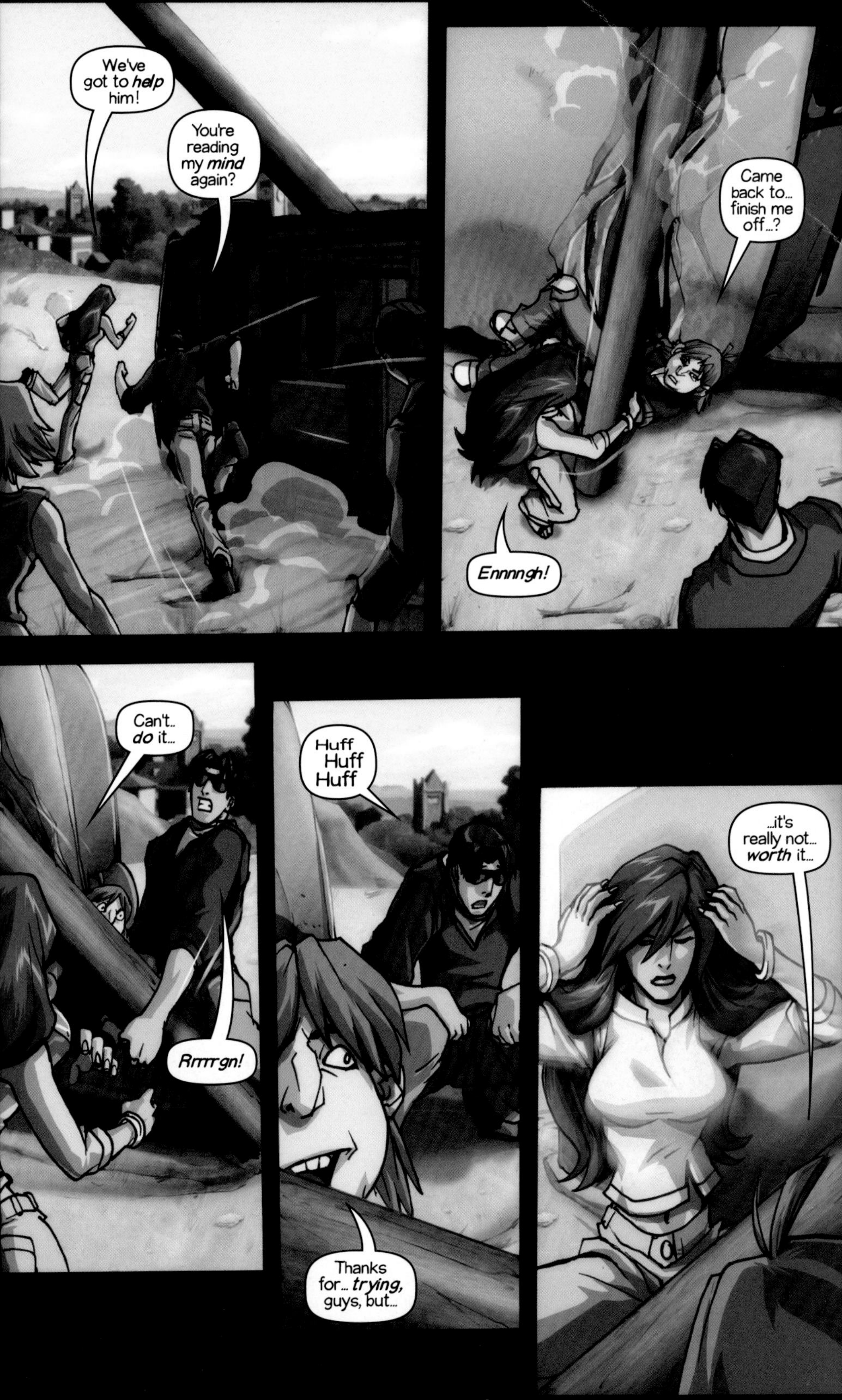

We've got to *help* him!
You're reading my *mind* again?
Came back to... finish me off...?
Ennnngh!
Can't.. *do* it...
Rrrrrgn!
Huff Huff Huff
Thanks for... *trying,* guys, but...
...it's really not... *worth* it...

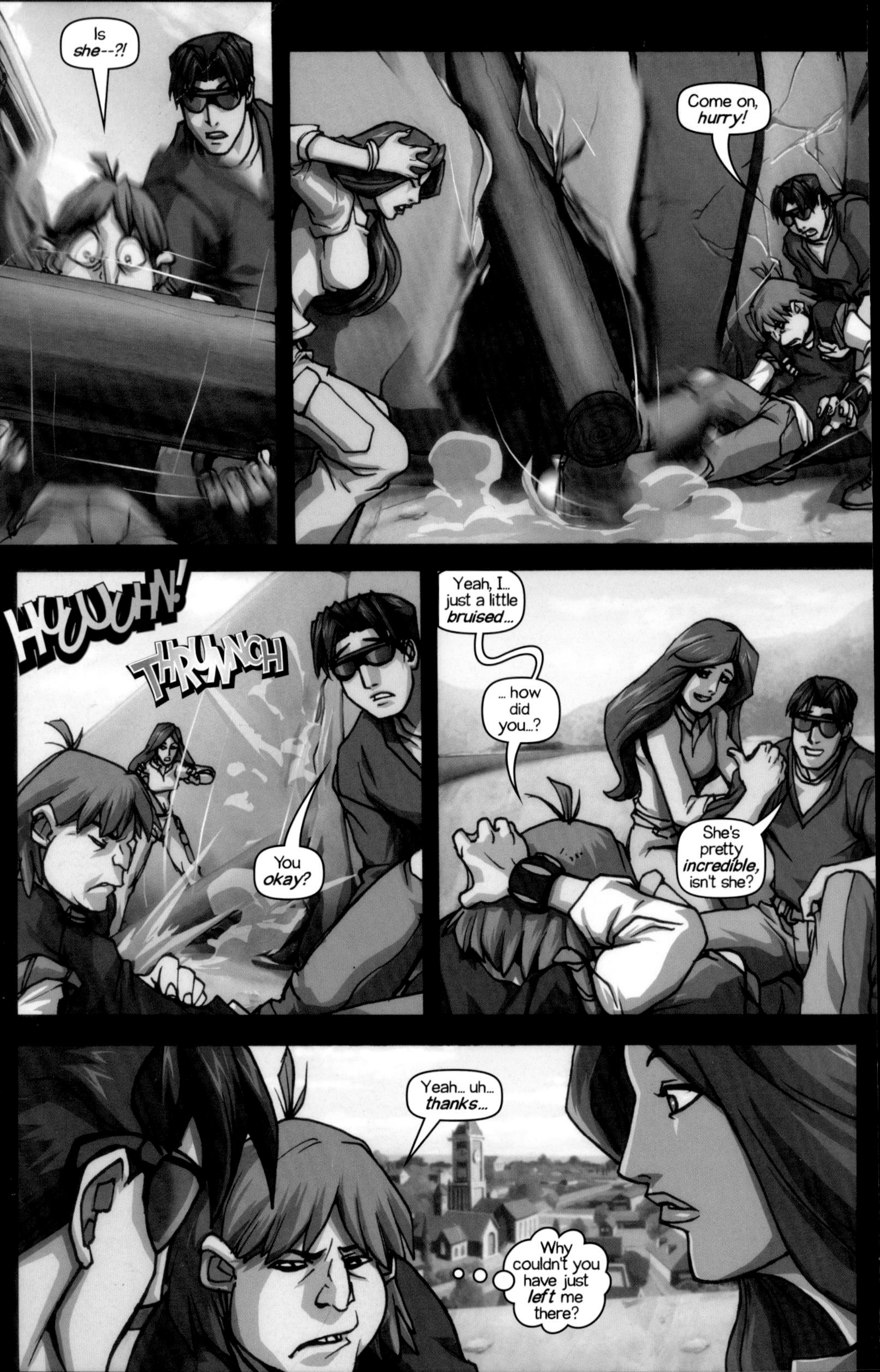
Is she--?!
Come on, hurry!
HWOOOHN!
THRUNNCH
You okay?
Yeah, I... just a little bruised...
... how did you...?
She's pretty incredible, isn't she?
Yeah... uh... thanks...
Why couldn't you have just left me there?

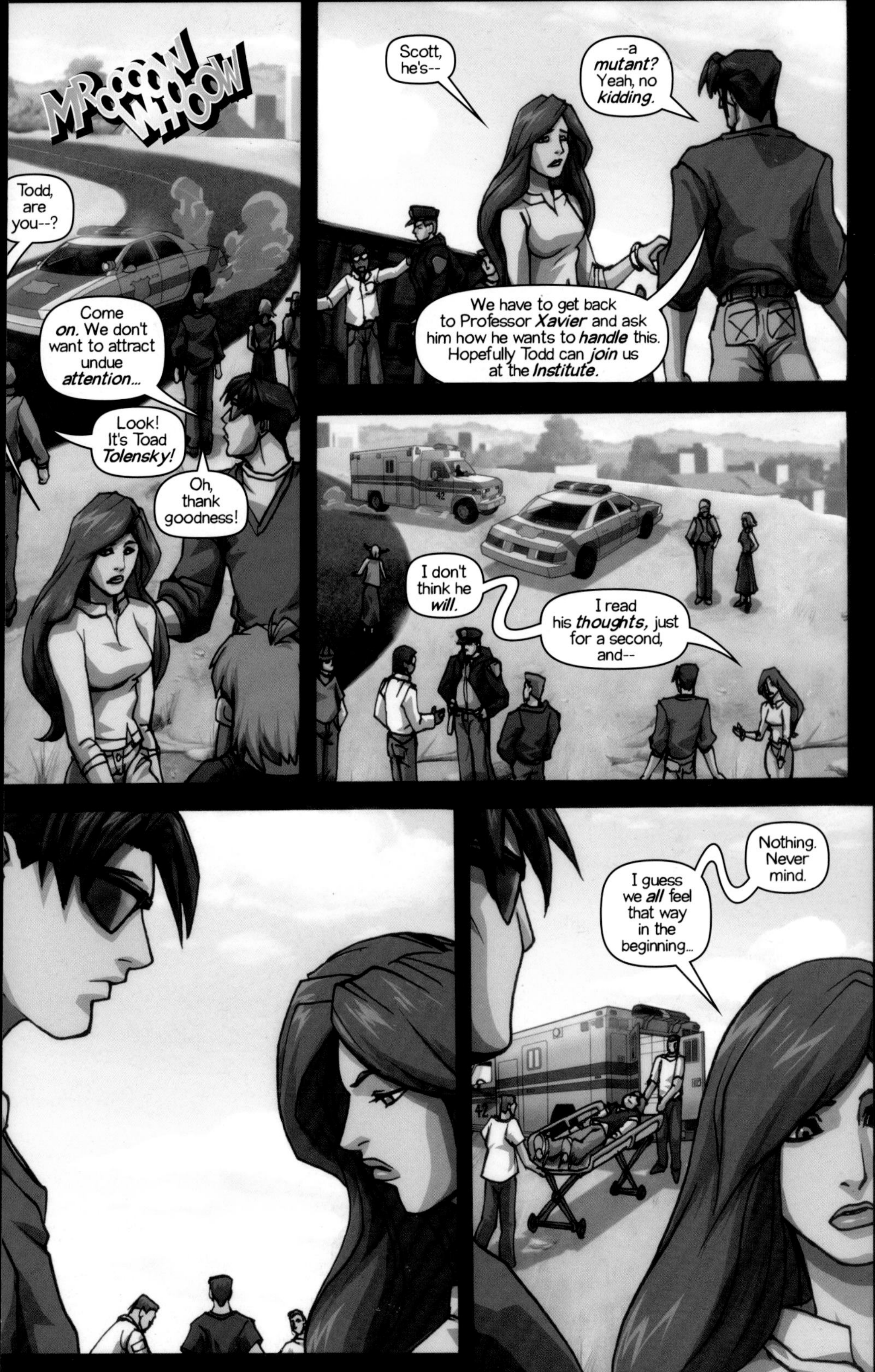
MROOOW WHOOW
Todd, are you--?
Come on. We don't want to attract undue attention...
Look! It's Toad Tolensky!
Oh, thank goodness!
Scott, he's--
--a mutant? Yeah, no kidding.
We have to get back to Professor Xavier and ask him how he wants to handle this. Hopefully Todd can join us at the Institute.
I don't think he will.
I read his thoughts, just for a second, and--
I guess we all feel that way in the beginning...
Nothing. Never mind.

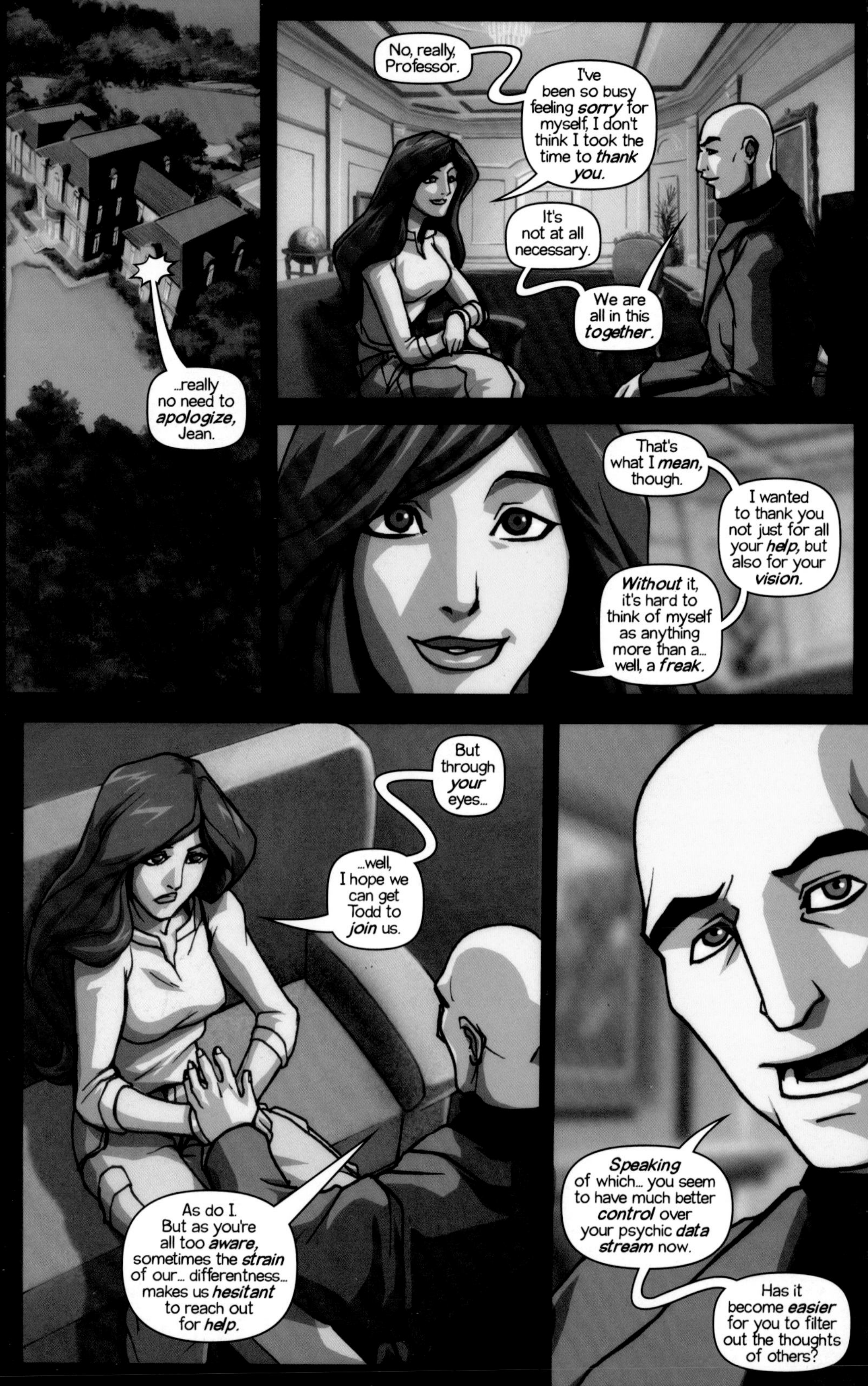
...really no need to *apologize,* Jean.
No, really, Professor.
I've been so busy feeling *sorry* for myself, I don't think I took the time to *thank you.*
It's not at all necessary.
We are all in this *together.*
That's what I *mean,* though.
I wanted to thank you not just for all your *help,* but also for your *vision.*
Without it, it's hard to think of myself as anything more than a... well, a *freak.*
But through *your* eyes...
...well, I hope we can get Todd to *join* us.
As do I. But as you're all too *aware,* sometimes the *strain* of our... differentness... makes us *hesitant* to reach out for *help.*
Speaking of which... you seem to have much better *control* over your psychic *data stream* now.
Has it become *easier* for you to filter out the thoughts of others?

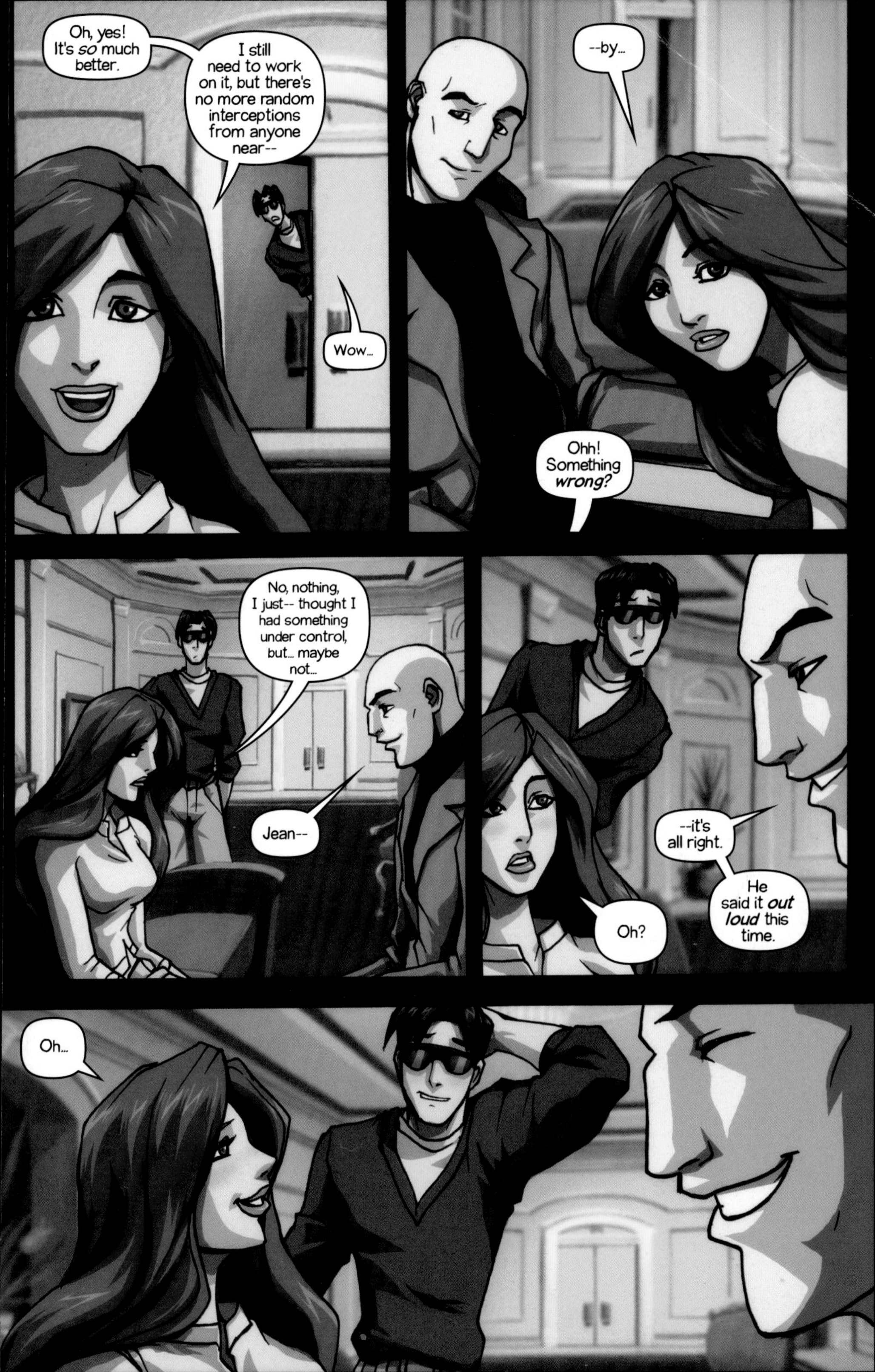
Oh, yes! It's *so* much better.
I still need to work on it, but there's no more random interceptions from anyone near--
Wow...
--by...
Ohh! Something ***wrong?***
No, nothing, I just-- thought I had something under control, but... maybe not...
Jean--
--it's all right.
He said it ***out loud*** this time.
Oh?
Oh...

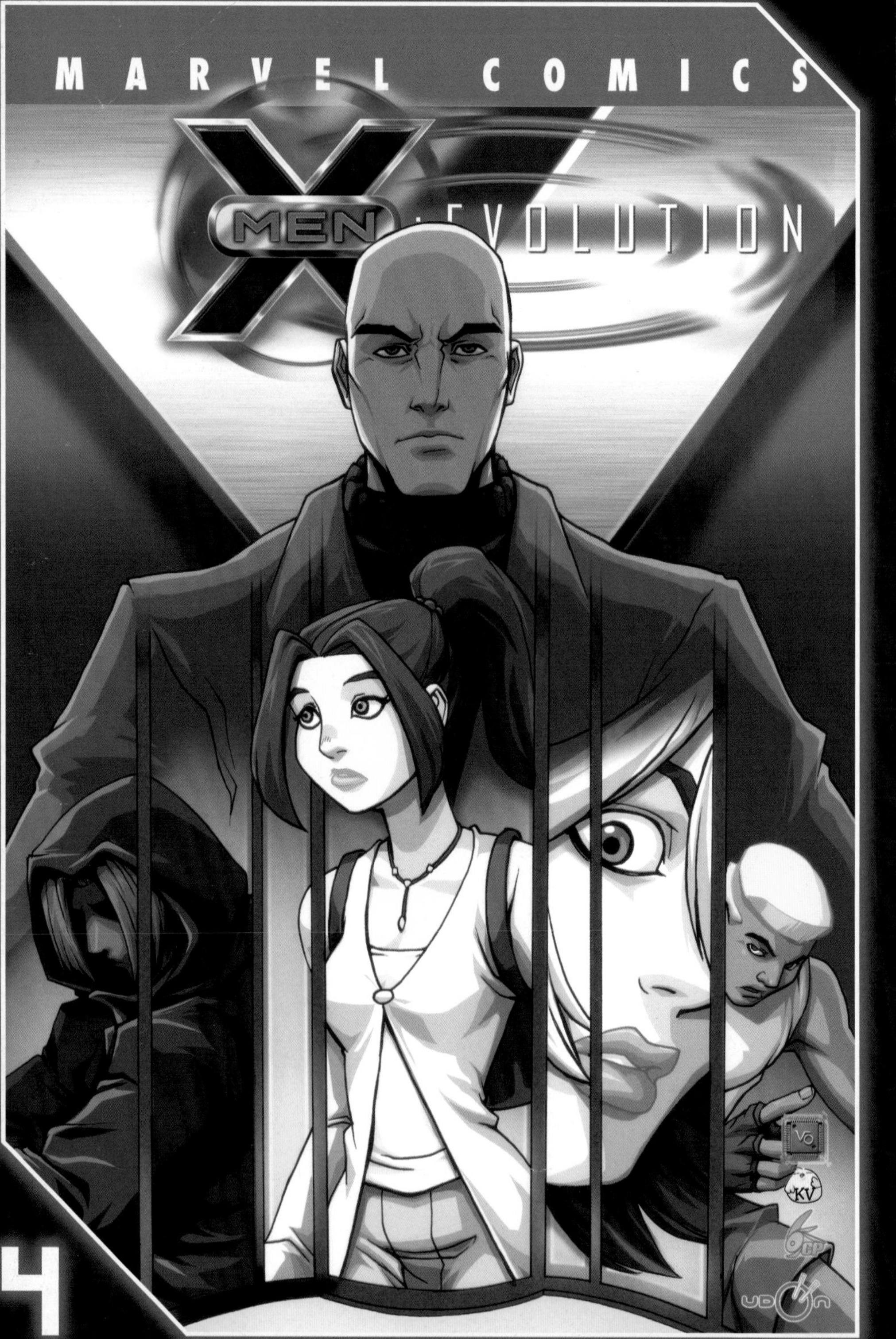
MARVEL COMICS
X-MEN: EVOLUTION
4

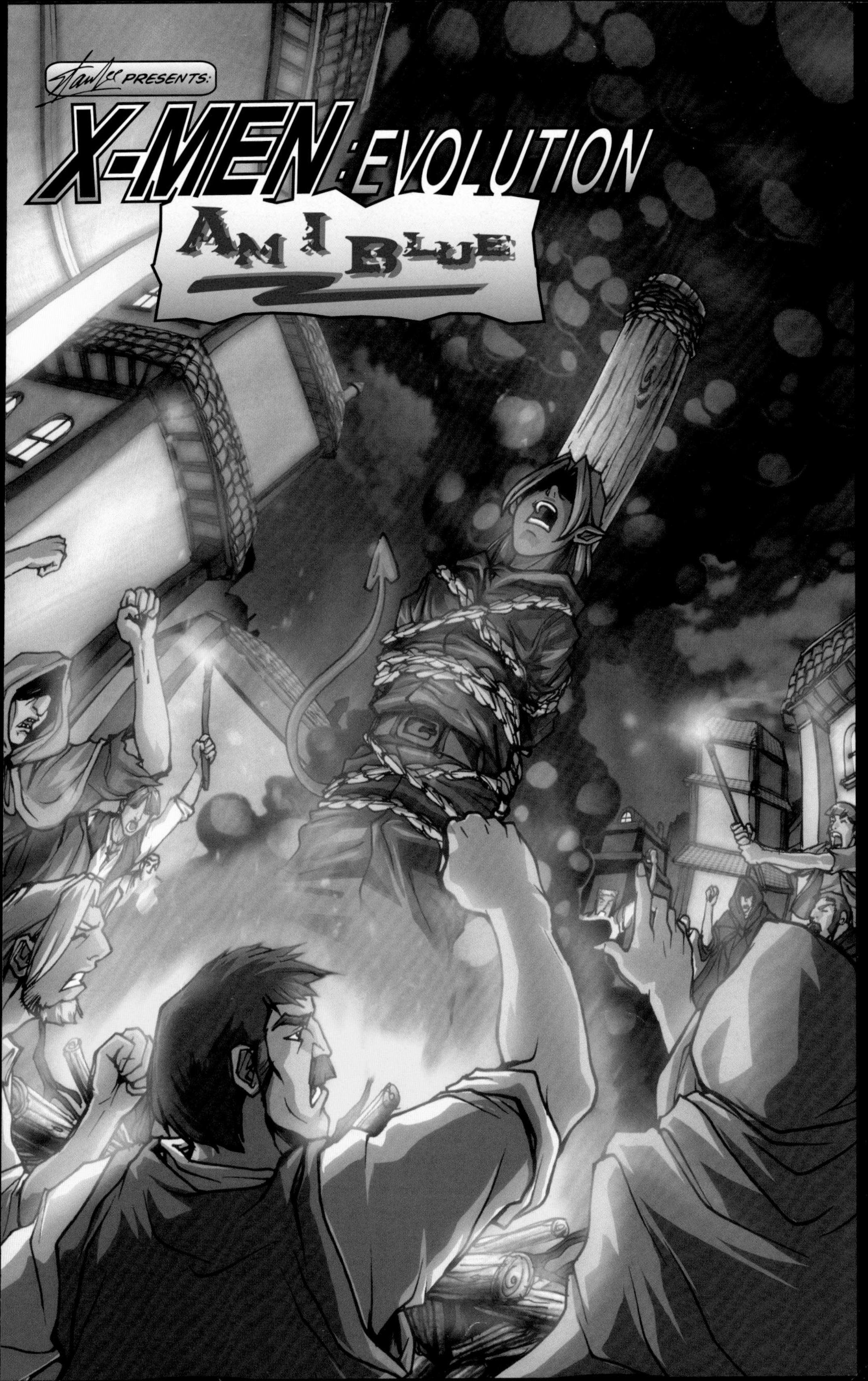
Stan Lee PRESENTS:
X-MEN: EVOLUTION
AM I BLUE

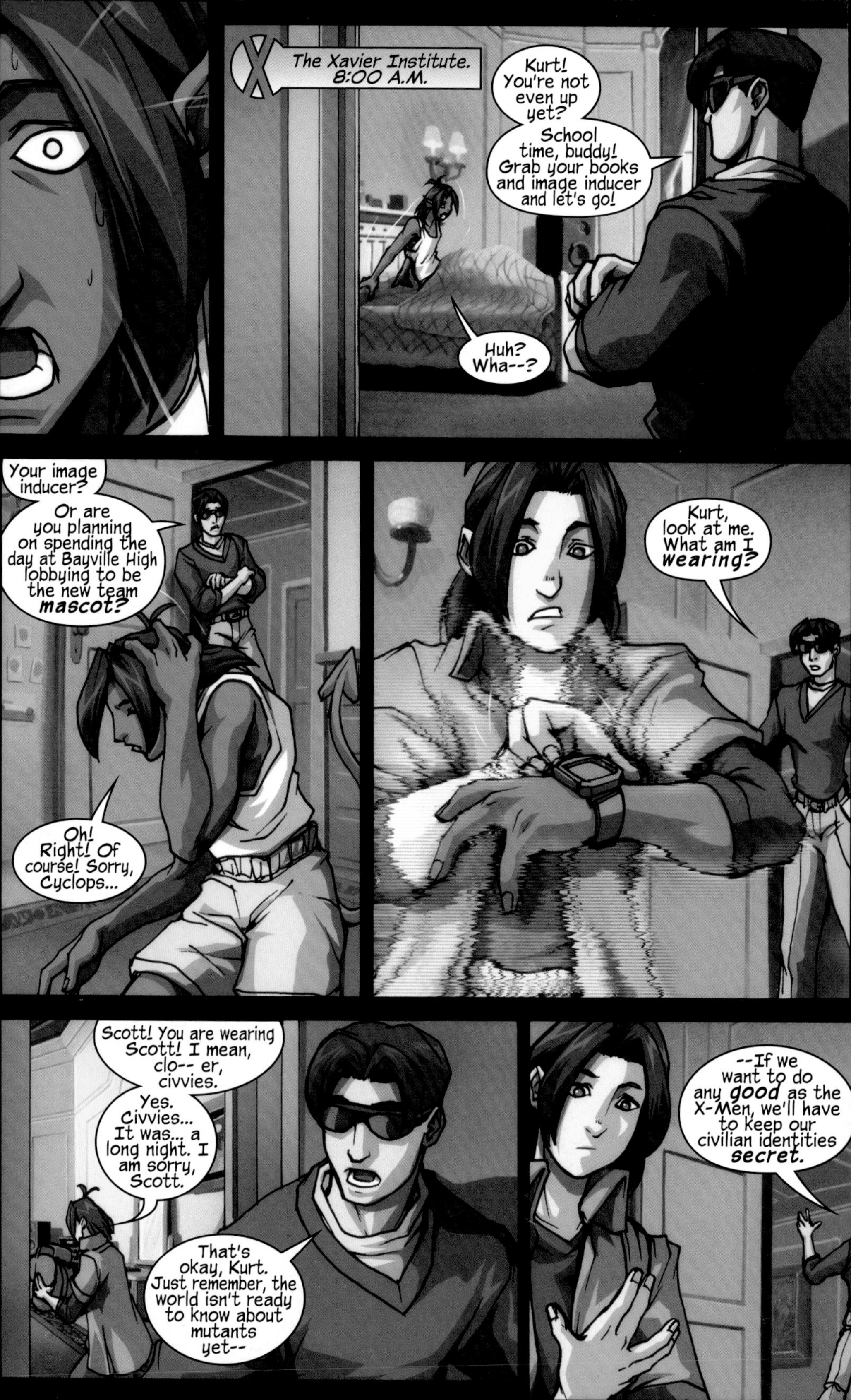
The Xavier Institute. 8:00 A.M.
Kurt! You're not even up yet?
School time, buddy! Grab your books and image inducer and let's go!
Huh? Wha--?
Your image inducer?
Or are you planning on spending the day at Bayville High lobbying to be the new team mascot?
Oh! Right! Of course! Sorry, Cyclops...
Kurt, look at me. What am I wearing?
Scott! You are wearing Scott! I mean, clo-- er, civvies.
Yes. Civvies... It was... a long night. I am sorry, Scott.
That's okay, Kurt. Just remember, the world isn't ready to know about mutants yet--
--If we want to do any good as the X-Men, we'll have to keep our civilian identities secret.

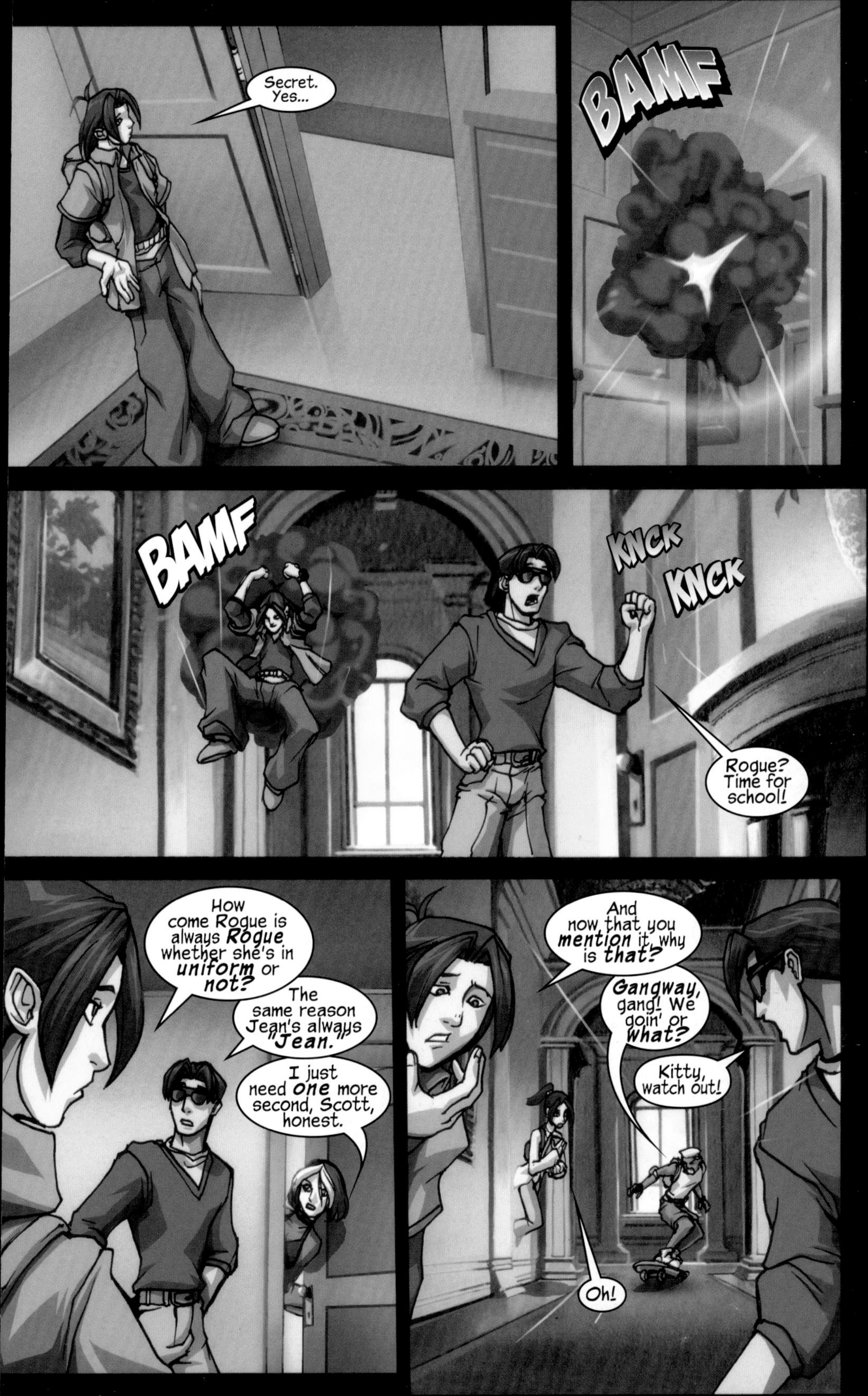
Secret. Yes...
BAMF
BAMF
KNCK
KNCK
Rogue? Time for school!
How come Rogue is always Rogue whether she's in uniform or not?
The same reason Jean's always "Jean."
I just need one more second, Scott, honest.
And now that you mention it, why is that?
Gangway, gang! We goin' or what?
Kitty, watch out!
Oh!

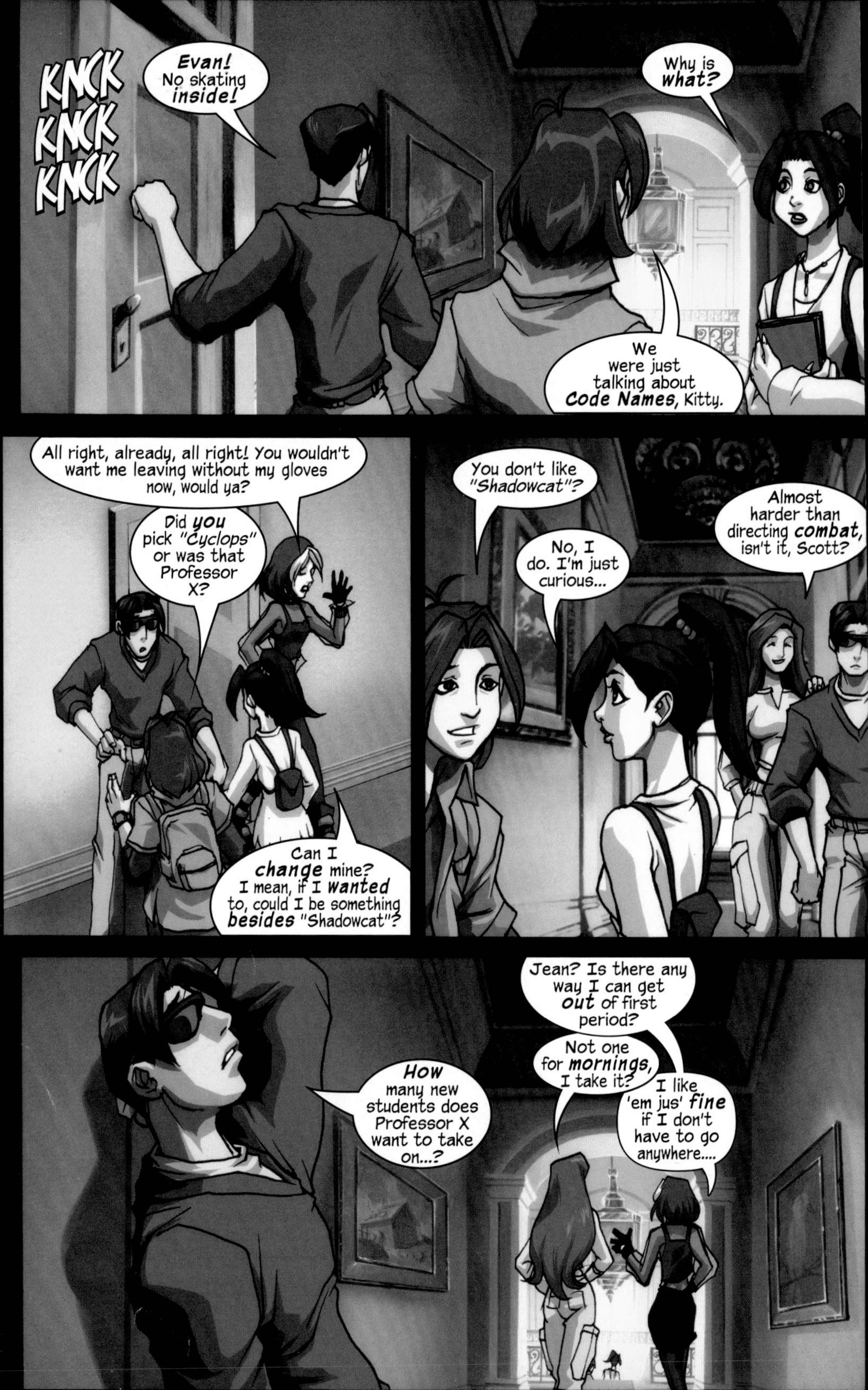
KNCK KNCK KNCK
Evan! No skating inside!
Why is what?
We were just talking about Code Names, Kitty.
All right, already, all right! You wouldn't want me leaving without my gloves now, would ya?
Did you pick "Cyclops" or was that Professor X?
Can I change mine? I mean, if I wanted to, could I be something besides "Shadowcat"?
You don't like "Shadowcat"?
No, I do. I'm just curious...
Almost harder than directing combat, isn't it, Scott?
How many new students does Professor X want to take on...?
Jean? Is there any way I can get out of first period?
Not one for mornings, I take it?
I like 'em jus' fine if I don't have to go anywhere....

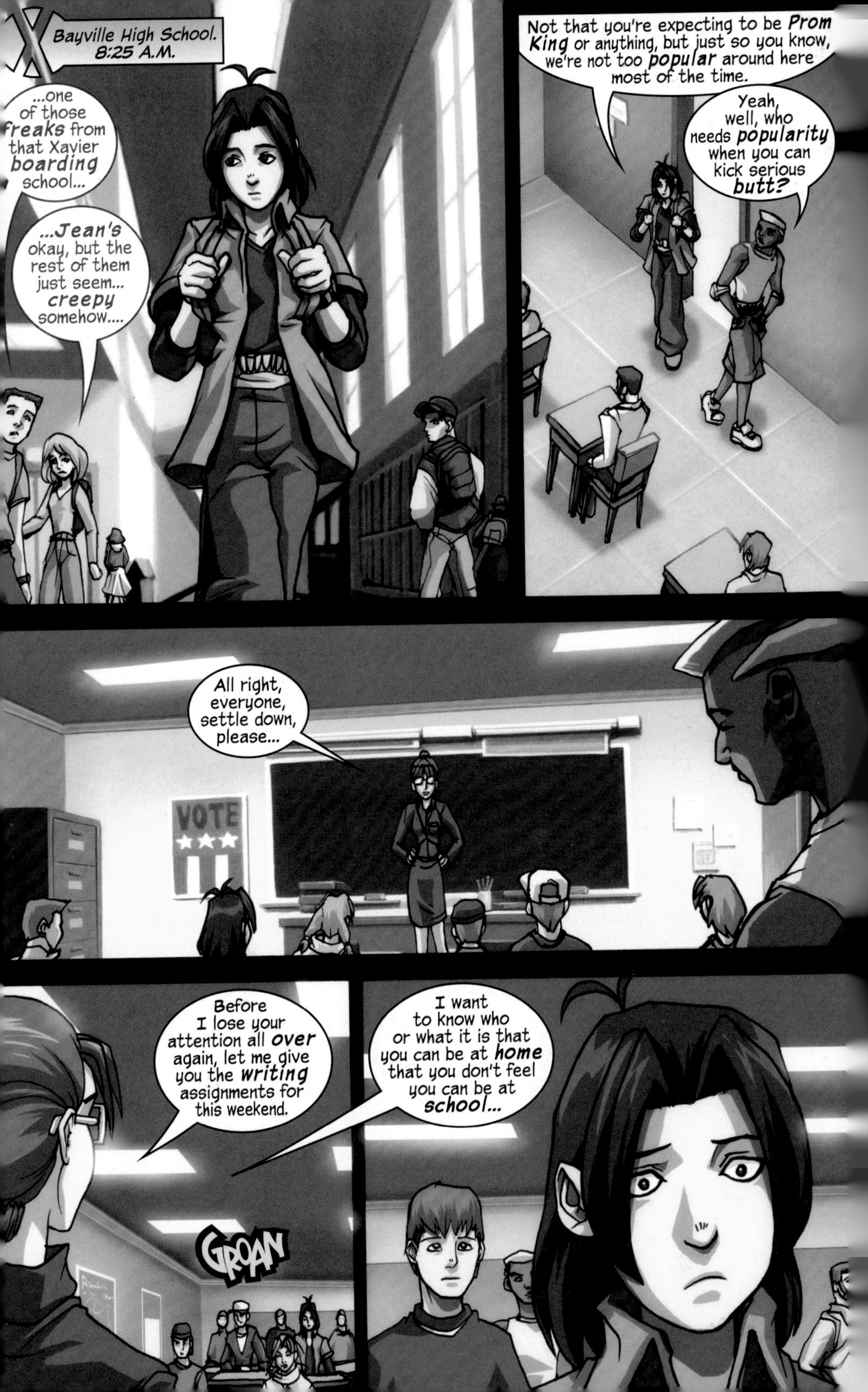
Bayville High School. 8:25 A.M.
...one of those freaks from that Xavier boarding school...
...Jean's okay, but the rest of them just seem... creepy somehow....
Not that you're expecting to be Prom King or anything, but just so you know, we're not too popular around here most of the time.
Yeah, well, who needs popularity when you can kick serious butt?
All right, everyone, settle down, please...
VOTE
Before I lose your attention all over again, let me give you the writing assignments for this weekend.
GROAN
I want to know who or what it is that you can be at home that you don't feel you can be at school...

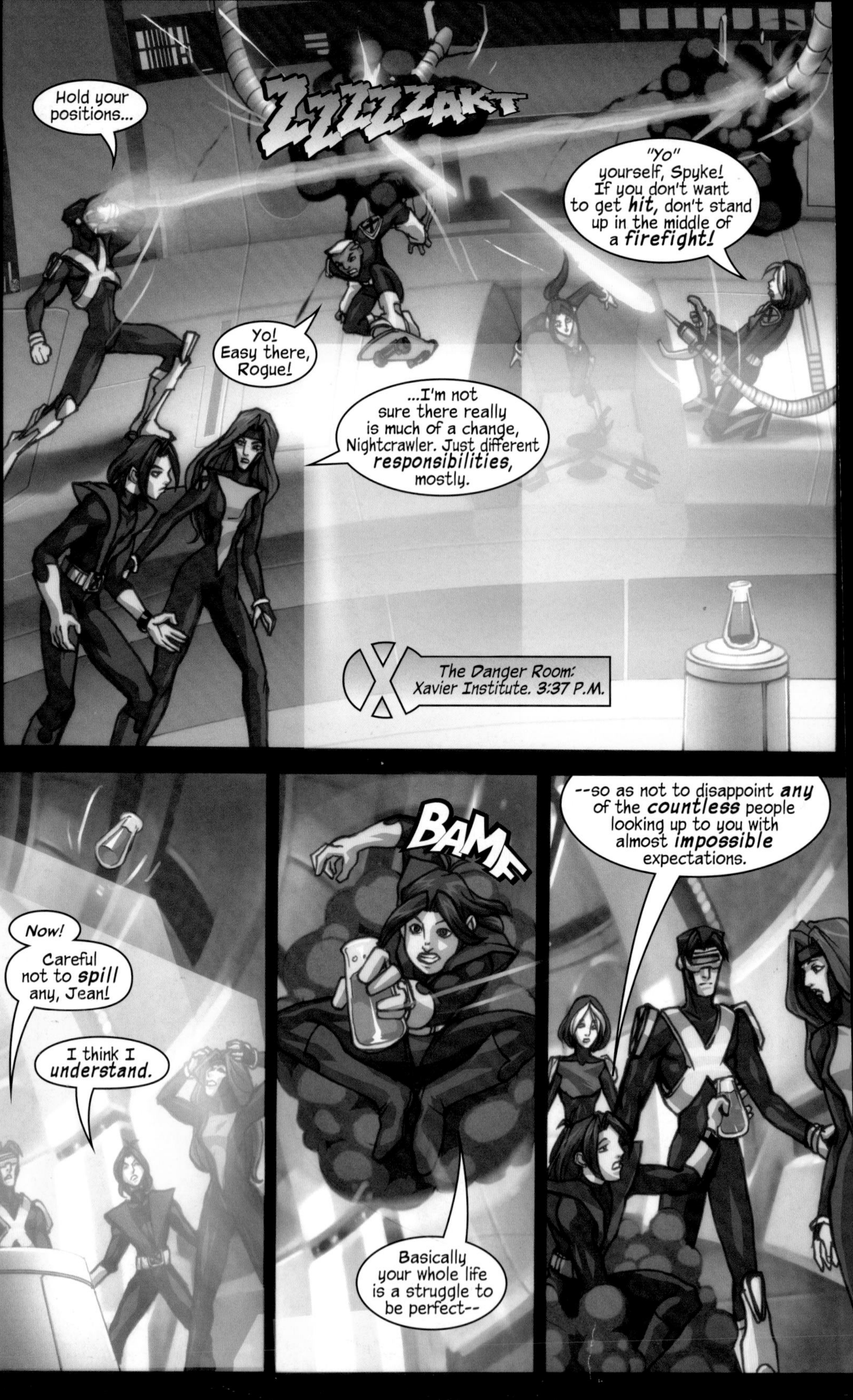
Hold your positions...
ZZZZZAKT
"Yo" yourself, Spyke! If you don't want to get hit, don't stand up in the middle of a firefight!
Yo! Easy there, Rogue!
...I'm not sure there really is much of a change, Nightcrawler. Just different responsibilities, mostly.
The Danger Room: Xavier Institute. 3:37 P.M.
Now!
Careful not to spill any, Jean!
I think I understand.
BAMF
Basically your whole life is a struggle to be perfect--
--so as not to disappoint any of the countless people looking up to you with almost impossible expectations.

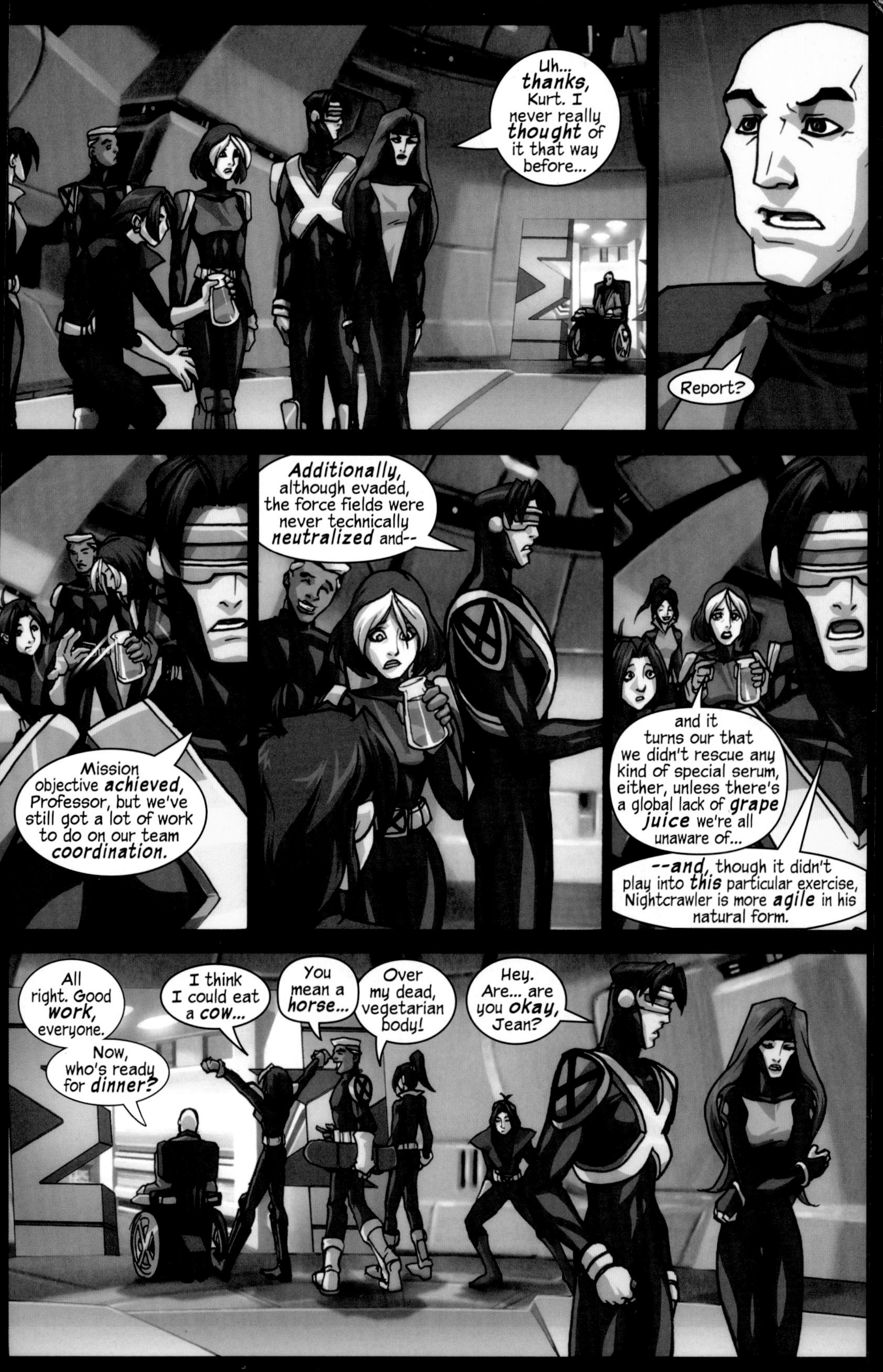
Uh... thanks, Kurt. I never really thought of it that way before...
Report?
Mission objective achieved, Professor, but we've still got a lot of work to do on our team coordination.
Additionally, although evaded, the force fields were never technically neutralized and--
and it turns our that we didn't rescue any kind of special serum, either, unless there's a global lack of grape juice we're all unaware of...
--and, though it didn't play into this particular exercise, Nightcrawler is more agile in his natural form.
All right. Good work, everyone.
Now, who's ready for dinner?
I think I could eat a cow...
You mean a horse...
Over my dead, vegetarian body!
Hey. Are... are you okay, Jean?

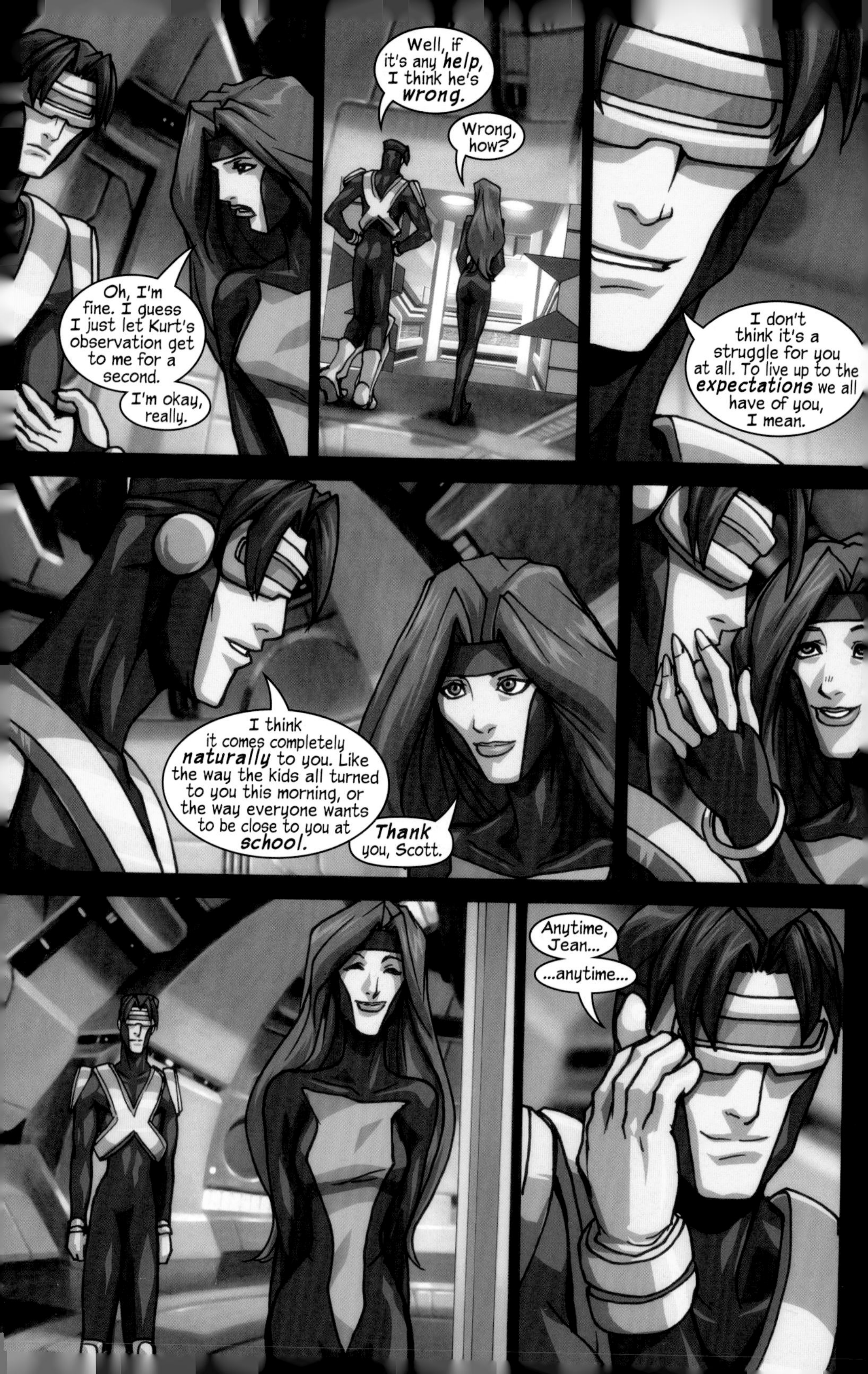
Oh, I'm fine. I guess I just let Kurt's observation get to me for a second.
I'm okay, really.
Well, if it's any help, I think he's wrong.
Wrong, how?
I don't think it's a struggle for you at all. To live up to the expectations we all have of you, I mean.
I think it comes completely naturally to you. Like the way the kids all turned to you this morning, or the way everyone wants to be close to you at school.
Thank you, Scott.
Anytime, Jean...
...anytime...

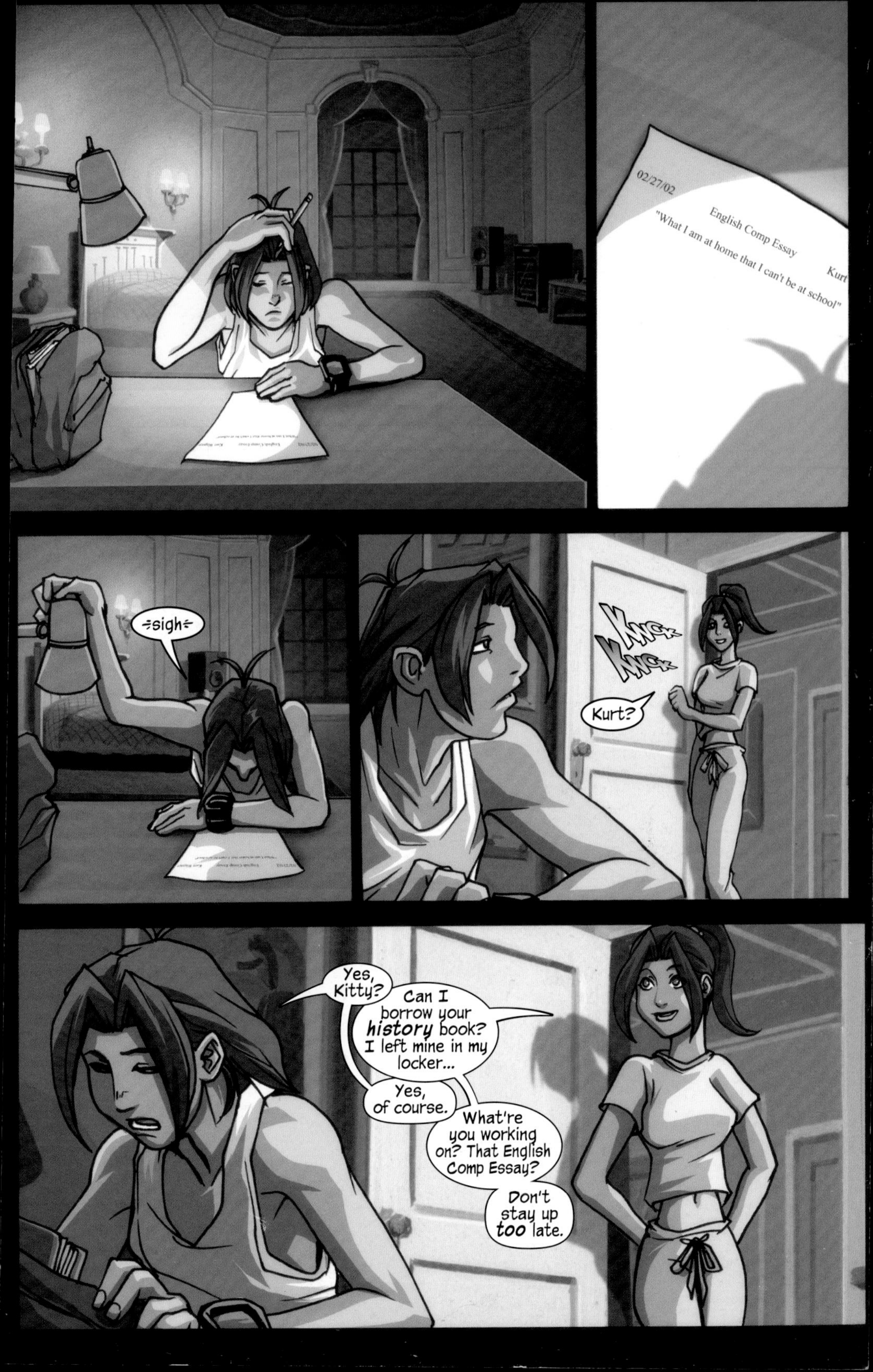
02/27/02
English Comp Essay
Kurt
"What I am at home that I can't be at school"
=sigh=
KNOCK KNOCK
Kurt?
Yes, Kitty?
Can I borrow your history book? I left mine in my locker...
Yes, of course.
What're you working on? That English Comp Essay?
Don't stay up too late.

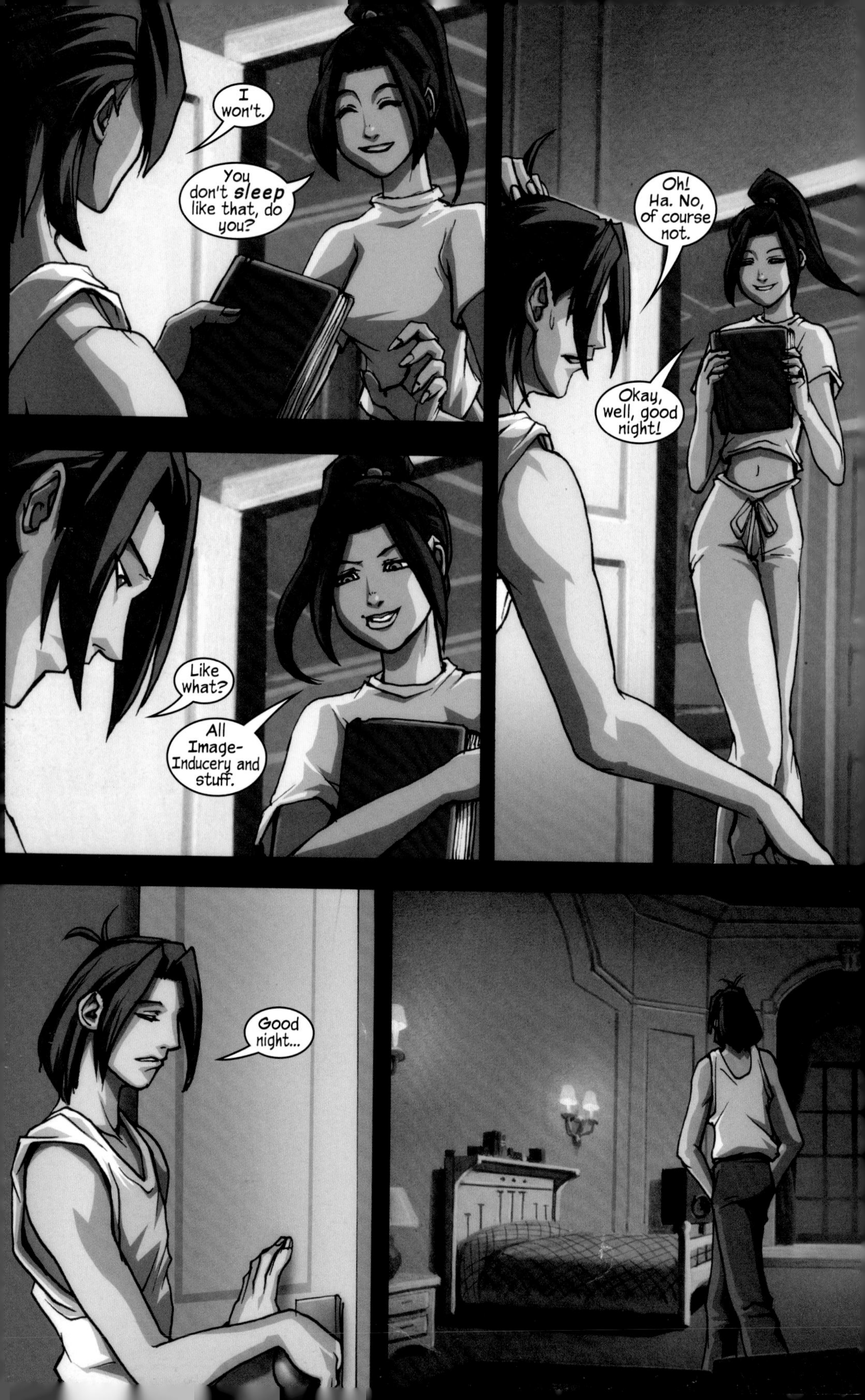

I won't.
You don't **sleep** like that, do you?
Oh! Ha. No, of course not.
Okay, well, good night!
Like what?
All Image-Inducery and stuff.
Good night...

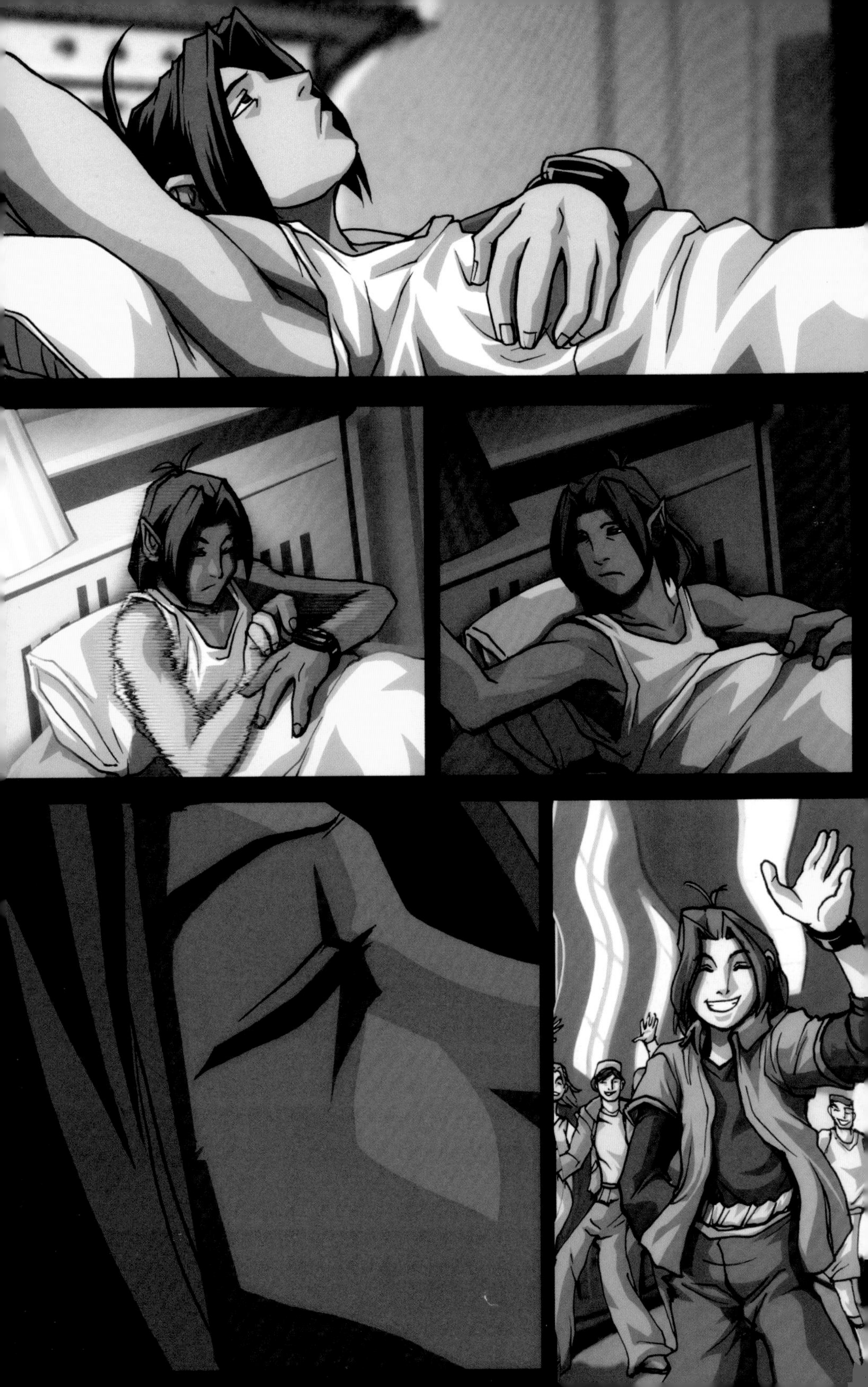

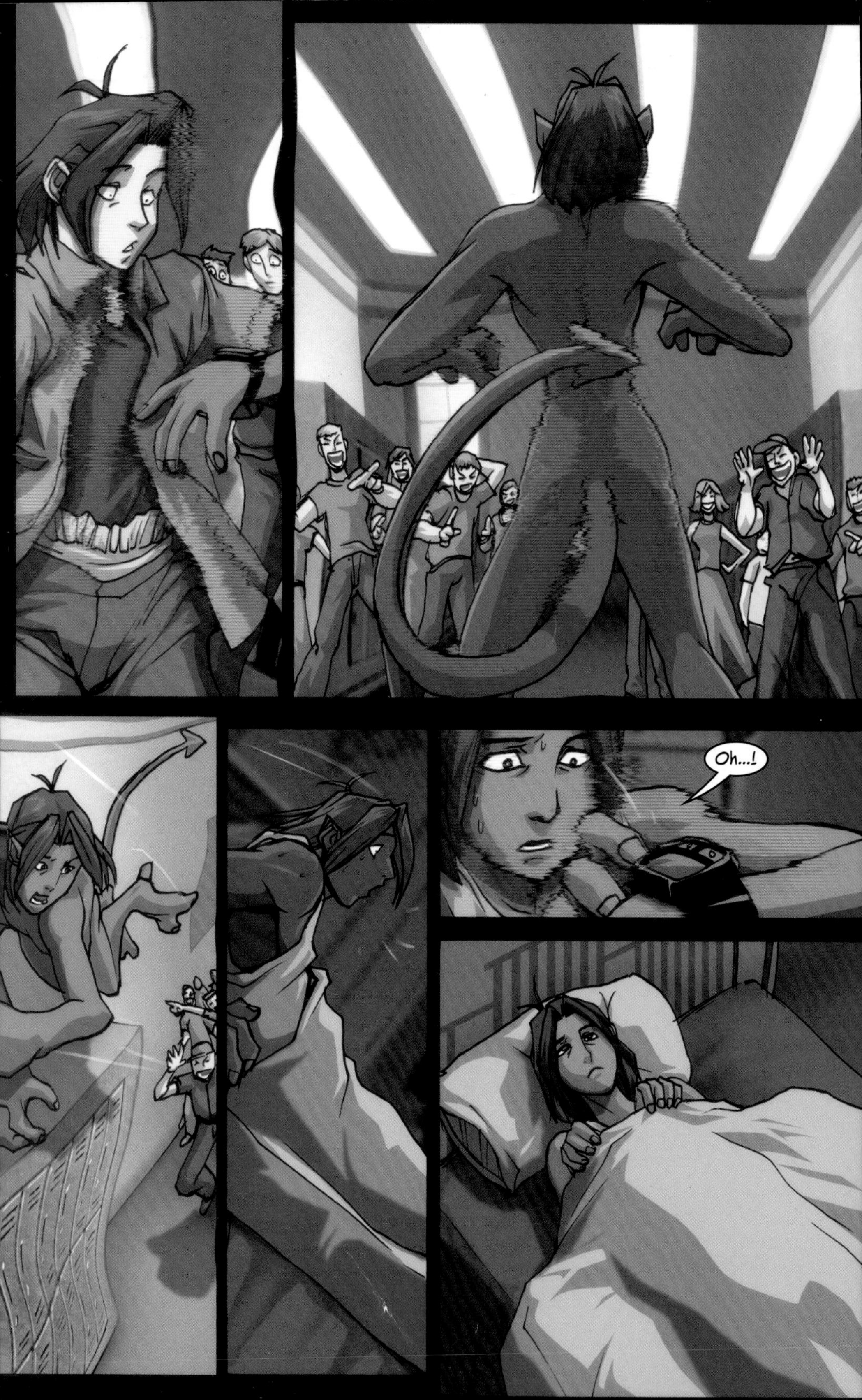
Oh...!

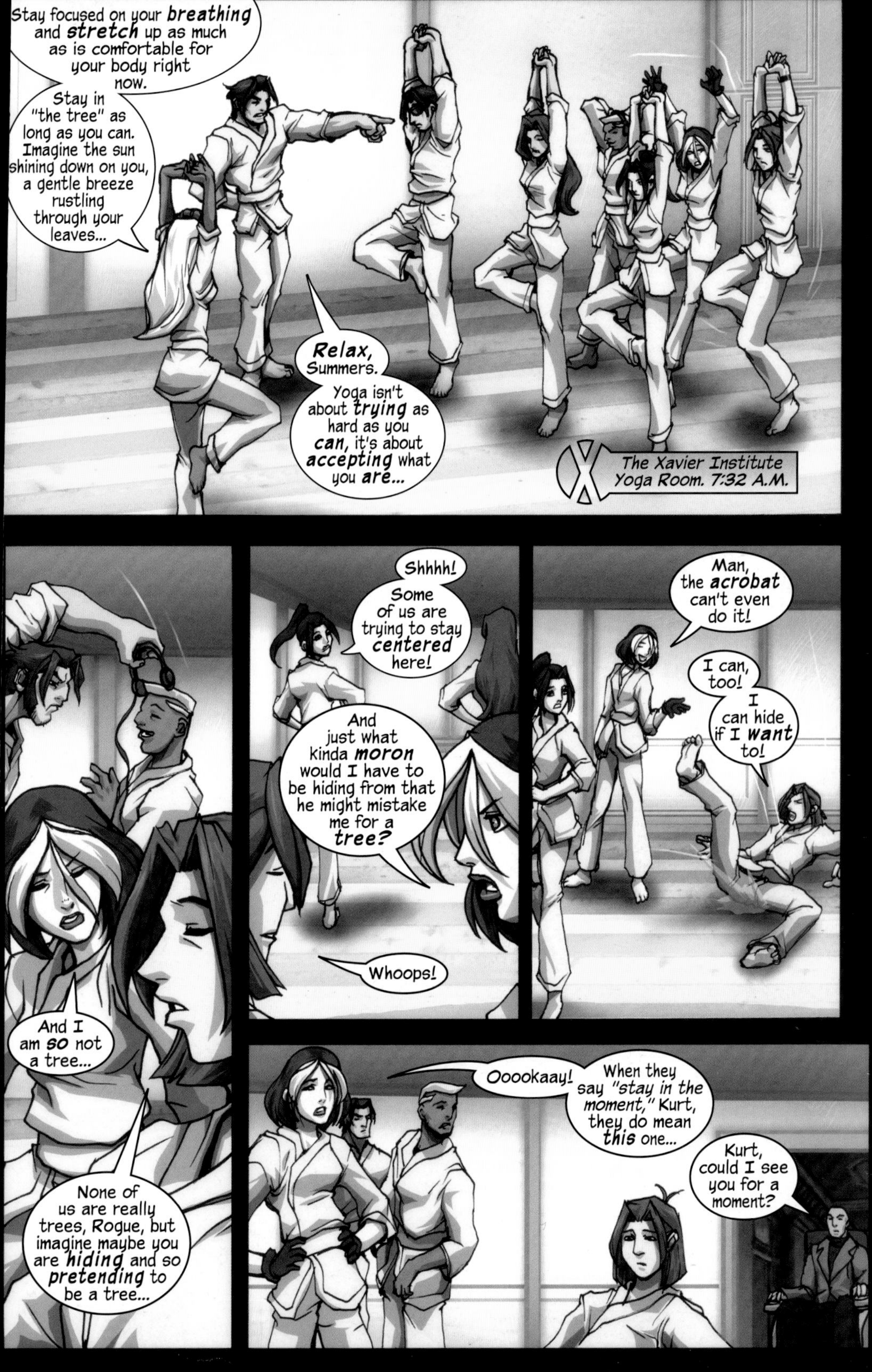
Stay focused on your breathing and stretch up as much as is comfortable for your body right now.
Stay in "the tree" as long as you can. Imagine the sun shining down on you, a gentle breeze rustling through your leaves...
Relax, Summers.
Yoga isn't about trying as hard as you can, it's about accepting what you are...
The Xavier Institute Yoga Room. 7:32 A.M.
Shhhh!
Some of us are trying to stay centered here!
And just what kinda moron would I have to be hiding from that he might mistake me for a tree?
Whoops!
Man, the acrobat can't even do it!
I can, too!
I can hide if I want to!
And I am so not a tree...
None of us are really trees, Rogue, but imagine maybe you are hiding and so pretending to be a tree...
Oooookaay!
When they say "stay in the moment," Kurt, they do mean this one...
Kurt, could I see you for a moment?

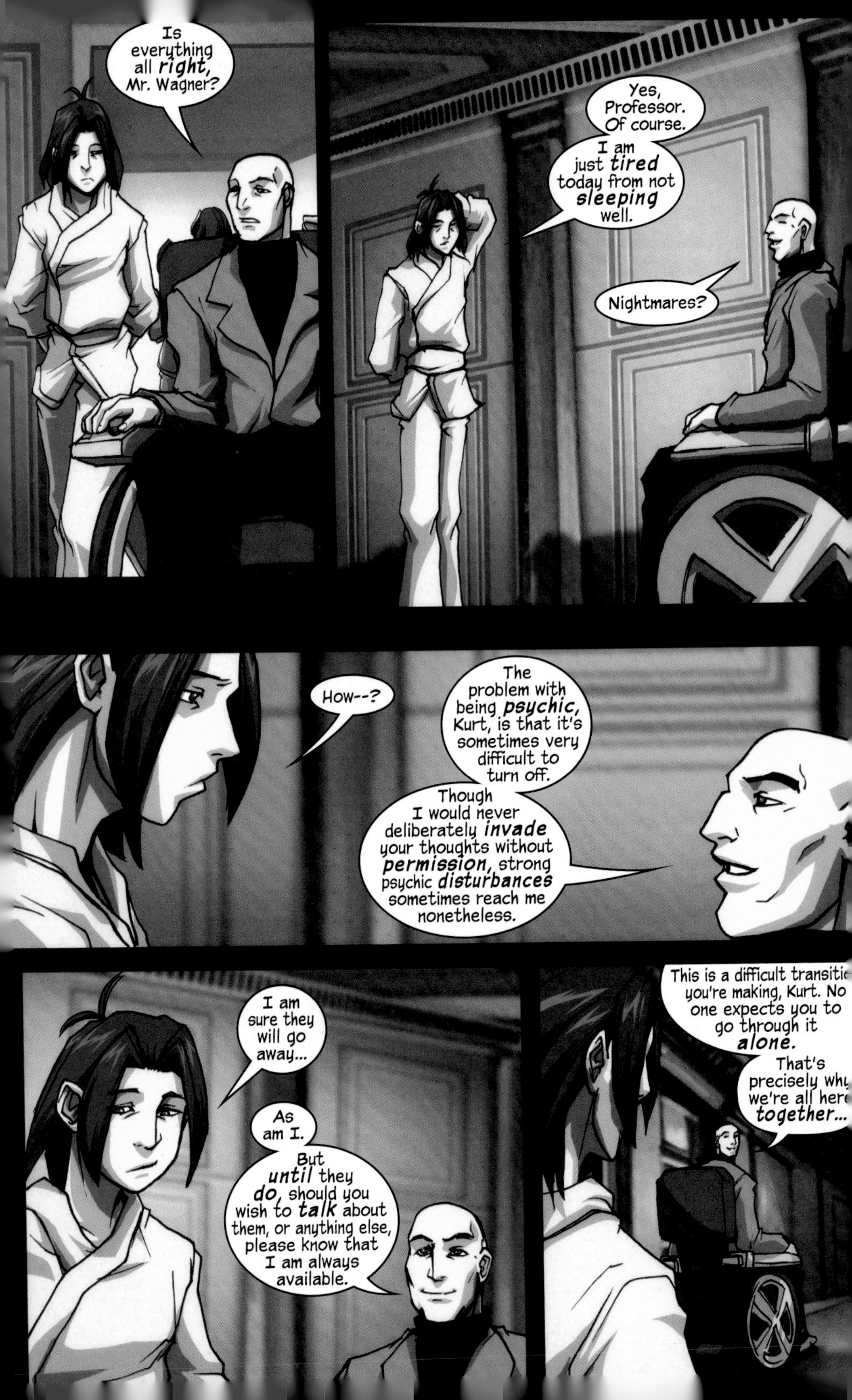

Is everything all right, Mr. Wagner?
Yes, Professor. Of course.
I am just tired today from not sleeping well.
Nightmares?
How--?
The problem with being psychic, Kurt, is that it's sometimes very difficult to turn off.
Though I would never deliberately invade your thoughts without permission, strong psychic disturbances sometimes reach me nonetheless.
I am sure they will go away...
As am I.
But until they do, should you wish to talk about them, or anything else, please know that I am always available.
This is a difficult transiti you're making, Kurt. No one expects you to go through it alone.
That's precisely why we're all here together...

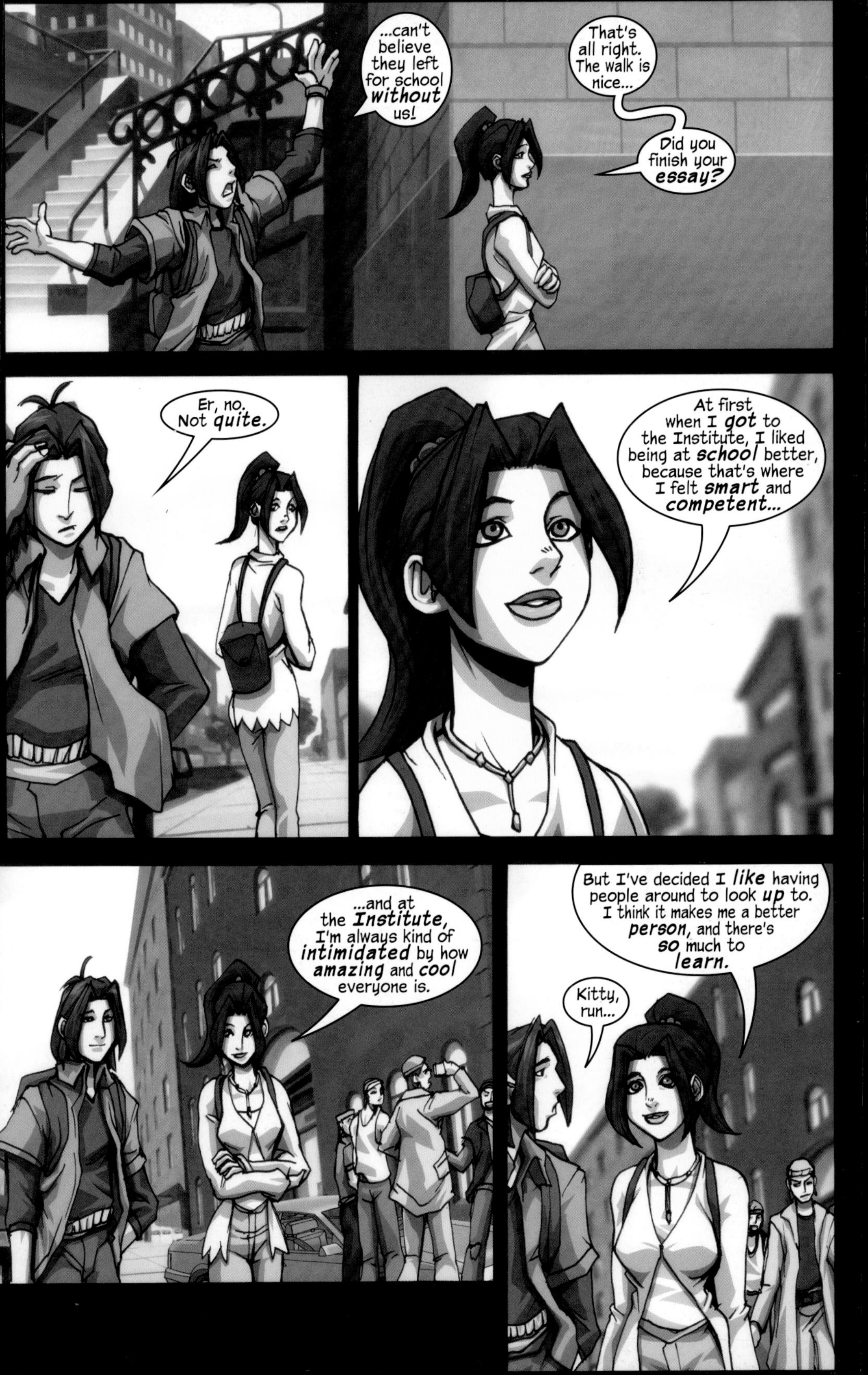
...can't believe they left for school without us!
That's all right. The walk is nice...
Did you finish your essay?
Er, no. Not quite.
At first when I got to the Institute, I liked being at school better, because that's where I felt smart and competent...
...and at the Institute, I'm always kind of intimidated by how amazing and cool everyone is.
But I've decided I like having people around to look up to. I think it makes me a better person, and there's so much to learn.
Kitty, run...

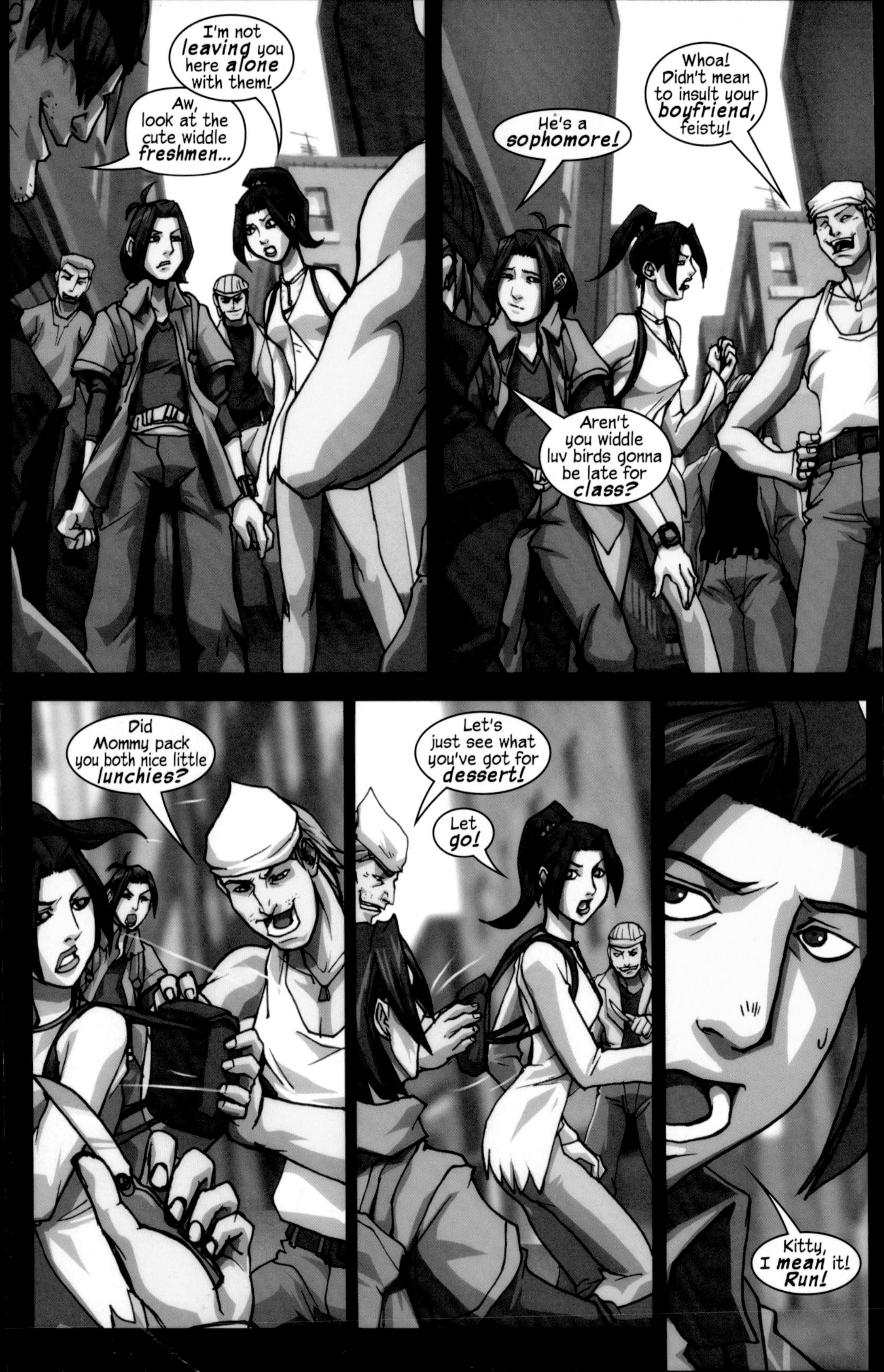
I'm not *leaving* you here *alone* with them!
Aw, look at the cute widdle *freshmen*...
He's a *sophomore!*
Whoa! Didn't mean to insult your *boyfriend,* feisty!
Aren't you widdle luv birds gonna be late for *class?*
Did Mommy pack you both nice little *lunchies?*
Let's just see what you've got for *dessert!*
Let *go!*
Kitty, I *mean* it! *Run!*

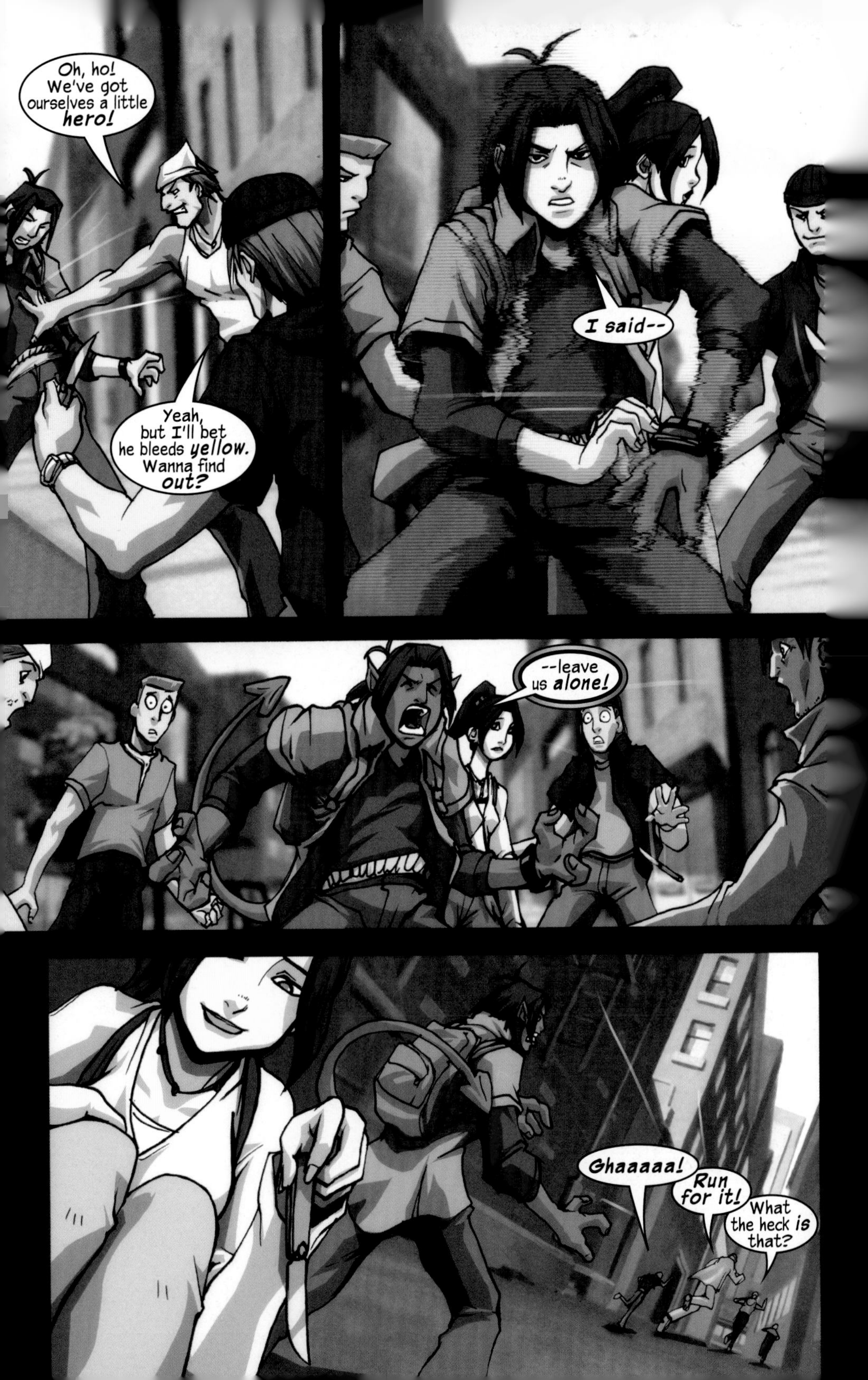

Oh, ho! We've got ourselves a little hero!
Yeah, but I'll bet he bleeds yellow. Wanna find out?
I said--
--leave us alone!
Ghaaaaa!
Run for it!
What the heck is that?

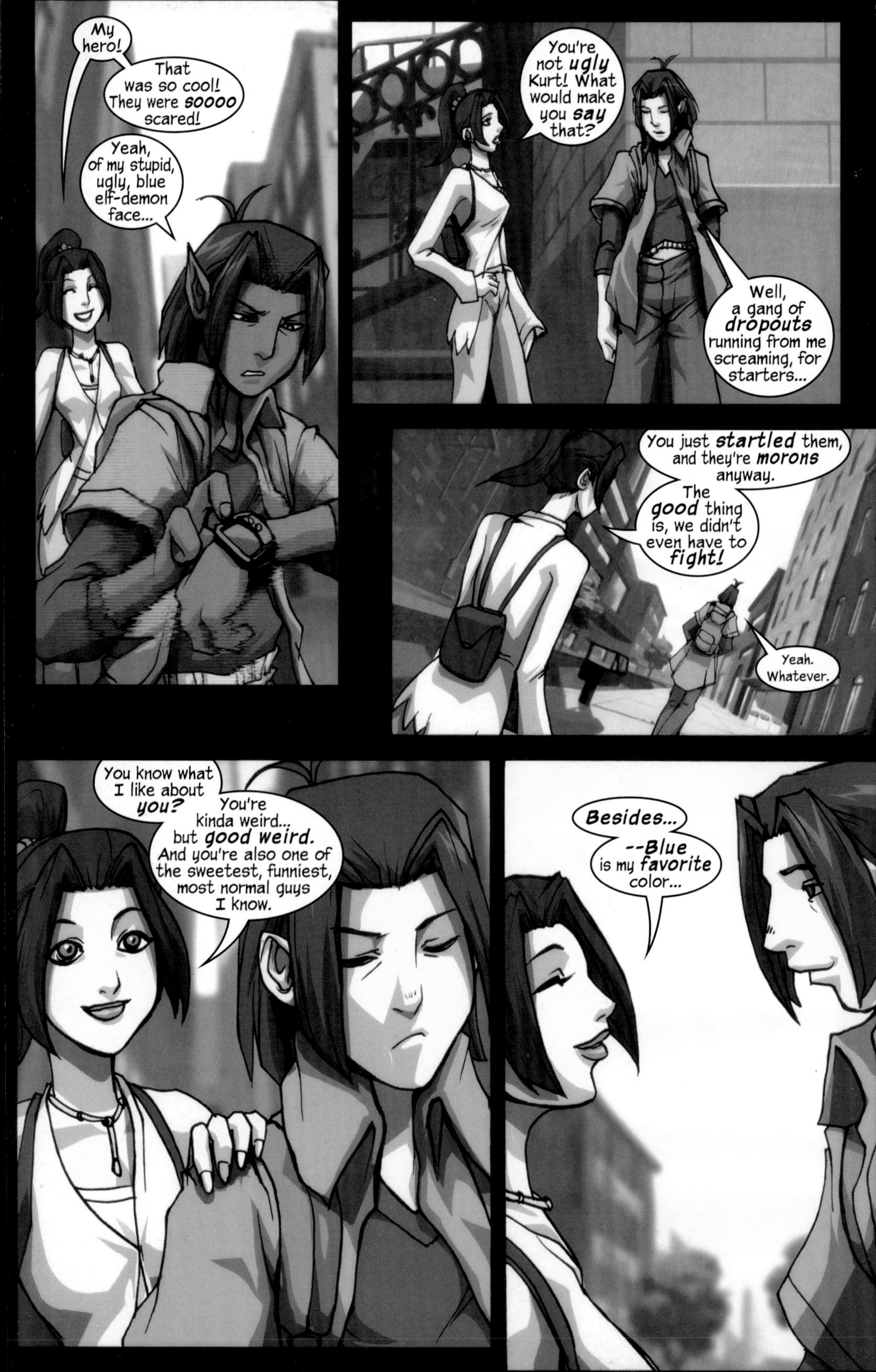
My hero!
That was so cool! They were SOOOO scared!
Yeah, of my stupid, ugly, blue elf-demon face...
You're not ugly Kurt! What would make you say that?
Well, a gang of dropouts running from me screaming, for starters...
You just startled them, and they're morons anyway.
The good thing is, we didn't even have to fight!
Yeah. Whatever.
You know what I like about you?
You're kinda weird... but good weird. And you're also one of the sweetest, funniest, most normal guys I know.
Besides...
--Blue is my favorite color...

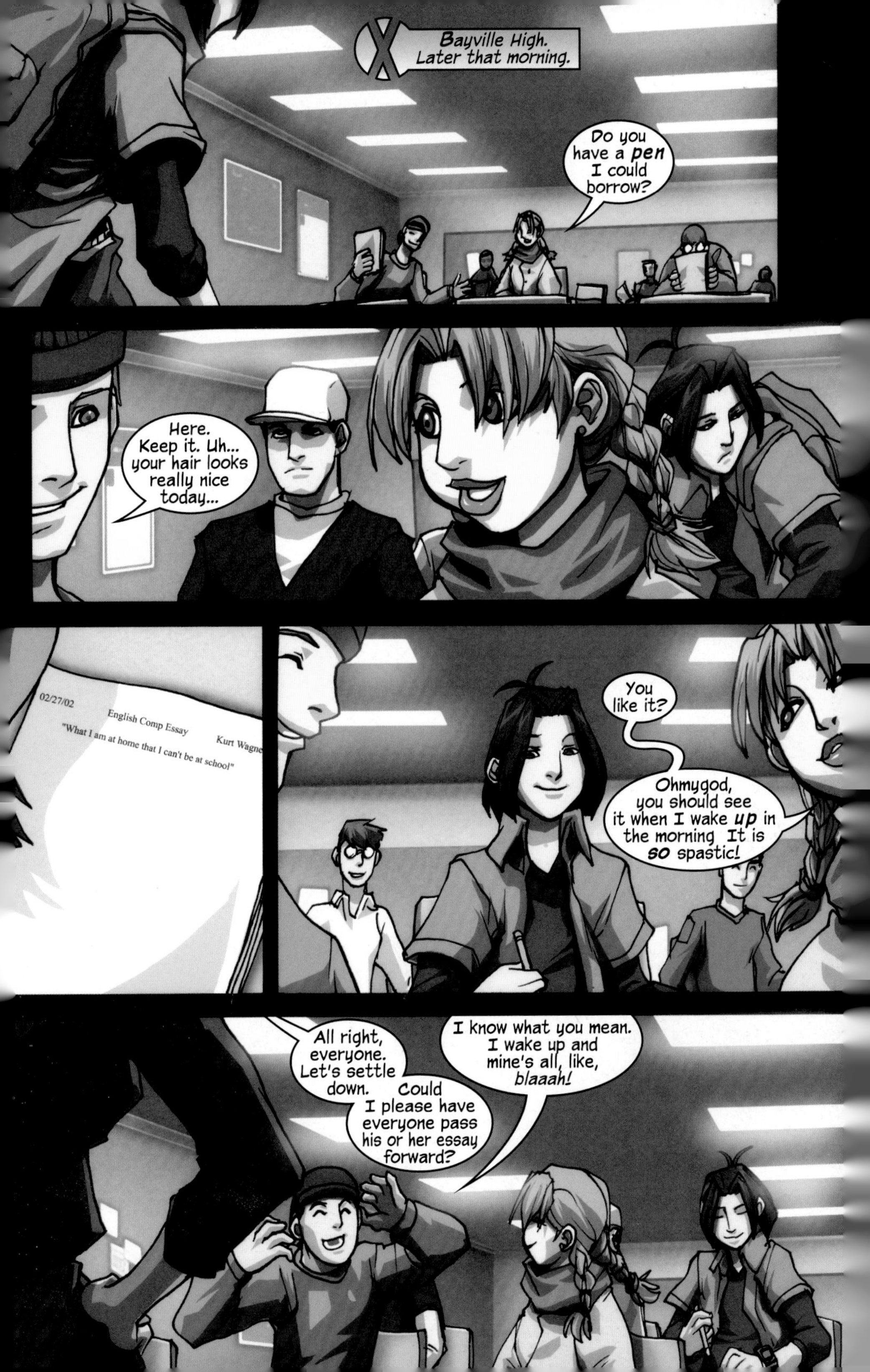
Bayville High. Later that morning.
Do you have a pen I could borrow?
Here. Keep it. Uh... your hair looks really nice today...
02/27/02
English Comp Essay
Kurt Wagne
"What I am at home that I can't be at school"
You like it?
Ohmygod, you should see it when I wake up in the morning It is so spastic!
All right, everyone. Let's settle down.
Could I please have everyone pass his or her essay forward?
I know what you mean. I wake up and mine's all, like, blaaah!

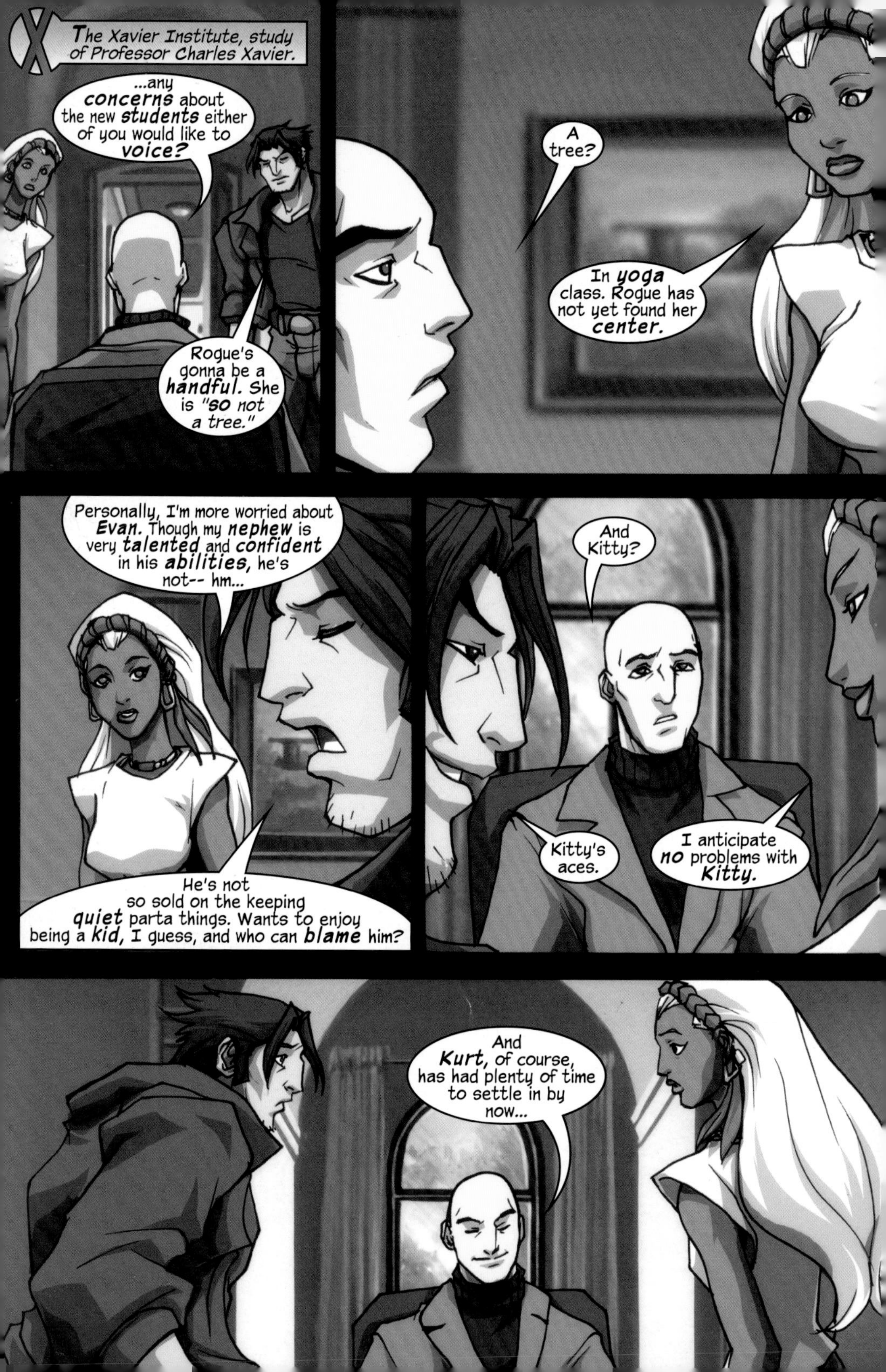

The Xavier Institute, study of Professor Charles Xavier.
...any concerns about the new students either of you would like to voice?
Rogue's gonna be a handful. She is "so not a tree."
A tree?
In yoga class. Rogue has not yet found her center.
Personally, I'm more worried about Evan. Though my nephew is very talented and confident in his abilities, he's not-- hm...
He's not so sold on the keeping quiet parta things. Wants to enjoy being a kid, I guess, and who can blame him?
And Kitty?
Kitty's aces.
I anticipate no problems with Kitty.
And Kurt, of course, has had plenty of time to settle in by now...

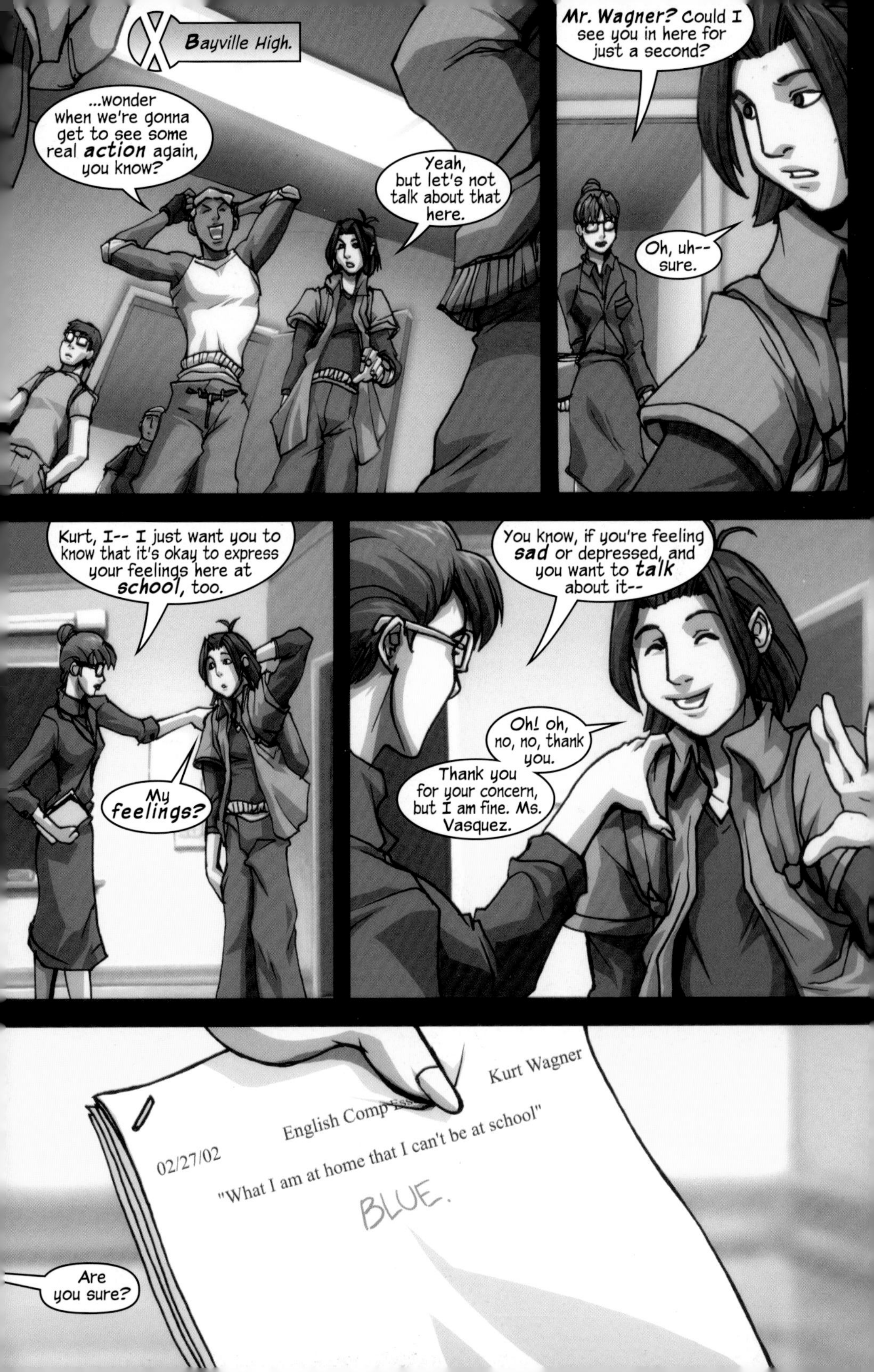
Bayville High.
...wonder when we're gonna get to see some real action again, you know?
Yeah, but let's not talk about that here.
Mr. Wagner? Could I see you in here for just a second?
Oh, uh-- sure.
Kurt, I-- I just want you to know that it's okay to express your feelings here at school, too.
My feelings?
You know, if you're feeling sad or depressed, and you want to talk about it--
Oh! oh, no, no, thank you.
Thank you for your concern, but I am fine. Ms. Vasquez.
Kurt Wagner
English Comp Ess
02/27/02
"What I am at home that I can't be at school"
BLUE.
Are you sure?

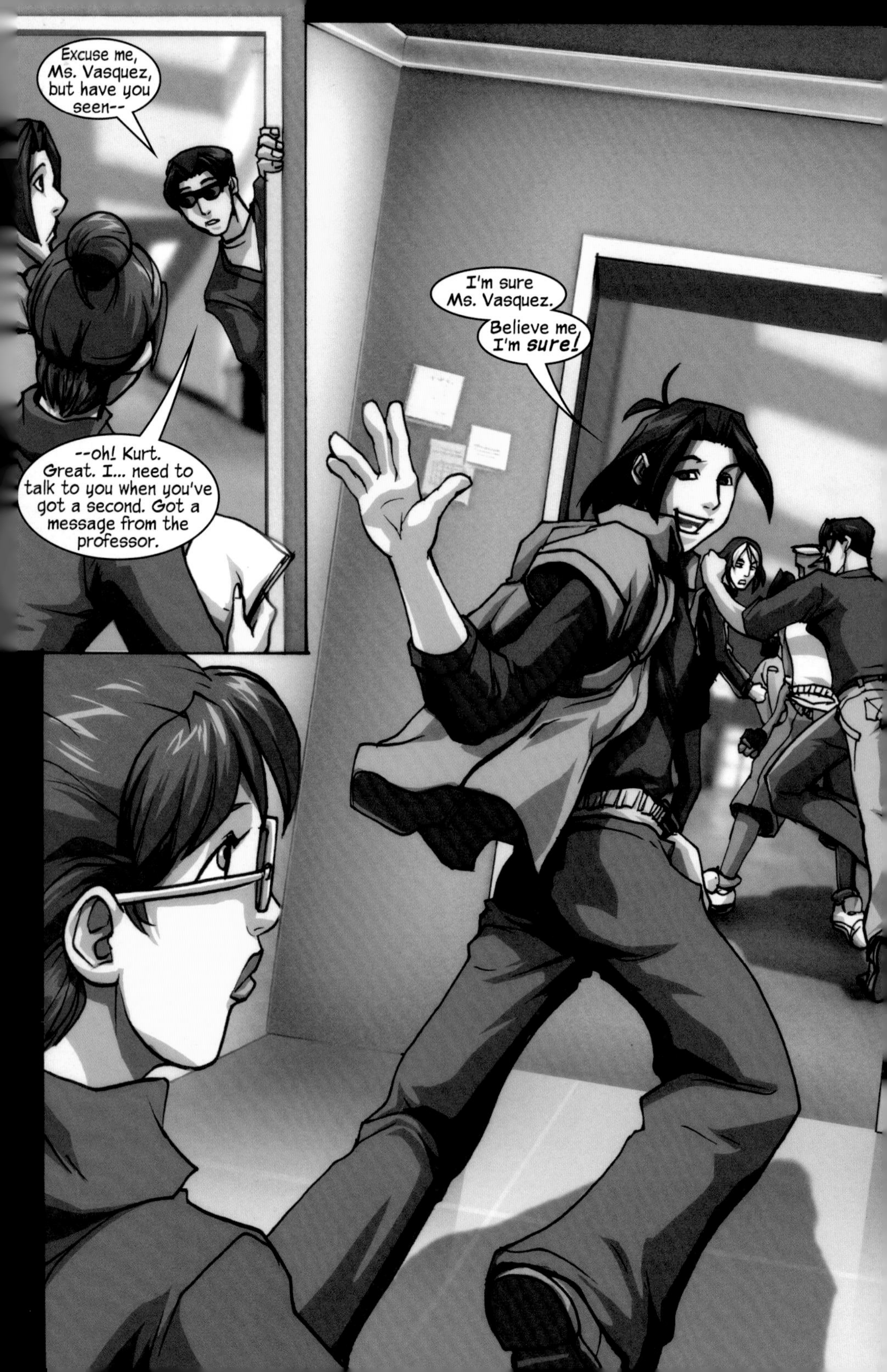
Excuse me, Ms. Vasquez, but have you seen--
--oh! Kurt. Great. I... need to talk to you when you've got a second. Got a message from the professor.
I'm sure Ms. Vasquez.
Believe me, I'm *sure!*

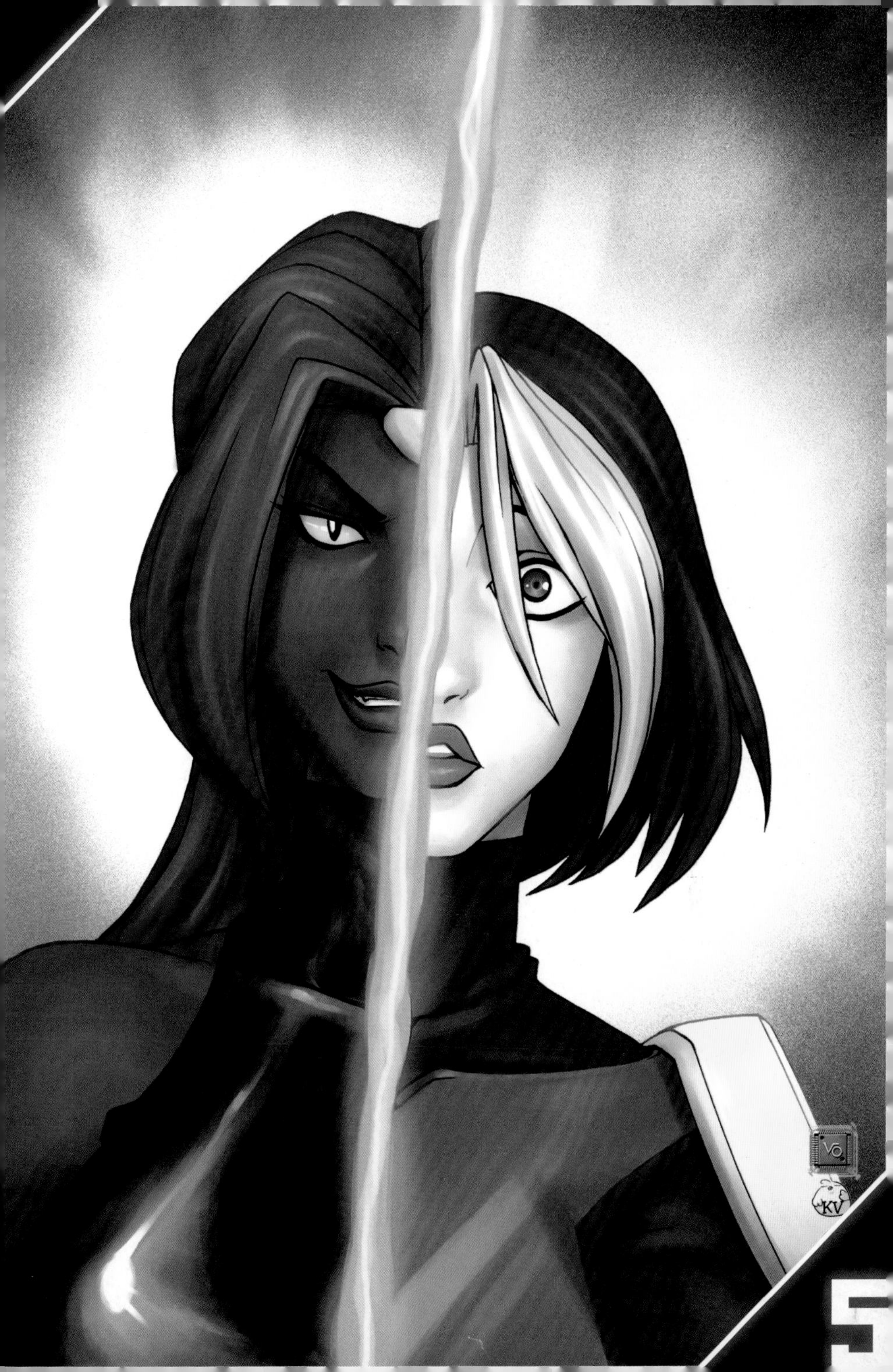
5

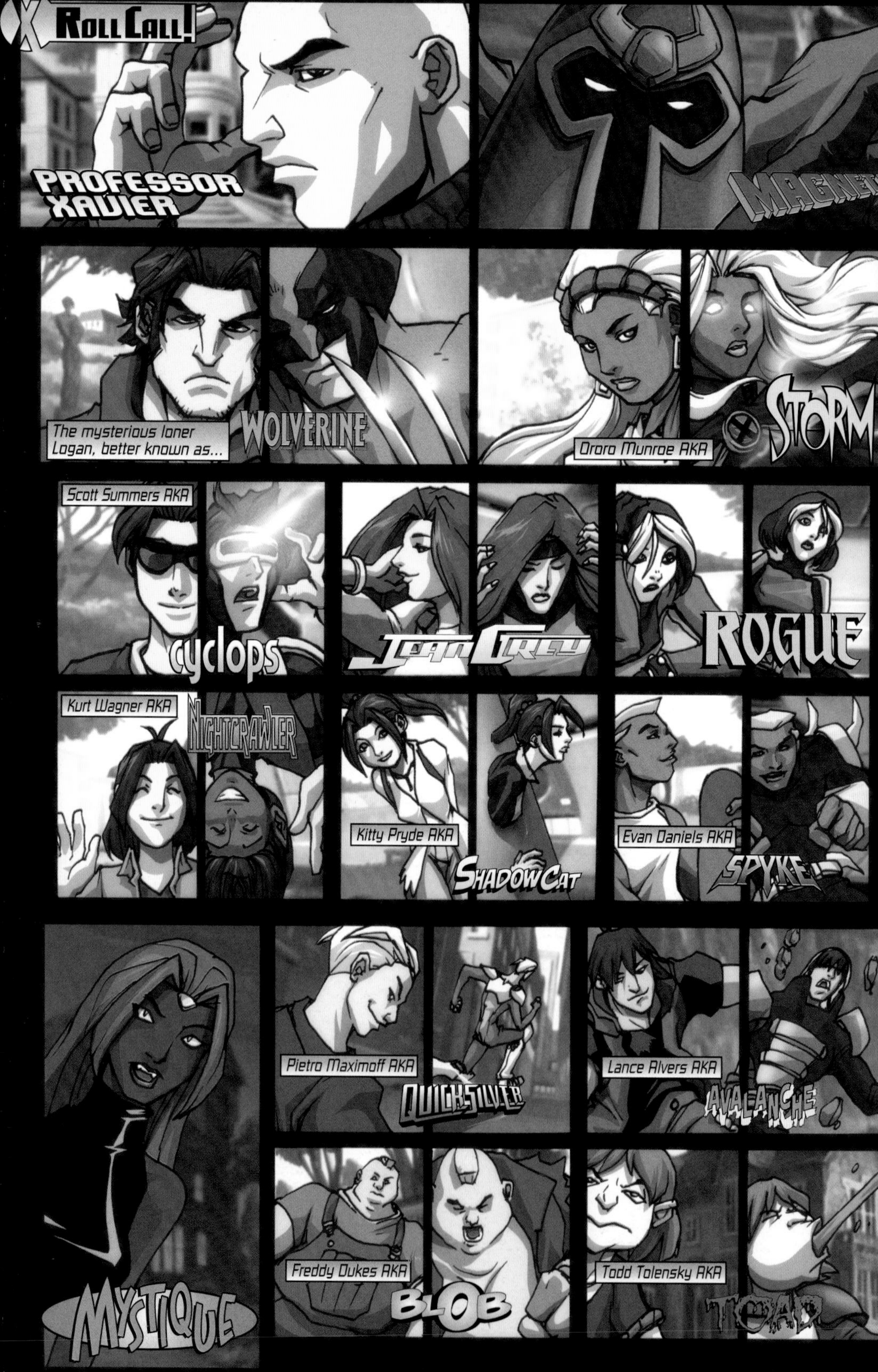

Roll Call!
PROFESSOR XAVIER
MAGNETO
The mysterious loner Logan, better known as...
WOLVERINE
Ororo Munroe AKA
STORM
Scott Summers AKA
cyclops
JEAN GREY
ROGUE
Kurt Wagner AKA
NIGHTCRAWLER
Kitty Pryde AKA
SHADOWCAT
Evan Daniels AKA
SPYKE
MYSTIQUE
Pietro Maximoff AKA
QUICKSILVER
Lance Alvers AKA
AVALANCHE
Freddy Dukes AKA
BLOB
Todd Tolensky AKA
TOAD

X-MEN: EVOLUTION
UNTOUCHABLE

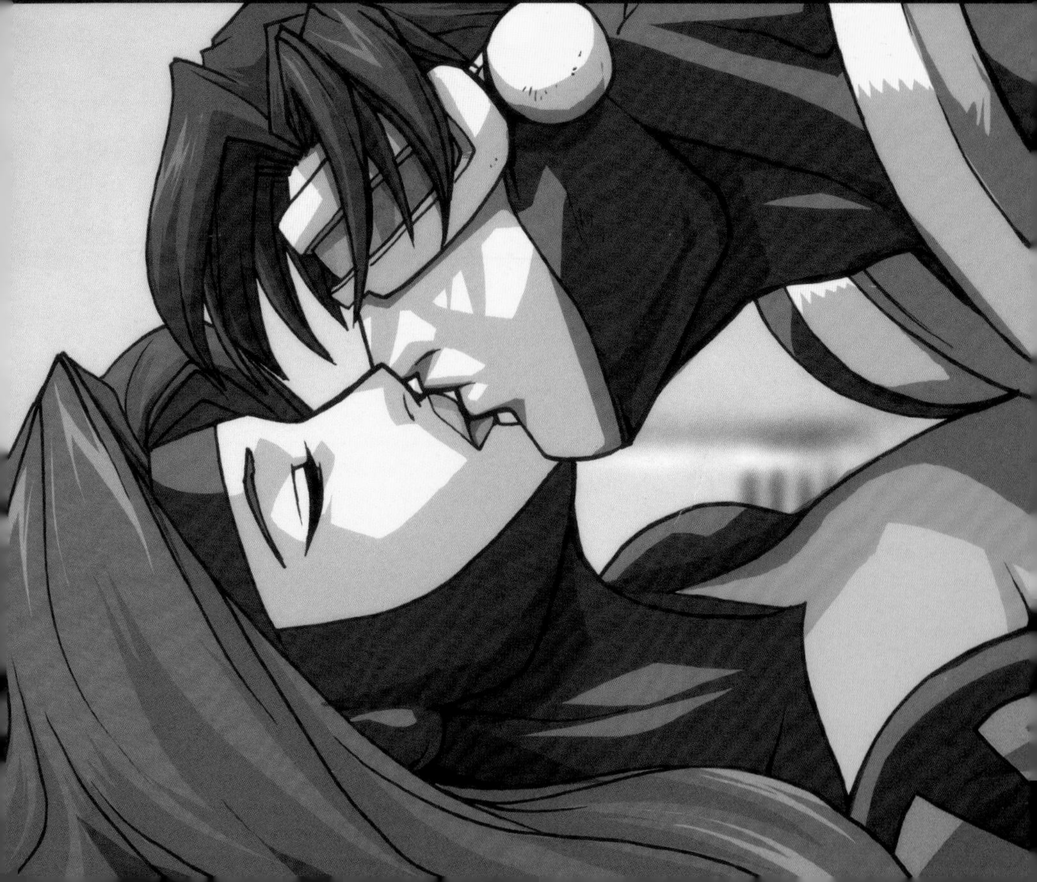

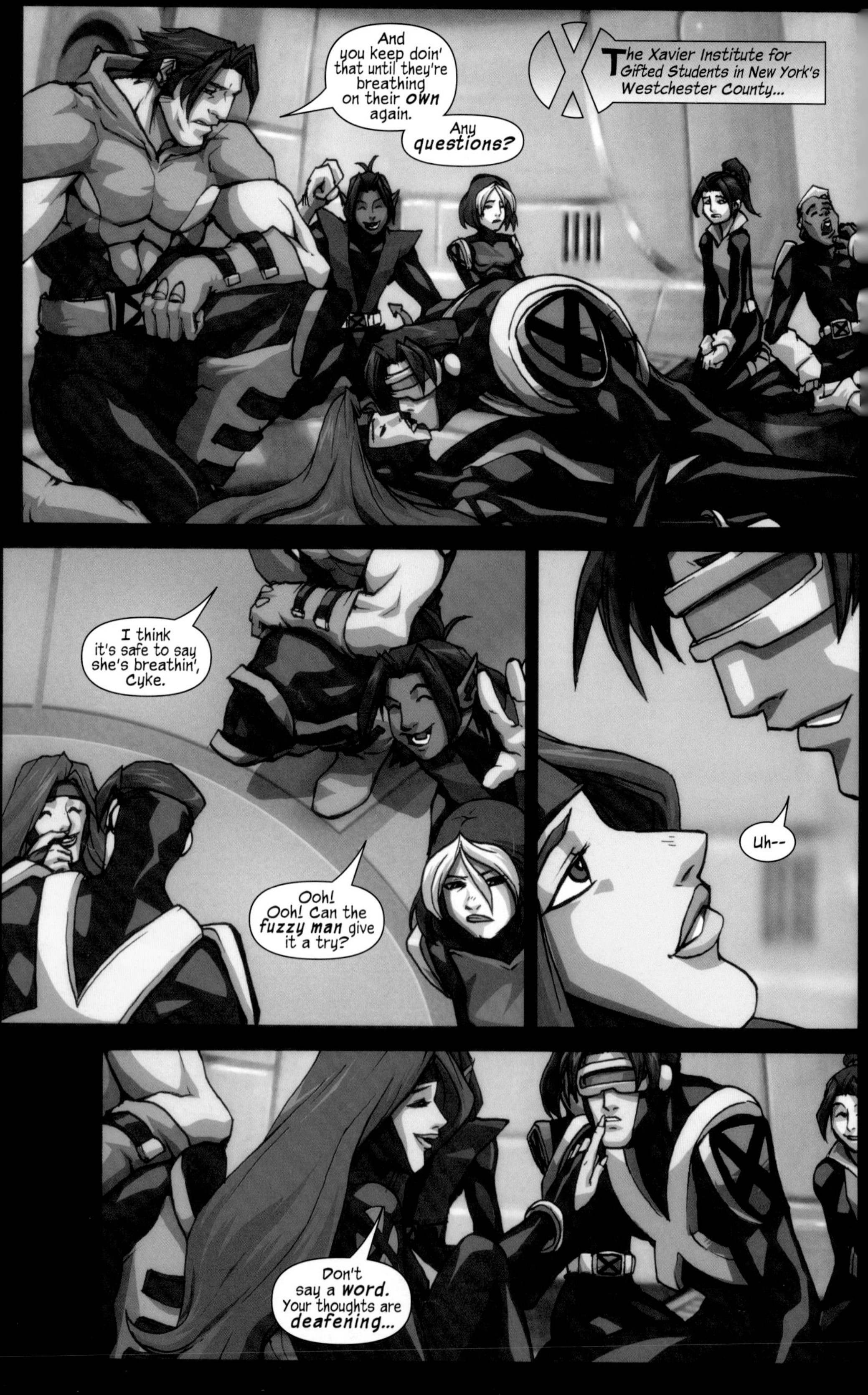

The Xavier Institute for Gifted Students in New York's Westchester County...
And you keep doin' that until they're breathing on their own again.
Any questions?
I think it's safe to say she's breathin', Cyke.
Ooh! Ooh! Can the fuzzy man give it a try?
Uh--
Don't say a word. Your thoughts are deafening...

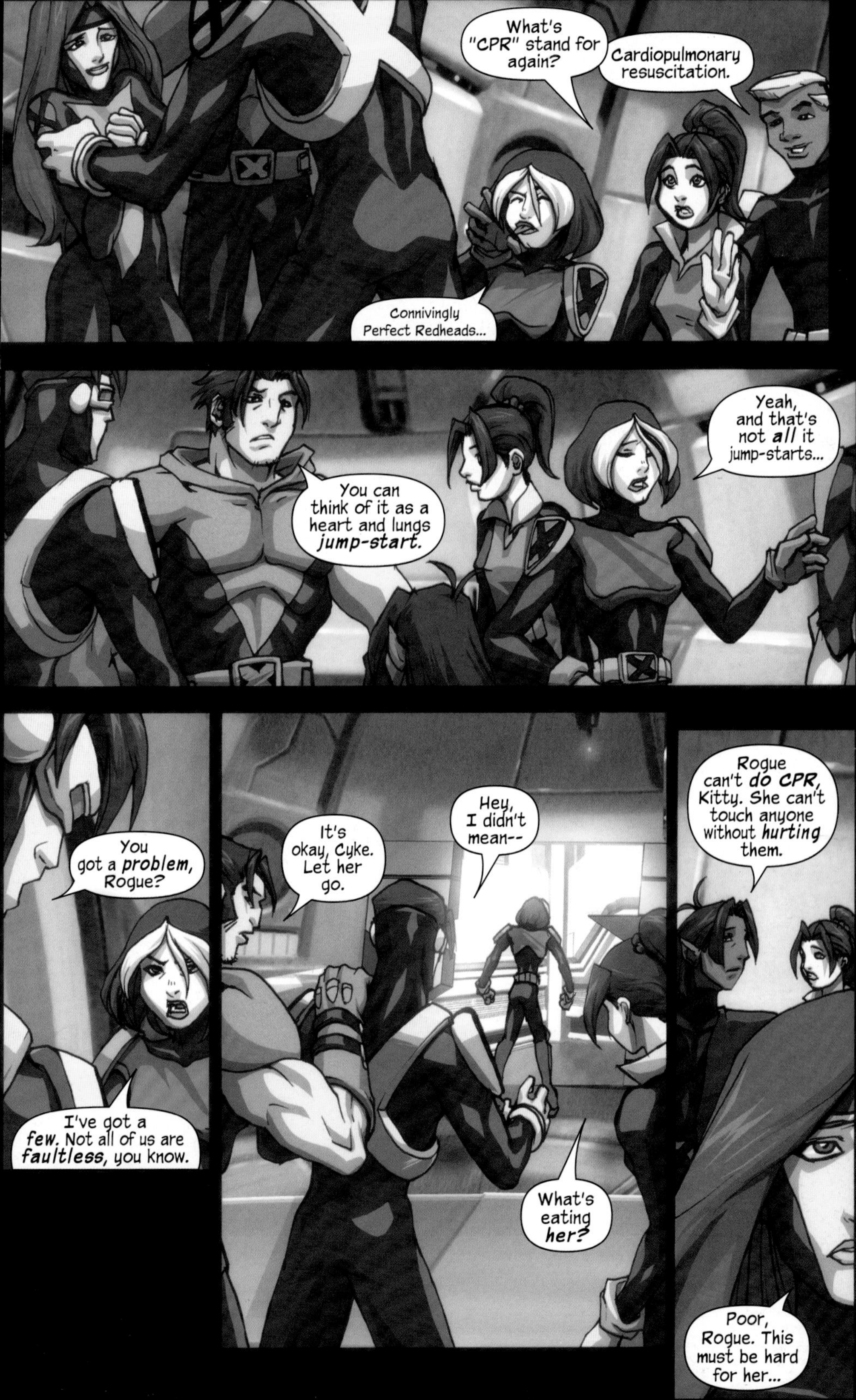
What's "CPR" stand for again?
Cardiopulmonary resuscitation.
Connivingly Perfect Redheads...
You can think of it as a heart and lungs *jump-start.*
Yeah, and that's not *all* it jump-starts...
You got a *problem,* Rogue?
I've got a *few.* Not all of us are *faultless,* you know.
It's okay, Cyke. Let her go.
Hey, I didn't mean--
What's eating *her?*
Rogue can't *do CPR,* Kitty. She can't touch anyone without *hurting* them.
Poor, Rogue. This must be hard for her...

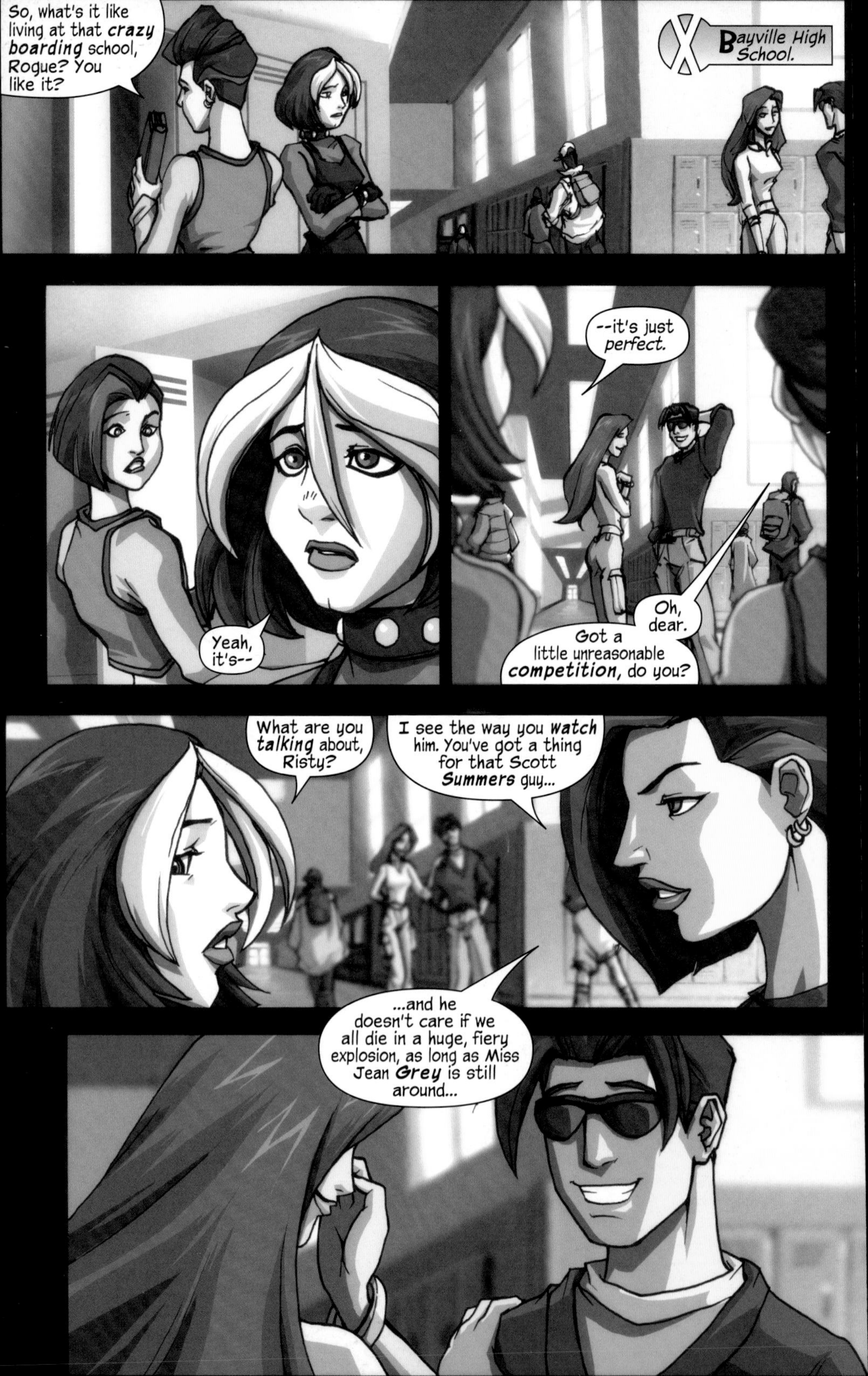
Bayville High School.
So, what's it like living at that crazy boarding school, Rogue? You like it?
Yeah, it's--
--it's just perfect.
Oh, dear.
Got a little unreasonable competition, do you?
What are you talking about, Risty?
I see the way you watch him. You've got a thing for that Scott Summers guy...
...and he doesn't care if we all die in a huge, fiery explosion, as long as Miss Jean Grey is still around...

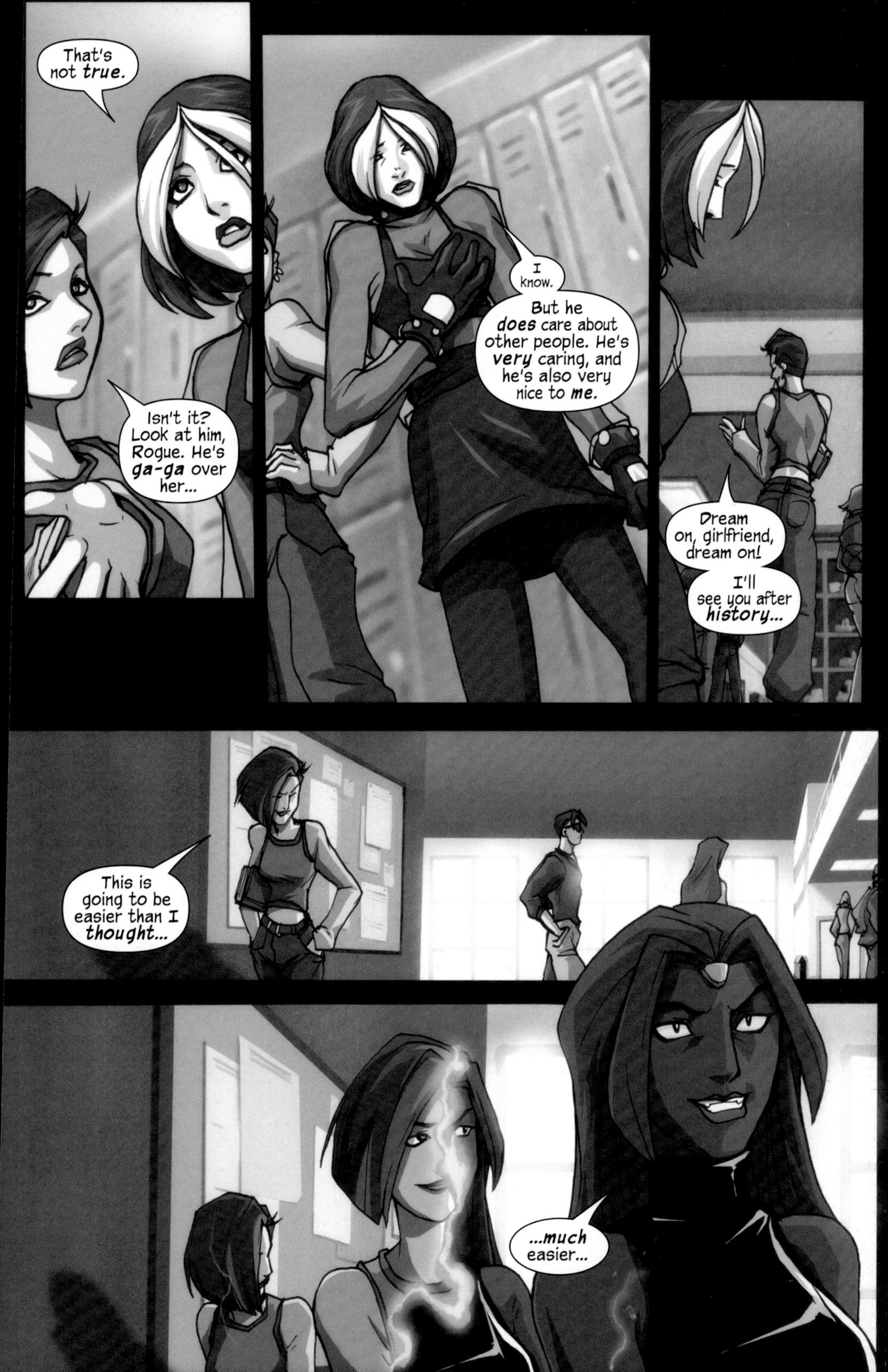
That's not *true.*
Isn't it? Look at him, Rogue. He's *ga-ga* over her...
I know.
But he *does* care about other people. He's *very* caring, and he's also very nice to *me.*
Dream on, girlfriend, dream on!
I'll see you after *history...*
This is going to be easier than I *thought...*
...much easier...

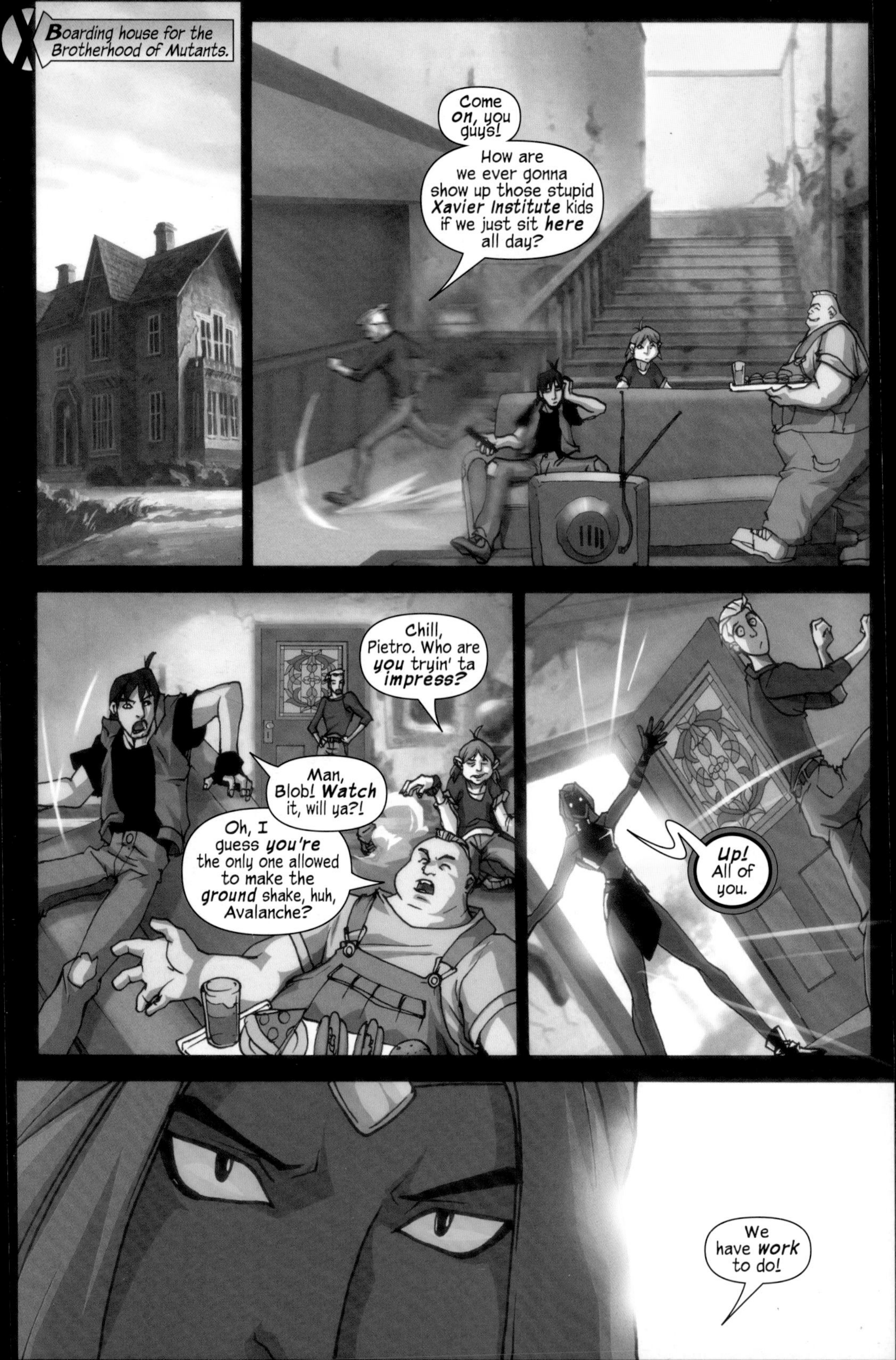
Boarding house for the Brotherhood of Mutants.
Come on, you guys!
How are we ever gonna show up those stupid Xavier Institute kids if we just sit here all day?
Chill, Pietro. Who are you tryin' ta impress?
Man, Blob! Watch it, will ya?!
Oh, I guess you're the only one allowed to make the ground shake, huh, Avalanche?
Up! All of you.
We have work to do!

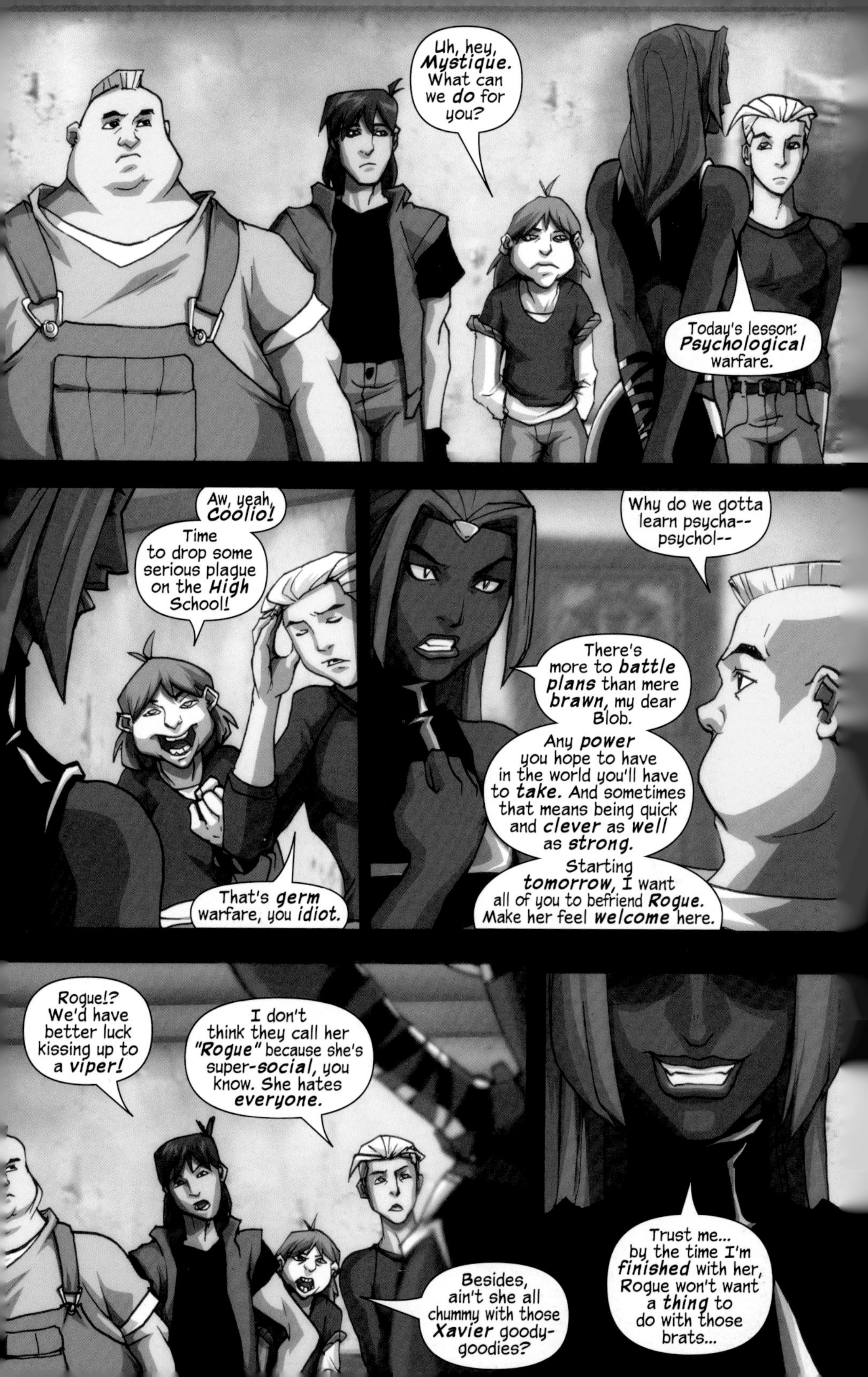

Uh, hey, Mystique. What can we do for you?
Today's lesson: Psychological warfare.
Aw, yeah, Coolio! Time to drop some serious plague on the High School!
That's germ warfare, you idiot.
Why do we gotta learn psycha-- psychol--
There's more to battle plans than mere brawn, my dear Blob.
Any power you hope to have in the world you'll have to take. And sometimes that means being quick and clever as well as strong.
Starting tomorrow, I want all of you to befriend Rogue. Make her feel welcome here.
Rogue!? We'd have better luck kissing up to a viper!
I don't think they call her "Rogue" because she's super-social, you know. She hates everyone.
Besides, ain't she all chummy with those Xavier goody-goodies?
Trust me... by the time I'm finished with her, Rogue won't want a thing to do with those brats...

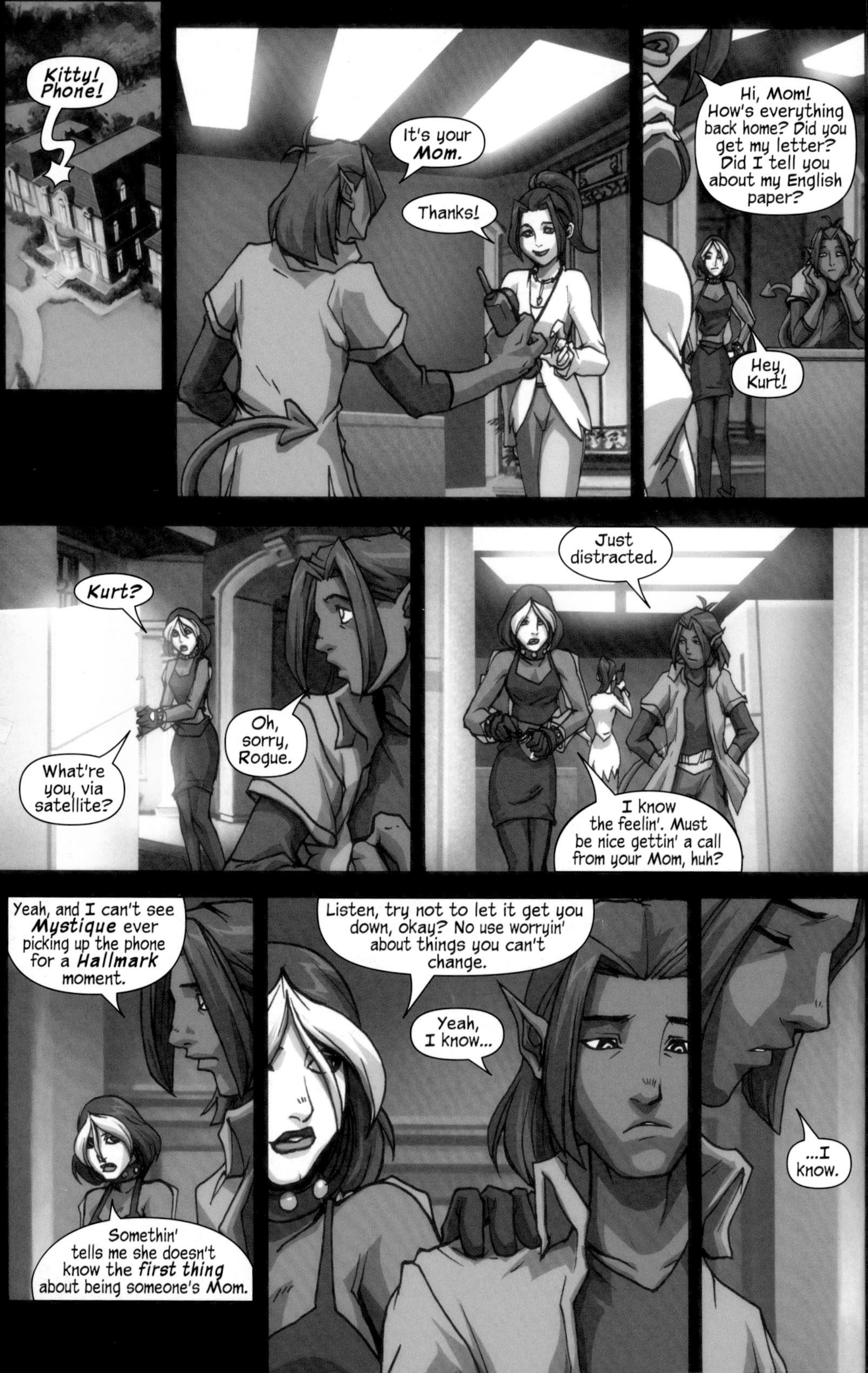
Kitty! Phone!
It's your Mom.
Thanks!
Hi, Mom! How's everything back home? Did you get my letter? Did I tell you about my English paper?
Hey, Kurt!
Kurt?
What're you, via satellite?
Oh, sorry, Rogue.
Just distracted.
I know the feelin'. Must be nice gettin' a call from your Mom, huh?
Yeah, and I can't see Mystique ever picking up the phone for a Hallmark moment.
Somethin' tells me she doesn't know the first thing about being someone's Mom.
Listen, try not to let it get you down, okay? No use worryin' about things you can't change.
Yeah, I know...
...I know.

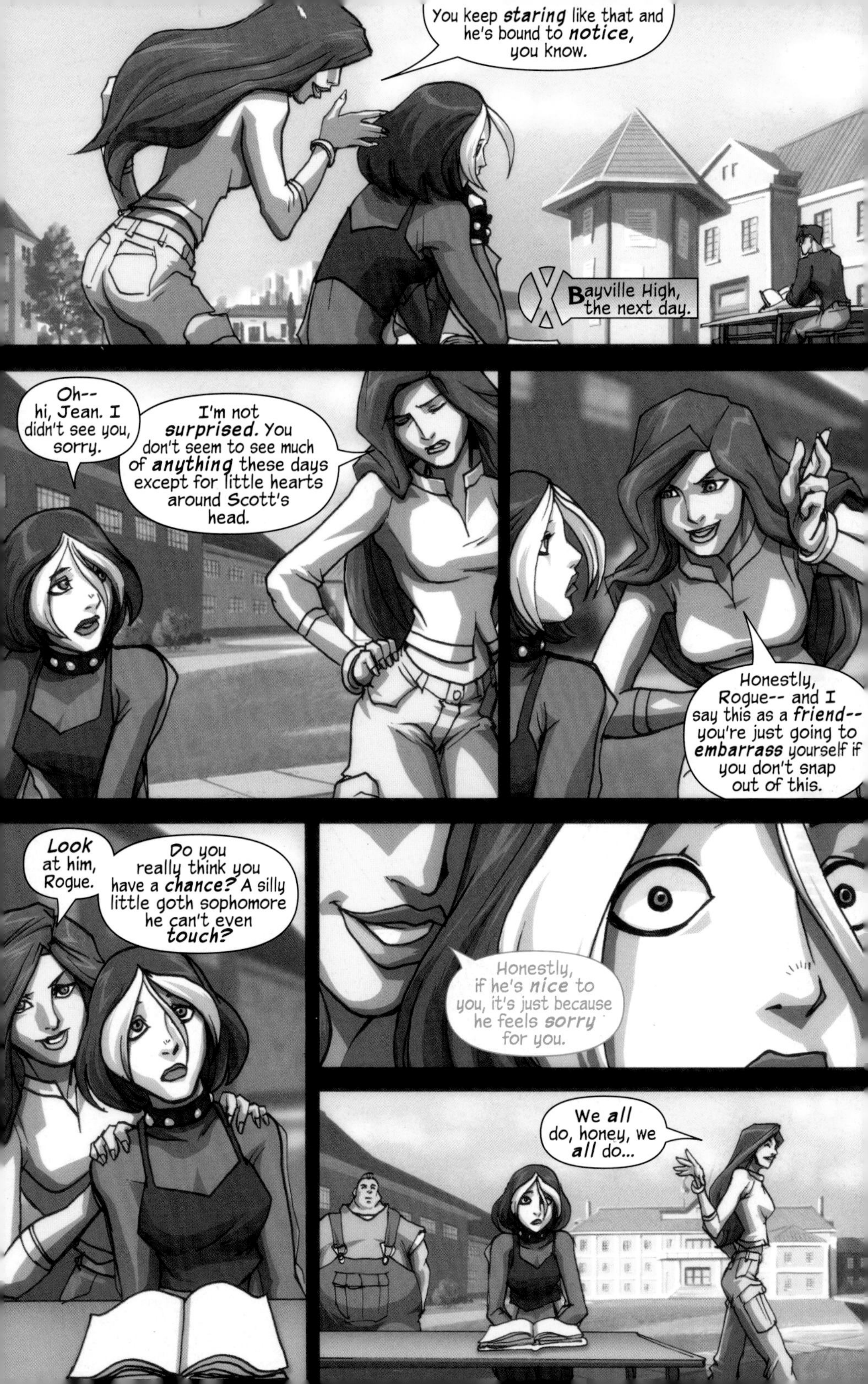

You keep staring like that and he's bound to notice, you know.
Bayville High, the next day.
Oh-- hi, Jean. I didn't see you, sorry.
I'm not surprised. You don't seem to see much of anything these days except for little hearts around Scott's head.
Honestly, Rogue-- and I say this as a friend-- you're just going to embarrass yourself if you don't snap out of this.
Look at him, Rogue.
Do you really think you have a chance? A silly little goth sophomore he can't even touch?
Honestly, if he's nice to you, it's just because he feels sorry for you.
We all do, honey, we all do...

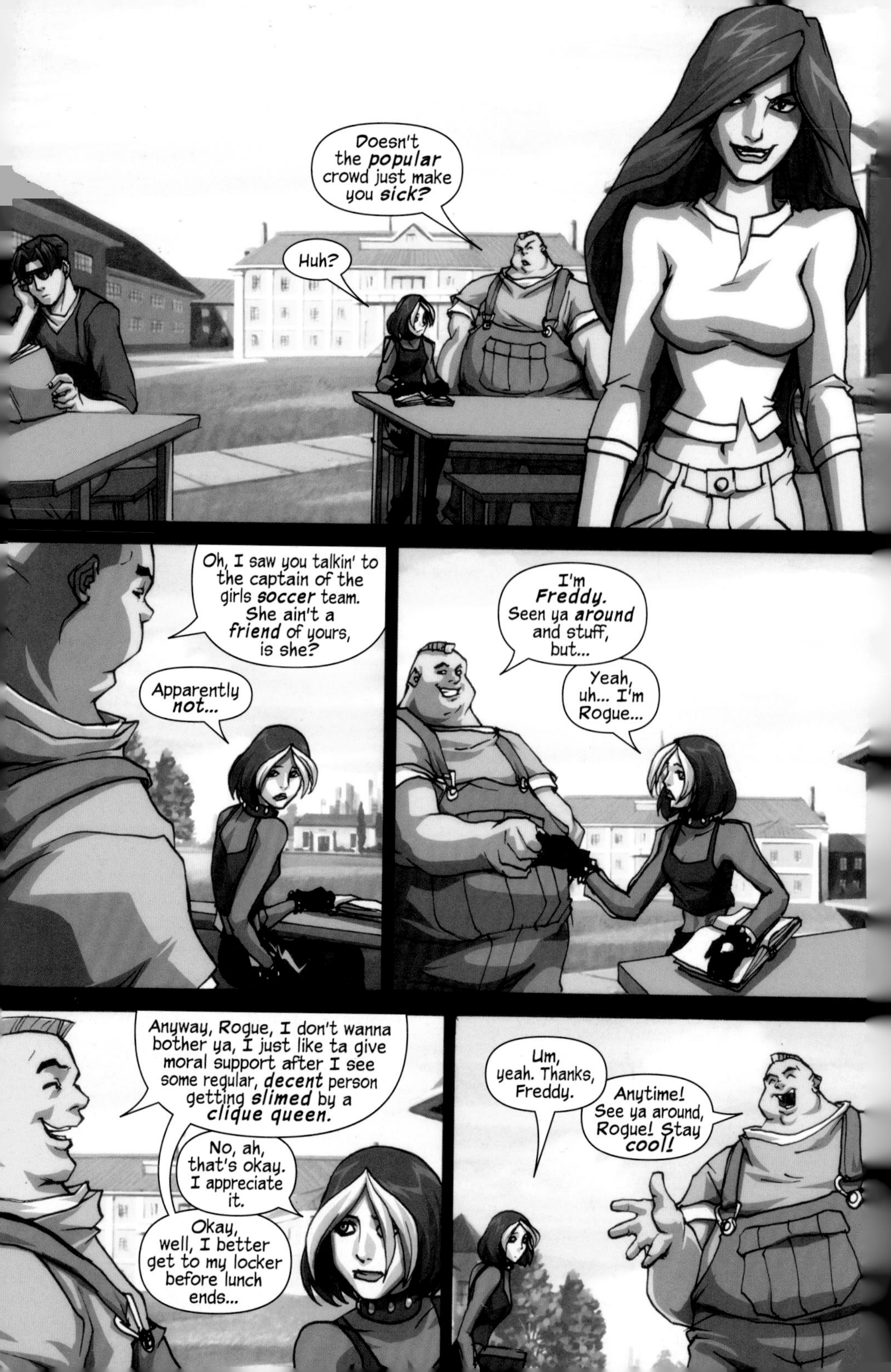
Doesn't the popular crowd just make you sick?
Huh?
Oh, I saw you talkin' to the captain of the girls soccer team. She ain't a friend of yours, is she?
Apparently not...
I'm Freddy. Seen ya around and stuff, but...
Yeah, uh... I'm Rogue...
Anyway, Rogue, I don't wanna bother ya, I just like ta give moral support after I see some regular, decent person getting slimed by a clique queen.
No, ah, that's okay. I appreciate it.
Okay, well, I better get to my locker before lunch ends...
Um, yeah. Thanks, Freddy.
Anytime! See ya around, Rogue! Stay cool!

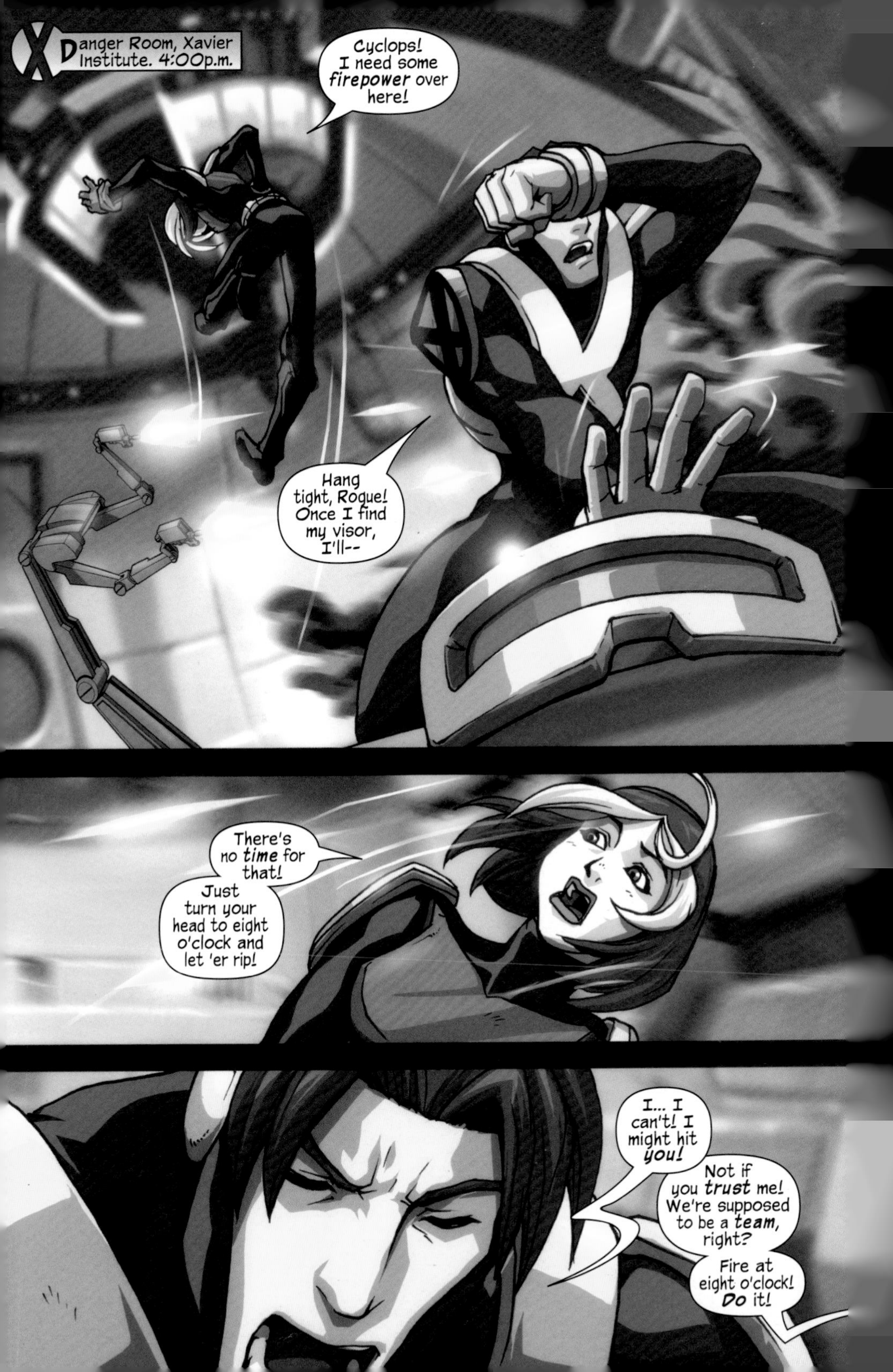
Danger Room, Xavier Institute. 4:00p.m.
Cyclops! I need some firepower over here!
Hang tight, Rogue! Once I find my visor, I'll--
There's no time for that!
Just turn your head to eight o'clock and let 'er rip!
I... I can't! I might hit you!
Not if you trust me! We're supposed to be a team, right?
Fire at eight o'clock! Do it!

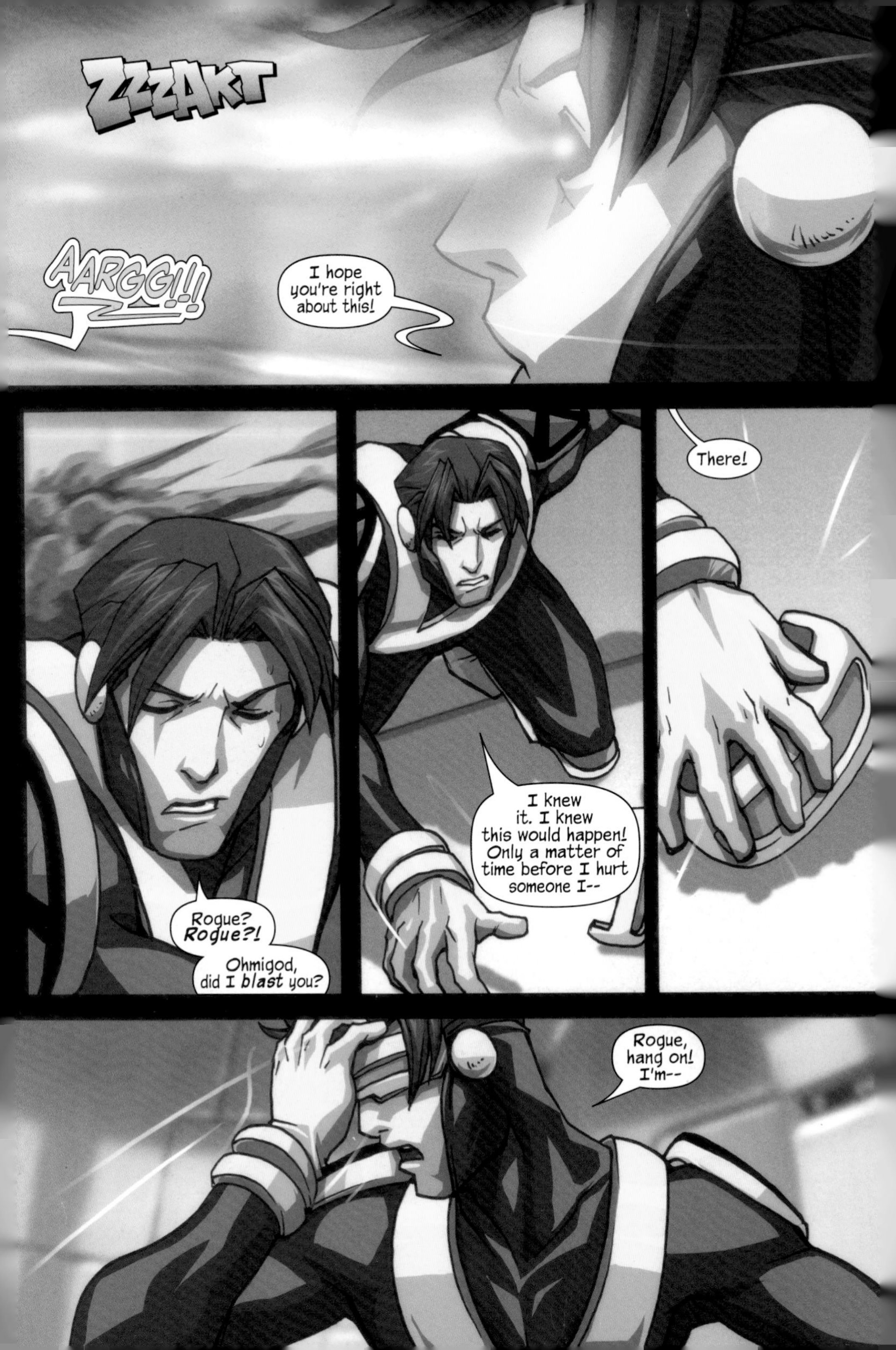
ZZZAKT
AARGG!!!
I hope you're right about this!
Rogue? Rogue?!
Ohmigod, did I blast you?
I knew it. I knew this would happen! Only a matter of time before I hurt someone I--
There!
Rogue, hang on! I'm--

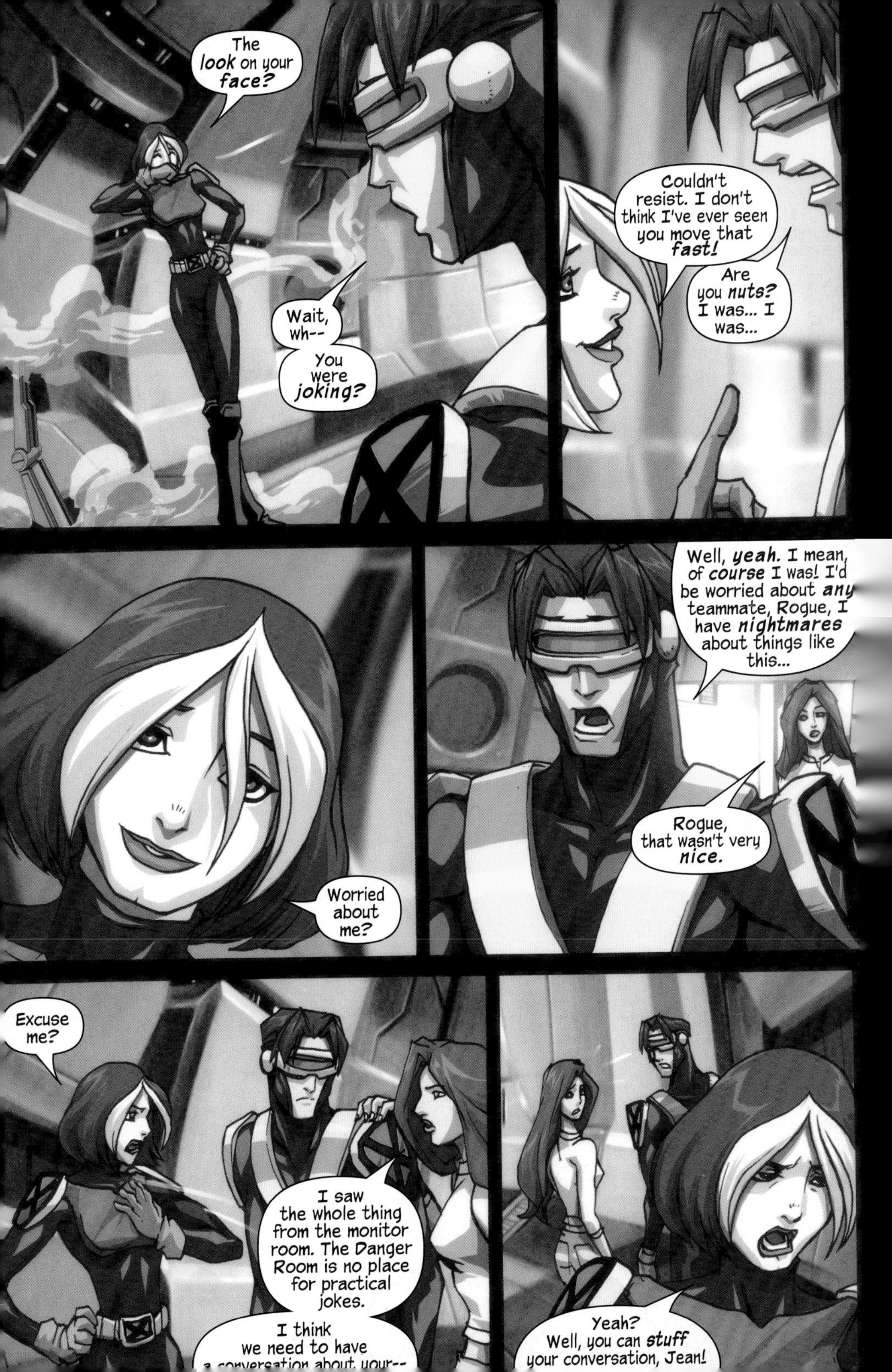
The look on your face?
Wait, wh--
You were joking?
Couldn't resist. I don't think I've ever seen you move that fast!
Are you nuts? I was... I was...
Worried about me?
Well, yeah. I mean, of course I was! I'd be worried about any teammate, Rogue, I have nightmares about things like this...
Rogue, that wasn't very nice.
Excuse me?
I saw the whole thing from the monitor room. The Danger Room is no place for practical jokes.
I think we need to have a conversation about your--
Yeah? Well, you can stuff your conversation, Jean!

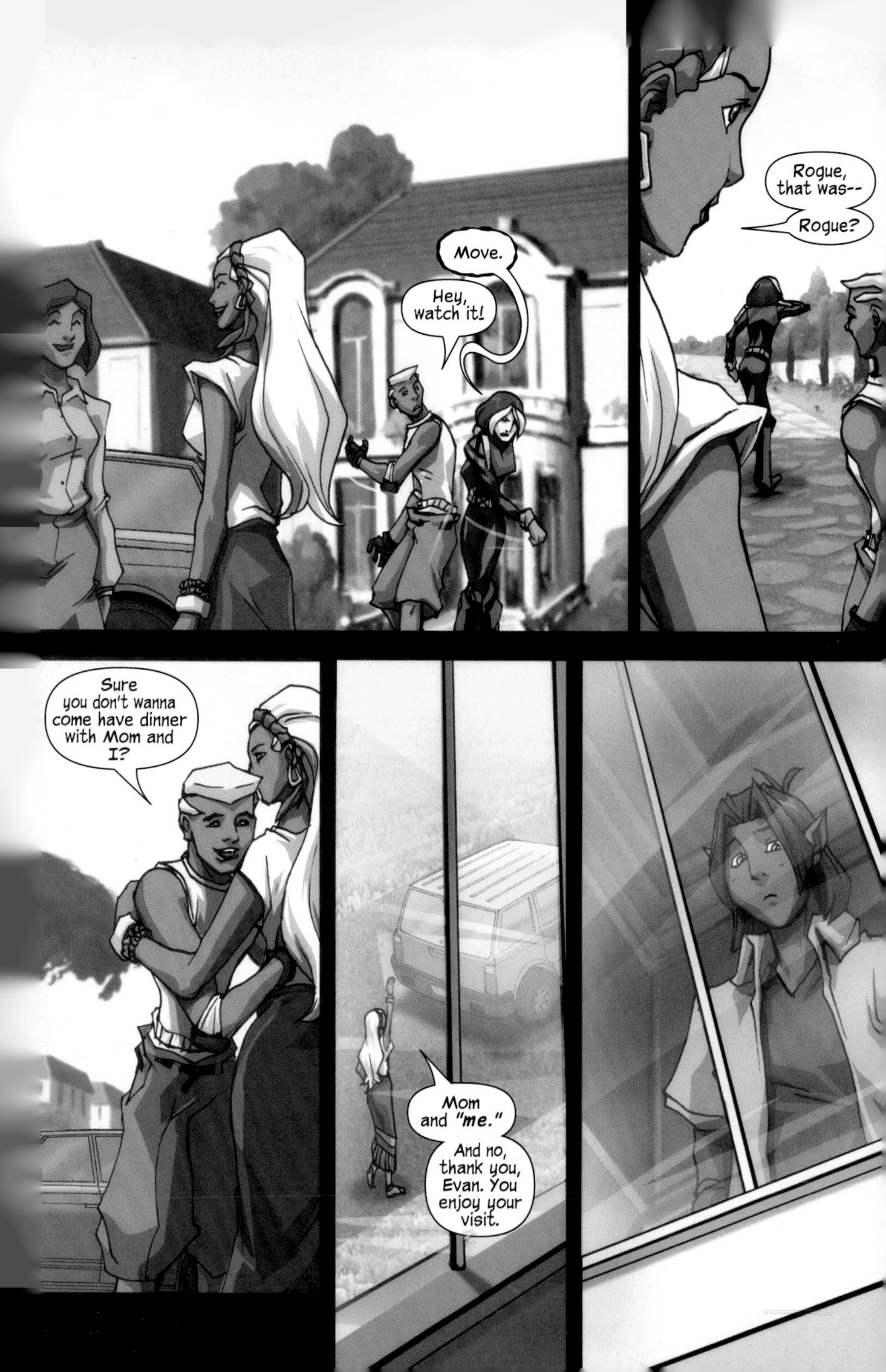

Move.
Hey, watch it!
Rogue, that was--
Rogue?
Sure you don't wanna come have dinner with Mom and I?
Mom and "me."
And no, thank you, Evan. You enjoy your visit.

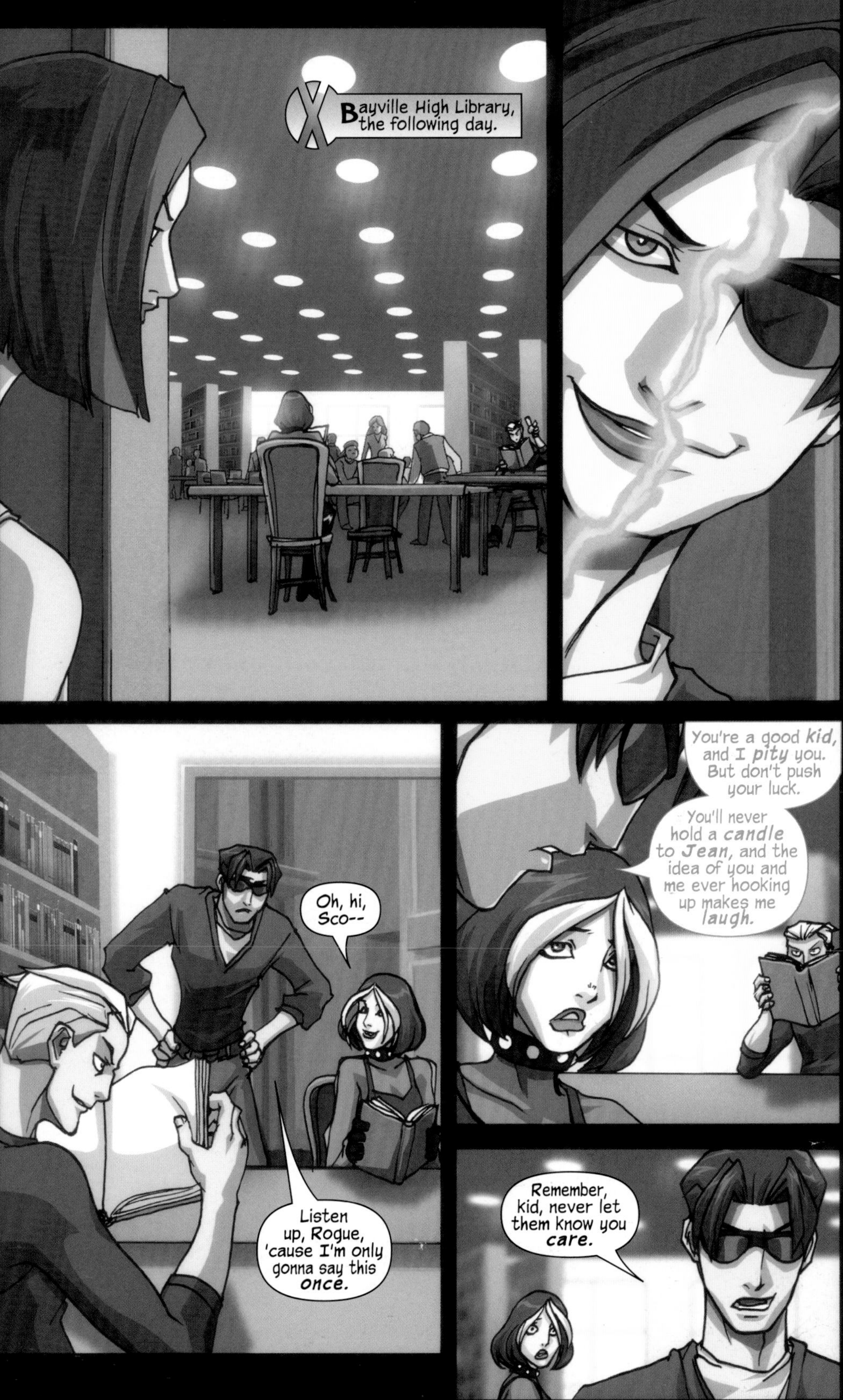
Bayville High Library, the following day.
Oh, hi, Sco--
Listen up, Rogue, 'cause I'm only gonna say this once.
You're a good kid, and I pity you. But don't push your luck.
You'll never hold a candle to Jean, and the idea of you and me ever hooking up makes me laugh.
Remember, kid, never let them know you care.

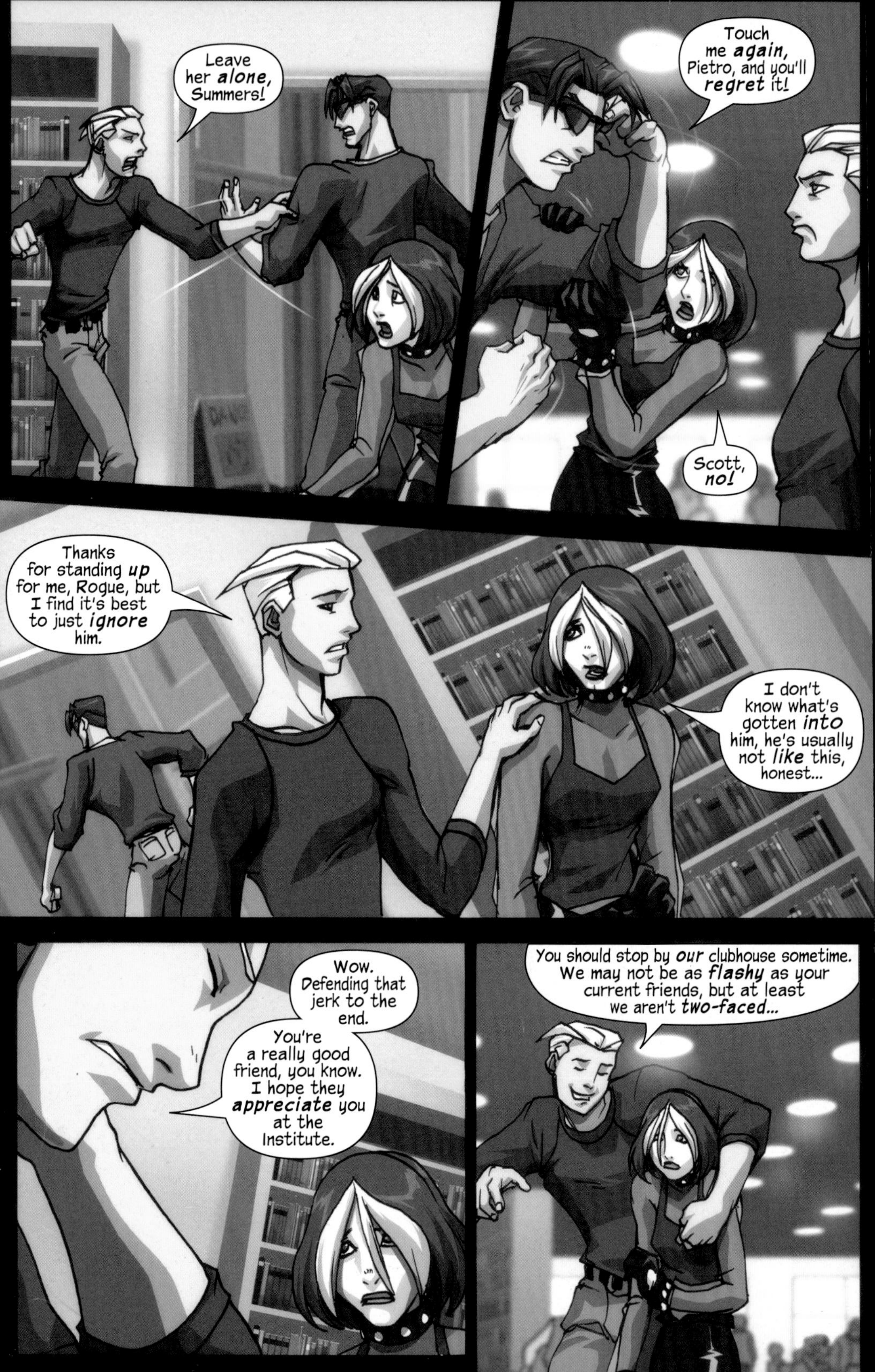

Leave her alone, Summers!
Touch me again, Pietro, and you'll regret it!
Scott, no!
Thanks for standing up for me, Rogue, but I find it's best to just ignore him.
I don't know what's gotten into him, he's usually not like this, honest...
Wow. Defending that jerk to the end.
You're a really good friend, you know. I hope they appreciate you at the Institute.
You should stop by our clubhouse sometime. We may not be as flashy as your current friends, but at least we aren't two-faced...

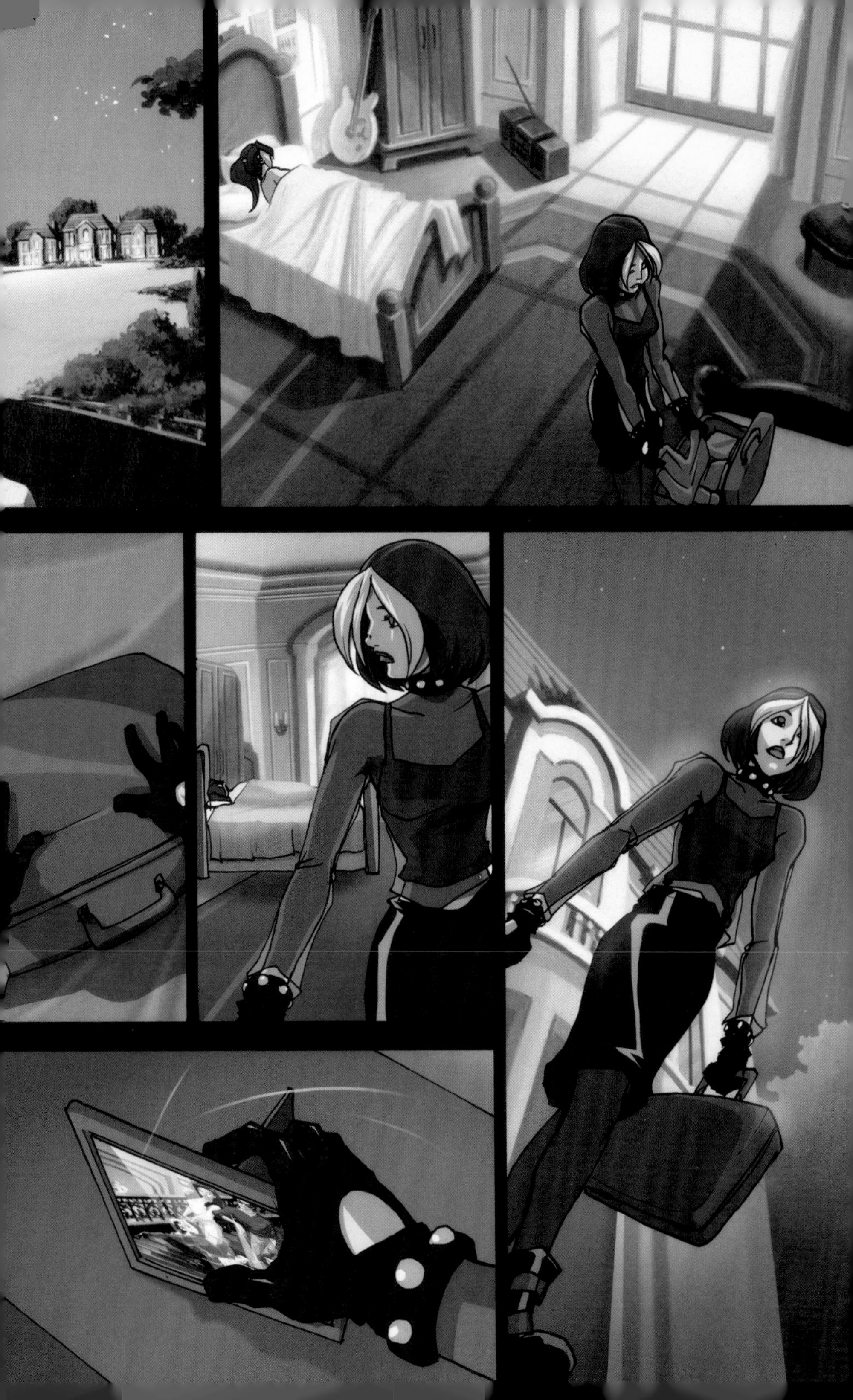

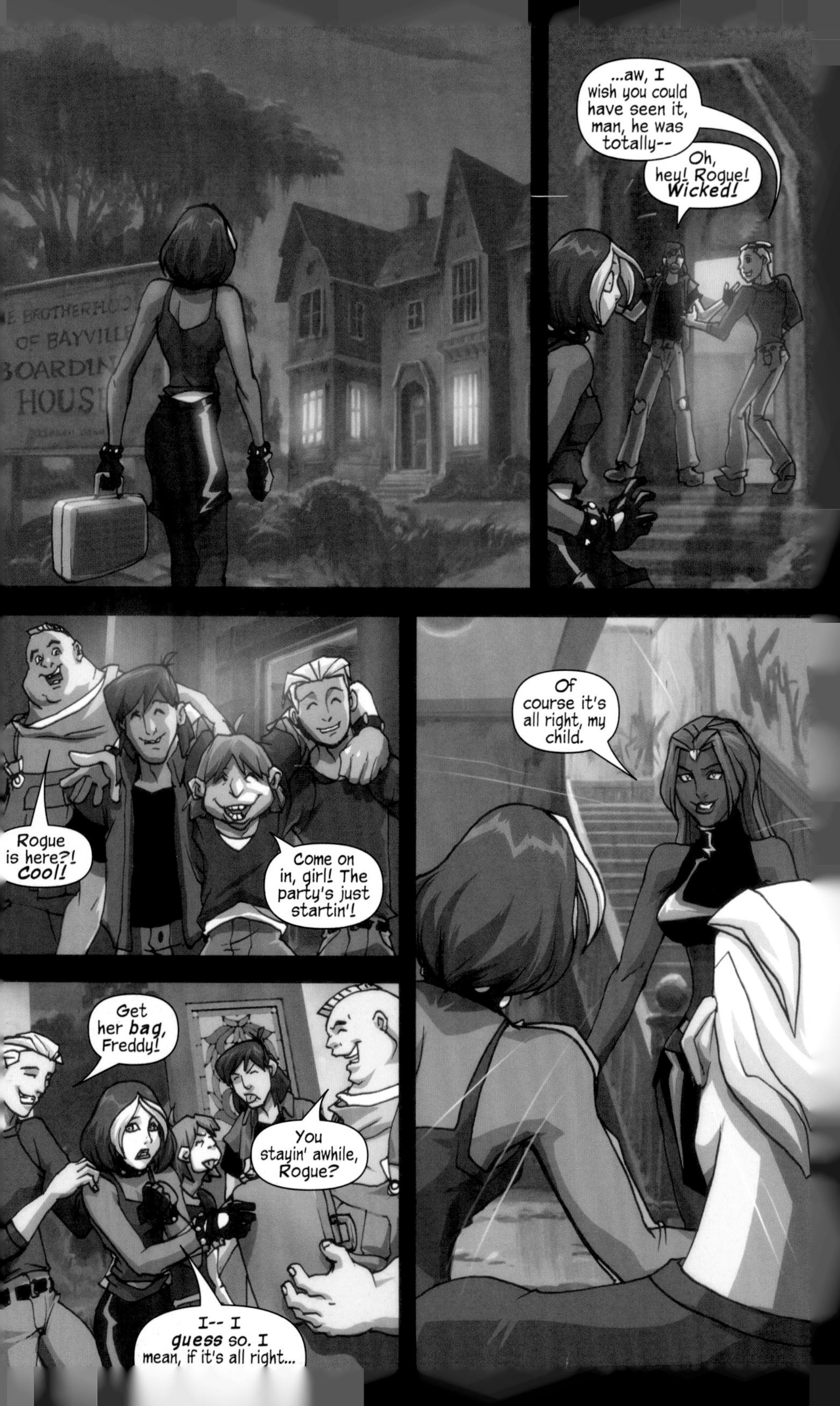

...aw, I wish you could have seen it, man, he was totally--
Oh, hey! Rogue! Wicked!
Rogue is here?! Cool!
Come on in, girl! The party's just startin'!
Get her bag, Freddy!
You stayin' awhile, Rogue?
I-- I guess so. I mean, if it's all right...
Of course it's all right, my child.

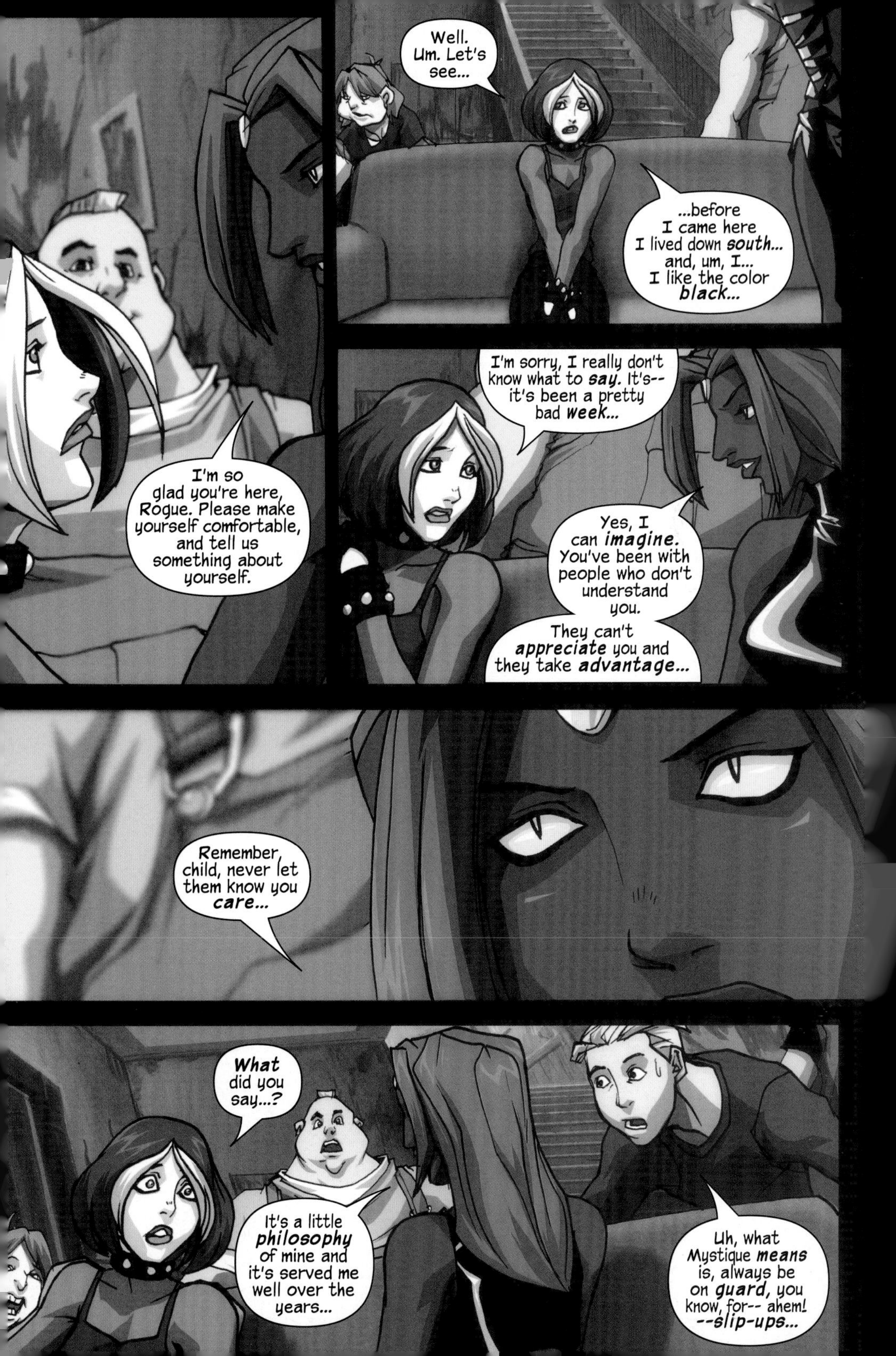
I'm so glad you're here, Rogue. Please make yourself comfortable, and tell us something about yourself.
Well. Um. Let's see...
...before I came here I lived down south... and, um, I... I like the color black...
I'm sorry, I really don't know what to say. It's-- it's been a pretty bad week...
Yes, I can imagine. You've been with people who don't understand you.
They can't appreciate you and they take advantage...
Remember child, never let them know you care...
What did you say...?
It's a little philosophy of mine and it's served me well over the years...
Uh, what Mystique means is, always be on guard, you know, for-- ahem! --slip-ups...

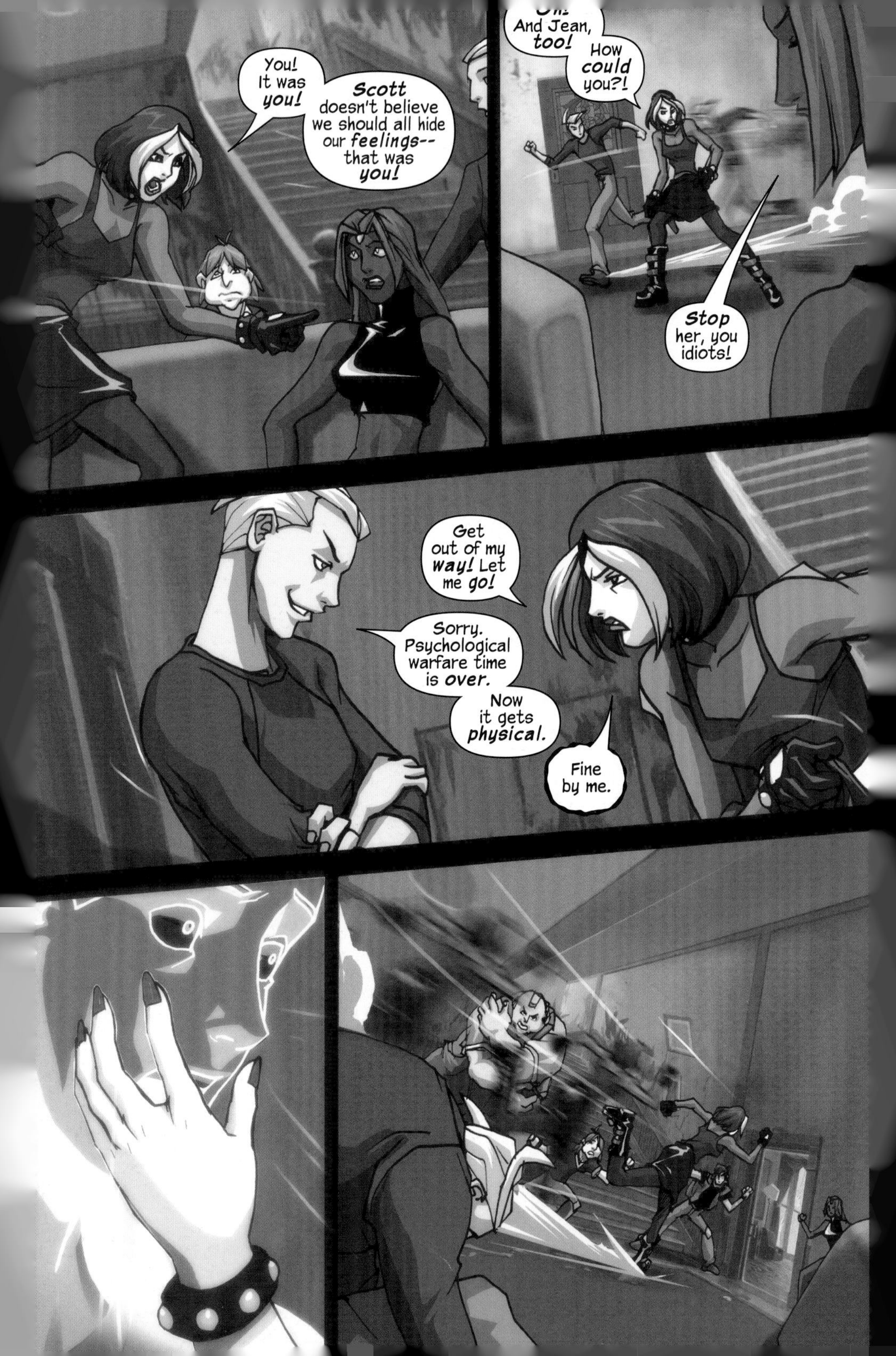
You! It was you!
Scott doesn't believe we should all hide our feelings-- that was you!
And Jean, too!
How could you?!
Stop her, you idiots!
Get out of my way! Let me go!
Sorry. Psychological warfare time is over.
Now it gets physical.
Fine by me.

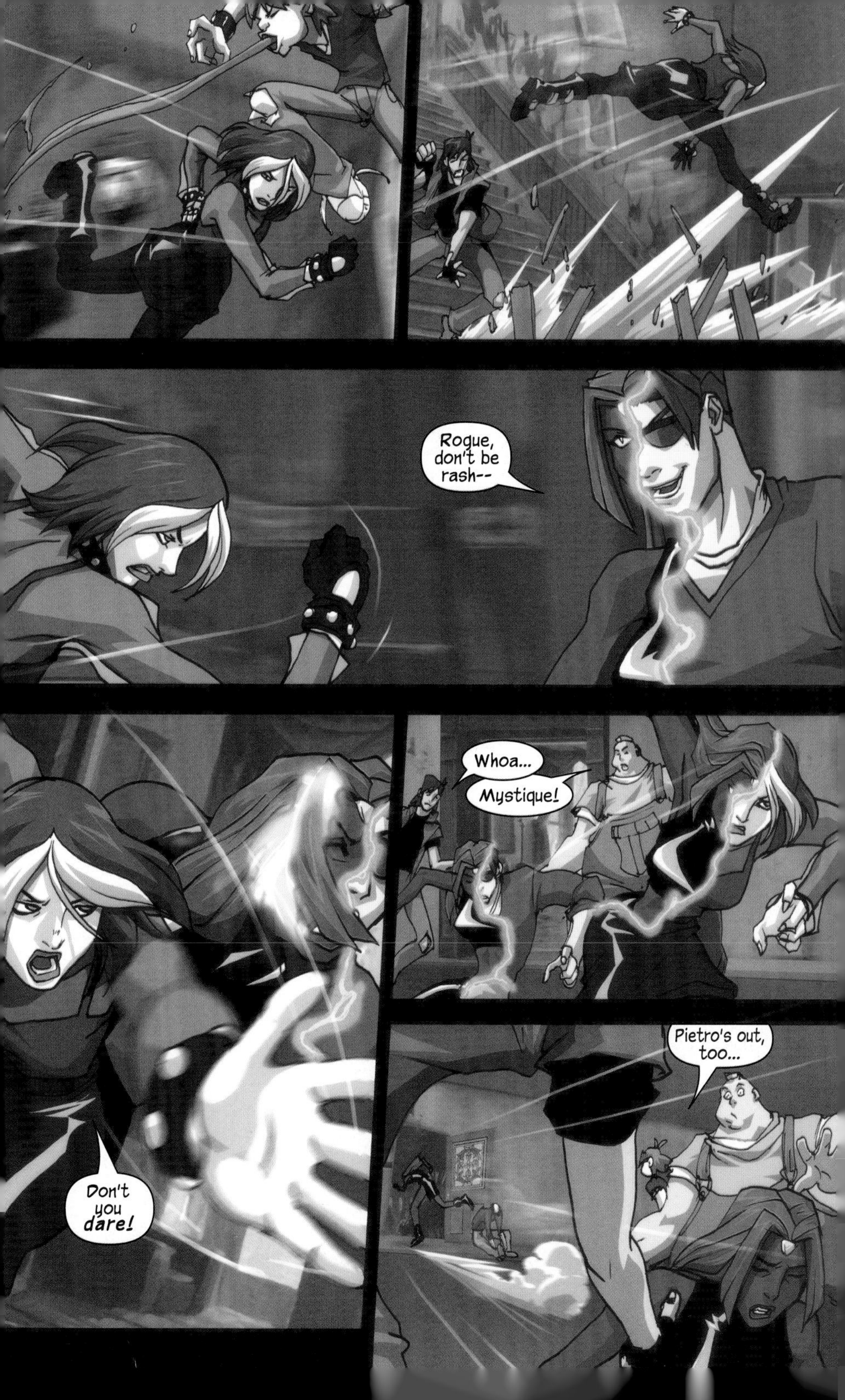
Rogue, don't be rash--
Whoa...
Mystique!
Don't you dare!
Pietro's out, too...

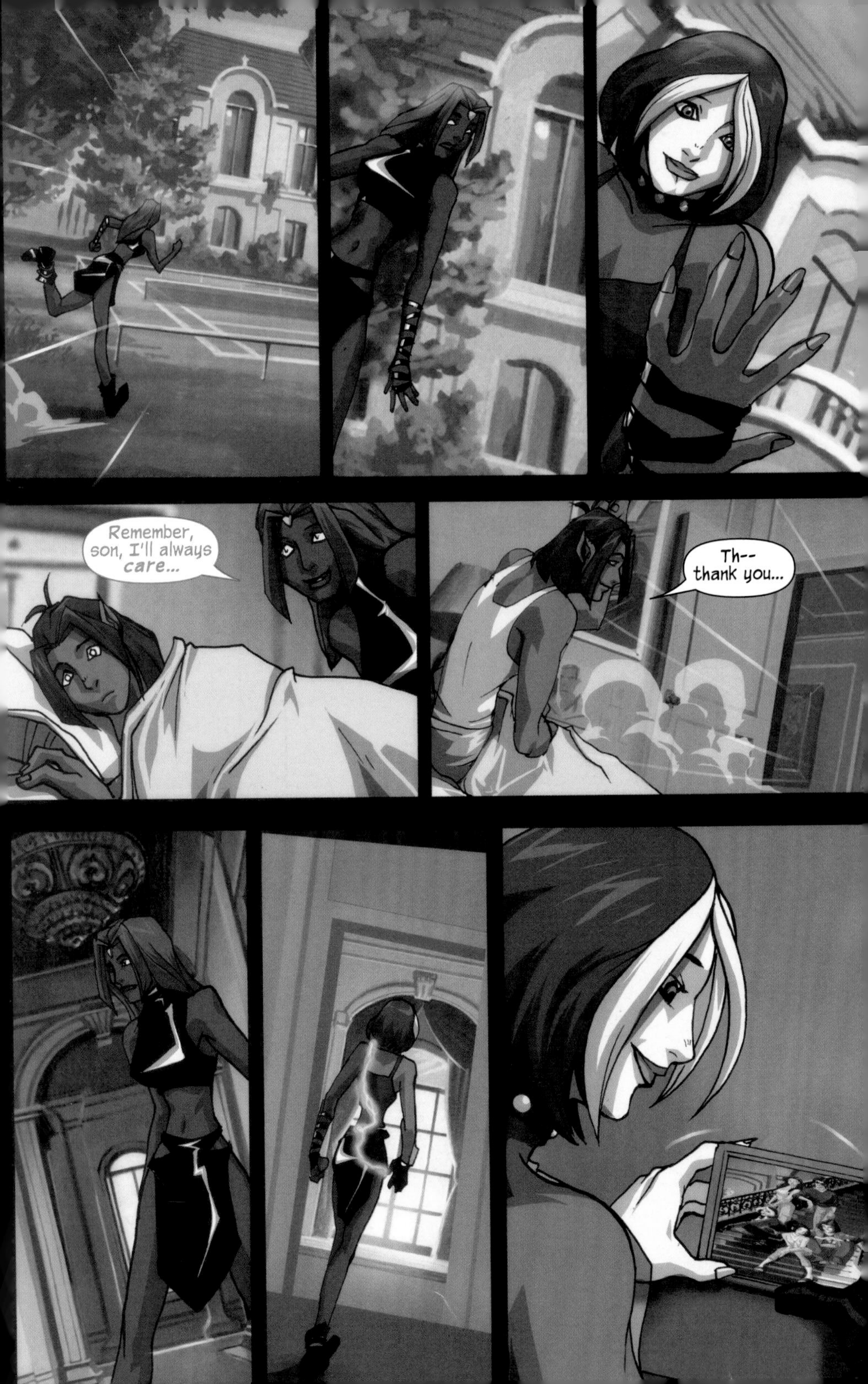
Remember, son, I'll always care...
Th-- thank you...

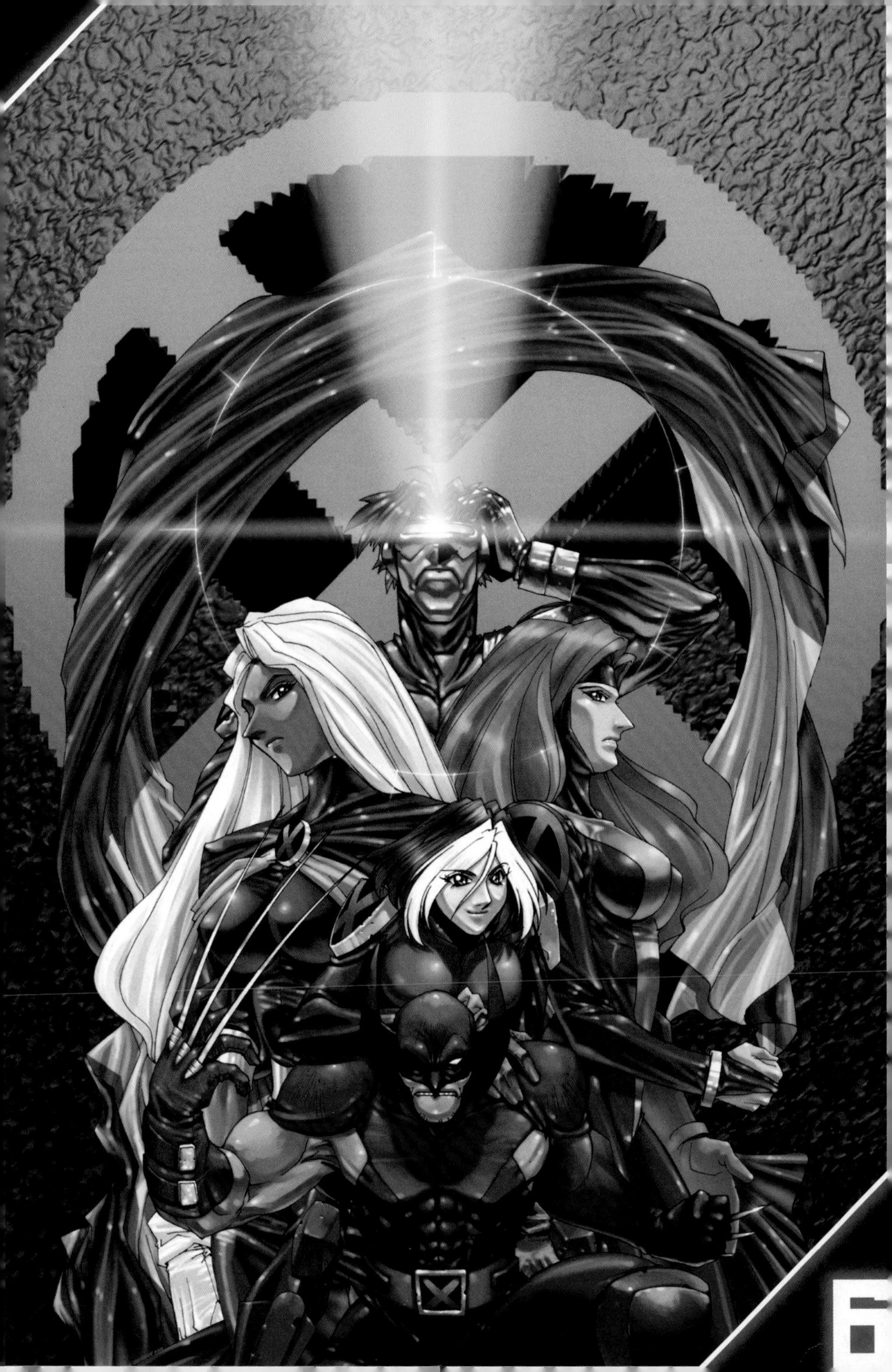
6

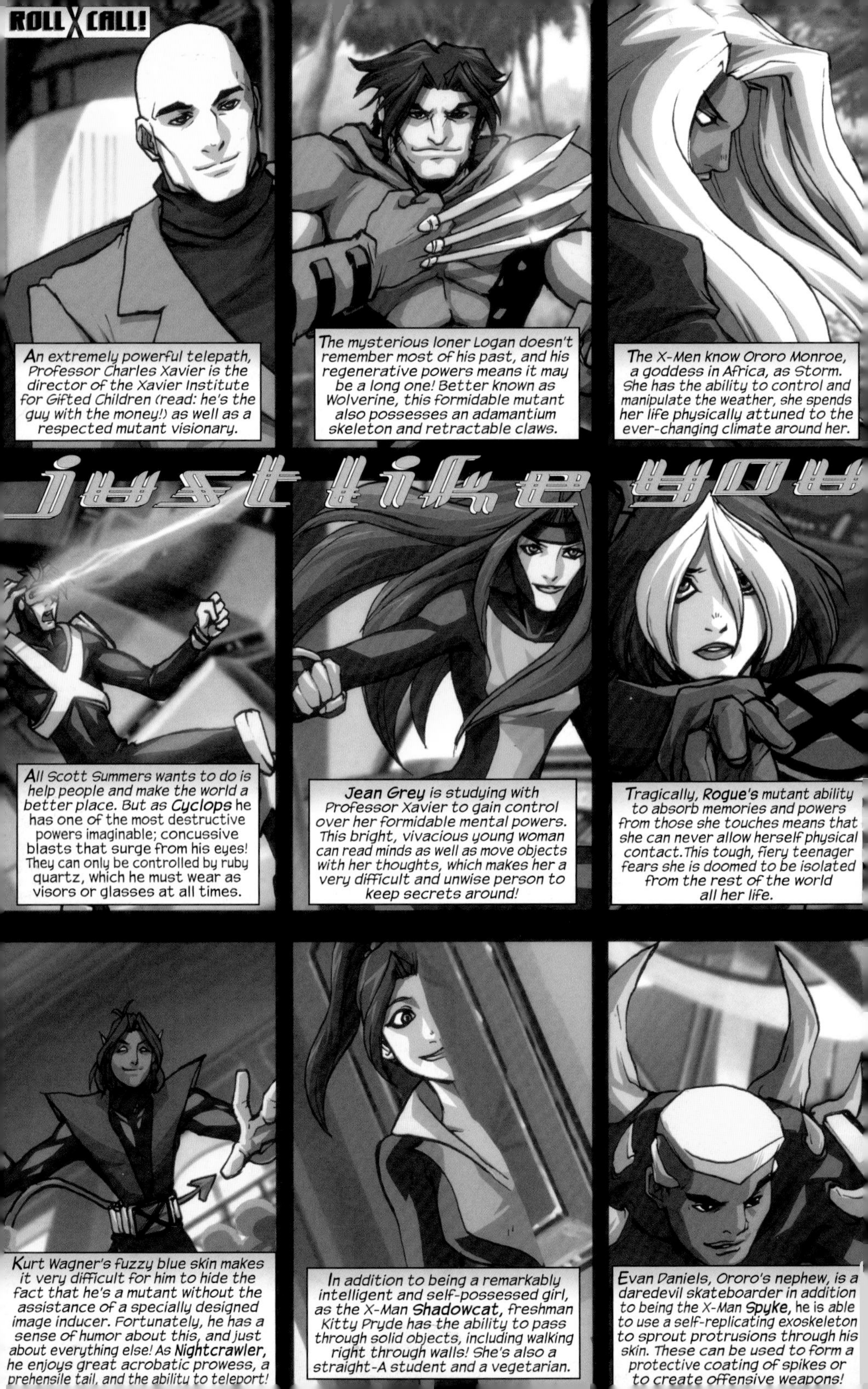
ROLL X CALL!
An extremely powerful telepath, Professor Charles Xavier is the director of the Xavier Institute for Gifted Children (read: he's the guy with the money!) as well as a respected mutant visionary.
The mysterious loner Logan doesn't remember most of his past, and his regenerative powers means it may be a long one! Better known as Wolverine, this formidable mutant also possesses an adamantium skeleton and retractable claws.
The X-Men know Ororo Monroe, a goddess in Africa, as Storm. She has the ability to control and manipulate the weather, she spends her life physically attuned to the ever-changing climate around her.
just like you
All Scott Summers wants to do is help people and make the world a better place. But as Cyclops he has one of the most destructive powers imaginable; concussive blasts that surge from his eyes! They can only be controlled by ruby quartz, which he must wear as visors or glasses at all times.
Jean Grey is studying with Professor Xavier to gain control over her formidable mental powers. This bright, vivacious young woman can read minds as well as move objects with her thoughts, which makes her a very difficult and unwise person to keep secrets around!
Tragically, Rogue's mutant ability to absorb memories and powers from those she touches means that she can never allow herself physical contact. This tough, fiery teenager fears she is doomed to be isolated from the rest of the world all her life.
Kurt Wagner's fuzzy blue skin makes it very difficult for him to hide the fact that he's a mutant without the assistance of a specially designed image inducer. Fortunately, he has a sense of humor about this, and just about everything else! As Nightcrawler, he enjoys great acrobatic prowess, a prehensile tail, and the ability to teleport!
In addition to being a remarkably intelligent and self-possessed girl, as the X-Man Shadowcat, freshman Kitty Pryde has the ability to pass through solid objects, including walking right through walls! She's also a straight-A student and a vegetarian.
Evan Daniels, Ororo's nephew, is a daredevil skateboarder in addition to being the X-Man Spyke, he is able to use a self-replicating exoskeleton to sprout protrusions through his skin. These can be used to form a protective coating of spikes or to create offensive weapons!

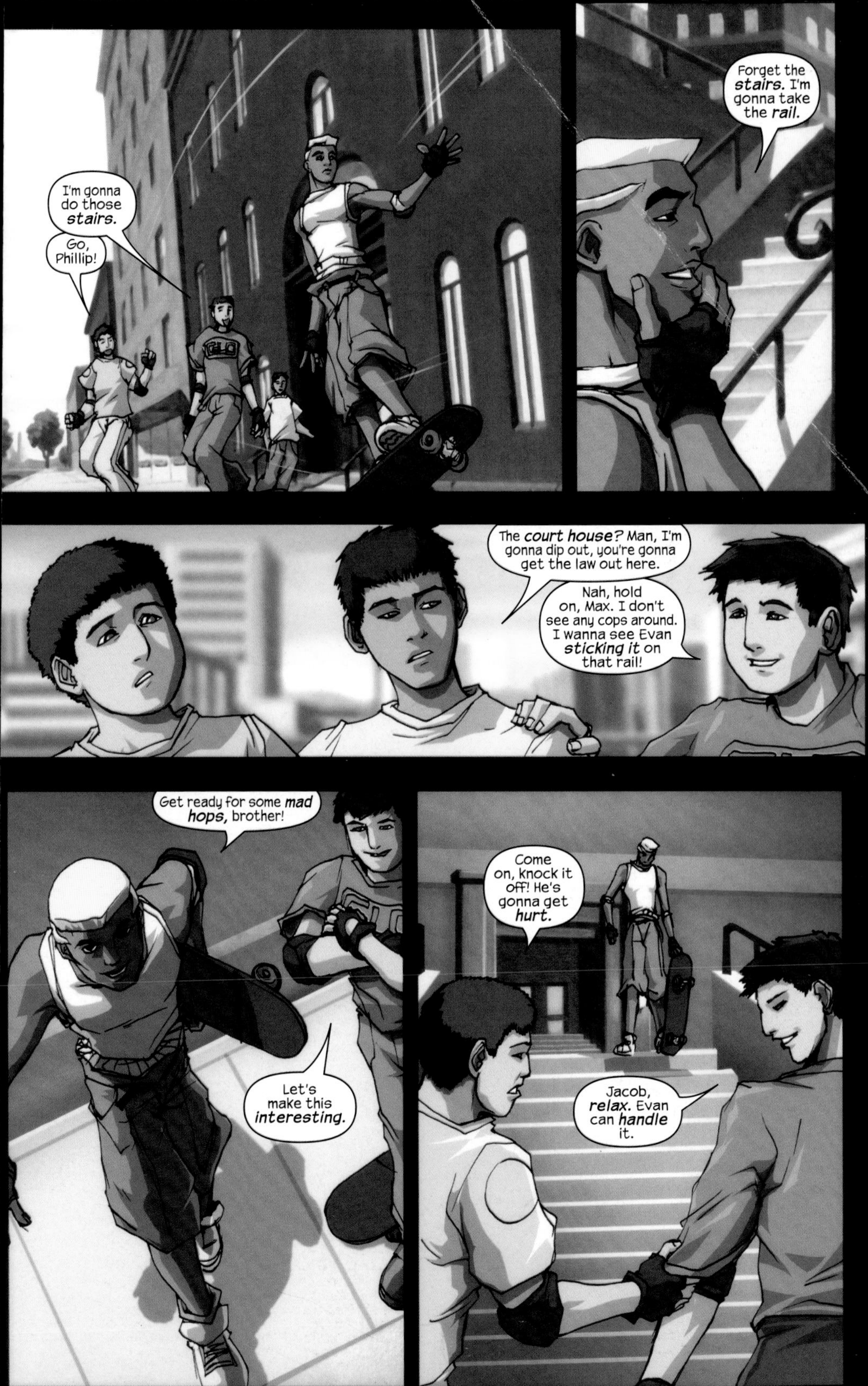
I'm gonna do those *stairs.*
Go, Phillip!
Forget the *stairs.* I'm gonna take the *rail.*
The *court house?* Man, I'm gonna dip out, you're gonna get the law out here.
Nah, hold on, Max. I don't see any cops around. I wanna see Evan *sticking it* on that rail!
Get ready for some *mad hops,* brother!
Let's make this *interesting.*
Come on, knock it off! He's gonna get *hurt.*
Jacob, *relax.* Evan can *handle* it.

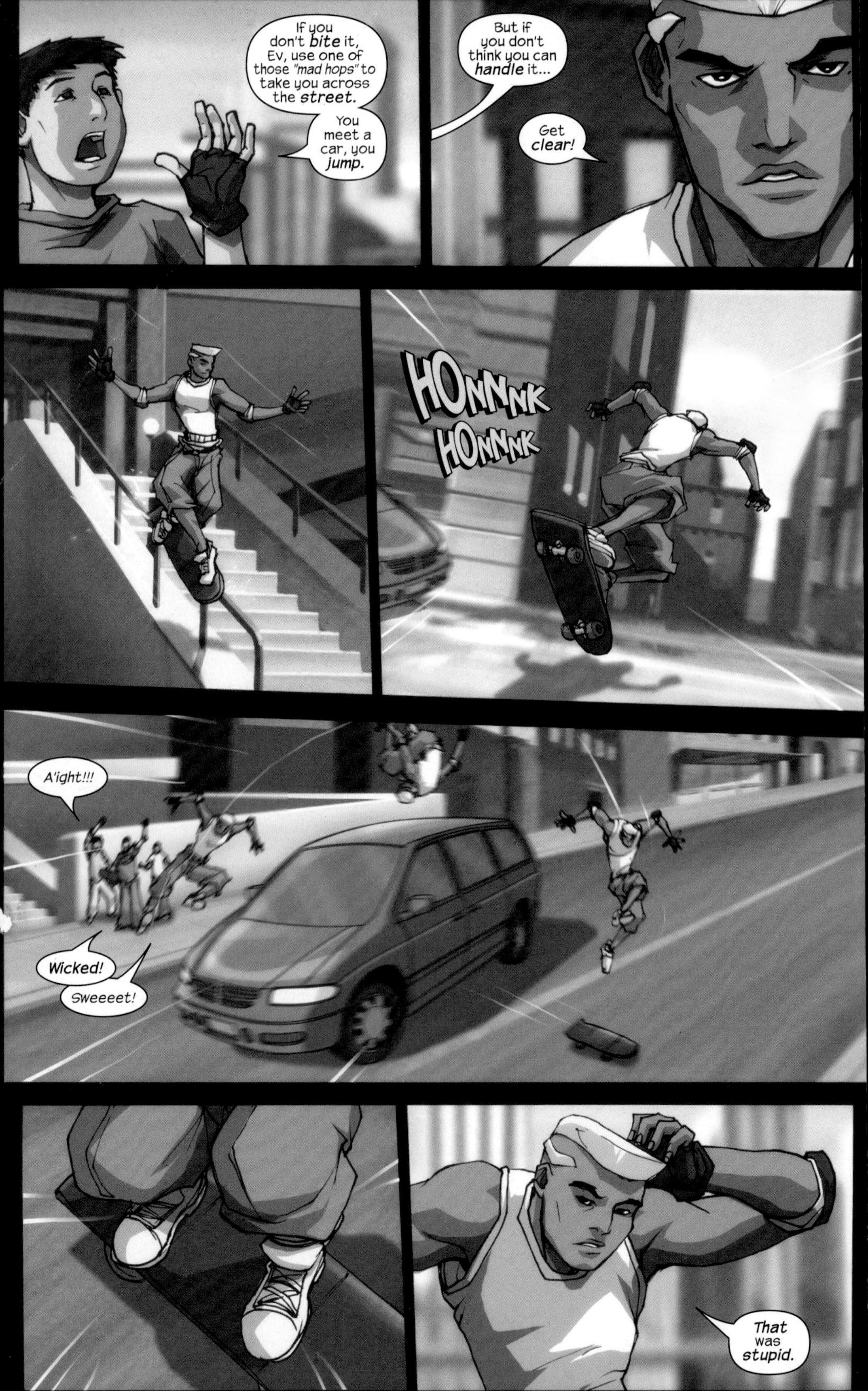
If you don't *bite* it, Ev, use one of those *"mad hops"* to take you across the *street.*
You meet a car, you *jump.*
But if you don't think you can *handle* it...
Get *clear!*
HONNNK
HONNNK
A'ight!!!
Wicked!
Sweeeet!
That was *stupid.*

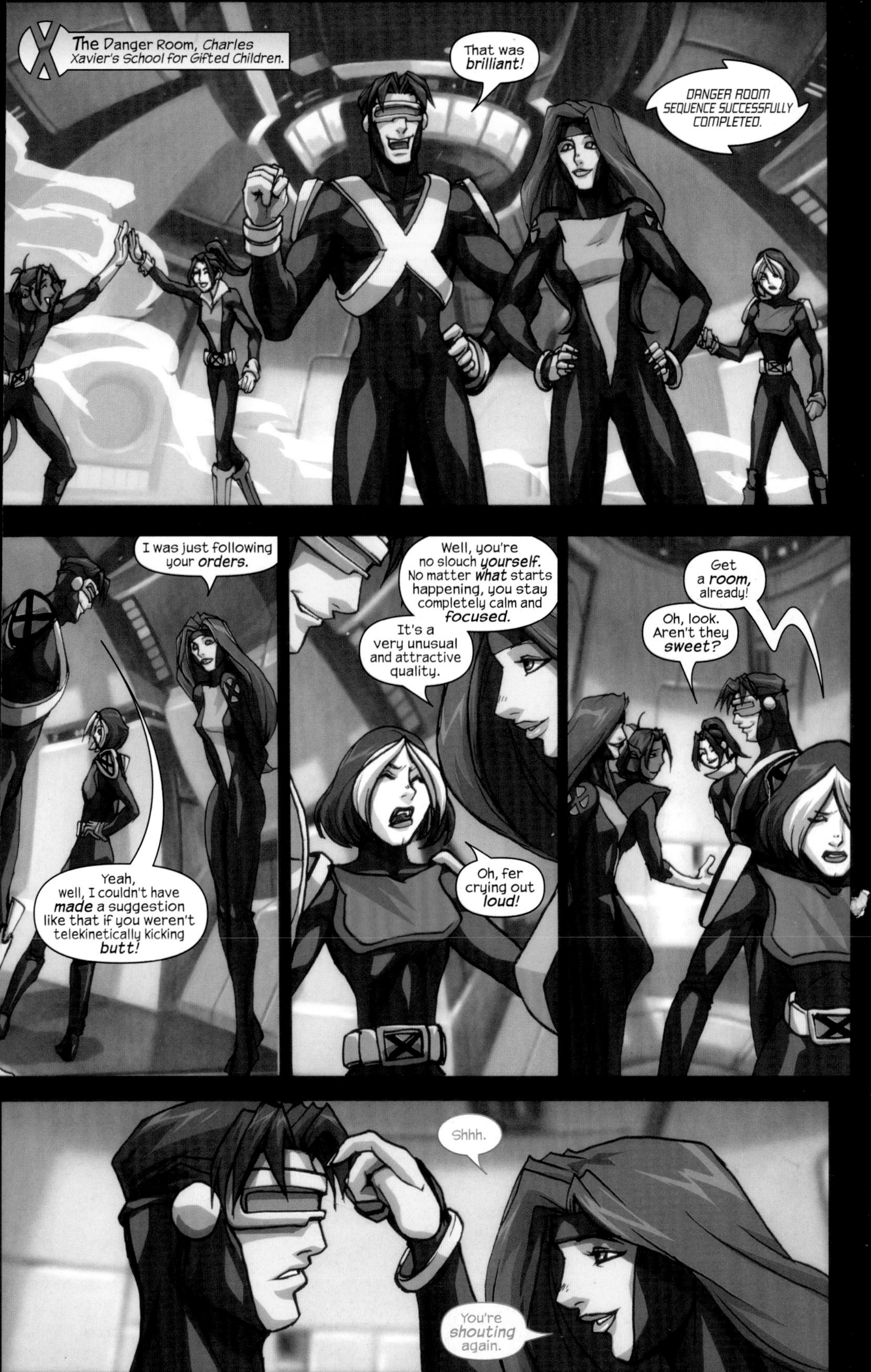
The Danger Room, Charles Xavier's School for Gifted Children.
That was brilliant!
DANGER ROOM SEQUENCE SUCCESSFULLY COMPLETED.
I was just following your orders.
Yeah, well, I couldn't have made a suggestion like that if you weren't telekinetically kicking butt!
Well, you're no slouch yourself. No matter what starts happening, you stay completely calm and focused.
It's a very unusual and attractive quality.
Oh, fer crying out loud!
Get a room, already!
Oh, look. Aren't they sweet?
Shhh.
You're shouting again.

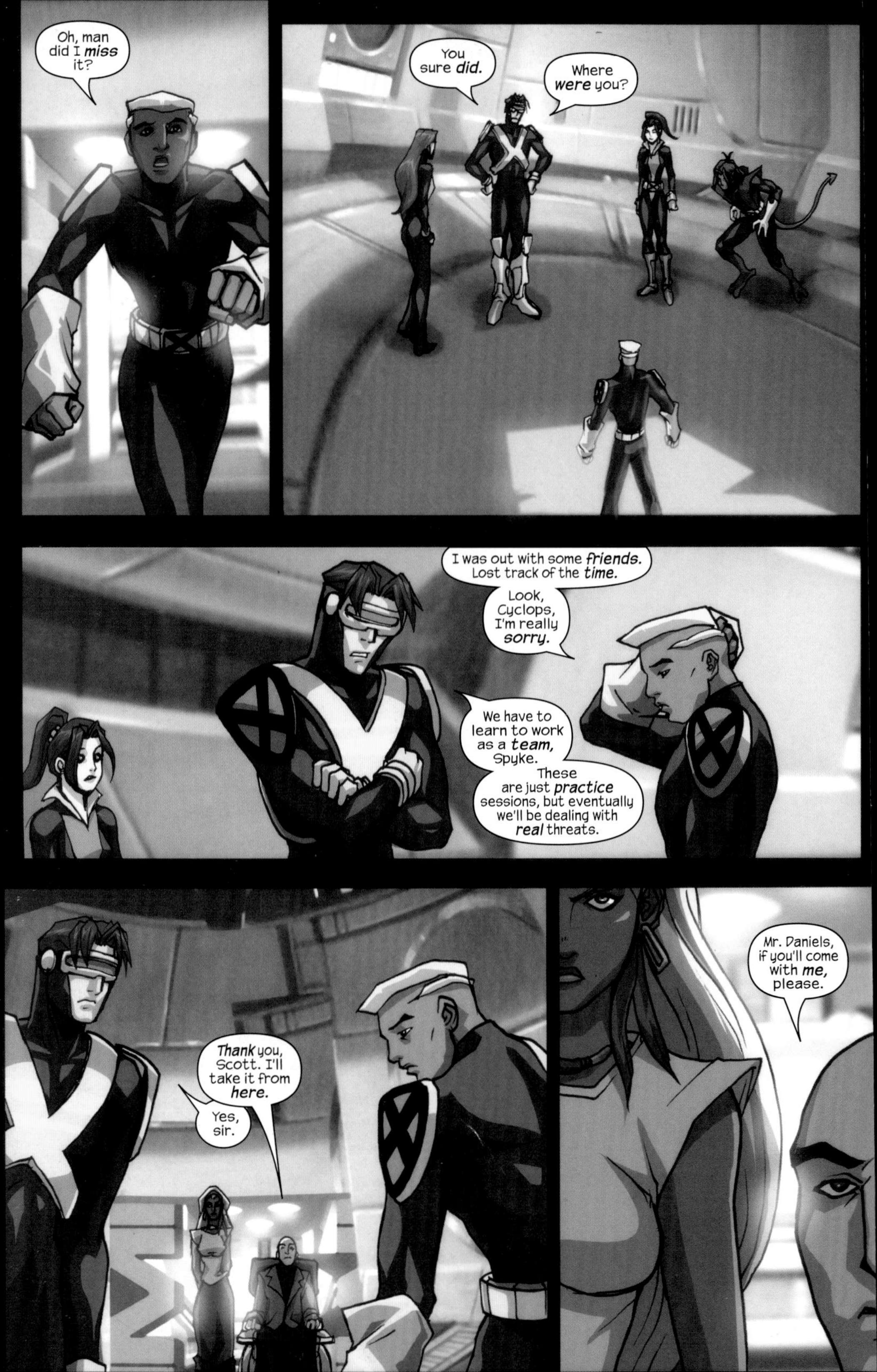
Oh, man did I *miss* it?
You sure *did.*
Where *were* you?
I was out with some *friends.* Lost track of the *time.*
Look, Cyclops, I'm really *sorry.*
We have to learn to work as a *team,* Spyke.
These are just *practice* sessions, but eventually we'll be dealing with *real* threats.
Thank you, Scott. I'll take it from *here.*
Yes, sir.
Mr. Daniels, if you'll come with *me,* please.

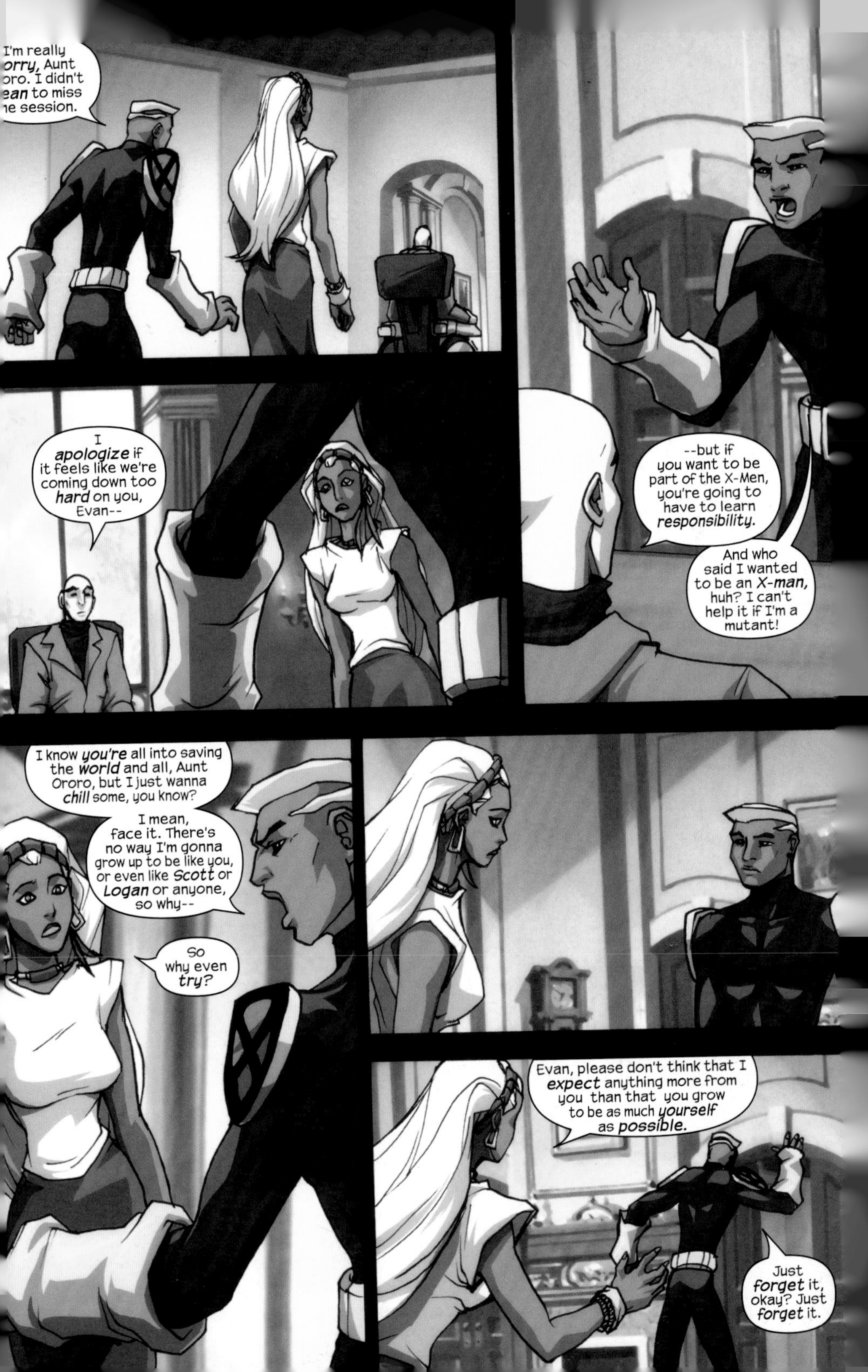

I'm really orry, Aunt oro. I didn't ean to miss e session.
I apologize if it feels like we're coming down too hard on you, Evan--
--but if you want to be part of the X-Men, you're going to have to learn responsibility.
And who said I wanted to be an X-man, huh? I can't help it if I'm a mutant!
I know you're all into saving the world and all, Aunt Ororo, but I just wanna chill some, you know?
I mean, face it. There's no way I'm gonna grow up to be like you, or even like Scott or Logan or anyone, so why--
So why even try?
Evan, please don't think that I expect anything more from you than that you grow to be as much yourself as possible.
Just forget it, okay? Just forget it.

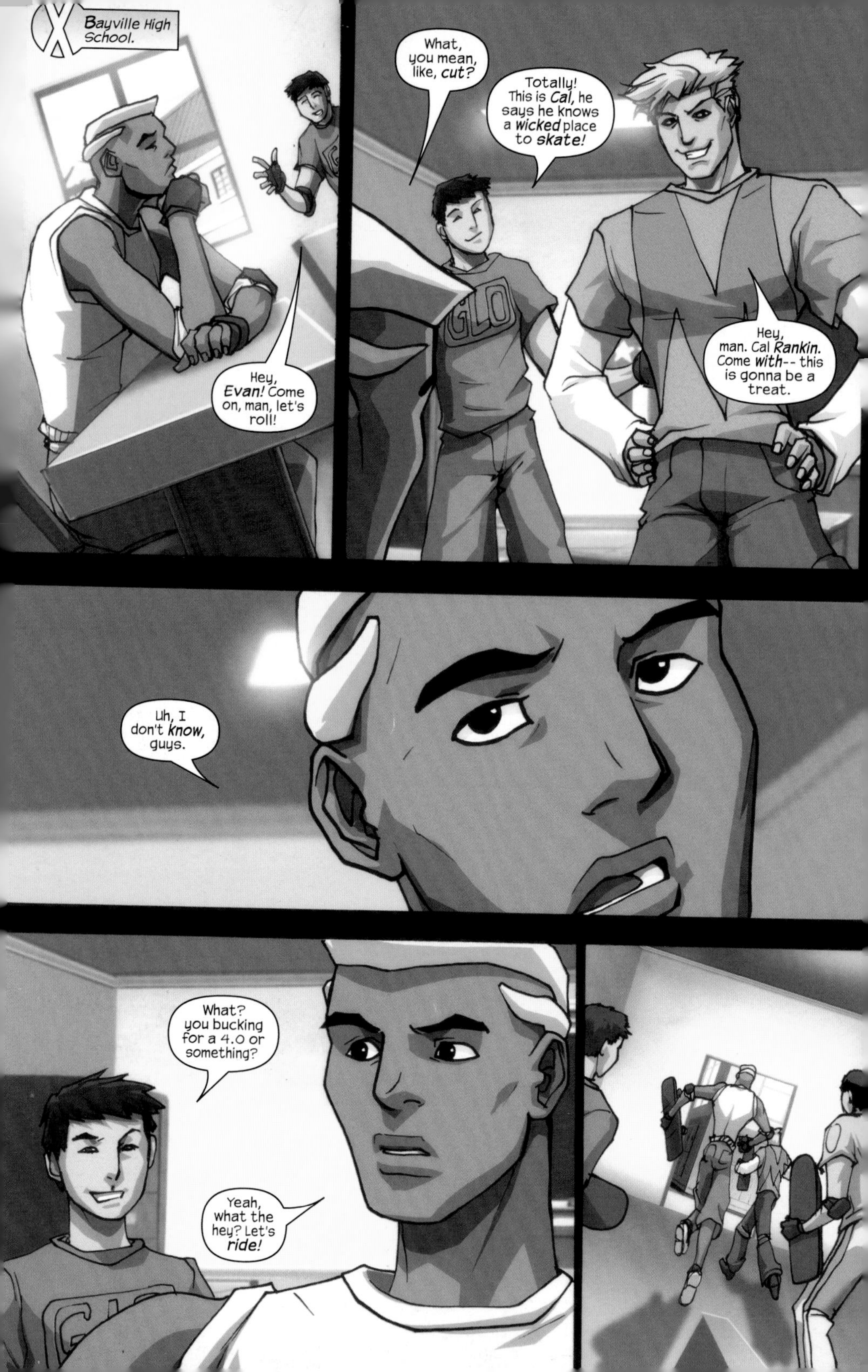
Bayville High School.
Hey, Evan! Come on, man, let's roll!
What, you mean, like, cut?
Totally! This is Cal, he says he knows a wicked place to skate!
Hey, man. Cal Rankin. Come with-- this is gonna be a treat.
Uh, I don't know, guys.
What? you bucking for a 4.0 or something?
Yeah, what the hey? Let's ride!

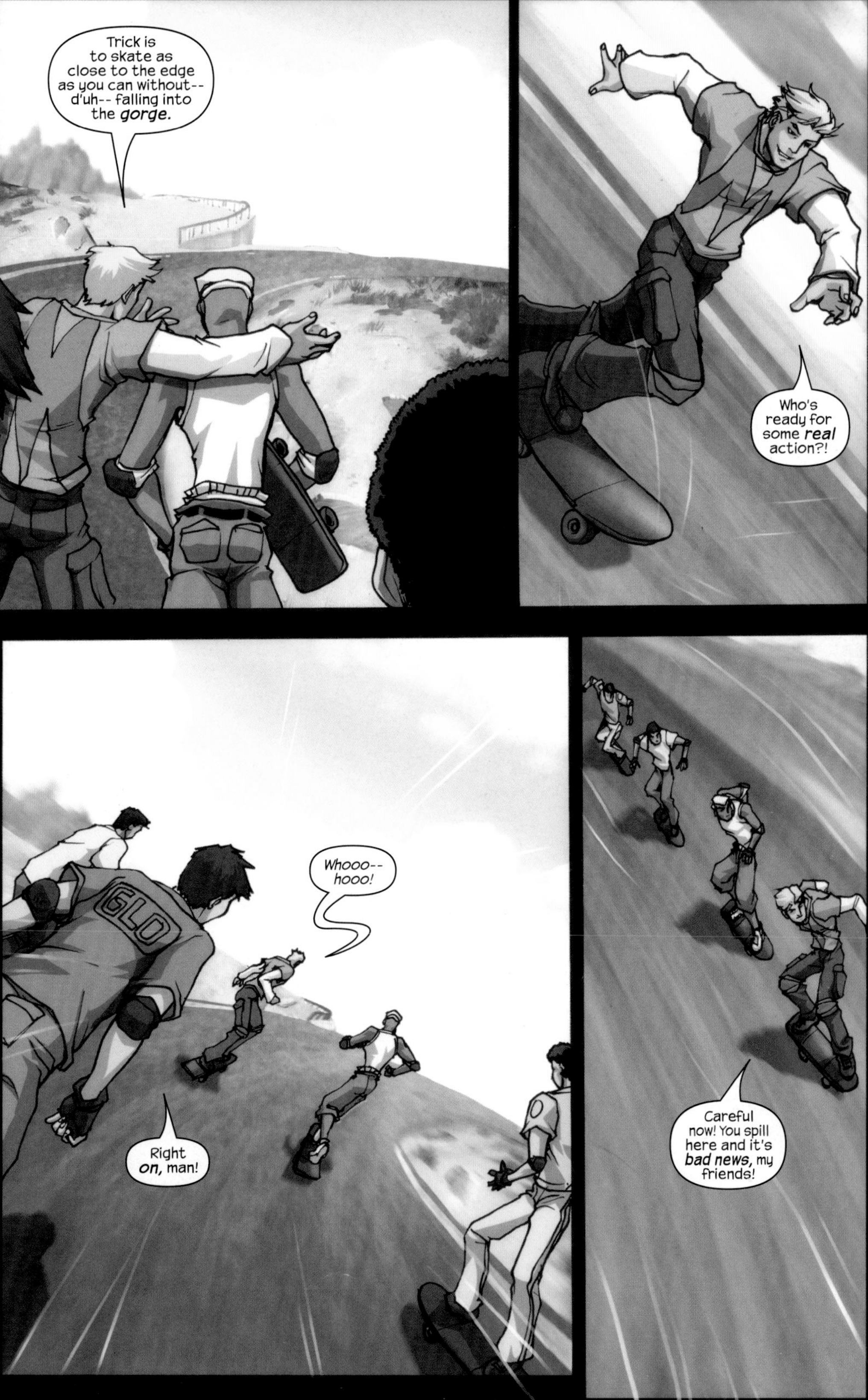
Trick is to skate as close to the edge as you can without-- d'uh-- falling into the *gorge.*
Who's ready for some *real* action?!
Whooo--hooo!
Right *on,* man!
Careful now! You spill here and it's *bad news,* my friends!

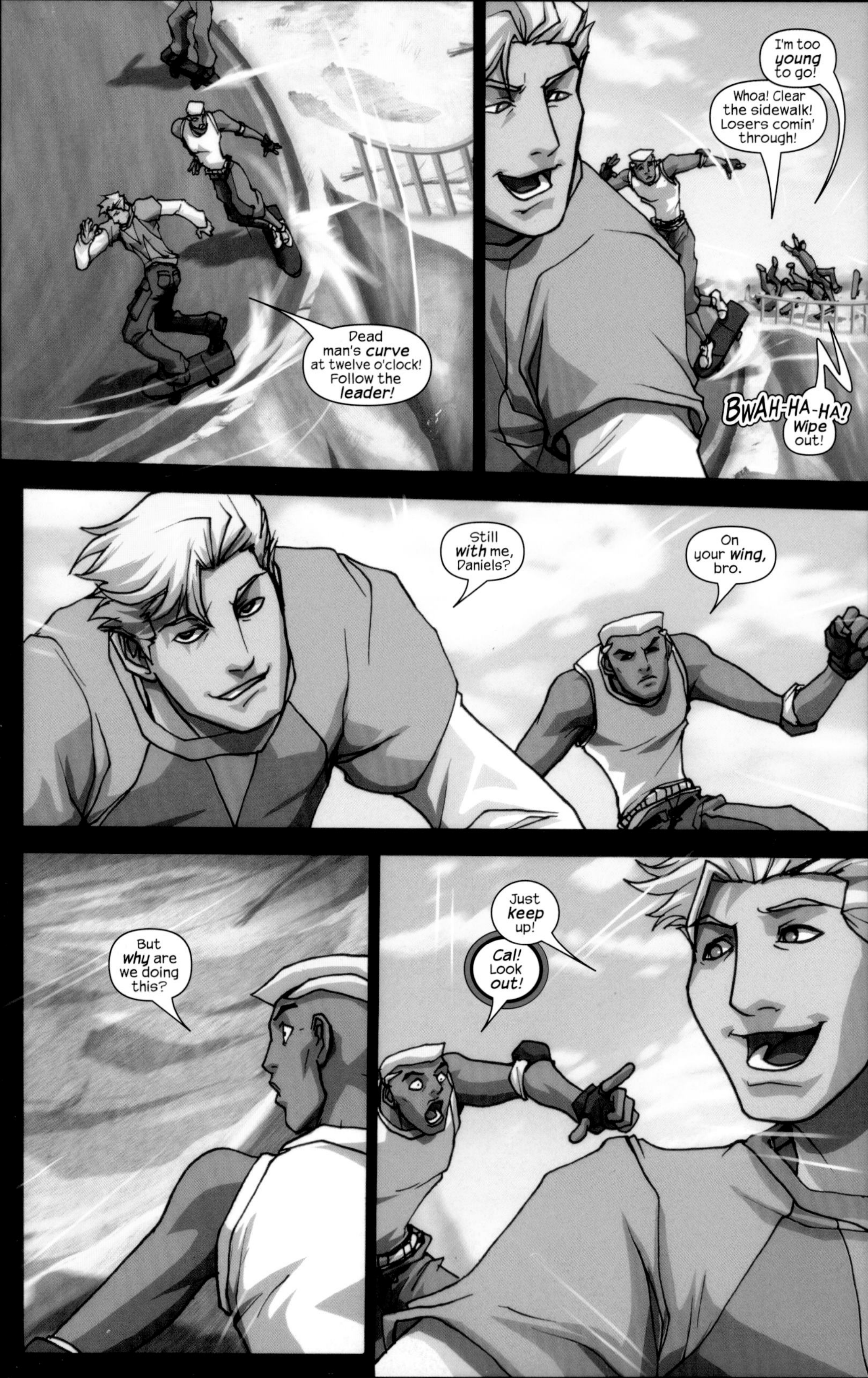

Dead man's *curve* at twelve o'clock! Follow the *leader!*
I'm too *young* to go!
Whoa! Clear the sidewalk! Losers comin' through!
BWAH-HA-HA! *Wipe* out!
Still *with* me, Daniels?
On your *wing,* bro.
But *why* are we doing this?
Just *keep* up!
Cal! Look *out!*

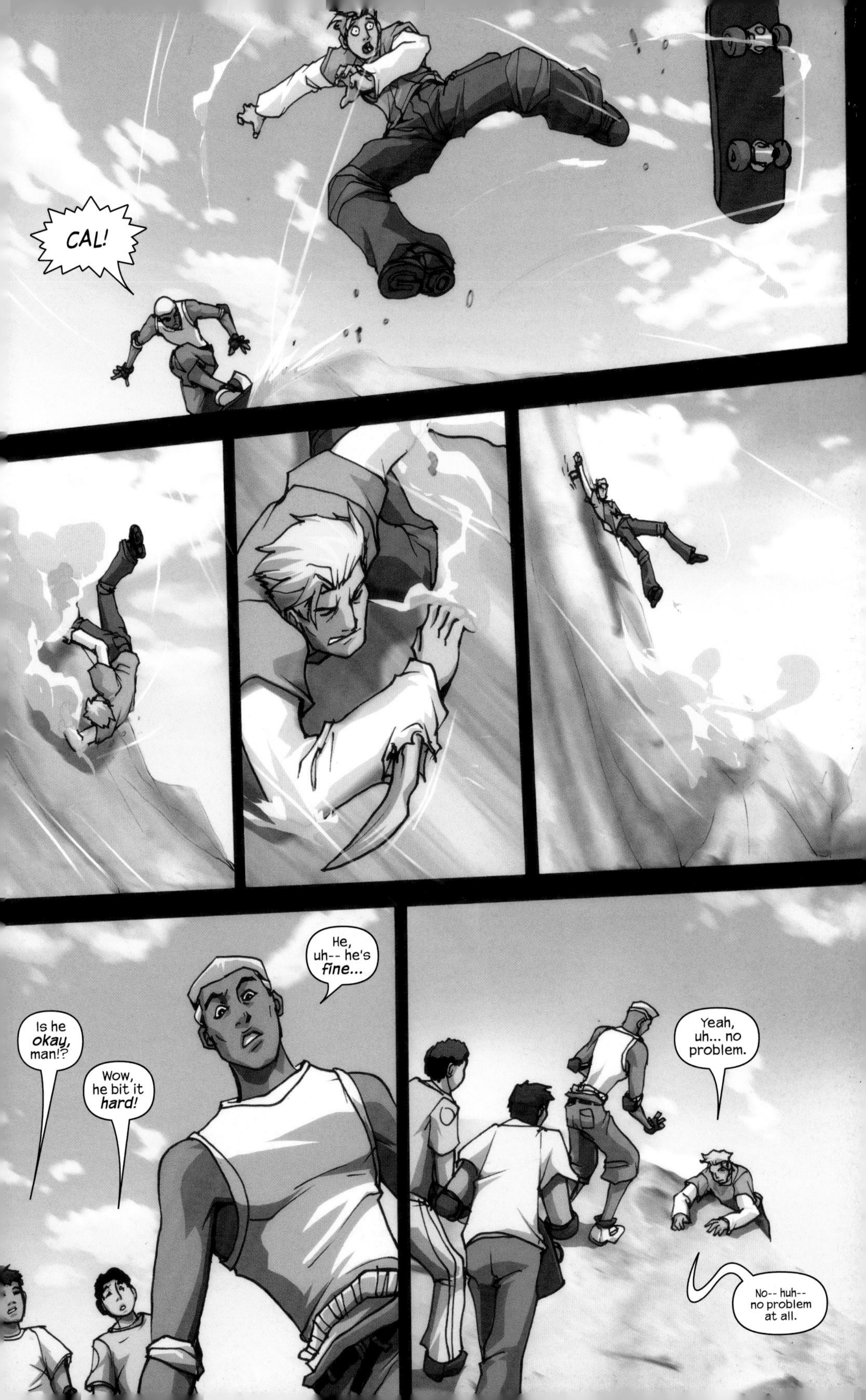
CAL!
Is he okay, man!?
Wow, he bit it hard!
He, uh-- he's fine...
Yeah, uh... no problem.
No-- huh-- no problem at all.

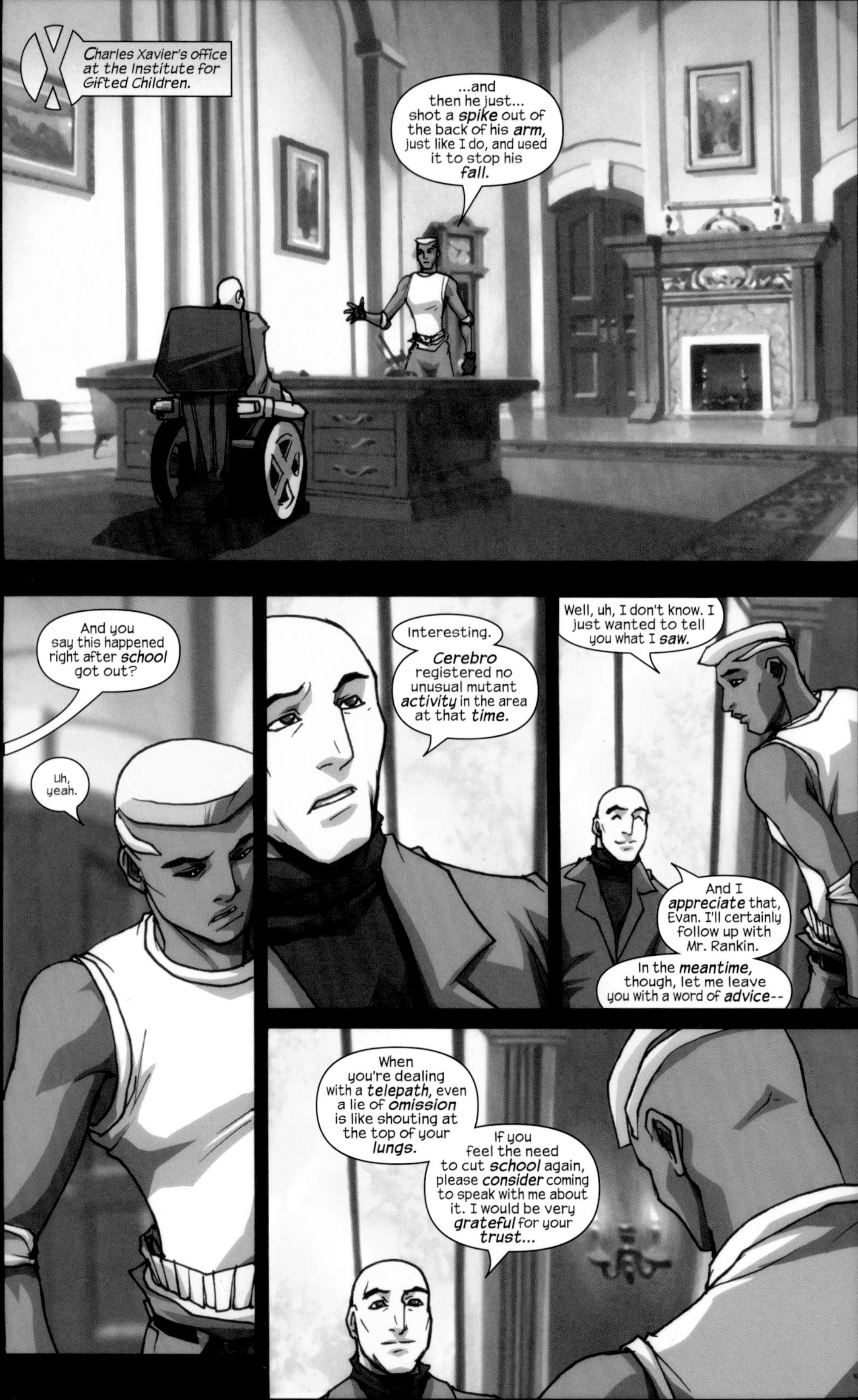
Charles Xavier's office at the Institute for Gifted Children.
...and then he just... shot a spike out of the back of his arm, just like I do, and used it to stop his fall.
And you say this happened right after school got out?
Uh, yeah.
Interesting.
Cerebro registered no unusual mutant activity in the area at that time.
Well, uh, I don't know. I just wanted to tell you what I saw.
And I appreciate that, Evan. I'll certainly follow up with Mr. Rankin.
In the meantime, though, let me leave you with a word of advice--
When you're dealing with a telepath, even a lie of omission is like shouting at the top of your lungs.
If you feel the need to cut school again, please consider coming to speak with me about it. I would be very grateful for your trust...

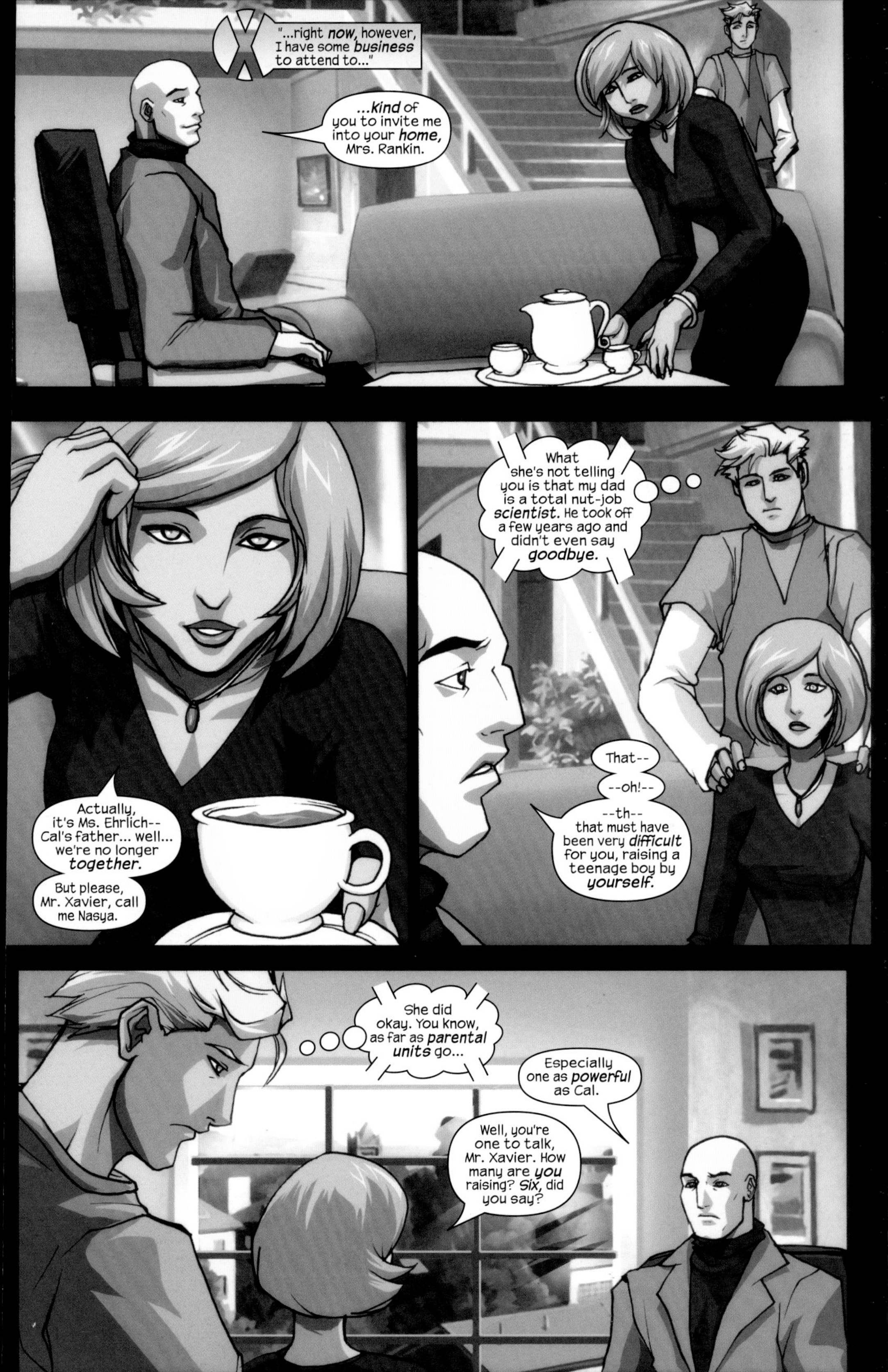
"...right now, however, I have some business to attend to..."
...kind of you to invite me into your home, Mrs. Rankin.
Actually, it's Ms. Ehrlich-- Cal's father... well... we're no longer together.
But please, Mr. Xavier, call me Nasya.
What she's not telling you is that my dad is a total nut-job scientist. He took off a few years ago and didn't even say goodbye.
That--
--oh!--
--th-- that must have been very difficult for you, raising a teenage boy by yourself.
She did okay. You know, as far as parental units go...
Especially one as powerful as Cal.
Well, you're one to talk, Mr. Xavier. How many are you raising? Six, did you say?

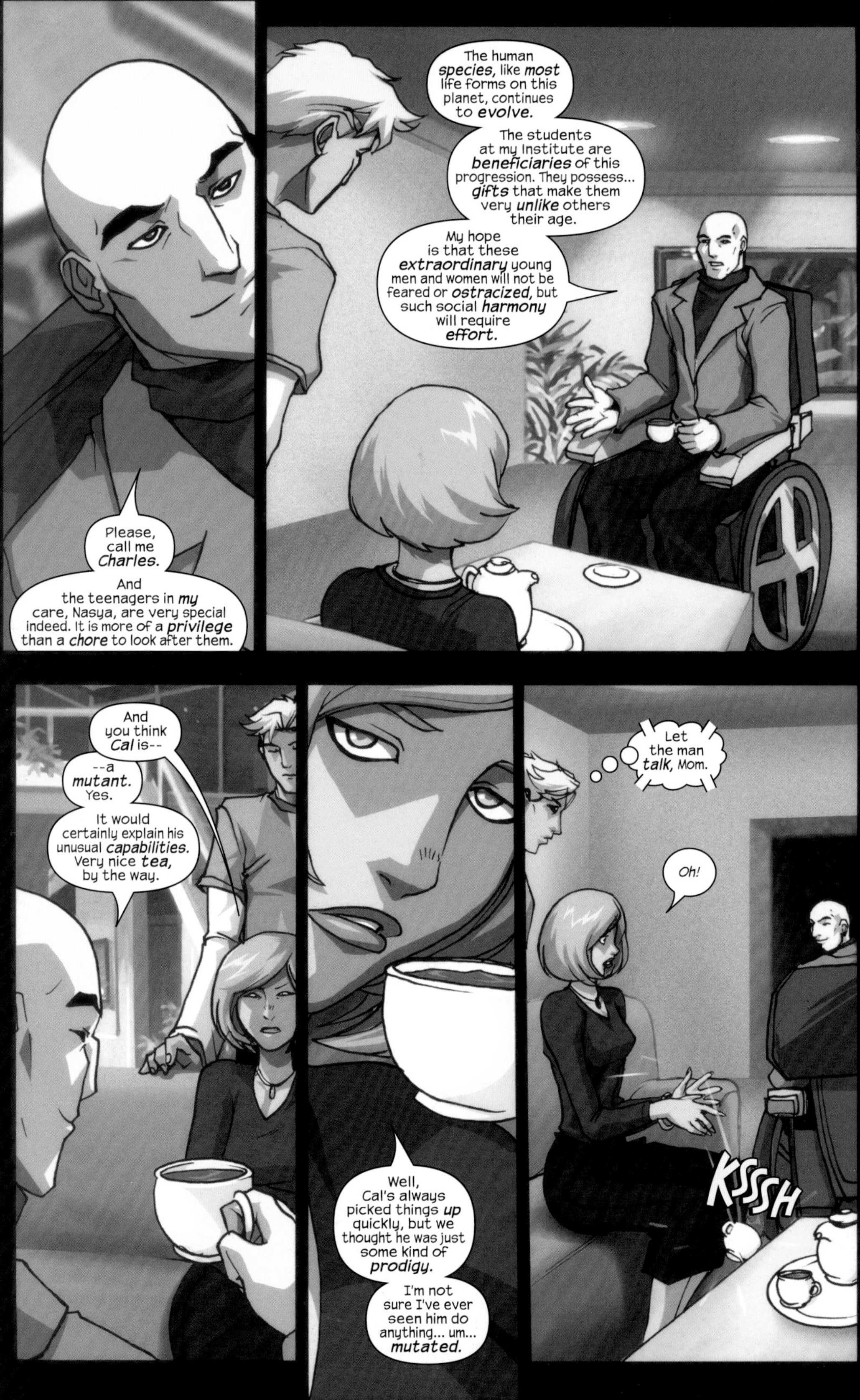
The human species, like most life forms on this planet, continues to evolve.
The students at my Institute are beneficiaries of this progression. They possess... gifts that make them very unlike others their age.
My hope is that these extraordinary young men and women will not be feared or ostracized, but such social harmony will require effort.
Please, call me Charles.
And the teenagers in my care, Nasya, are very special indeed. It is more of a privilege than a chore to look after them.
And you think Cal is--
--a mutant. Yes.
It would certainly explain his unusual capabilities. Very nice tea, by the way.
Well, Cal's always picked things up quickly, but we thought he was just some kind of prodigy.
I'm not sure I've ever seen him do anything... um... mutated.
Let the man talk, Mom.
Oh!
KSSSH

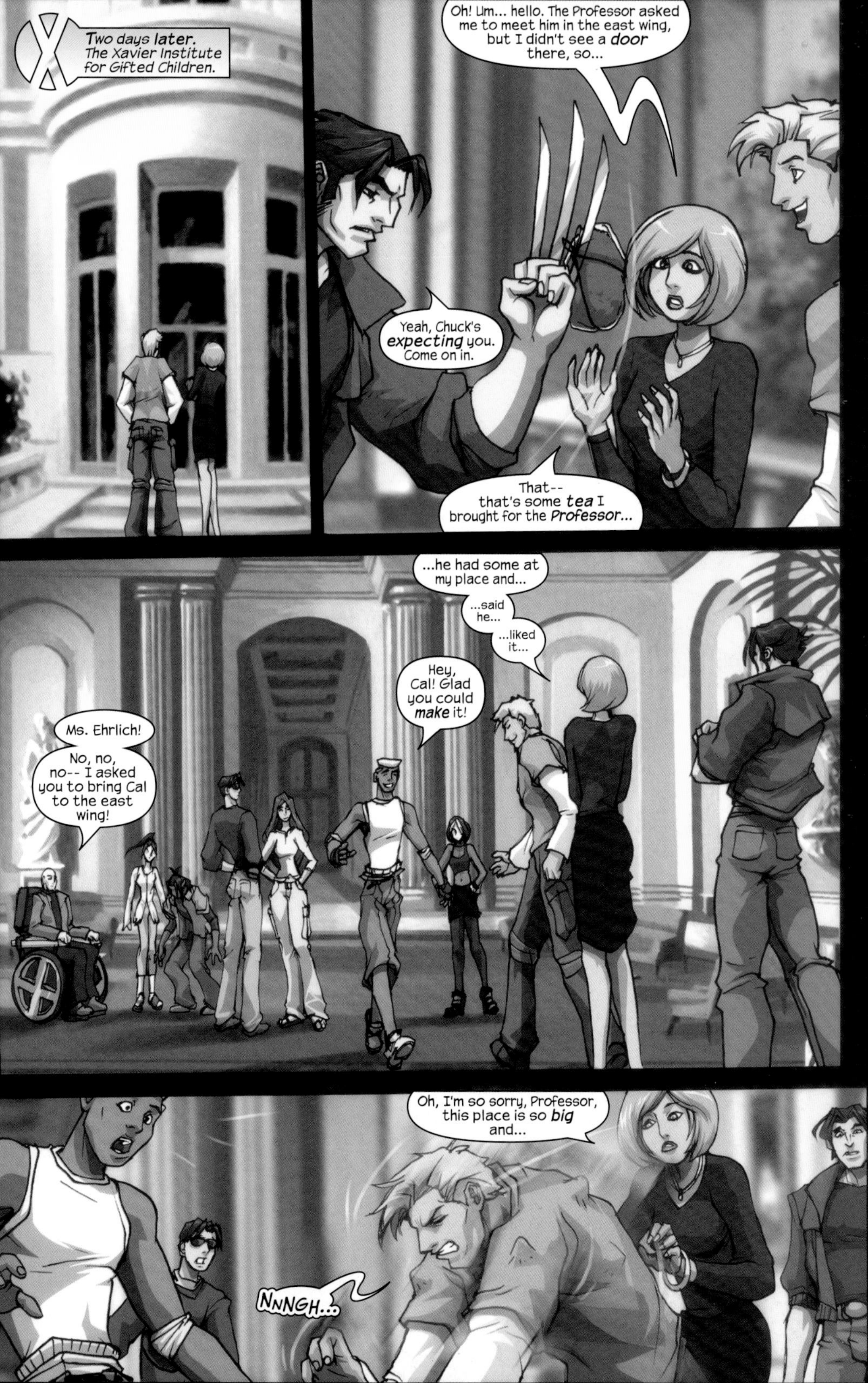
Two days later. The Xavier Institute for Gifted Children.
Oh! Um... hello. The Professor asked me to meet him in the east wing, but I didn't see a door there, so...
Yeah, Chuck's expecting you. Come on in.
That-- that's some tea I brought for the Professor...
...he had some at my place and...
...said he...
...liked it...
Hey, Cal! Glad you could make it!
Ms. Ehrlich!
No, no, no-- I asked you to bring Cal to the east wing!
Oh, I'm so sorry, Professor, this place is so big and...
NNNGH...

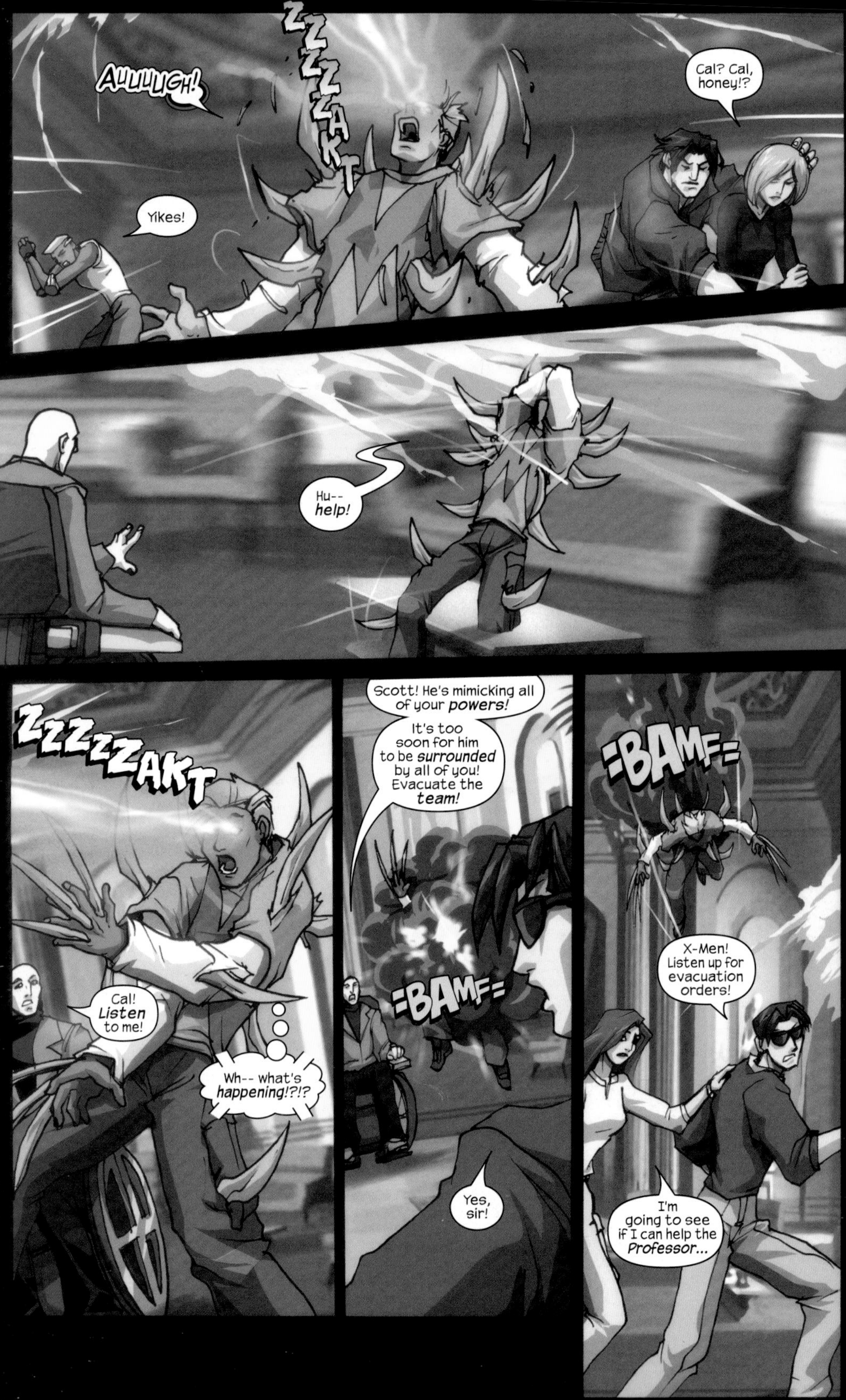

AUUUUGH!
ZZZZAKT
Cal? Cal, honey!?
Yikes!
Hu-- help!
ZZZZZAKT
Cal! Listen to me!
Wh-- what's happening!?!?
Scott! He's mimicking all of your powers!
It's too soon for him to be surrounded by all of you! Evacuate the team!
=BAMF=
Yes, sir!
=BAMF=
X-Men! Listen up for evacuation orders!
I'm going to see if I can help the Professor...

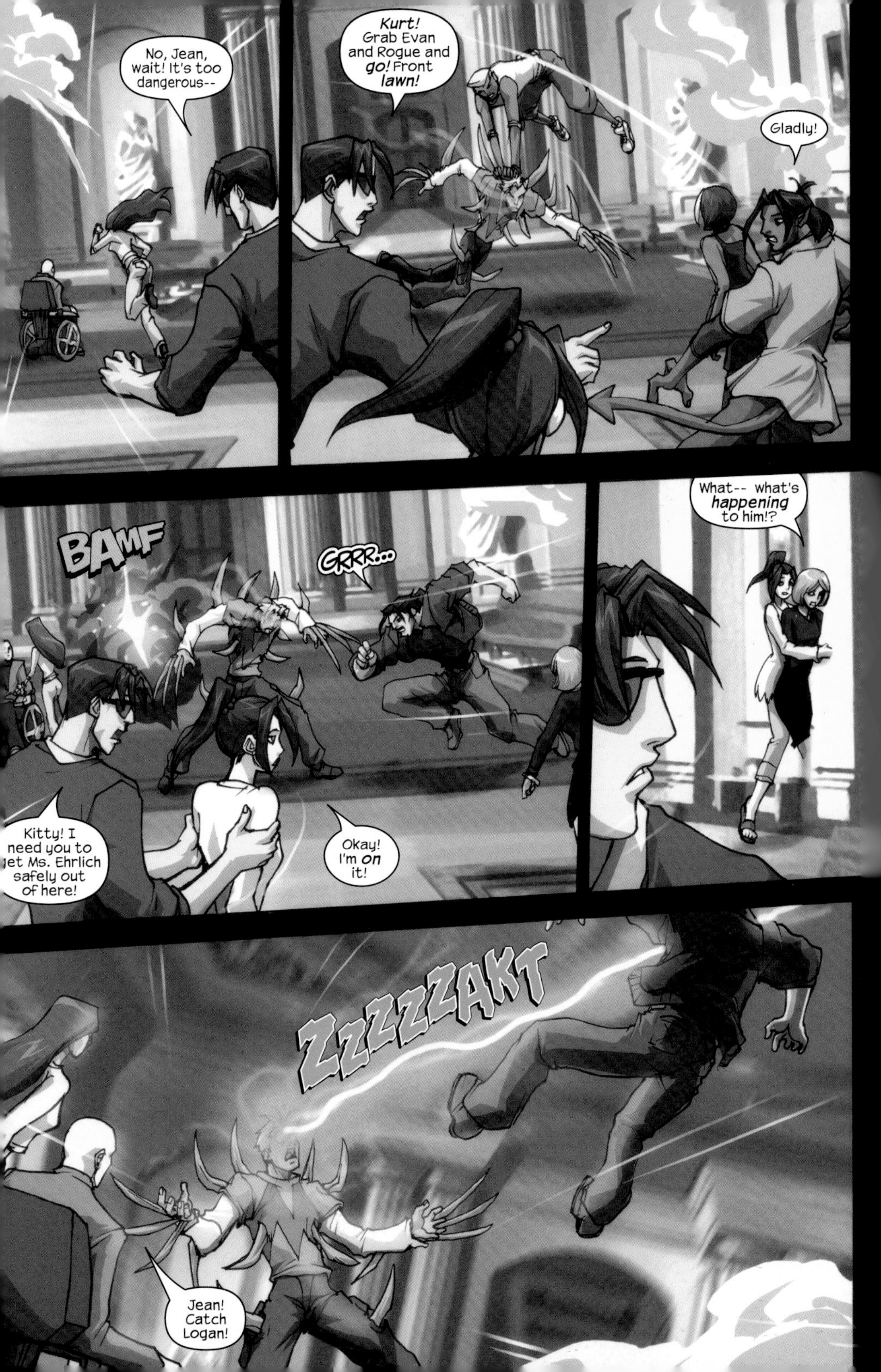
No, Jean, wait! It's too dangerous--
Kurt! Grab Evan and Rogue and go! Front lawn!
Gladly!
BAMF
GRRR...
Kitty! I need you to get Ms. Ehrlich safely out of here!
Okay! I'm on it!
What-- what's happening to him!?
ZZZZZAKT
Jean! Catch Logan!

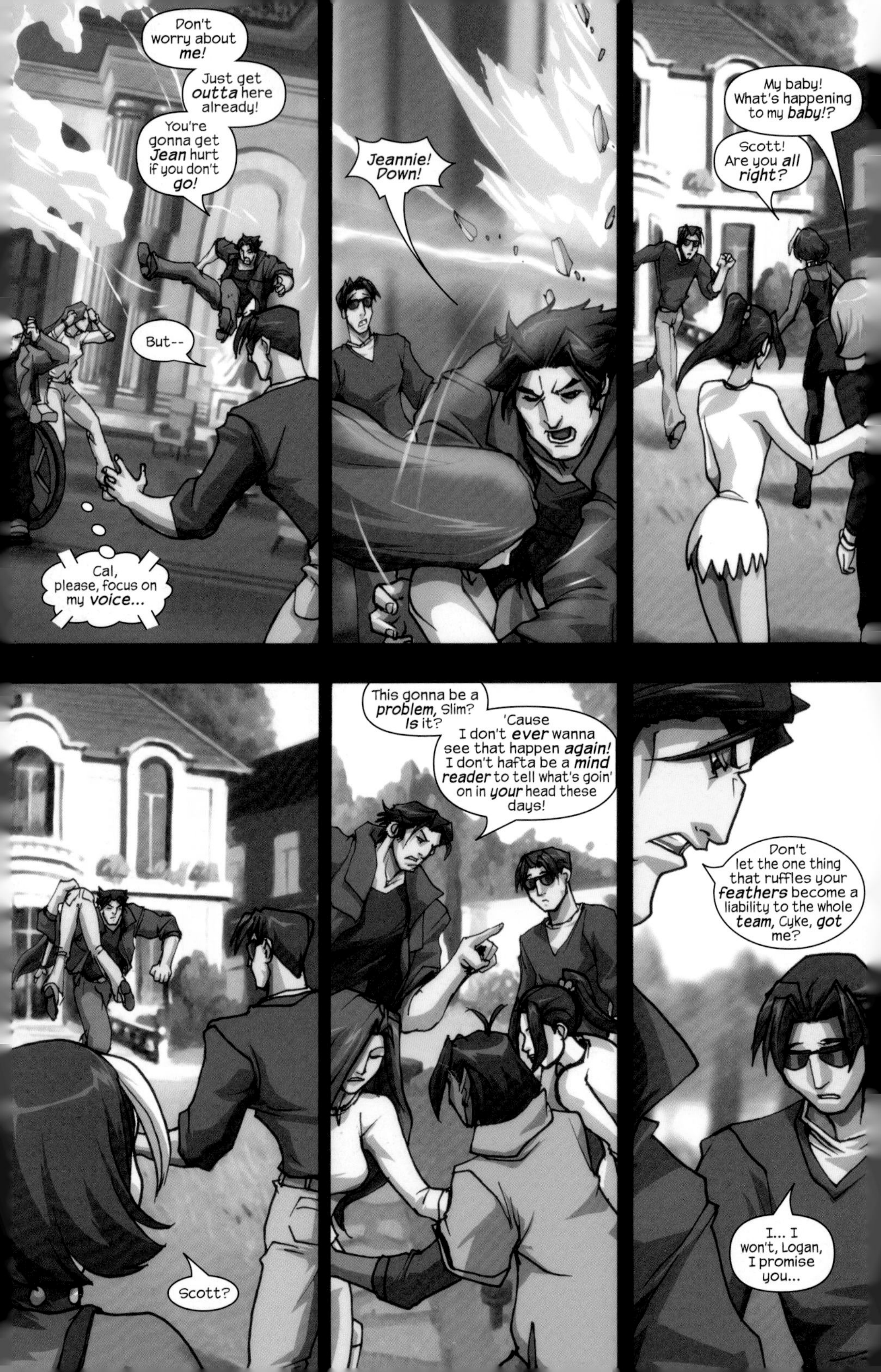
Don't worry about me!
Just get outta here already!
You're gonna get Jean hurt if you don't go!
But--
Cal, please, focus on my voice...
Jeannie! Down!
My baby! What's happening to my baby!?
Scott! Are you all right?
Scott?
This gonna be a problem, Slim? Is it?
'Cause I don't ever wanna see that happen again! I don't hafta be a mind reader to tell what's goin' on in your head these days!
Don't let the one thing that ruffles your feathers become a liability to the whole team, Cyke, got me?
I... I won't, Logan, I promise you...

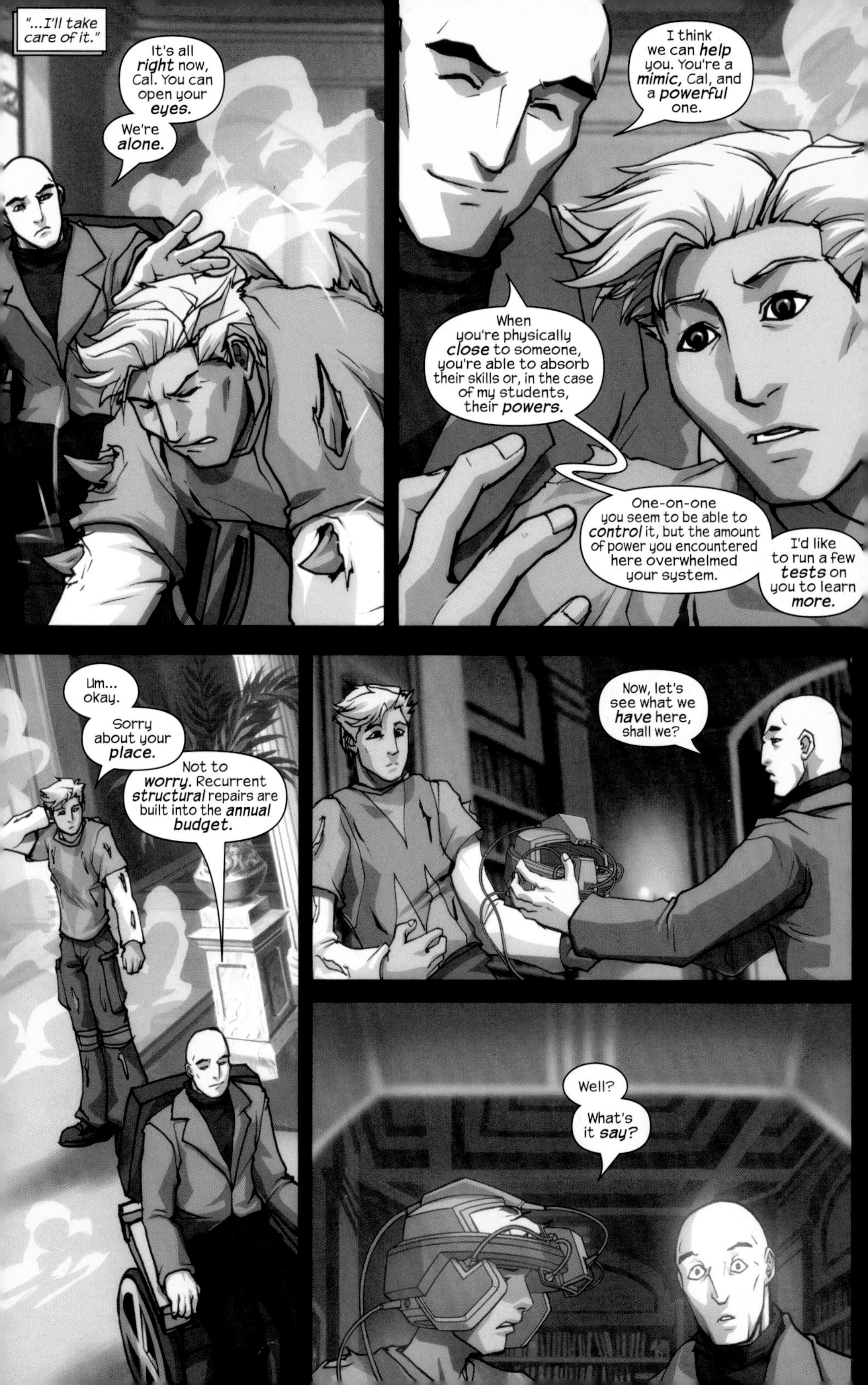
"...I'll take care of it."
It's all right now, Cal. You can open your eyes.
We're alone.
I think we can help you. You're a mimic, Cal, and a powerful one.
When you're physically close to someone, you're able to absorb their skills or, in the case of my students, their powers.
One-on-one you seem to be able to control it, but the amount of power you encountered here overwhelmed your system.
I'd like to run a few tests on you to learn more.
Um... okay.
Sorry about your place.
Not to worry. Recurrent structural repairs are built into the annual budget.
Now, let's see what we have here, shall we?
Well?
What's it say?

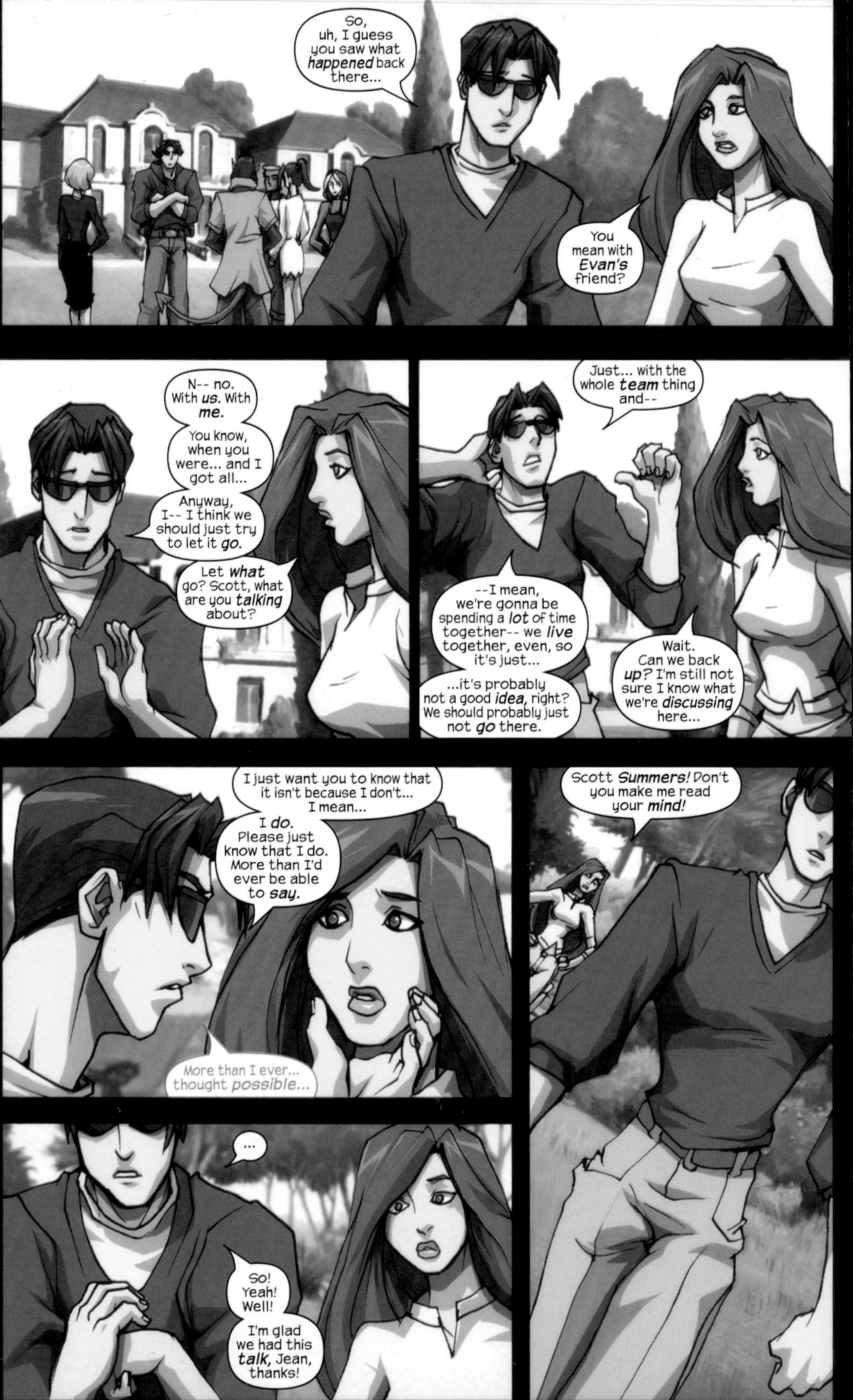
So, uh, I guess you saw what happened back there...
You mean with Evan's friend?
N-- no. With us. With me.
You know, when you were... and I got all...
Anyway, I-- I think we should just try to let it go.
Let what go? Scott, what are you talking about?
Just... with the whole team thing and--
--I mean, we're gonna be spending a lot of time together-- we live together, even, so it's just...
...it's probably not a good idea, right? We should probably just not go there.
Wait. Can we back up? I'm still not sure I know what we're discussing here...
I just want you to know that it isn't because I don't... I mean...
I do. Please just know that I do. More than I'd ever be able to say.
More than I ever... thought possible...
...
So! Yeah! Well!
I'm glad we had this talk, Jean, thanks!
Scott Summers! Don't you make me read your mind!

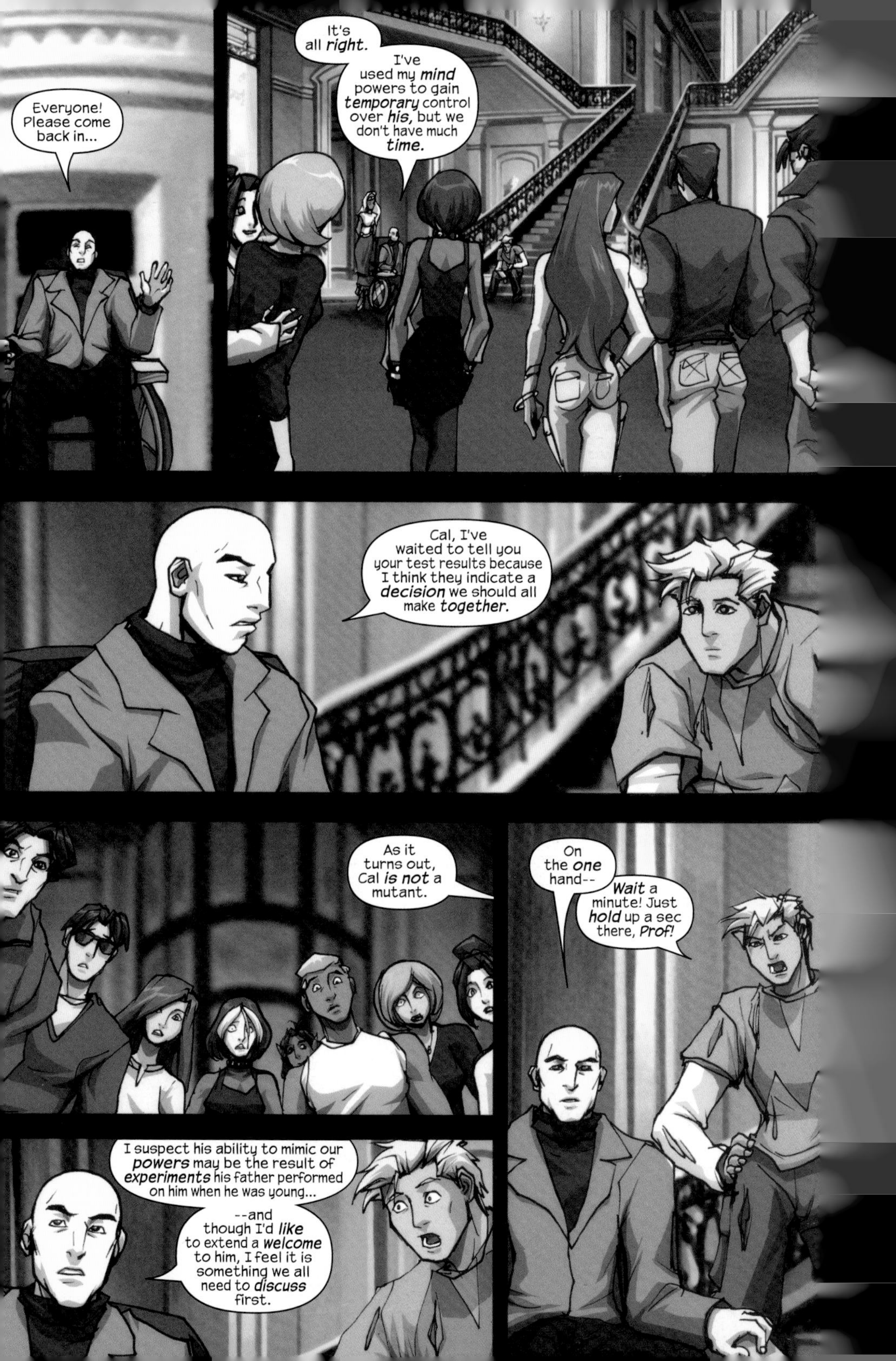
Everyone! Please come back in...
It's all right.
I've used my mind powers to gain temporary control over his, but we don't have much time.
Cal, I've waited to tell you your test results because I think they indicate a decision we should all make together.
As it turns out, Cal is not a mutant.
I suspect his ability to mimic our powers may be the result of experiments his father performed on him when he was young...
--and though I'd like to extend a welcome to him, I feel it is something we all need to discuss first.
On the one hand--
Wait a minute! Just hold up a sec there, Prof!

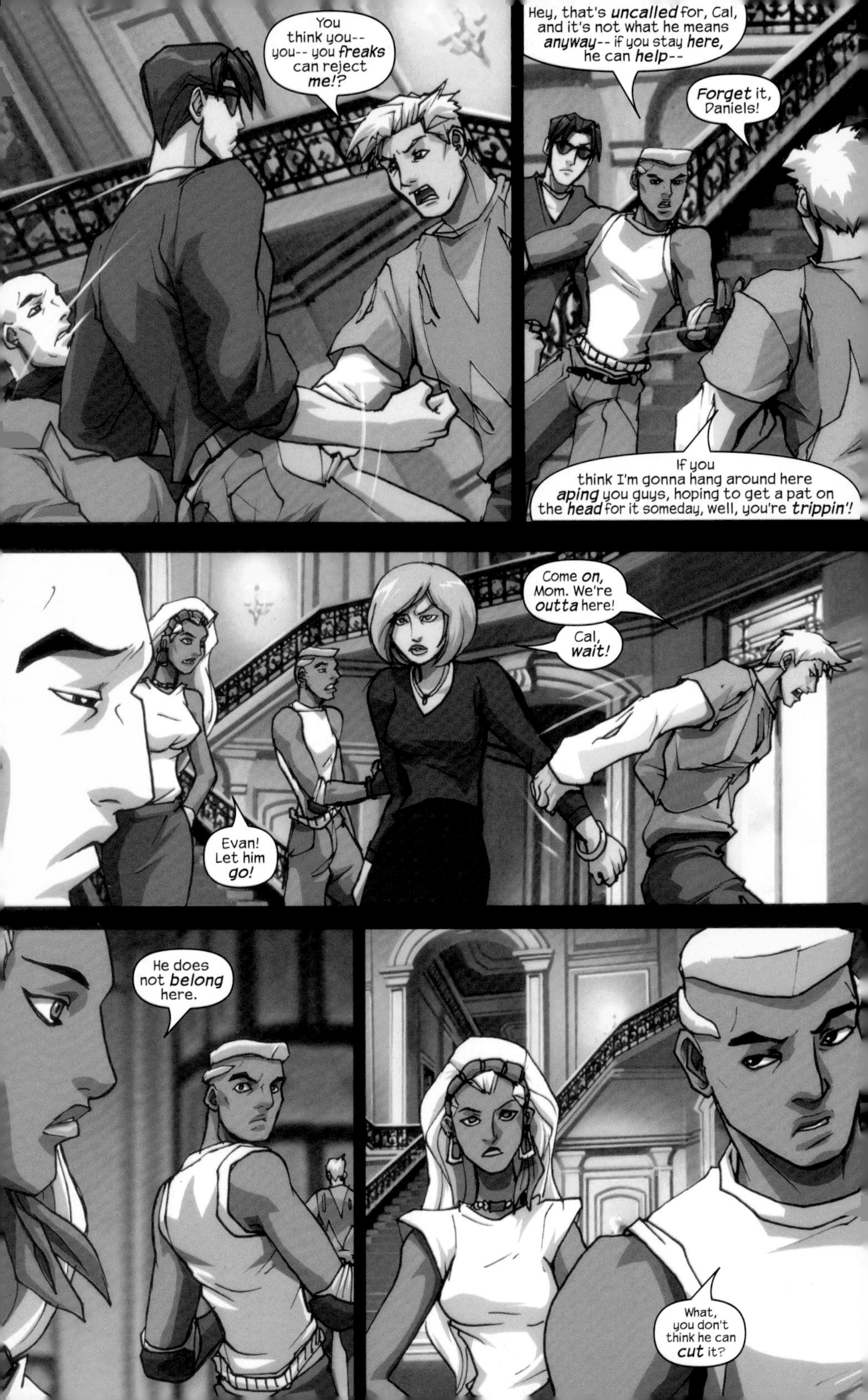
You think you-- you-- you freaks can reject me!?
Hey, that's uncalled for, Cal, and it's not what he means anyway-- if you stay here, he can help--
Forget it, Daniels!
If you think I'm gonna hang around here aping you guys, hoping to get a pat on the head for it someday, well, you're trippin'!
Come on, Mom. We're outta here!
Cal, wait!
Evan! Let him go!
He does not belong here.
What, you don't think he can cut it?

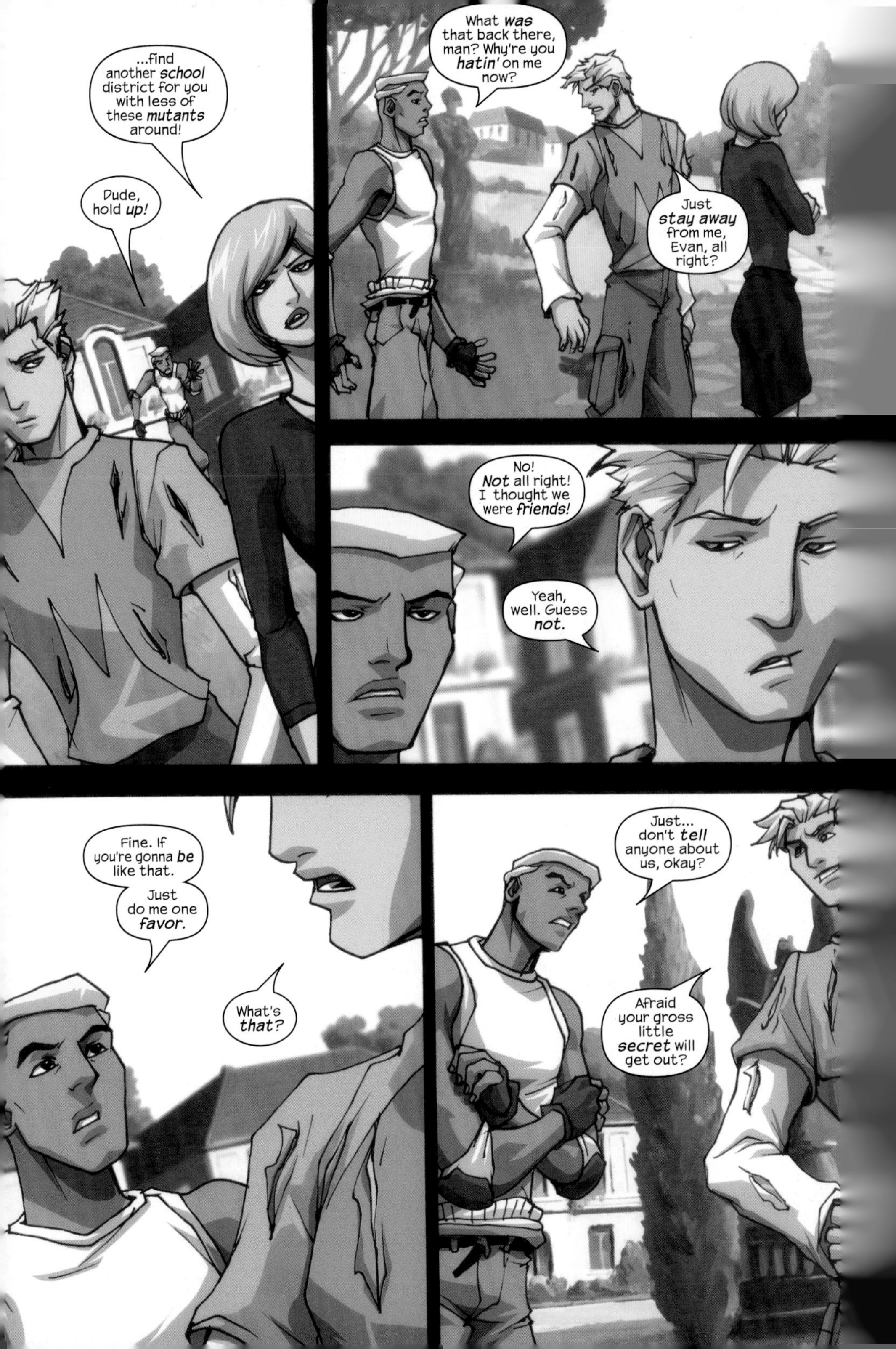
...find another school district for you with less of these mutants around!
Dude, hold up!
What was that back there, man? Why're you hatin' on me now?
Just stay away from me, Evan, all right?
No! Not all right! I thought we were friends!
Yeah, well. Guess not.
Fine. If you're gonna be like that.
Just do me one favor.
What's that?
Just... don't tell anyone about us, okay?
Afraid your gross little secret will get out?

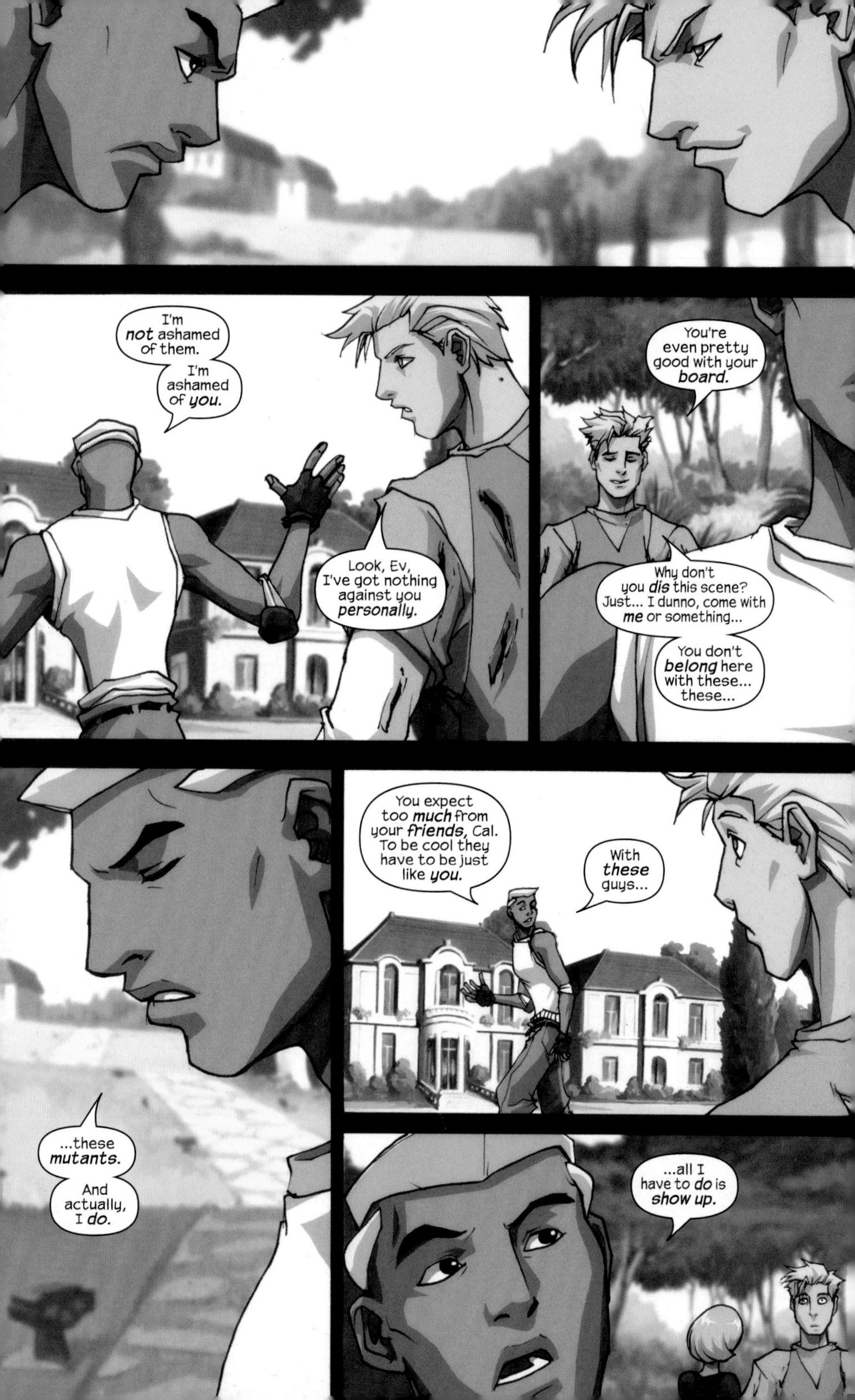

I'm not ashamed of them.
I'm ashamed of you.
Look, Ev, I've got nothing against you personally.
You're even pretty good with your board.
Why don't you dis this scene? Just... I dunno, come with me or something...
You don't belong here with these... these...
...these mutants.
And actually, I do.
You expect too much from your friends, Cal. To be cool they have to be just like you.
With these guys...
...all I have to do is show up.

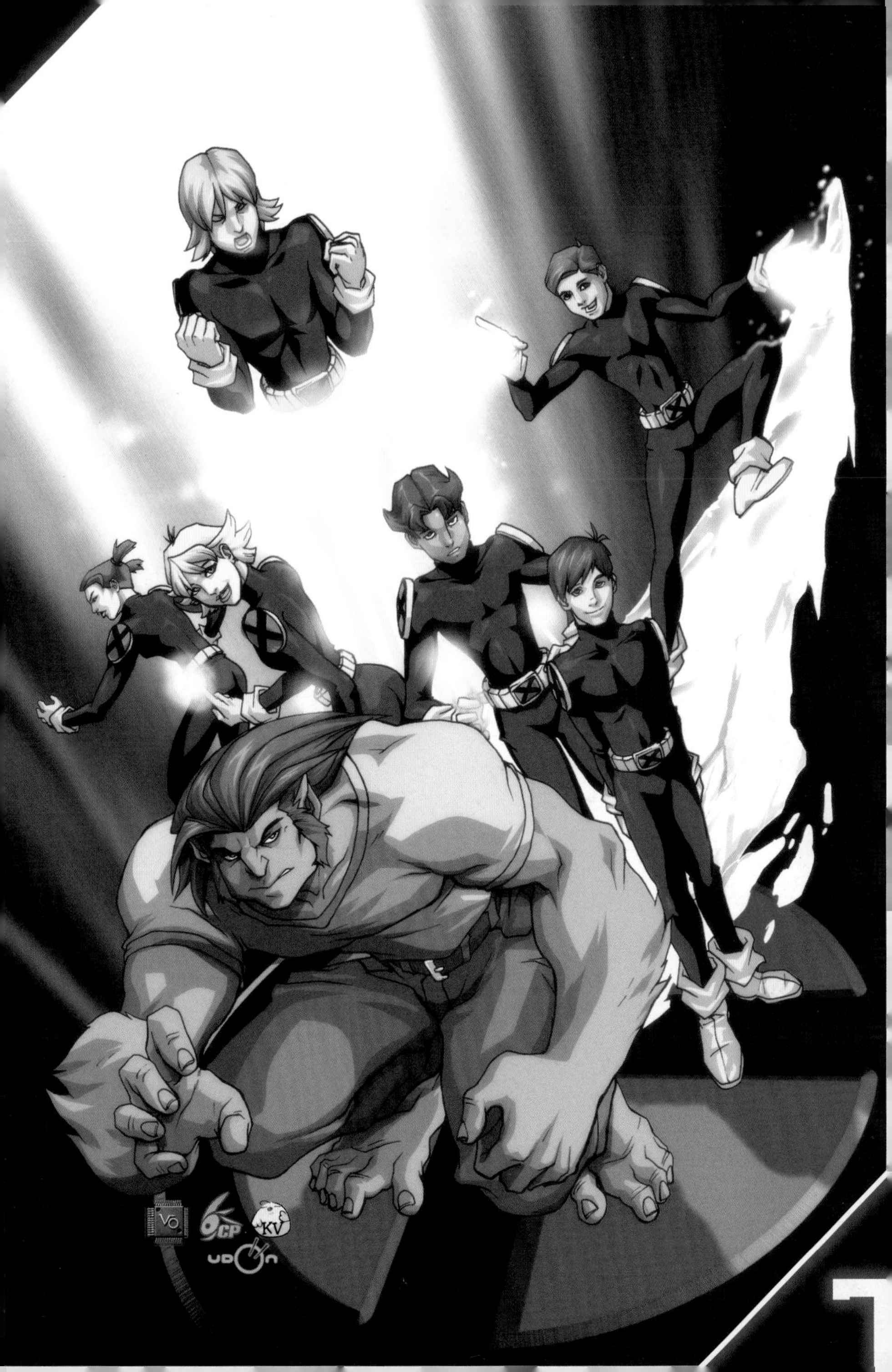

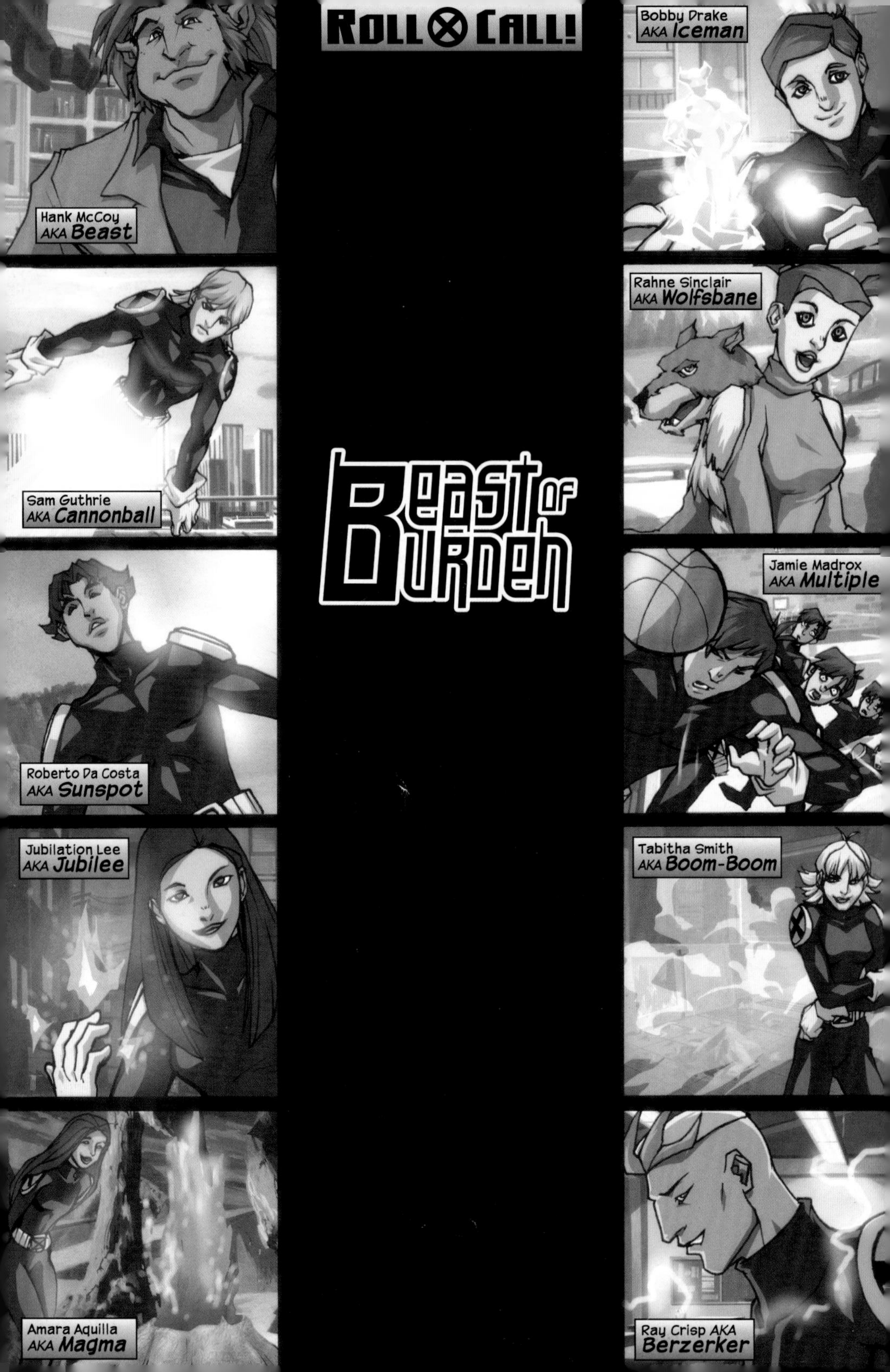
ROLL CALL!
BEAST OF BURDEN
Hank McCoy AKA Beast
Sam Guthrie AKA Cannonball
Roberto Da Costa AKA Sunspot
Jubilation Lee AKA Jubilee
Amara Aquilla AKA Magma
Bobby Drake AKA Iceman
Rahne Sinclair AKA Wolfsbane
Jamie Madrox AKA Multiple
Tabitha Smith AKA Boom-Boom
Ray Crisp AKA Berzerker

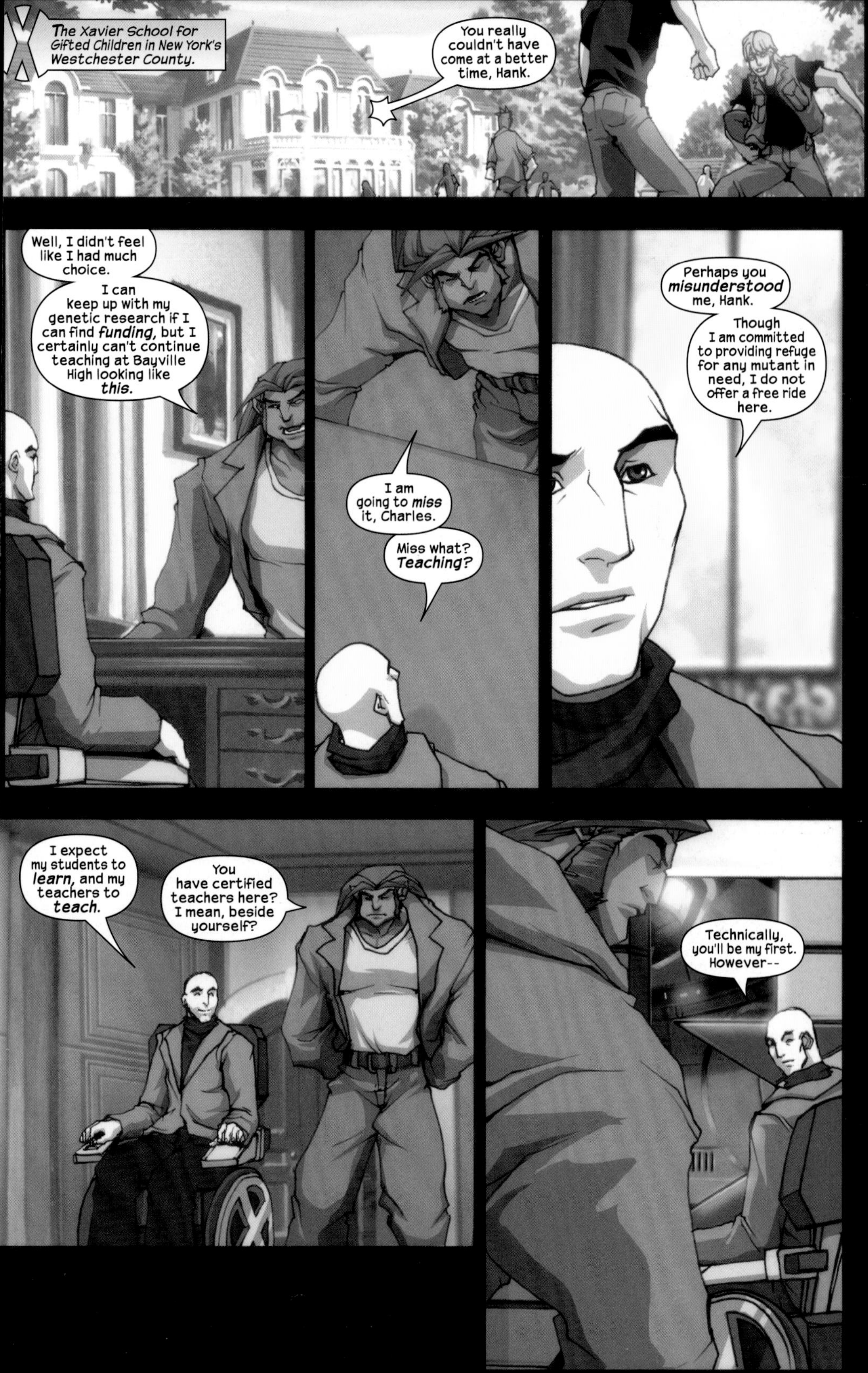
The Xavier School for Gifted Children in New York's Westchester County.
You really couldn't have come at a better time, Hank.
Well, I didn't feel like I had much choice.
I can keep up with my genetic research if I can find funding, but I certainly can't continue teaching at Bayville High looking like this.
I am going to miss it, Charles.
Miss what? Teaching?
Perhaps you misunderstood me, Hank.
Though I am committed to providing refuge for any mutant in need, I do not offer a free ride here.
I expect my students to learn, and my teachers to teach.
You have certified teachers here? I mean, beside yourself?
Technically, you'll be my first. However--

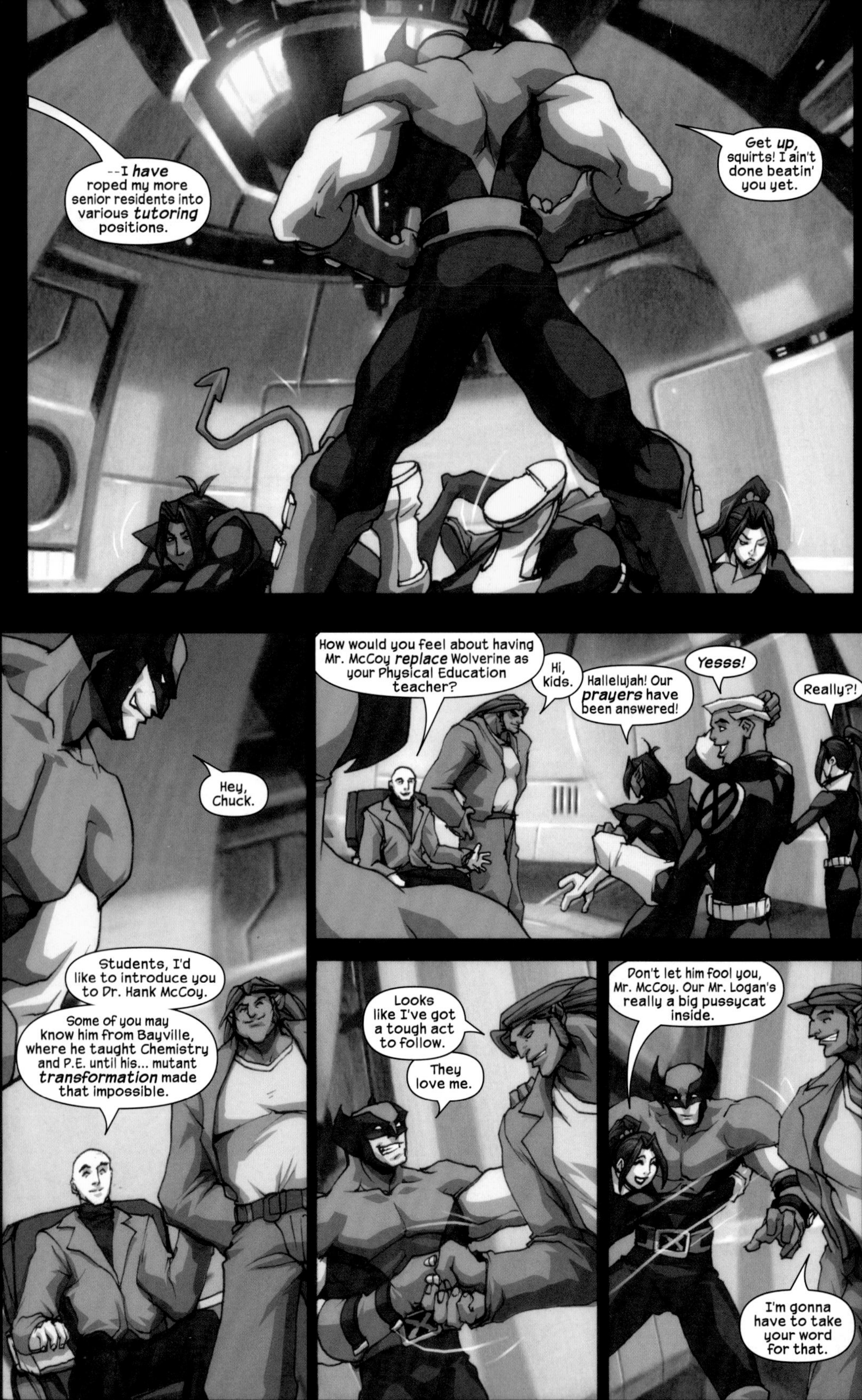

--I have roped my more senior residents into various tutoring positions.
Get up, squirts! I ain't done beatin' you yet.
Hey, Chuck.
Students, I'd like to introduce you to Dr. Hank McCoy.
Some of you may know him from Bayville, where he taught Chemistry and P.E. until his... mutant transformation made that impossible.
How would you feel about having Mr. McCoy replace Wolverine as your Physical Education teacher?
Hi, kids.
Hallelujah! Our prayers have been answered!
Yesss!
Really?!
Looks like I've got a tough act to follow.
They love me.
Don't let him fool you, Mr. McCoy. Our Mr. Logan's really a big pussycat inside.
I'm gonna have to take your word for that.

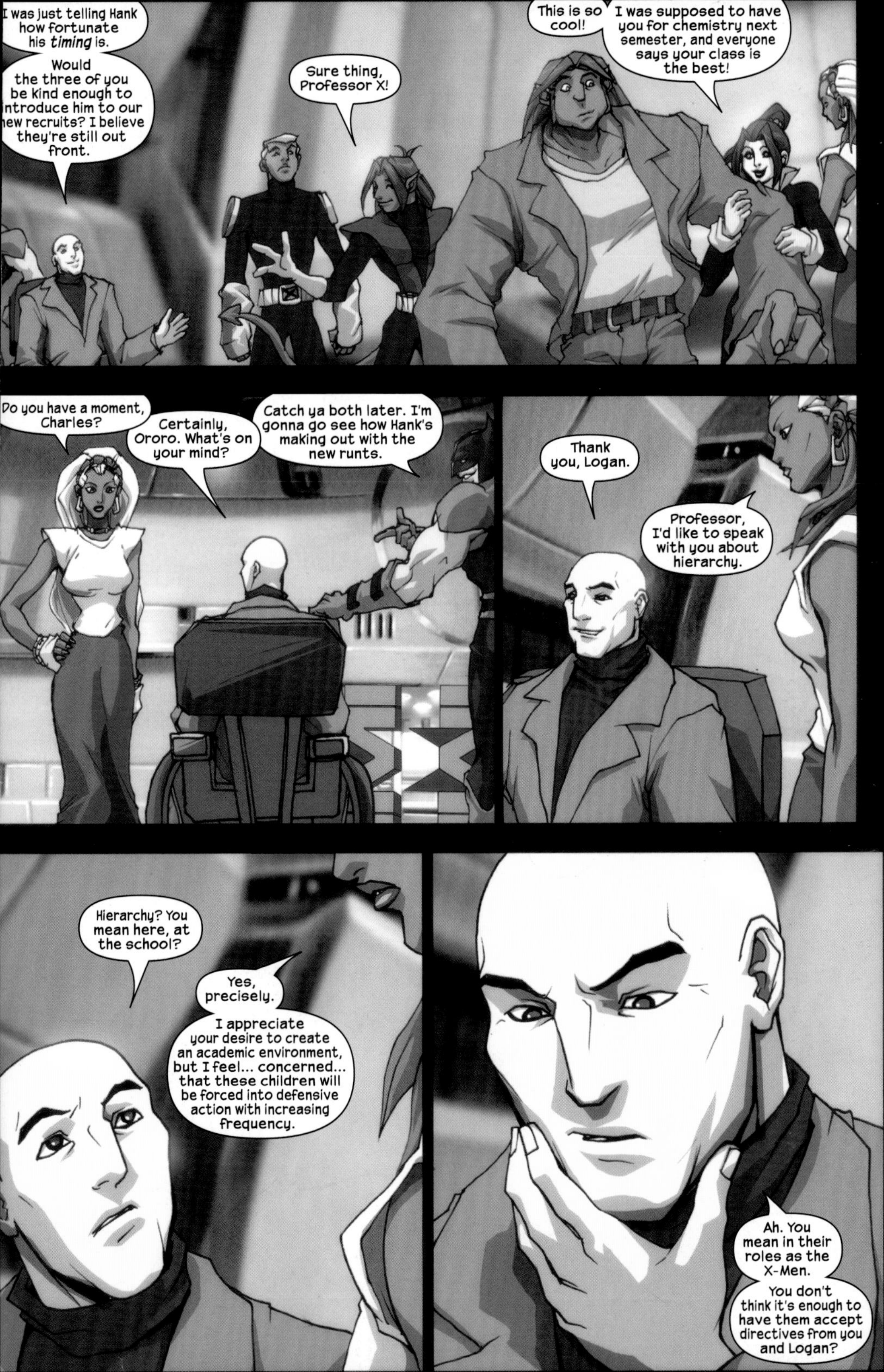
I was just telling Hank how fortunate his *timing* is.
Would the three of you be kind enough to introduce him to our new recruits? I believe they're still out front.
Sure thing, Professor X!
This is so cool!
I was supposed to have you for chemistry next semester, and everyone says your class is the best!
Do you have a moment, Charles?
Certainly, Ororo. What's on your mind?
Catch ya both later. I'm gonna go see how Hank's making out with the new runts.
Thank you, Logan.
Professor, I'd like to speak with you about hierarchy.
Hierarchy? You mean here, at the school?
Yes, precisely.
I appreciate your desire to create an academic environment, but I feel... concerned... that these children will be forced into defensive action with increasing frequency.
Ah. You mean in their roles as the X-Men.
You don't think it's enough to have them accept directives from you and Logan?

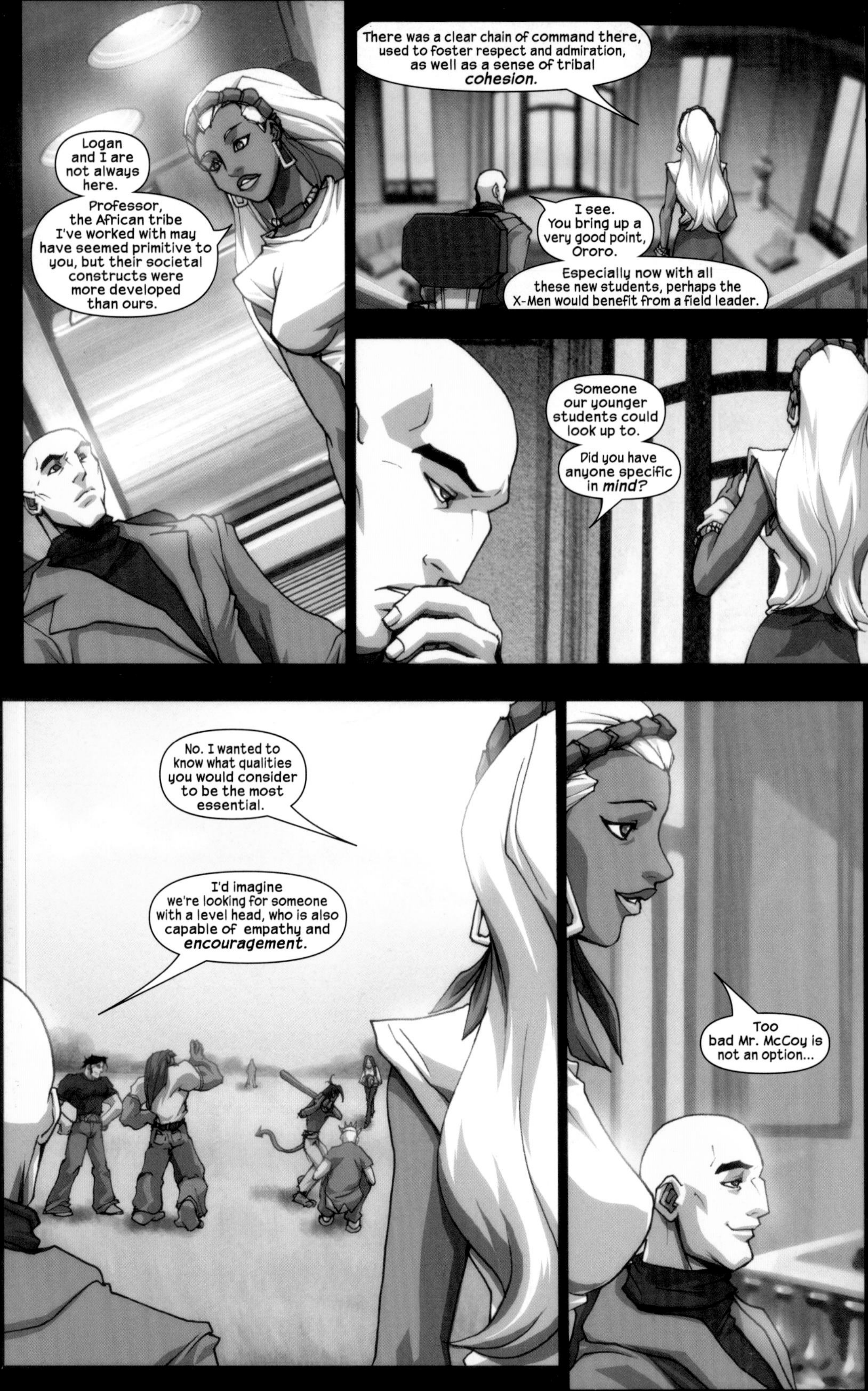
Logan and I are not always here.
Professor, the African tribe I've worked with may have seemed primitive to you, but their societal constructs were more developed than ours.
There was a clear chain of command there, used to foster respect and admiration, as well as a sense of tribal *cohesion.*
I see. You bring up a very good point, Ororo.
Especially now with all these new students, perhaps the X-Men would benefit from a field leader.
Someone our younger students could look up to.
Did you have anyone specific in *mind?*
No. I wanted to know what qualities you would consider to be the most essential.
I'd imagine we're looking for someone with a level head, who is also capable of empathy and *encouragement.*
Too bad Mr. McCoy is not an option...

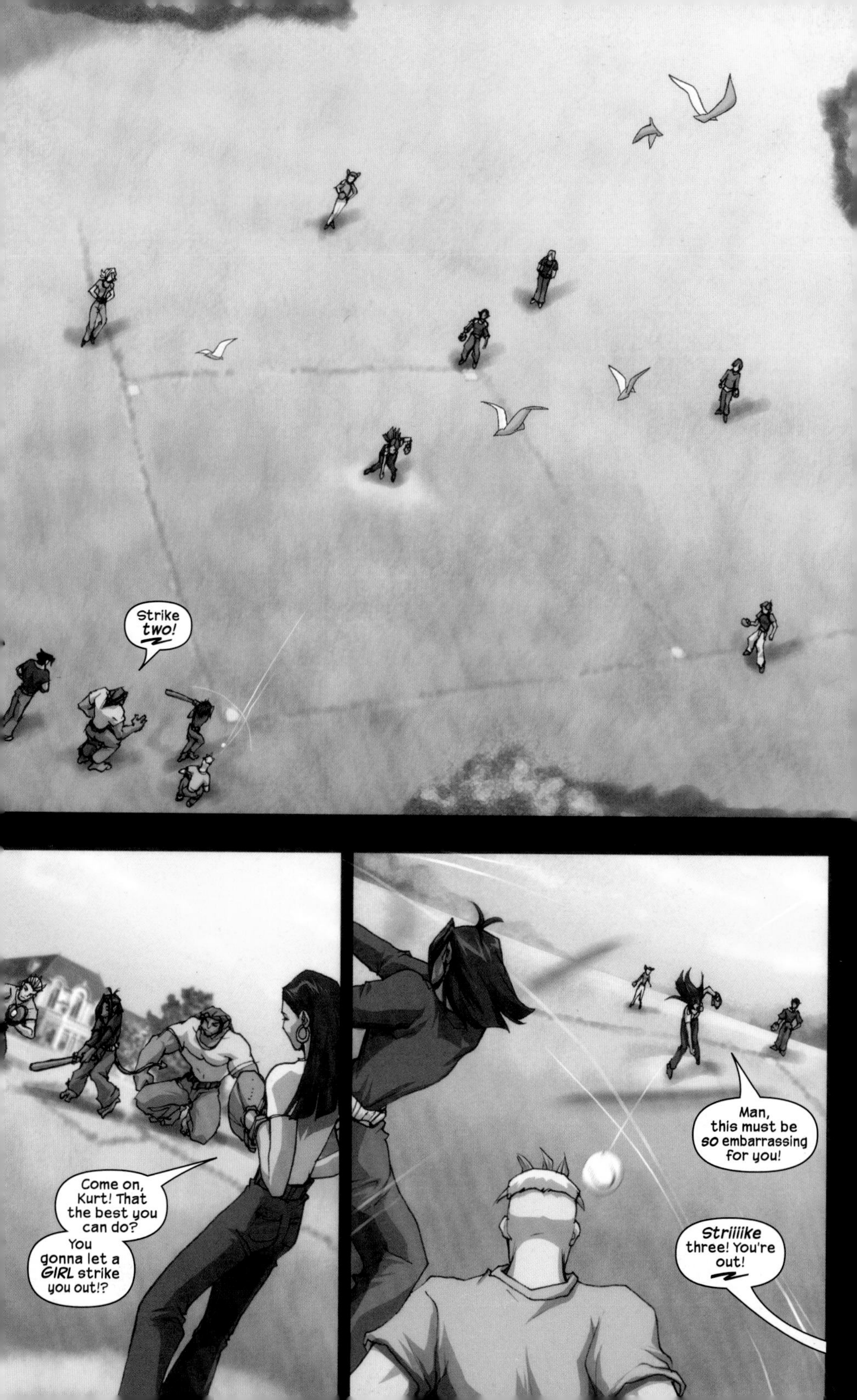
Strike two!
Come on, Kurt! That the best you can do?
You gonna let a GIRL strike you out!?
Man, this must be SO embarrassing for you!
Striiiike three! You're out!

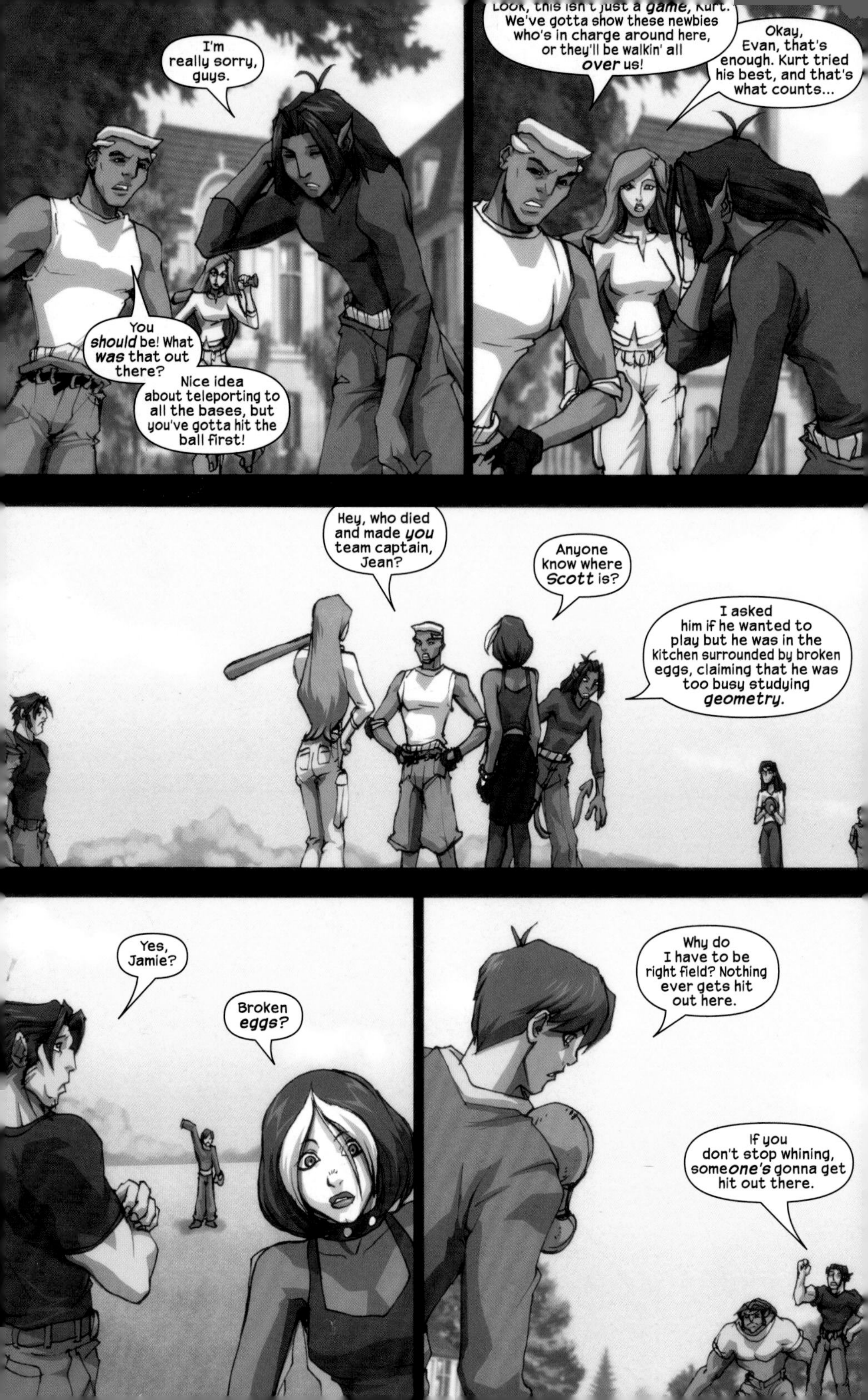
I'm really sorry, guys.
You should be! What was that out there?
Nice idea about teleporting to all the bases, but you've gotta hit the ball first!
Look, this isn't just a game, Kurt. We've gotta show these newbies who's in charge around here, or they'll be walkin' all over us!
Okay, Evan, that's enough. Kurt tried his best, and that's what counts...
Hey, who died and made you team captain, Jean?
Anyone know where Scott is?
I asked him if he wanted to play but he was in the kitchen surrounded by broken eggs, claiming that he was too busy studying geometry.
Yes, Jamie?
Broken eggs?
Why do I have to be right field? Nothing ever gets hit out here.
If you don't stop whining, someone's gonna get hit out there.

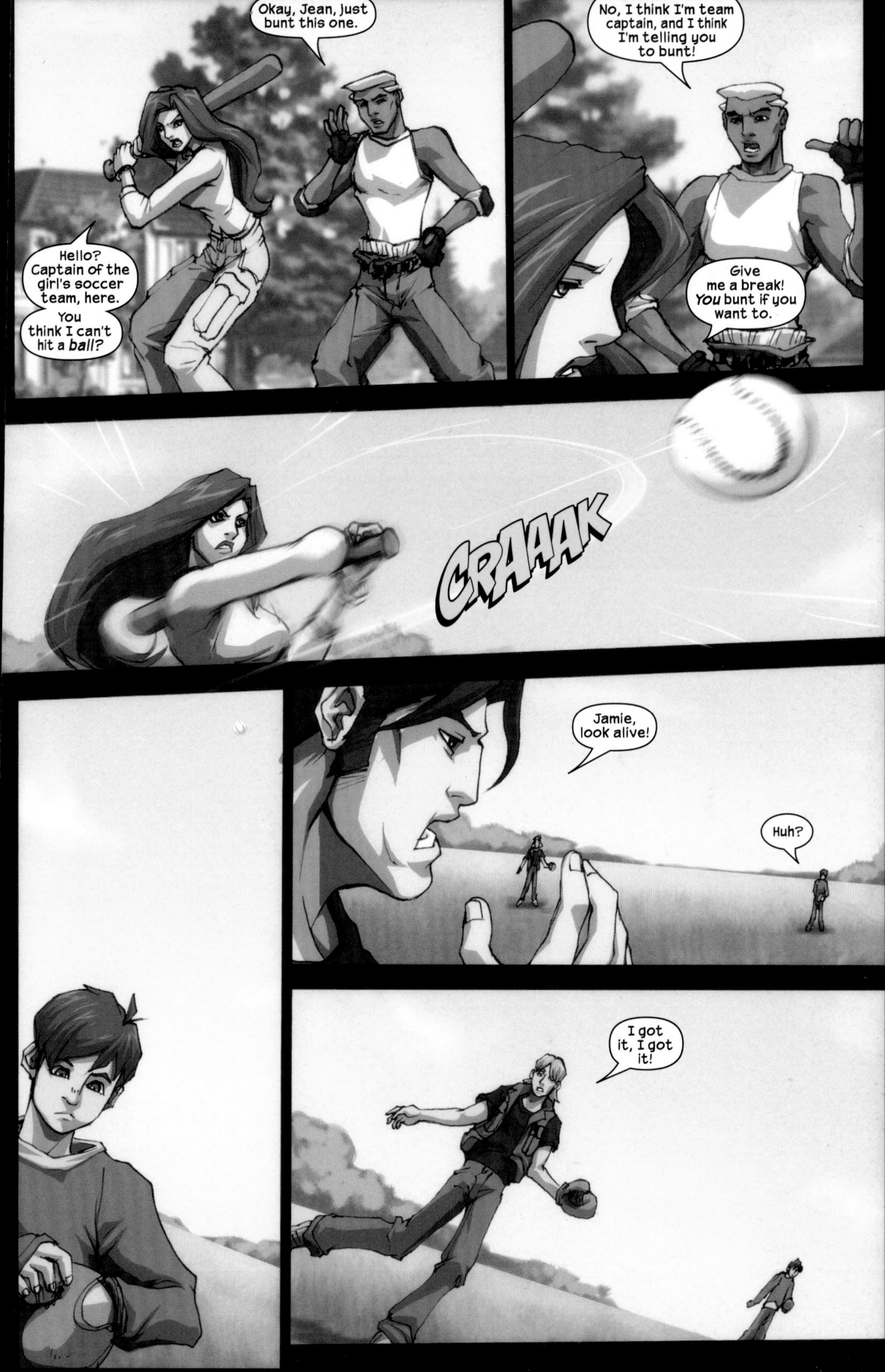
Okay, Jean, just bunt this one.
Hello? Captain of the girl's soccer team, here.
You think I can't hit a *ball*?
No, I think I'm team captain, and I think I'm telling you to bunt!
Give me a break! *You* bunt if you want to.
CRAAAK
Jamie, look alive!
Huh?
I got it, I got it!

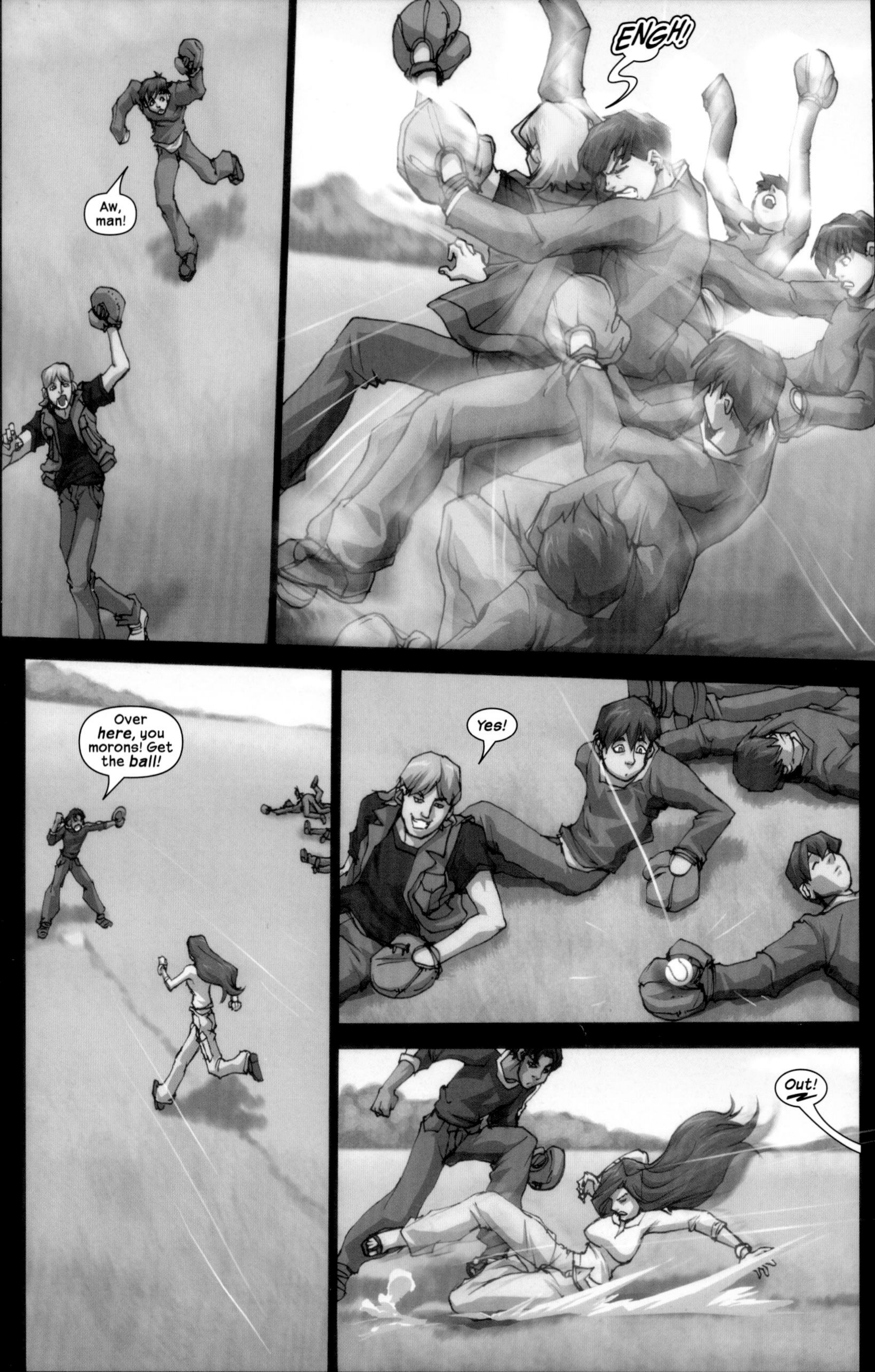
Aw, man!
ENGH!
Over here, you morons! Get the ball!
Yes!
Out!

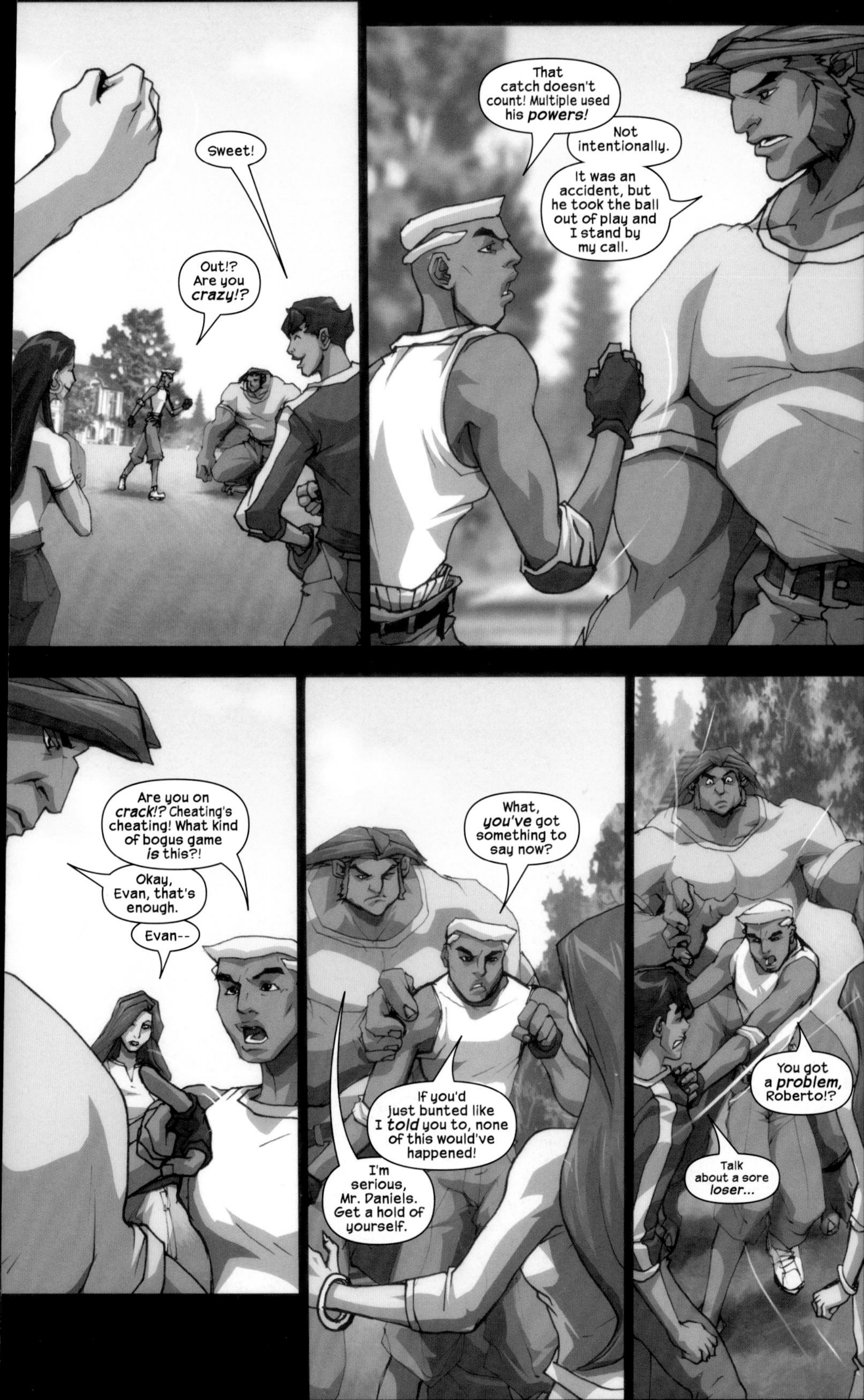
Sweet!
Out!? Are you *crazy!?*
That catch doesn't count! Multiple used his *powers!*
Not intentionally.
It was an accident, but he took the ball out of play and I stand by my call.
Are you on *crack!?* Cheating's cheating! What kind of bogus game *is* this?!
Okay, Evan, that's enough.
Evan--
What, *you've* got something to say now?
If you'd just bunted like I *told* you to, none of this would've happened!
I'm serious, Mr. Daniels. Get a hold of yourself.
You got a *problem,* Roberto!?
Talk about a sore *loser...*

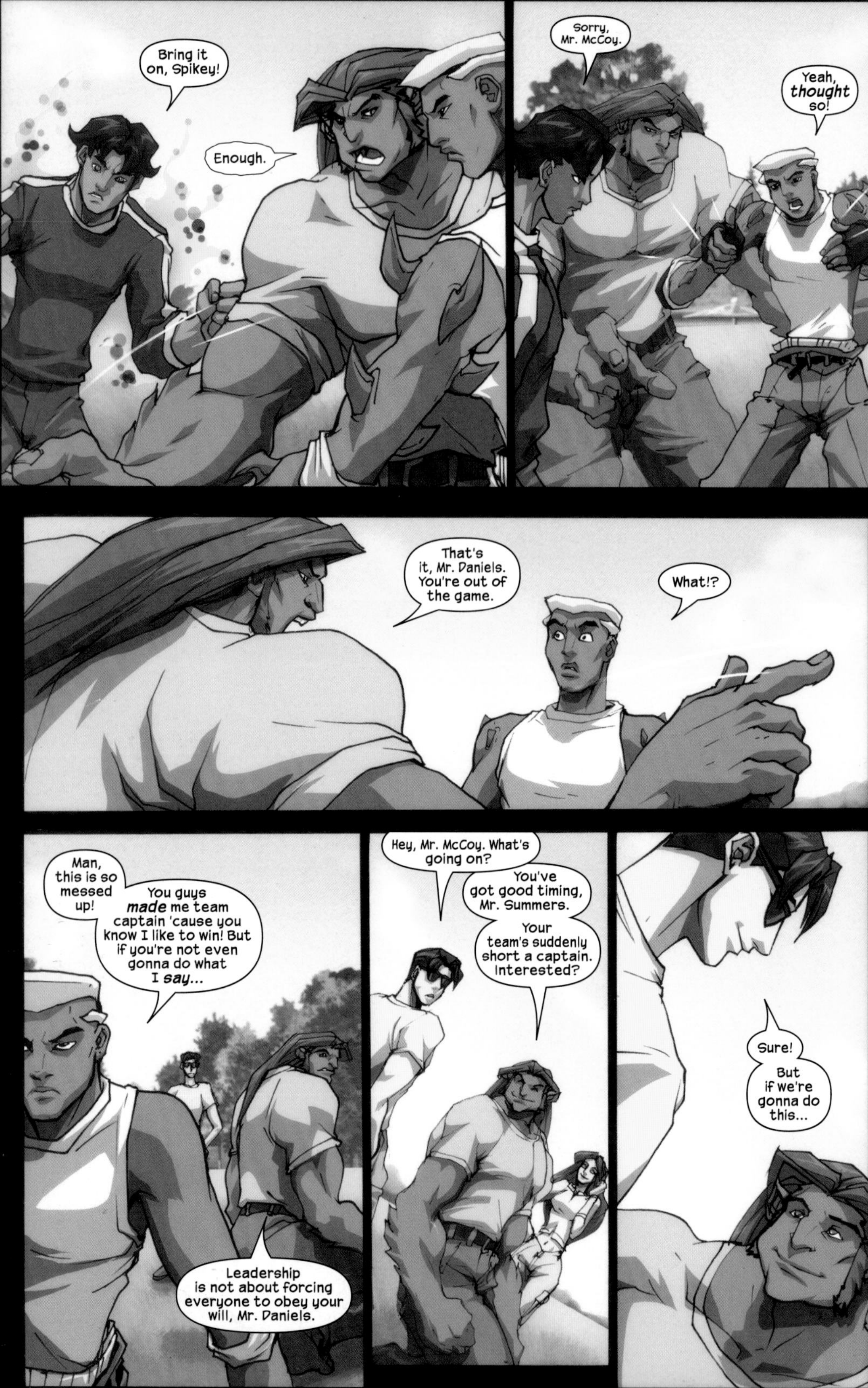
Bring it on, Spikey!
Enough.
Sorry, Mr. McCoy.
Yeah, *thought* so!
That's it, Mr. Daniels. You're out of the game.
What!?
Man, this is so messed up!
You guys *made* me team captain 'cause you know I like to win! But if you're not even gonna do what I *say*...
Leadership is not about forcing everyone to obey your will, Mr. Daniels.
Hey, Mr. McCoy. What's going on?
You've got good timing, Mr. Summers.
Your team's suddenly short a captain. Interested?
Sure!
But if we're gonna do this...

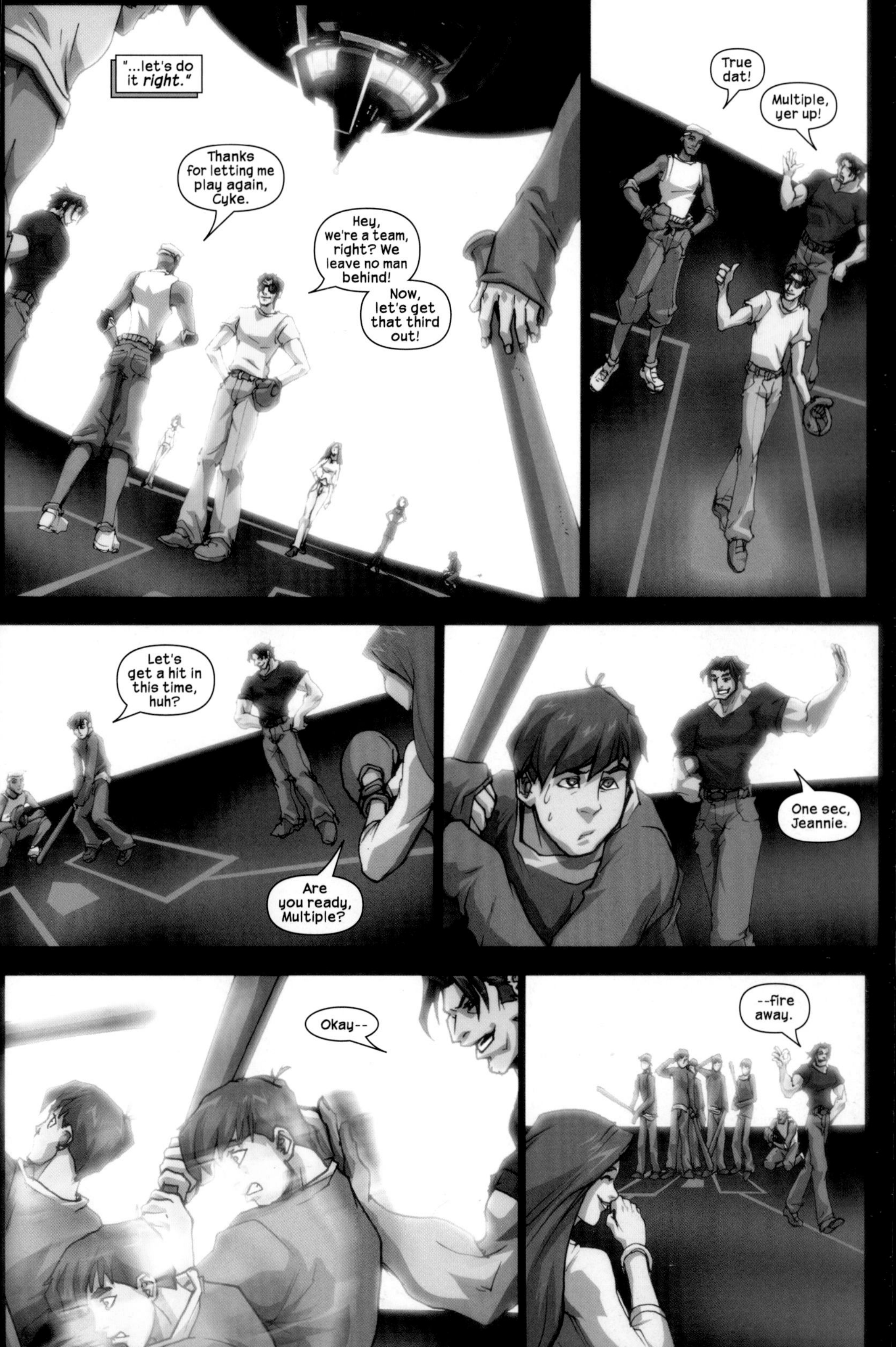
"...let's do it *right.*"
Thanks for letting me play again, Cyke.
Hey, we're a team, right? We leave no man behind!
Now, let's get that third out!
True dat!
Multiple, yer up!
Let's get a hit in this time, huh?
Are you ready, Multiple?
One sec, Jeannie.
Okay--
--fire away.

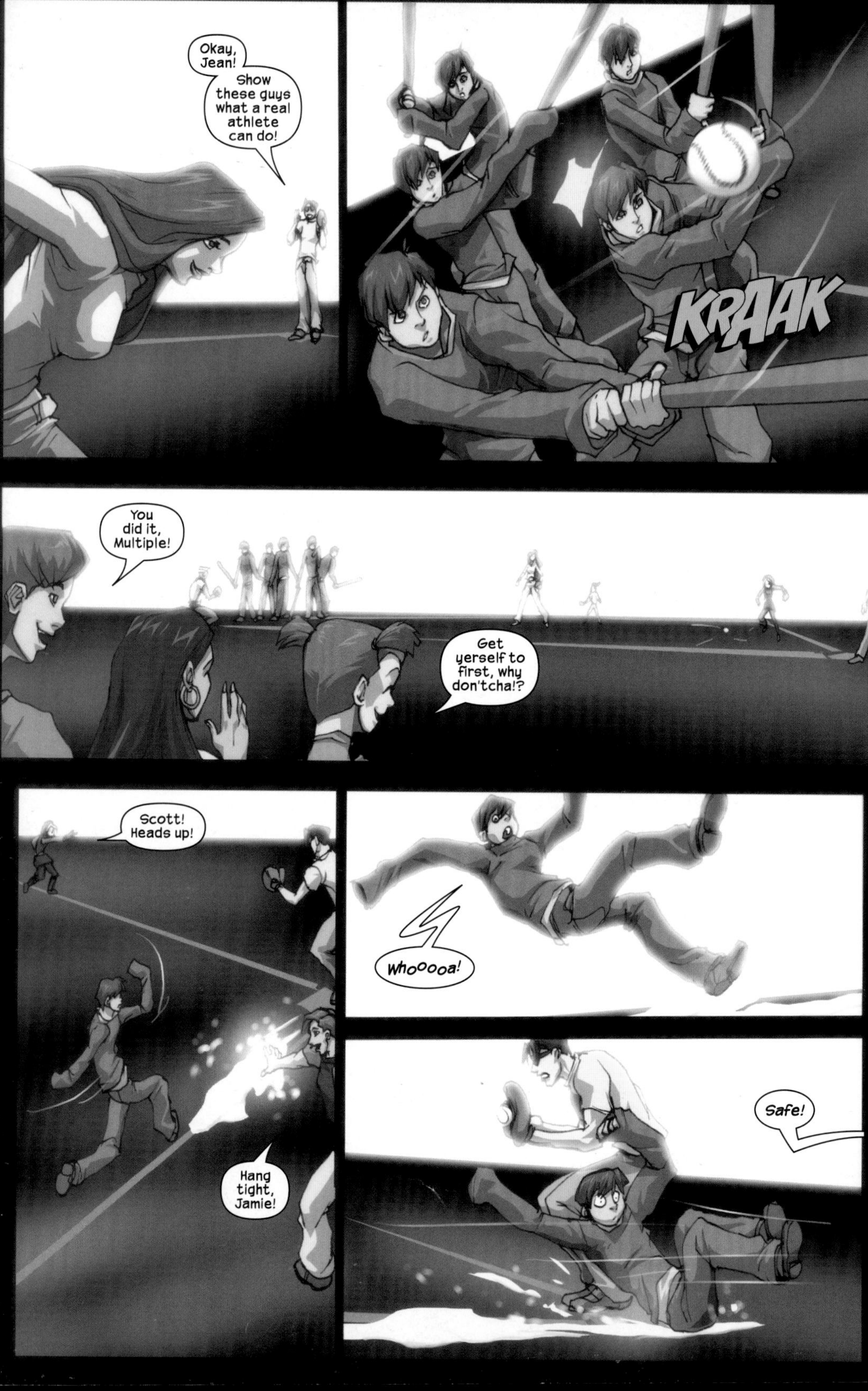
Okay, Jean!
Show these guys what a real athlete can do!
KRAAK
You did it, Multiple!
Get yerself to first, why don'tcha!?
Scott! Heads up!
Hang tight, Jamie!
Whoooooa!
Safe!

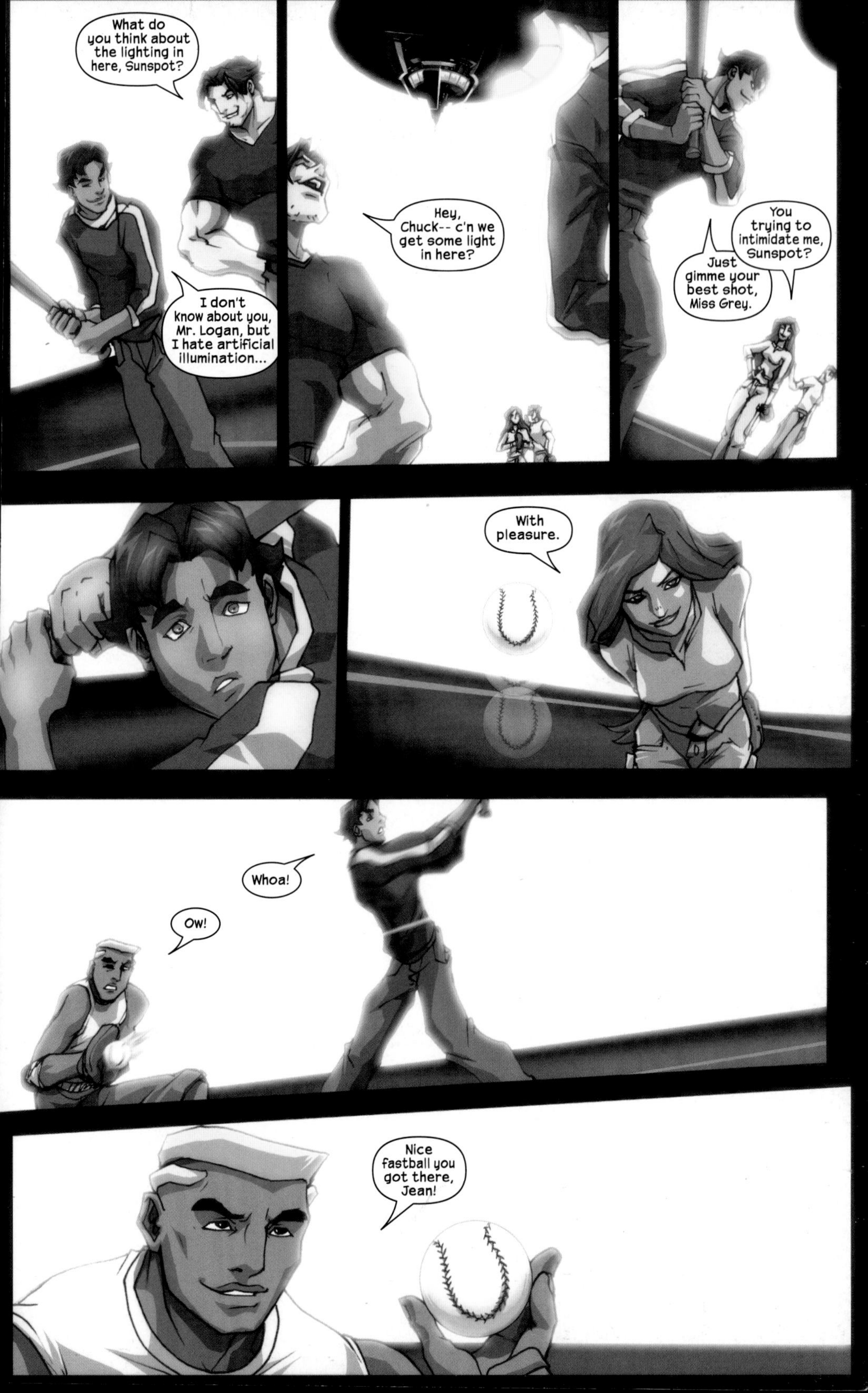
What do you think about the lighting in here, Sunspot?
I don't know about you, Mr. Logan, but I hate artificial illumination...
Hey, Chuck-- c'n we get some light in here?
You trying to intimidate me, Sunspot?
Just gimme your best shot, Miss Grey.
With pleasure.
Whoa!
Ow!
Nice fastball you got there, Jean!

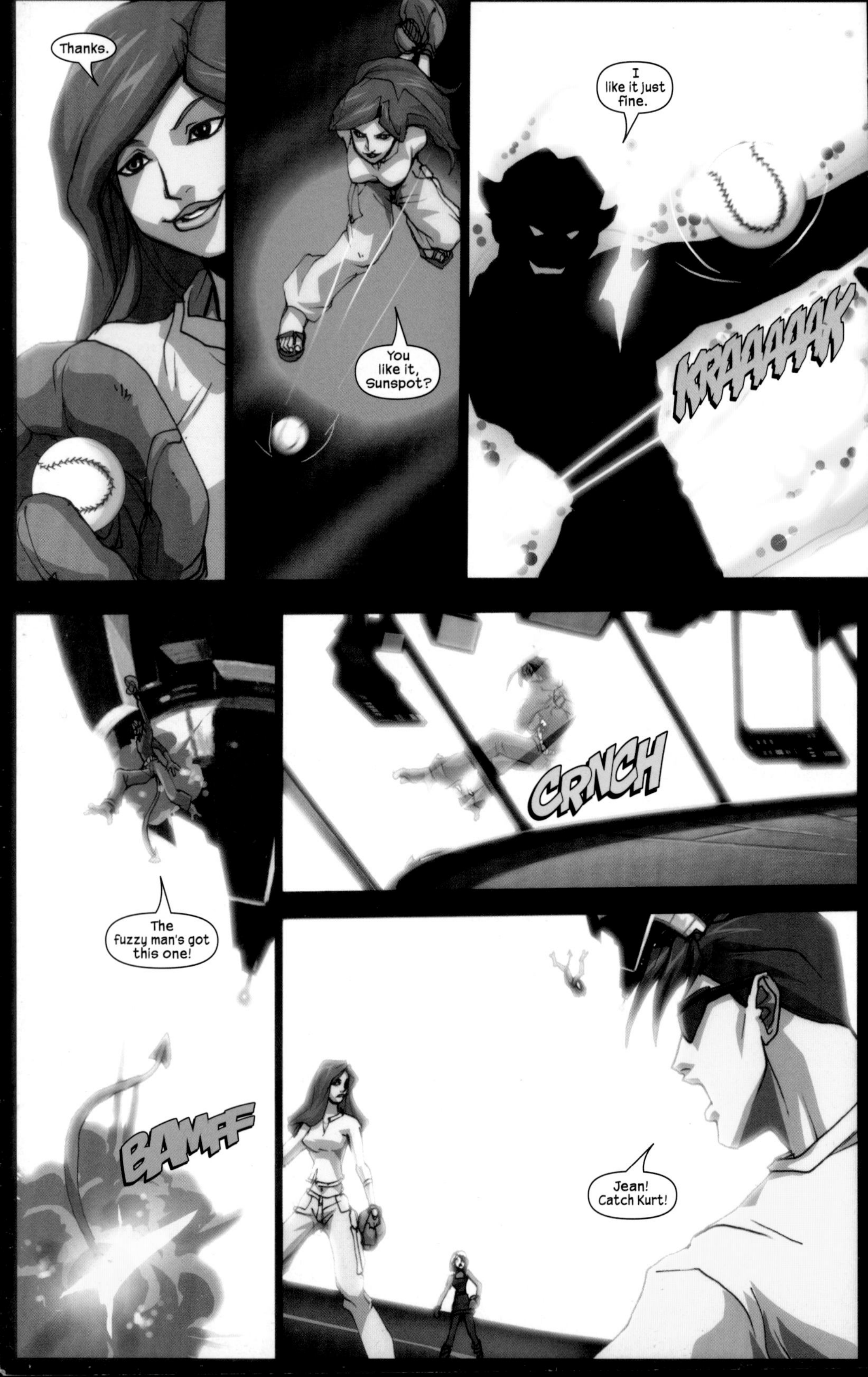
Thanks.
You like it, Sunspot?
I like it just fine.
KRAAAAAK
CRNCH
The fuzzy man's got this one!
BAMFF
Jean! Catch Kurt!

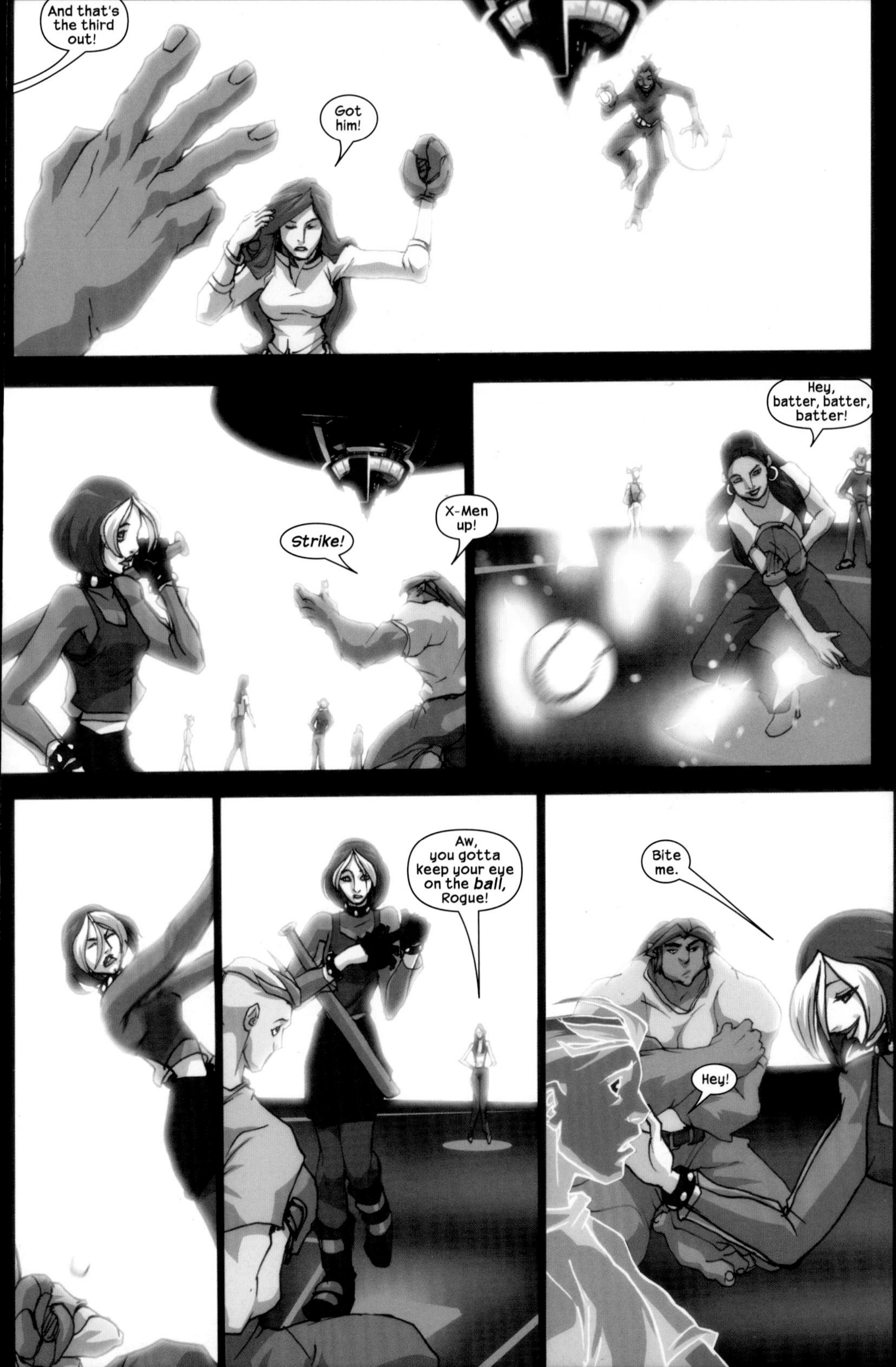

And that's the third out!
Got him!
Strike!
X-Men up!
Hey, batter, batter, batter!
Aw, you gotta keep your eye on the *ball,* Rogue!
Bite me.
Hey!

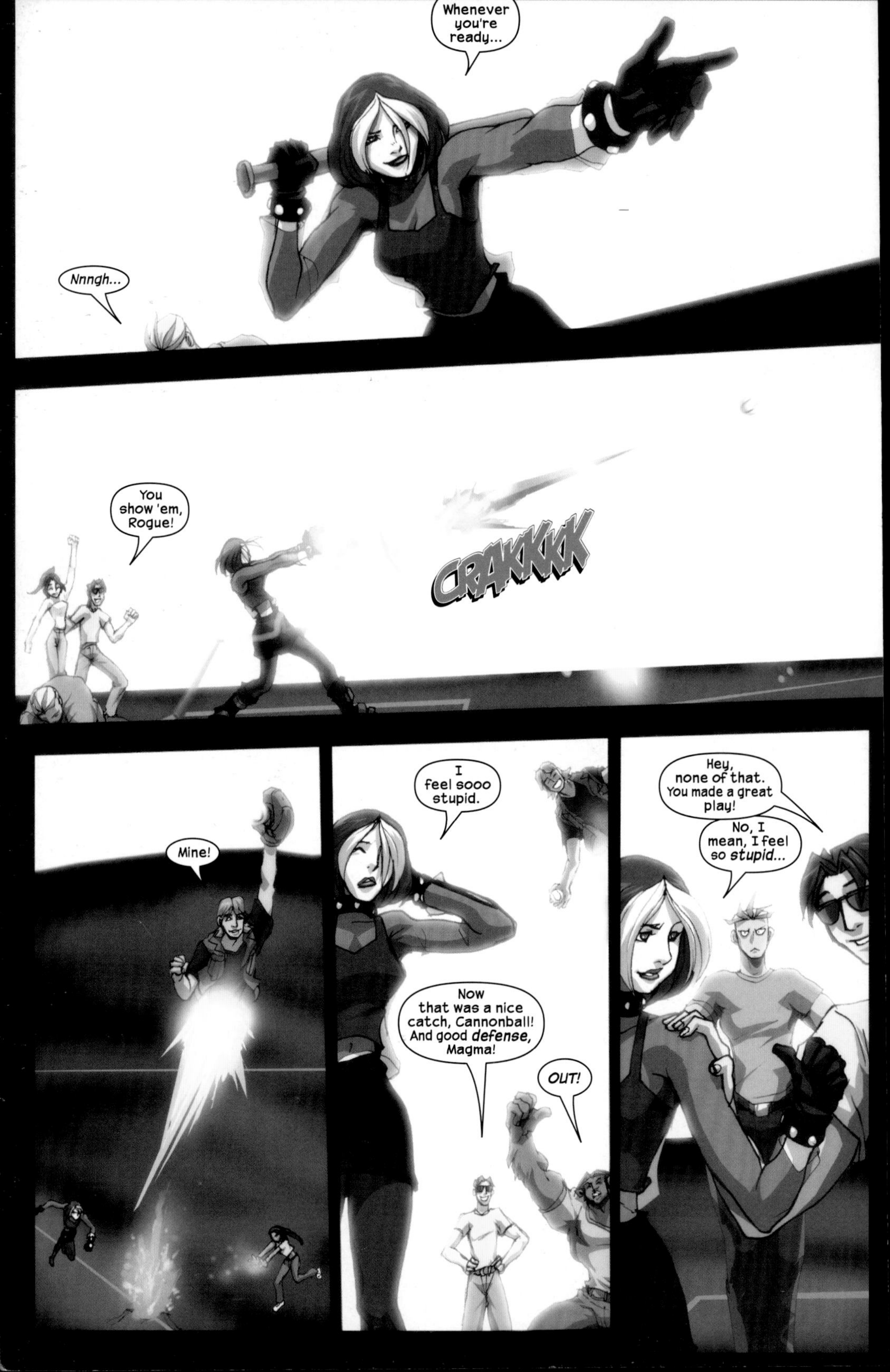
Whenever you're ready...
Nnngh...
You show 'em, Rogue!
CRAKKKK
Mine!
I feel sooo stupid.
Now that was a nice catch, Cannonball! And good *defense*, Magma!
OUT!
Hey, none of that. You made a great play!
No, I mean, I feel so *stupid*...

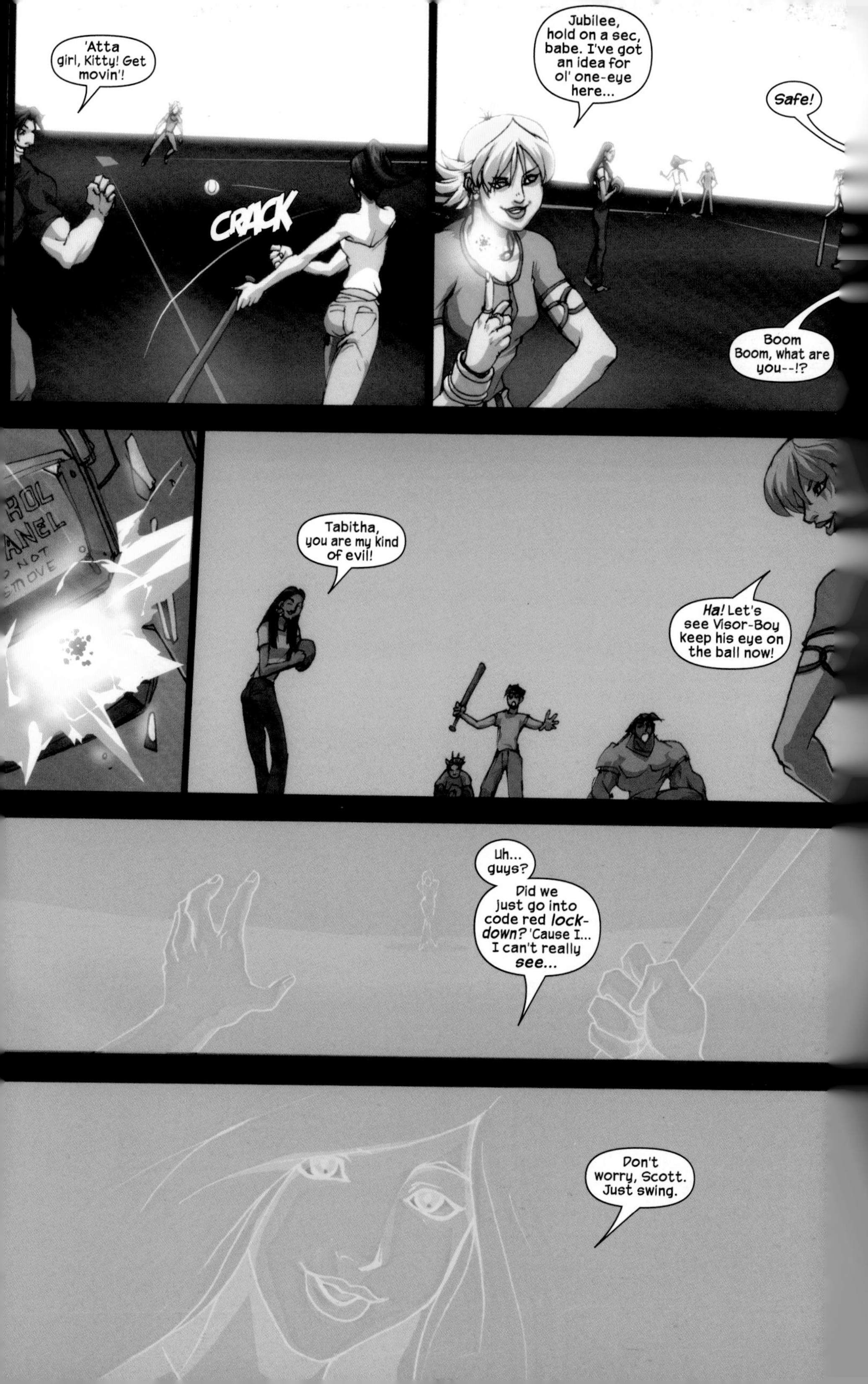
'Atta girl, Kitty! Get movin'!
CRACK
Jubilee, hold on a sec, babe. I've got an idea for ol' one-eye here...
Safe!
Boom Boom, what are you--!?
ROL
ANEL
O NOT
EMOVE
Tabitha, you are my kind of evil!
Ha! Let's see Visor-Boy keep his eye on the ball now!
Uh... guys?
Did we just go into code red lock-down? 'Cause I... I can't really see...
Don't worry, Scott. Just swing.

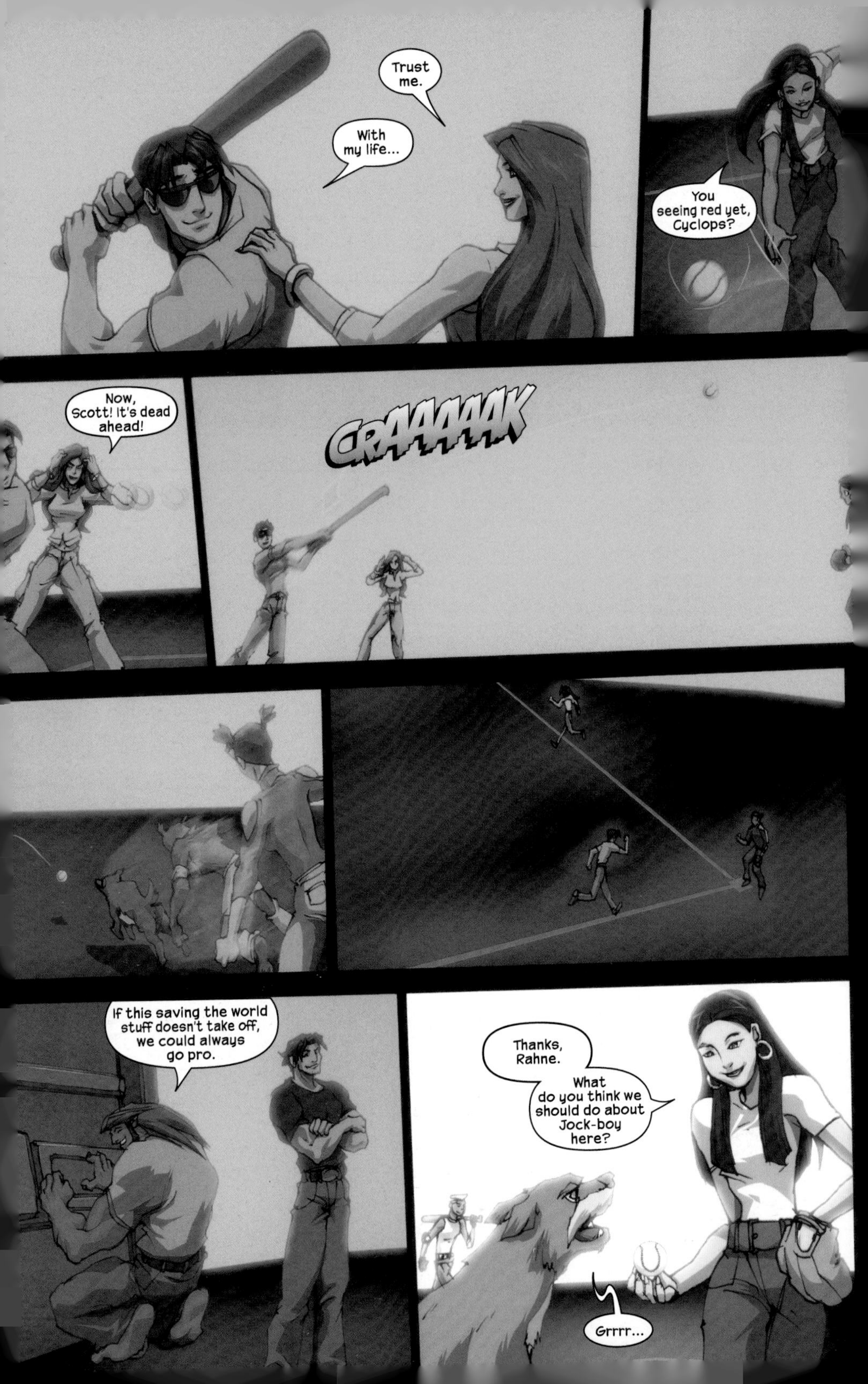
Trust me.
With my life...
You seeing red yet, Cyclops?
Now, Scott! It's dead ahead!
CRAAAAAK
If this saving the world stuff doesn't take off, we could always go pro.
Thanks, Rahne.
What do you think we should do about Jock-boy here?
Grrrr...

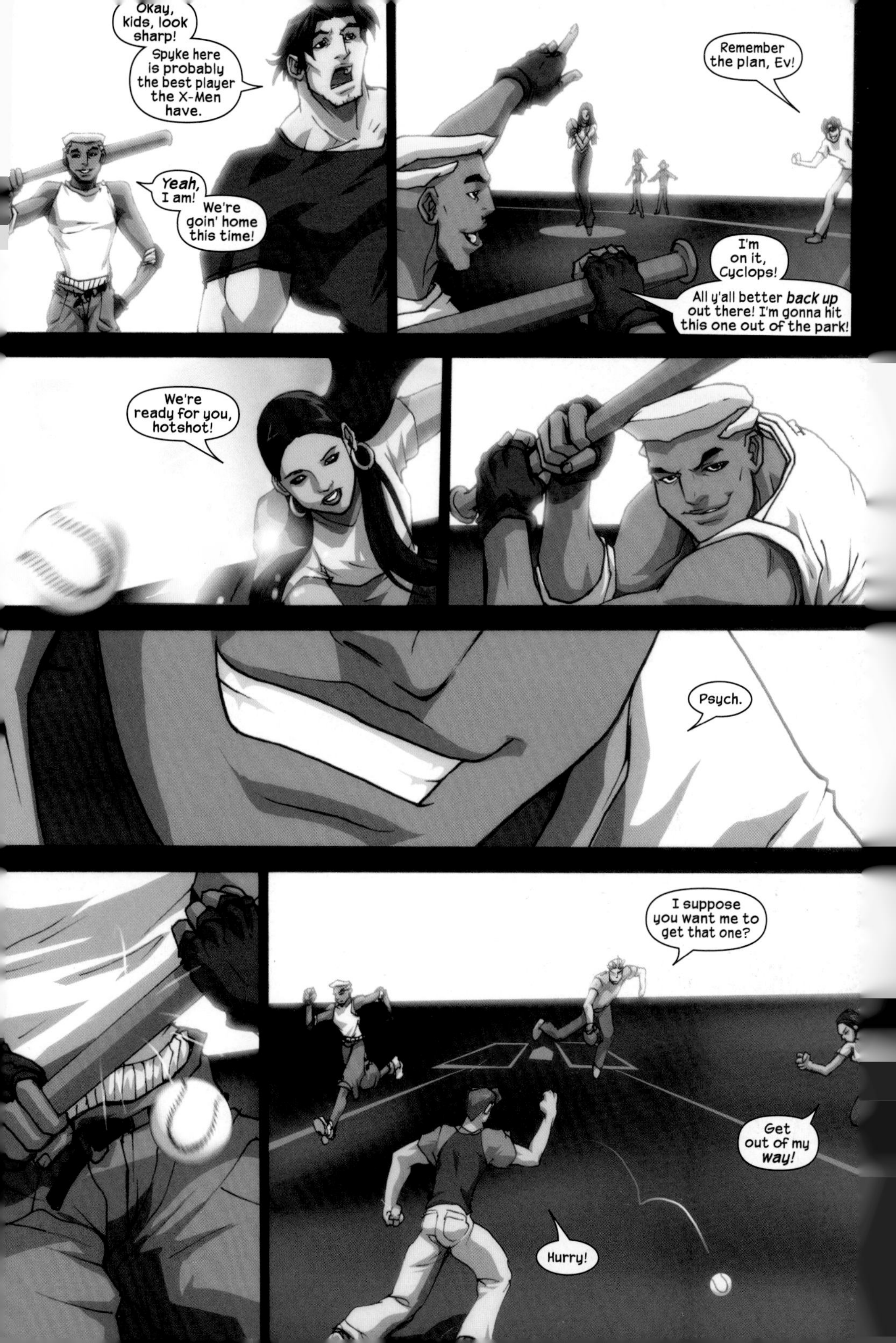
Okay, kids, look sharp!
Spyke here is probably the best player the X-Men have.
Yeah, I am!
We're goin' home this time!
Remember the plan, Ev!
I'm on it, Cyclops!
All y'all better back up out there! I'm gonna hit this one out of the park!
We're ready for you, hotshot!
Psych.
I suppose you want me to get that one?
Get out of my way!
Hurry!

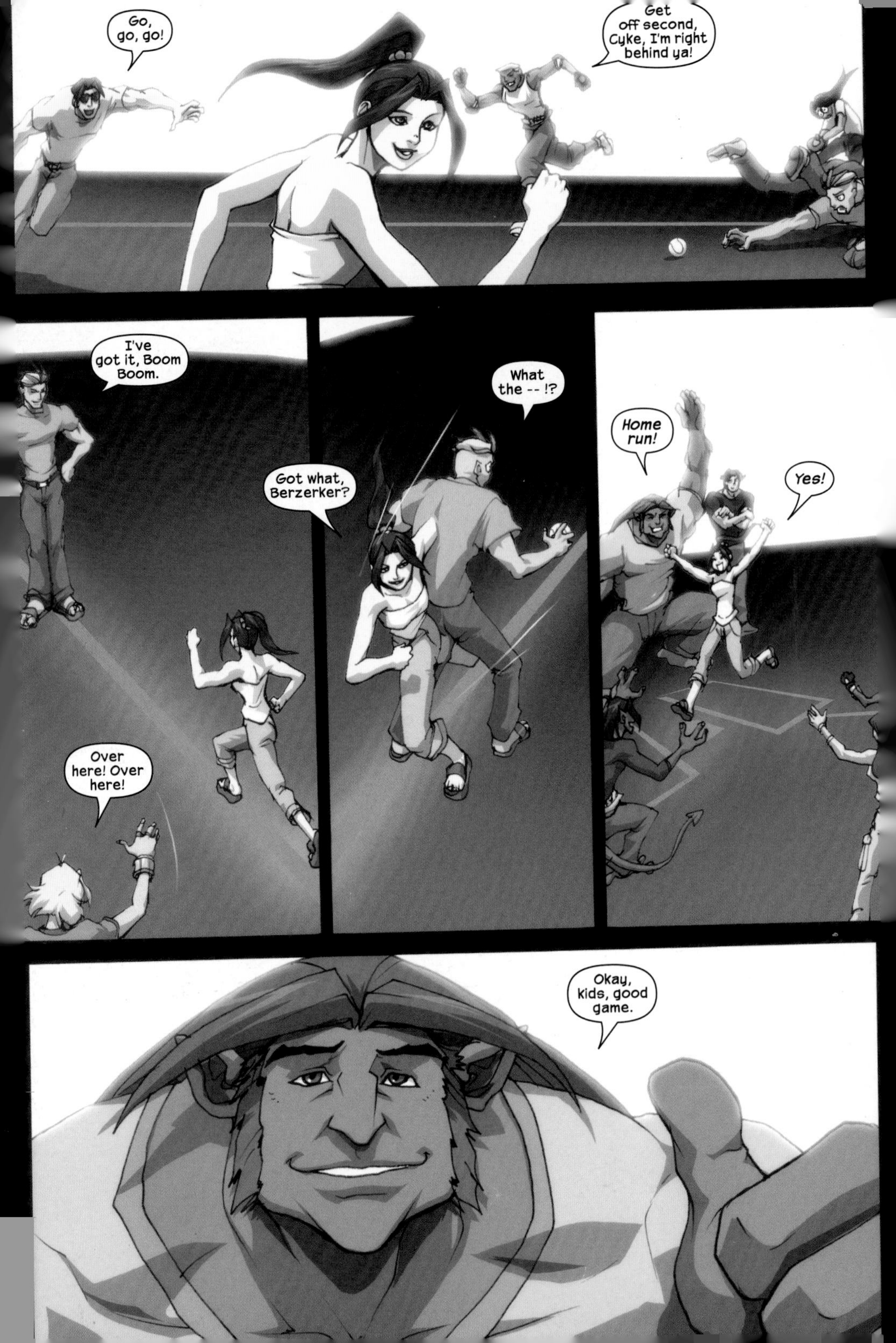
Go, go, go!
Get off second, Cyke, I'm right behind ya!
I've got it, Boom Boom.
Over here! Over here!
Got what, Berzerker?
What the -- !?
Home run!
Yes!
Okay, kids, good game.

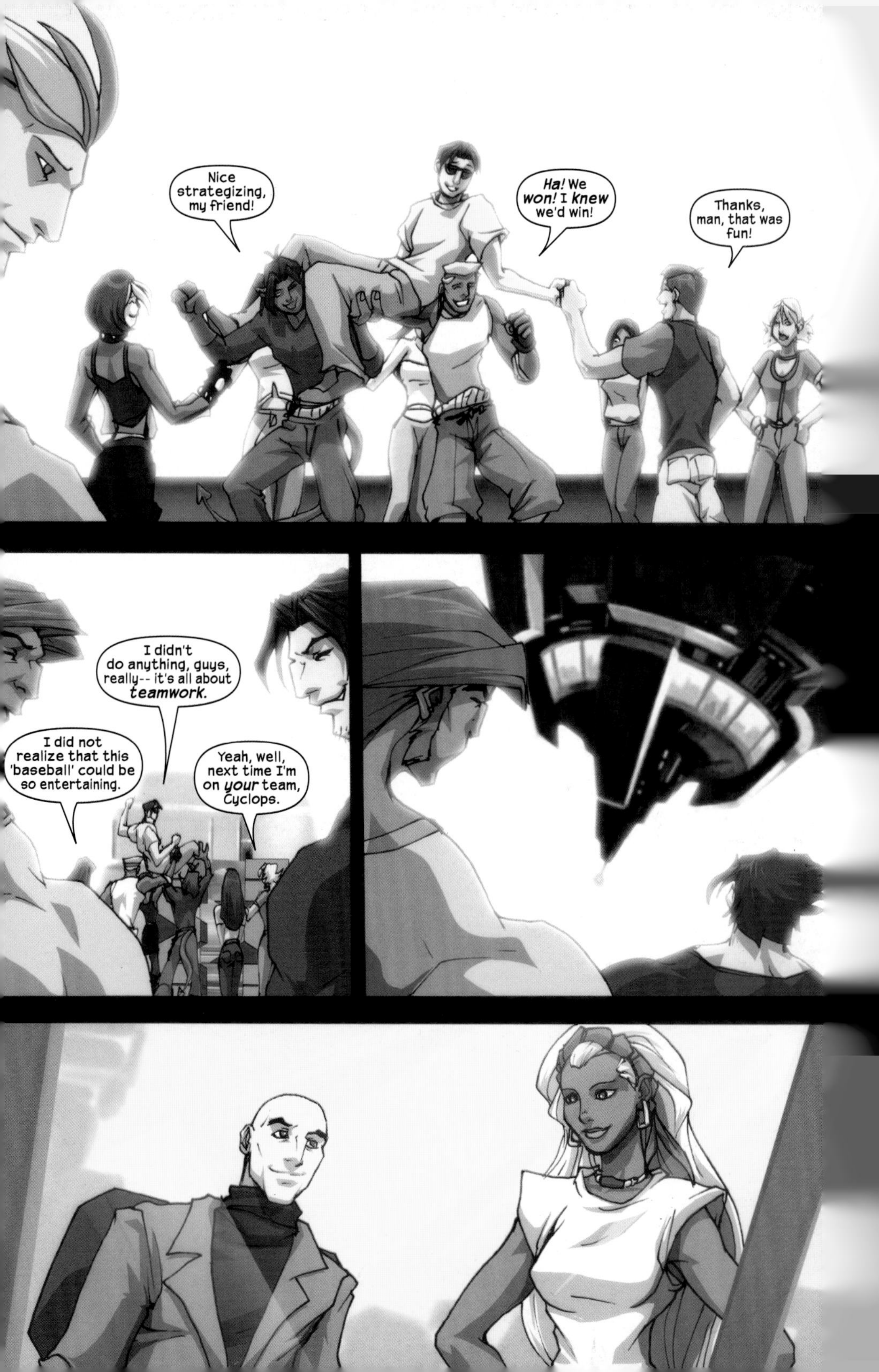
Nice strategizing, my friend!
Ha! We won! I knew we'd win!
Thanks, man, that was fun!
I didn't do anything, guys, really-- it's all about teamwork.
I did not realize that this 'baseball' could be so entertaining.
Yeah, well, next time I'm on your team, Cyclops.

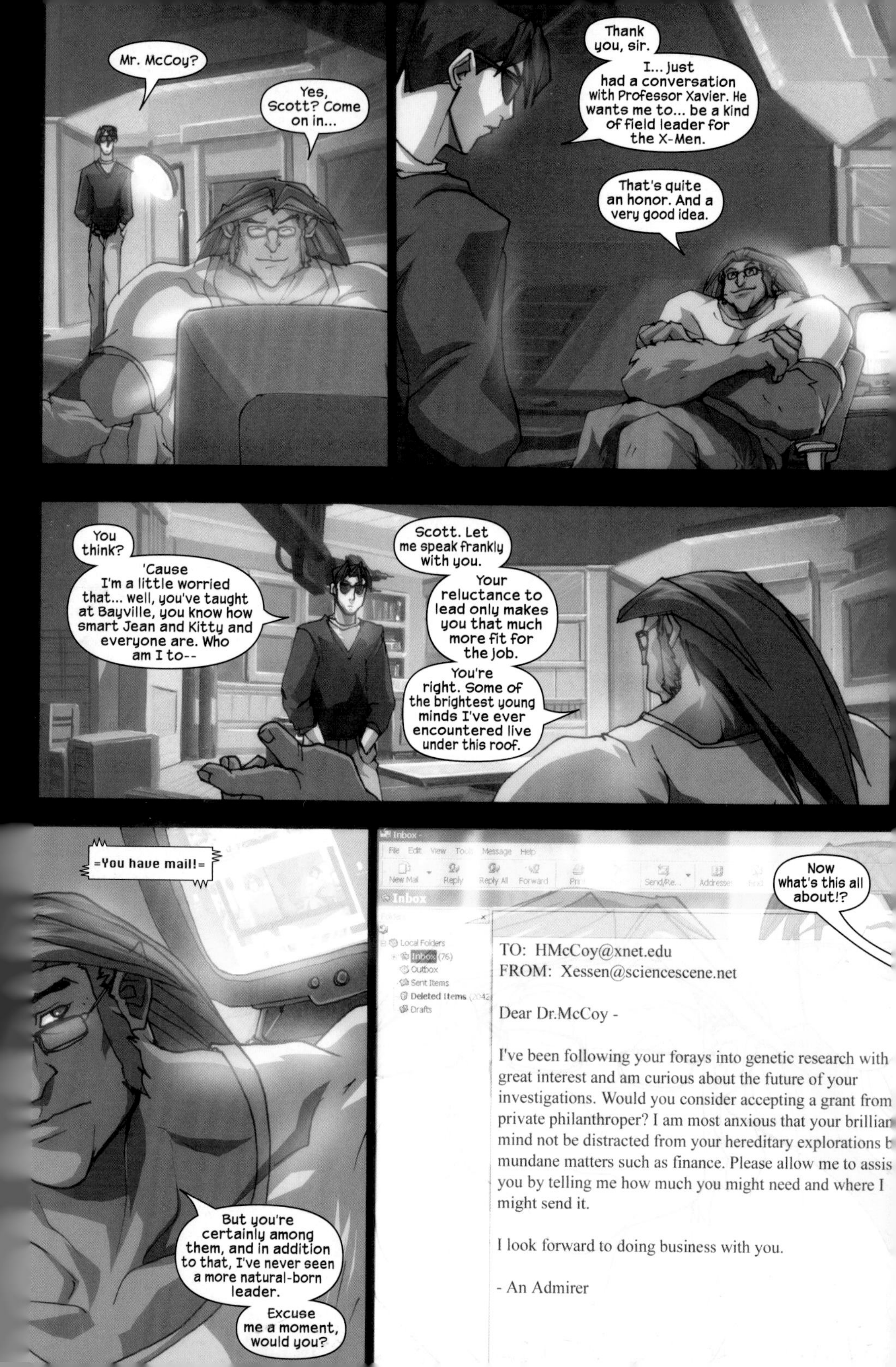
Mr. McCoy?
Yes, Scott? Come on in...
Thank you, sir.
I... just had a conversation with Professor Xavier. He wants me to... be a kind of field leader for the X-Men.
That's quite an honor. And a very good idea.
You think?
'Cause I'm a little worried that... well, you've taught at Bayville, you know how smart Jean and Kitty and everyone are. Who am I to--
Scott. Let me speak frankly with you.
Your reluctance to lead only makes you that much more fit for the job.
You're right. Some of the brightest young minds I've ever encountered live under this roof.
=You have mail!=
But you're certainly among them, and in addition to that, I've never seen a more natural-born leader.
Excuse me a moment, would you?
Inbox
File Edit View Message Help
New Mail Reply Reply All Forward Send/Re... Addresses
Inbox
Local Folders
Inbox (76)
Outbox
Sent Items
Deleted Items
Drafts
TO: HMcCoy@xnet.edu
FROM: Xessen@sciencescene.net
Dear Dr.McCoy -
I've been following your forays into genetic research with great interest and am curious about the future of your investigations. Would you consider accepting a grant from private philanthroper? I am most anxious that your brillian mind not be distracted from your hereditary explorations b mundane matters such as finance. Please allow me to assis you by telling me how much you might need and where I might send it.
I look forward to doing business with you.
- An Admirer
Now what's this all about!?

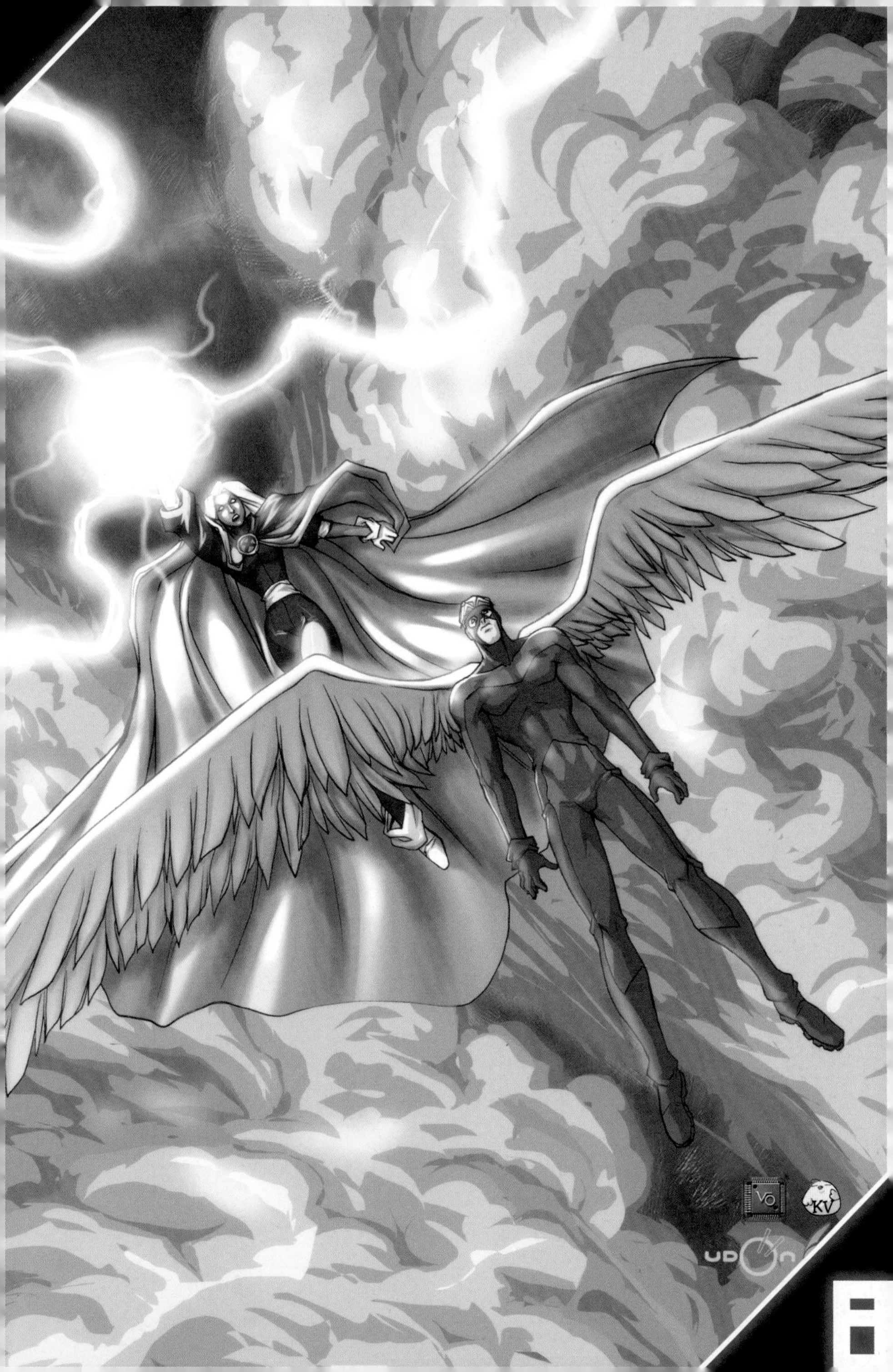

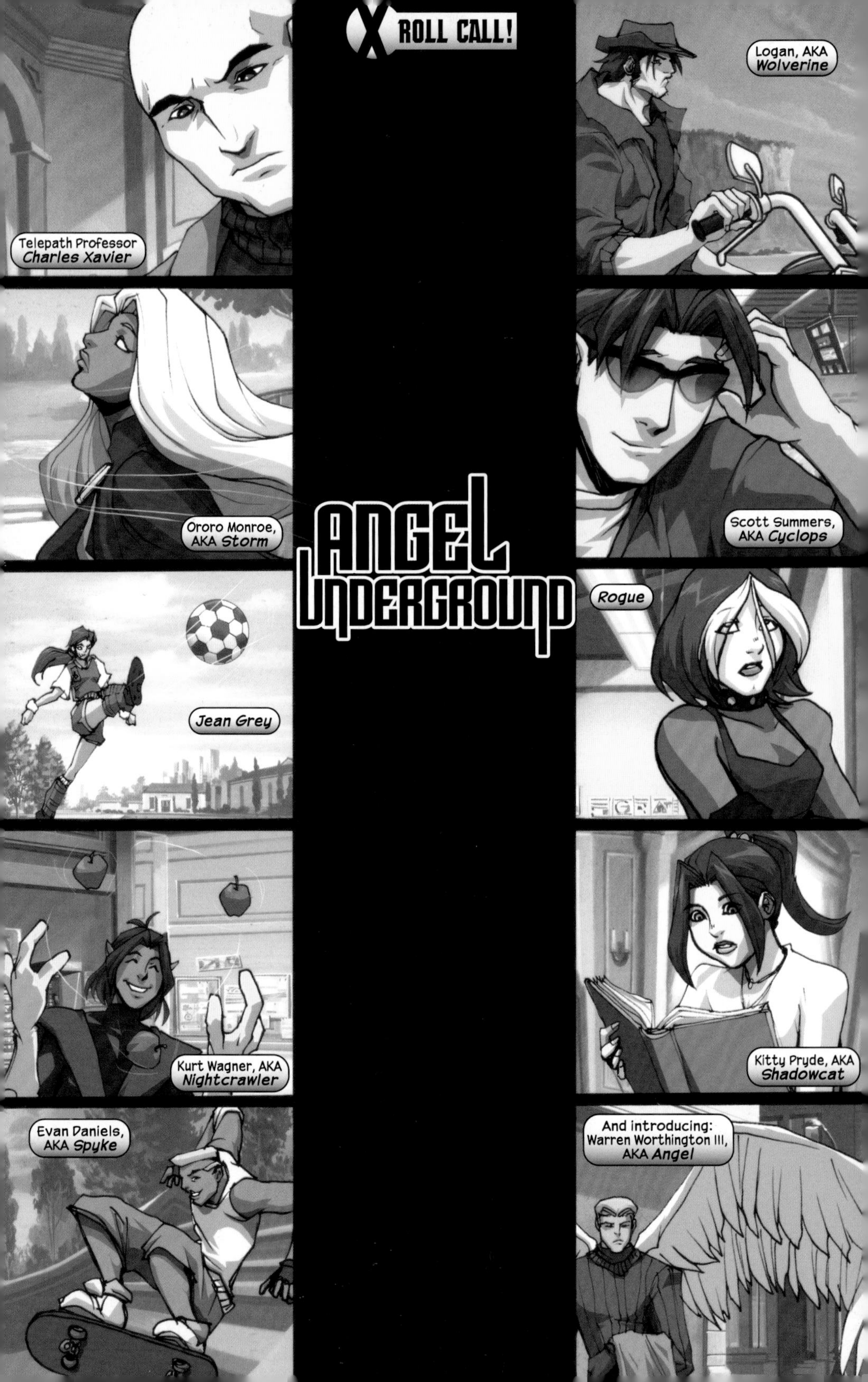

ROLL CALL!
Telepath Professor Charles Xavier
Logan, AKA Wolverine
Ororo Monroe, AKA Storm
Scott Summers, AKA Cyclops
ANGEL UNDERGROUND
Jean Grey
Rogue
Kurt Wagner, AKA Nightcrawler
Kitty Pryde, AKA Shadowcat
Evan Daniels, AKA Spyke
And introducing: Warren Worthington III, AKA Angel

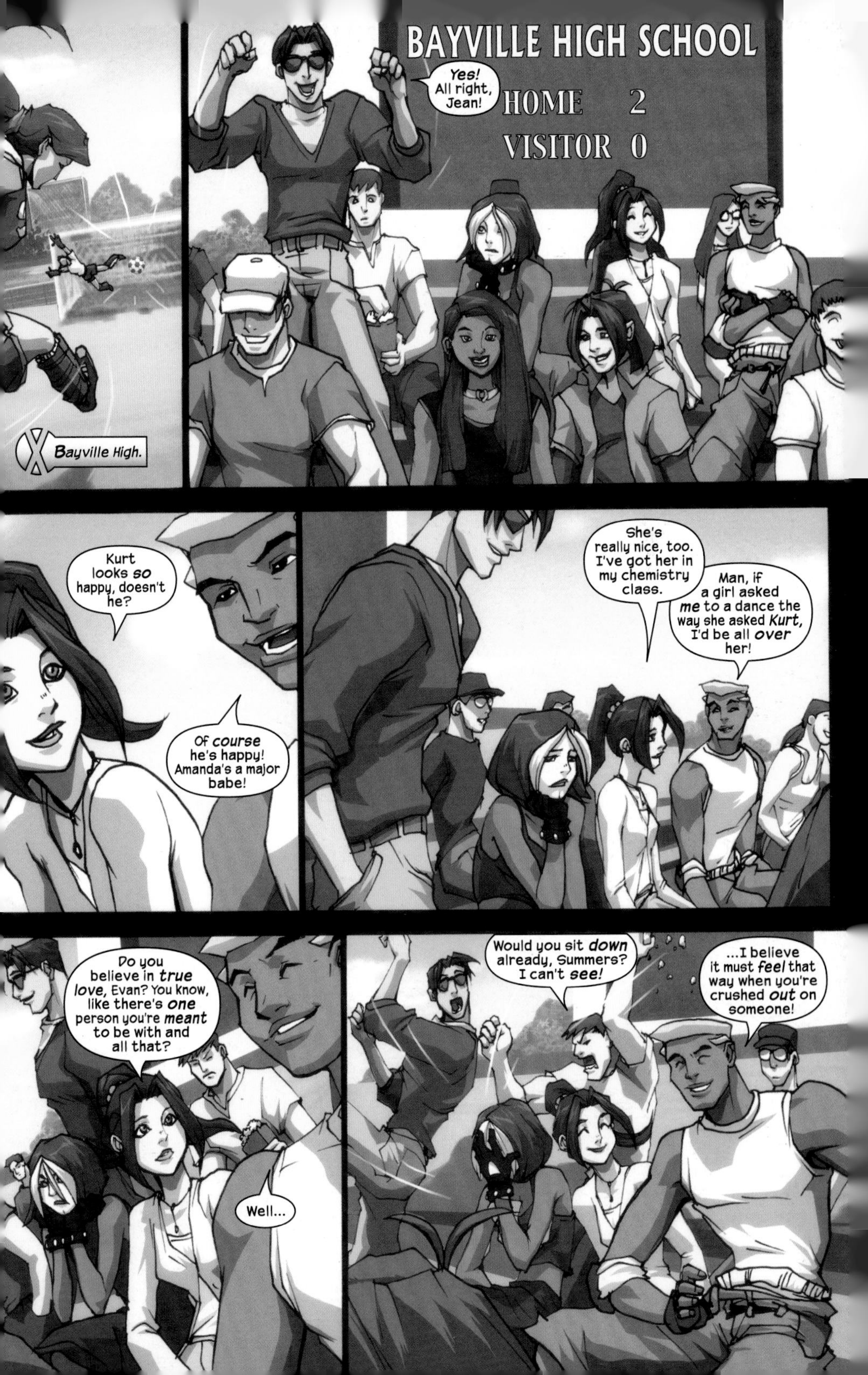

Bayville High.
BAYVILLE HIGH SCHOOL
HOME 2
VISITOR 0
Yes! All right, Jean!
Kurt looks so happy, doesn't he?
Of course he's happy! Amanda's a major babe!
She's really nice, too. I've got her in my chemistry class.
Man, if a girl asked me to a dance the way she asked Kurt, I'd be all over her!
Do you believe in true love, Evan? You know, like there's one person you're meant to be with and all that?
Well...
Would you sit down already, Summers? I can't see!
...I believe it must feel that way when you're crushed out on someone!

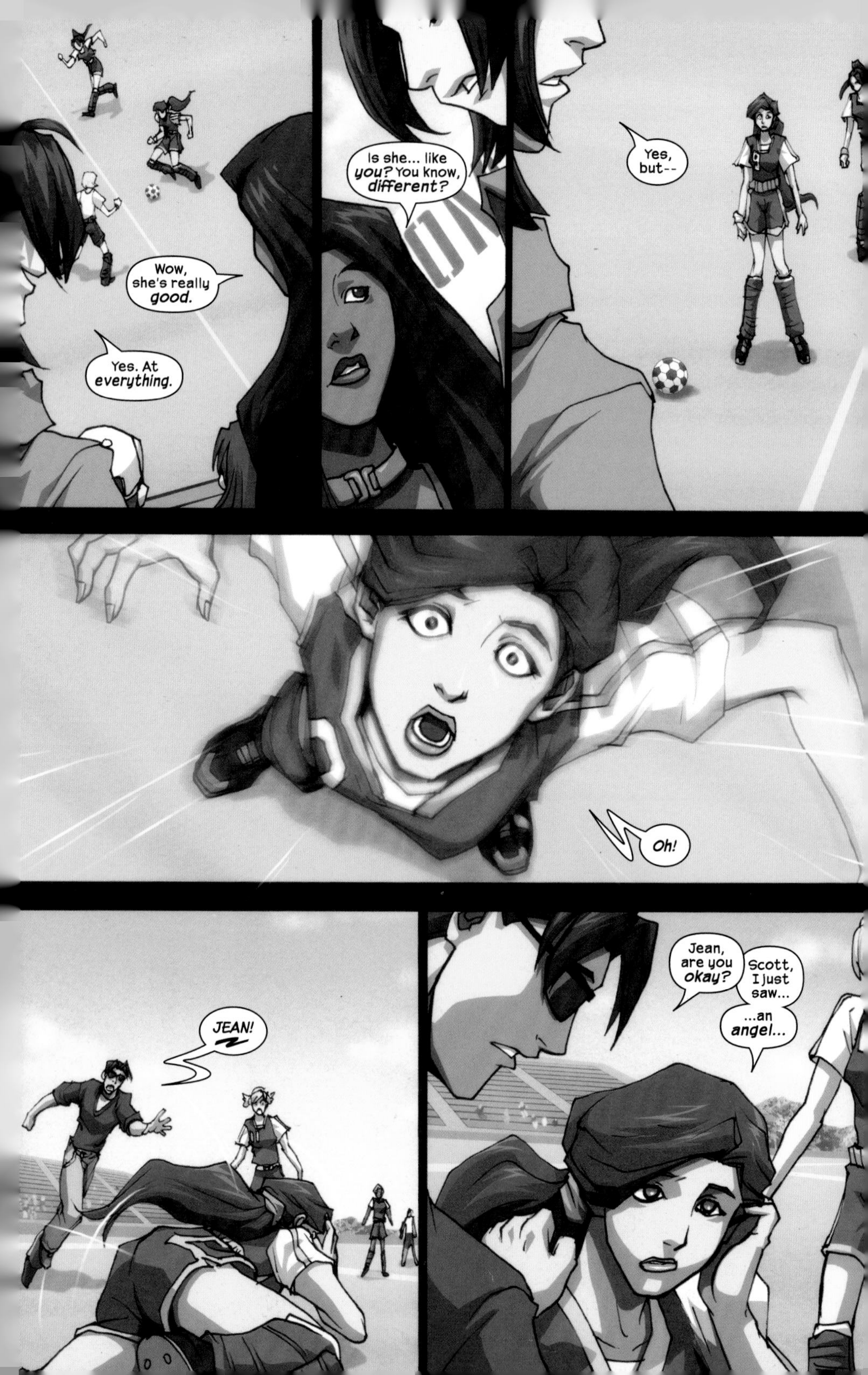
Wow, she's really good.
Yes. At everything.
Is she... like you? You know, different?
Yes, but--
Oh!
JEAN!
Jean, are you okay?
Scott, I just saw...
...an angel...

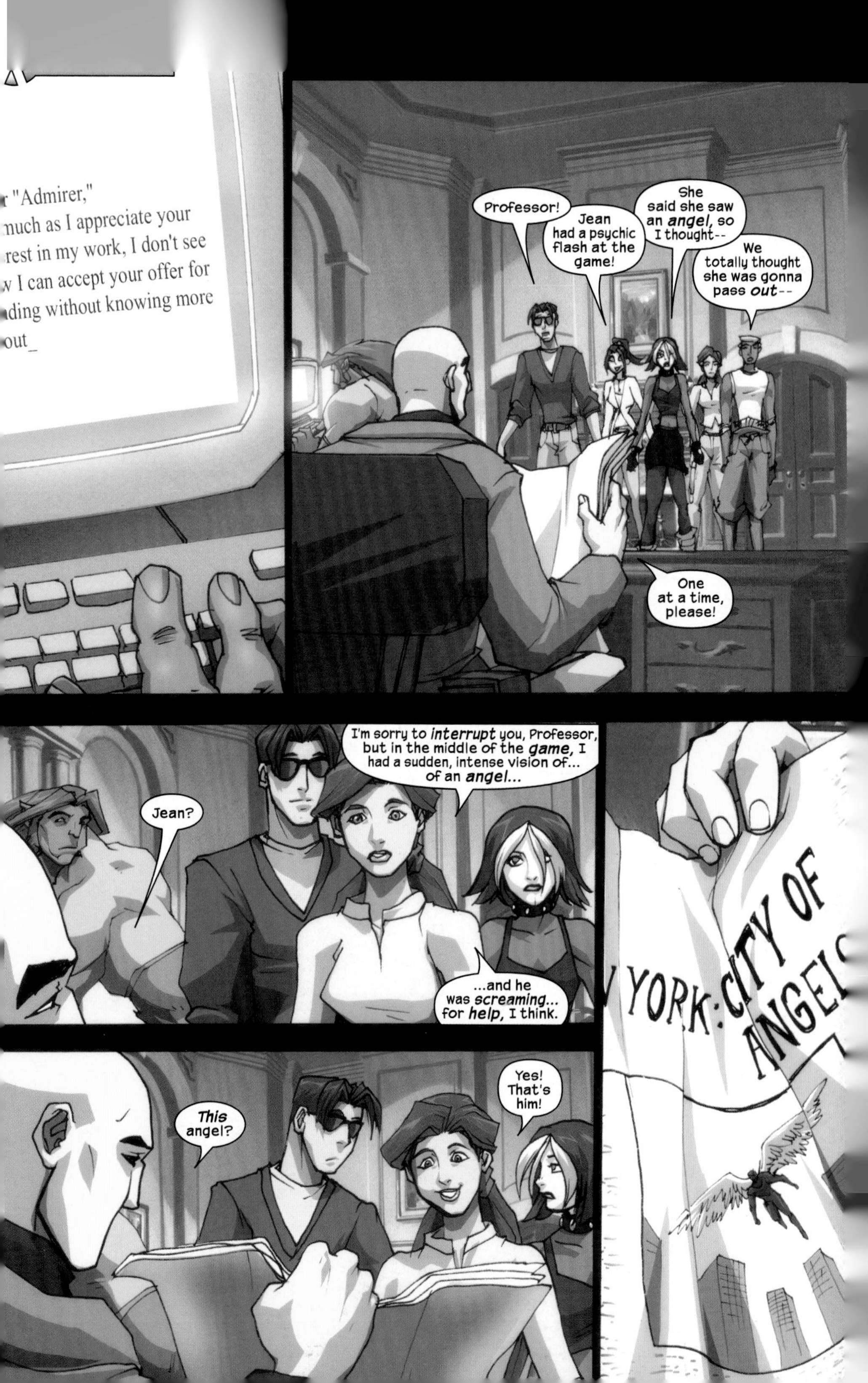
"Admirer,"
much as I appreciate your
rest in my work, I don't see
w I can accept your offer for
ding without knowing more
out_
Professor!
Jean had a psychic flash at the game!
She said she saw an *angel*, so I thought--
We totally thought she was gonna pass *out*--
One at a time, please!
Jean?
I'm sorry to *interrupt* you, Professor, but in the middle of the *game*, I had a sudden, intense vision of... of an *angel*...
...and he was *screaming*... for *help*, I think.
This angel?
Yes! That's him!
YORK: CITY OF ANGELS

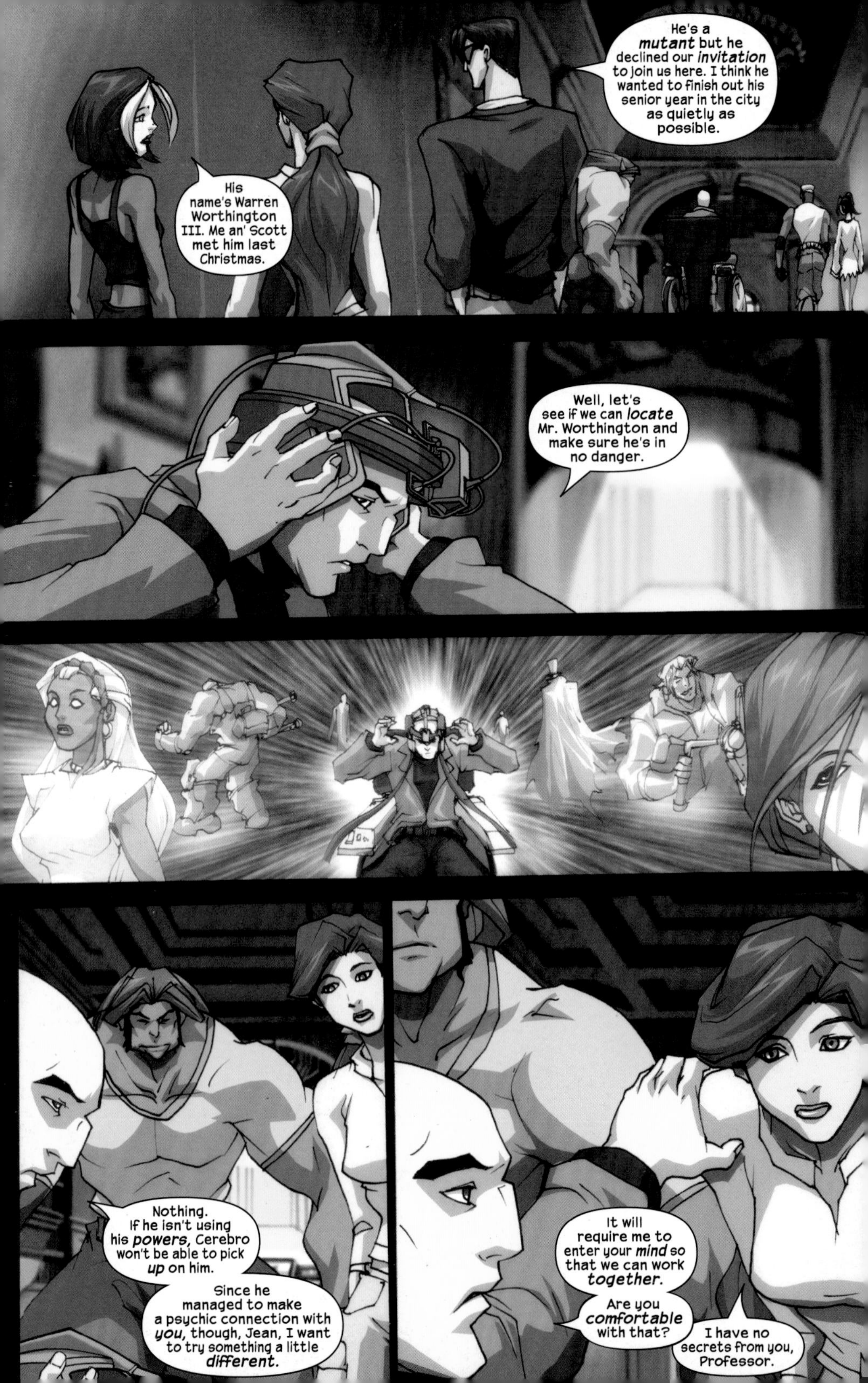
He's a *mutant* but he declined our *invitation* to join us here. I think he wanted to finish out his senior year in the city as quietly as possible.
His name's Warren Worthington III. Me an' Scott met him last Christmas.
Well, let's see if we can *locate* Mr. Worthington and make sure he's in no danger.
Nothing. If he isn't using his *powers*, Cerebro won't be able to pick *up* on him.
Since he managed to make a psychic connection with *you*, though, Jean, I want to try something a little *different.*
It will require me to enter your *mind* so that we can work *together.*
Are you *comfortable* with that?
I have no secrets from you, Professor.

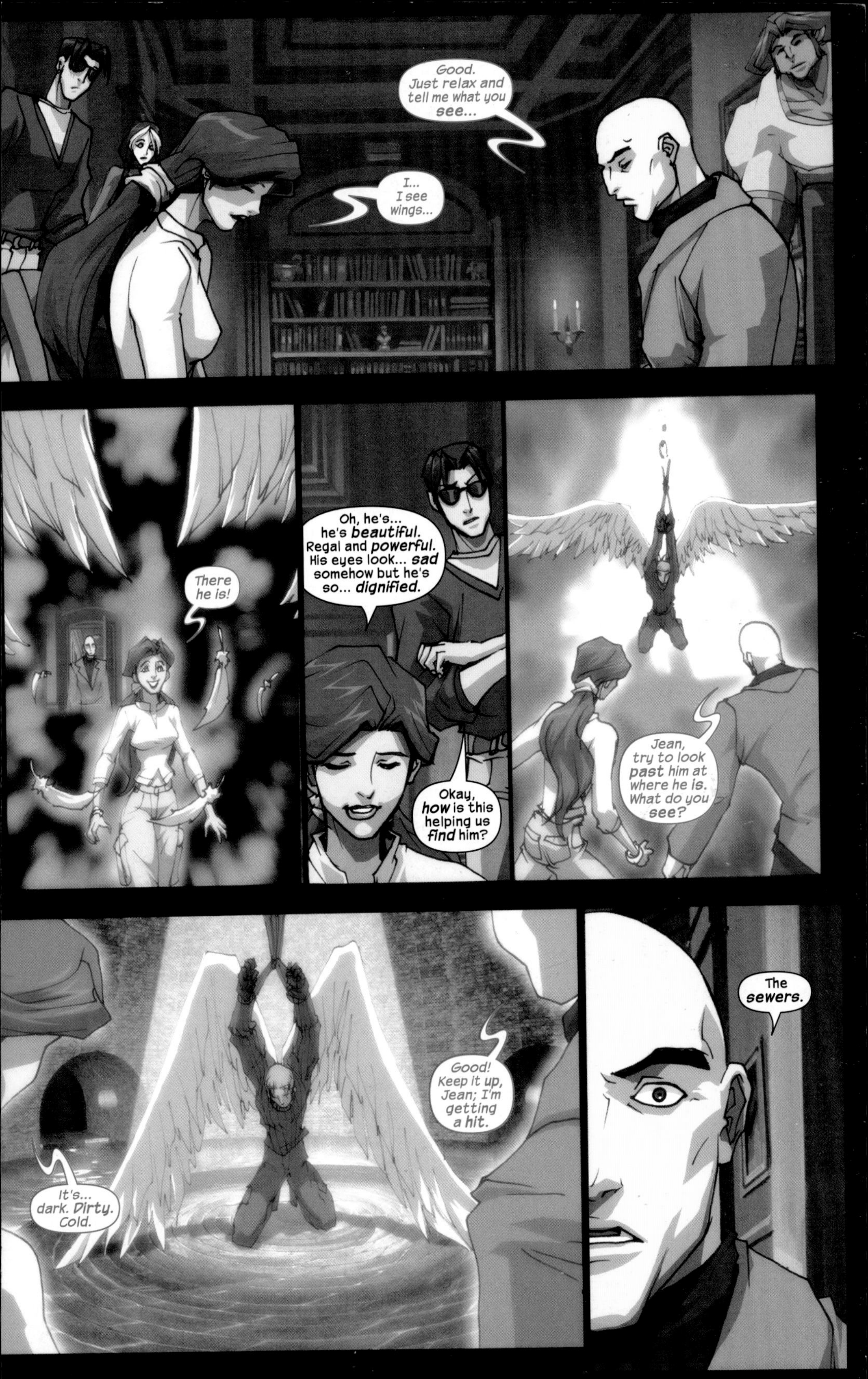
Good. Just relax and tell me what you see...
I... I see wings...
There he is!
Oh, he's... he's beautiful. Regal and powerful. His eyes look... sad somehow but he's so... dignified.
Okay, how is this helping us find him?
Jean, try to look past him at where he is. What do you see?
It's... dark. Dirty. Cold.
Good! Keep it up, Jean; I'm getting a hit.
The sewers.

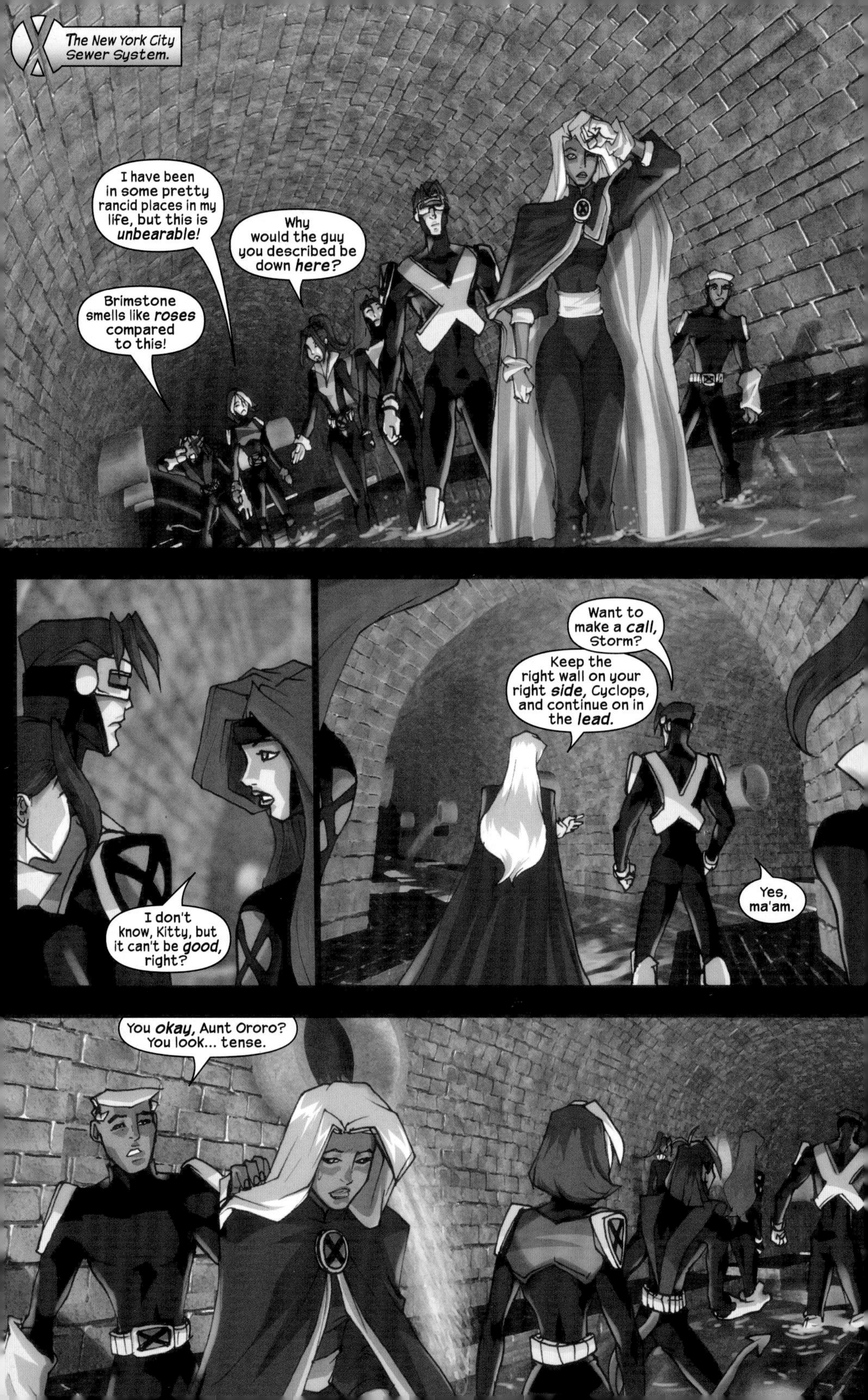
The New York City Sewer System.
I have been in some pretty rancid places in my life, but this is *unbearable!*
Why would the guy you described be down *here?*
Brimstone smells like *roses* compared to this!
I don't know, Kitty, but it can't be *good,* right?
Want to make a *call,* Storm?
Keep the right wall on your right *side,* Cyclops, and continue on in the *lead.*
Yes, ma'am.
You *okay,* Aunt Ororo? You look... tense.

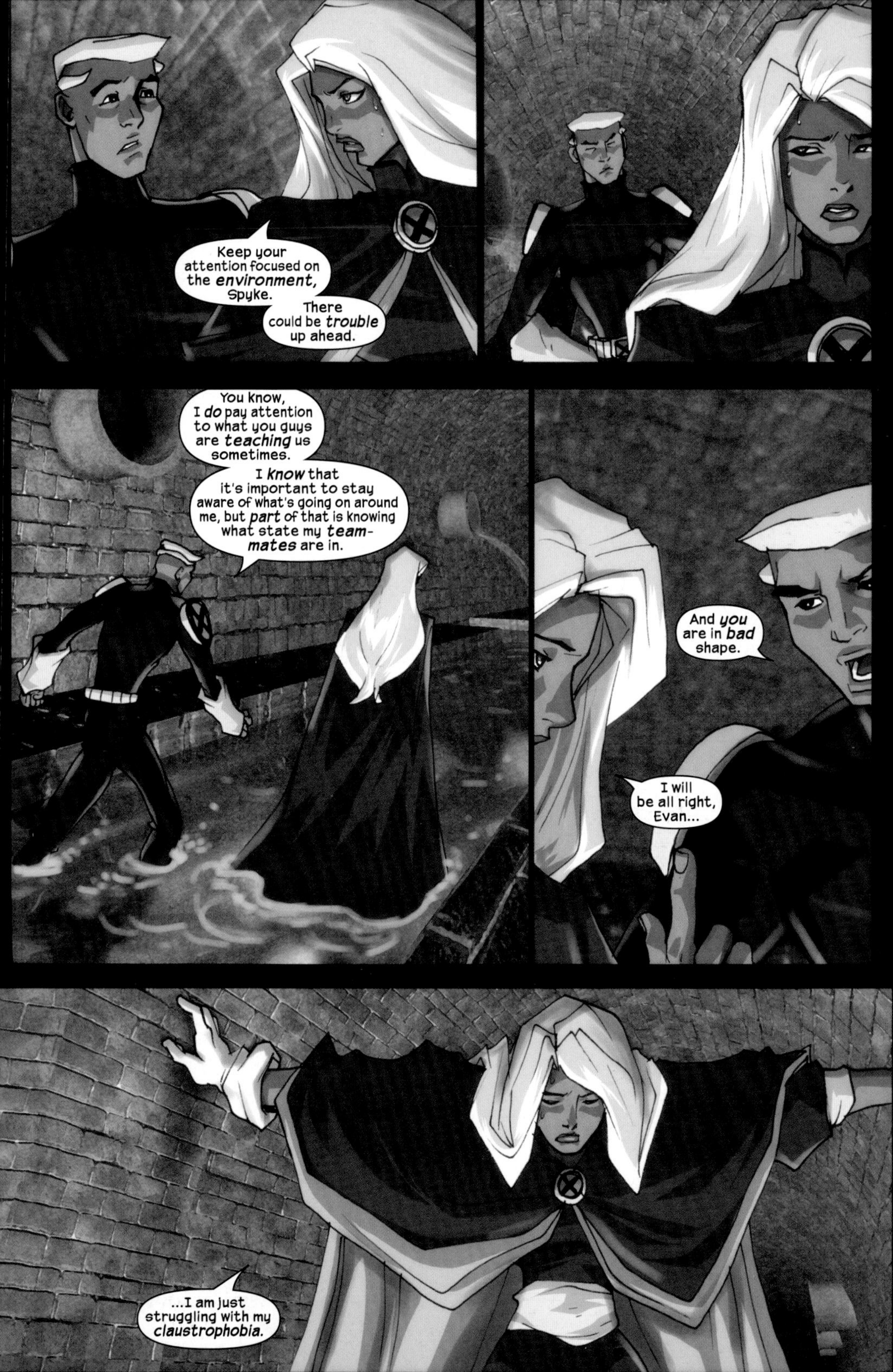
Keep your attention focused on the *environment,* Spyke.
There could be *trouble* up ahead.
You know, I *do* pay attention to what you guys are *teaching* us sometimes.
I *know* that it's important to stay aware of what's going on around me, but *part* of that is knowing what state my *team-mates* are in.
And *you* are in *bad* shape.
I will be all right, Evan...
...I am just struggling with my *claustrophobia.*

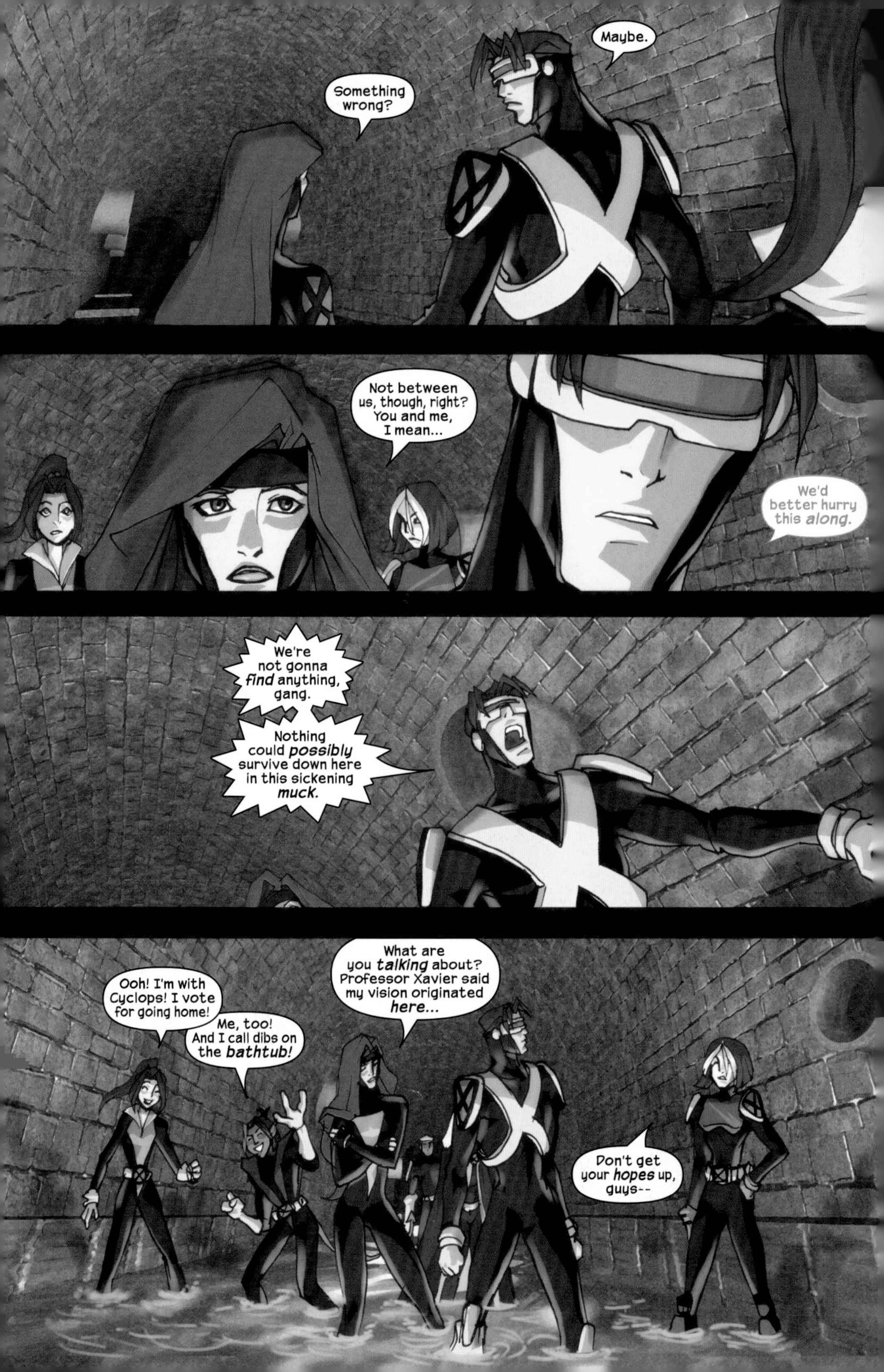
Something wrong?
Maybe.
Not between us, though, right? You and me, I mean...
We'd better hurry this *along*.
We're not gonna *find* anything, gang.
Nothing could *possibly* survive down here in this sickening *muck*.
Ooh! I'm with Cyclops! I vote for going home!
Me, too! And I call dibs on the *bathtub*!
What are you *talking* about? Professor Xavier said my vision originated *here*...
Don't get your *hopes* up, guys--

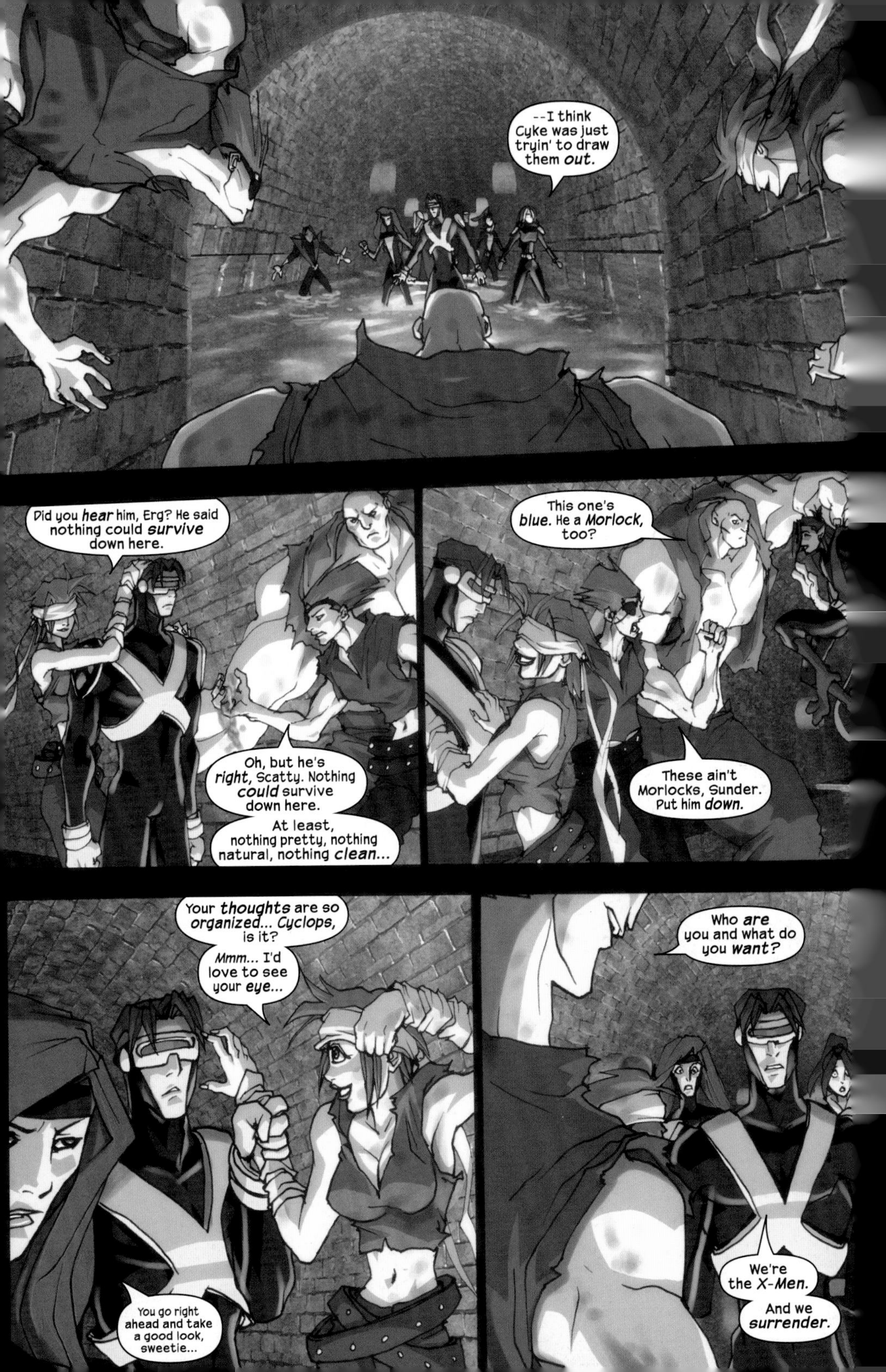
--I think Cyke was just tryin' to draw them out.
Did you hear him, Erg? He said nothing could survive down here.
Oh, but he's right, Scatty. Nothing could survive down here.
At least, nothing pretty, nothing natural, nothing clean...
This one's blue. He a Morlock, too?
These ain't Morlocks, Sunder. Put him down.
Your thoughts are so organized... Cyclops, is it?
Mmm... I'd love to see your eye...
You go right ahead and take a good look, sweetie...
Who are you and what do you want?
We're the X-Men.
And we surrender.

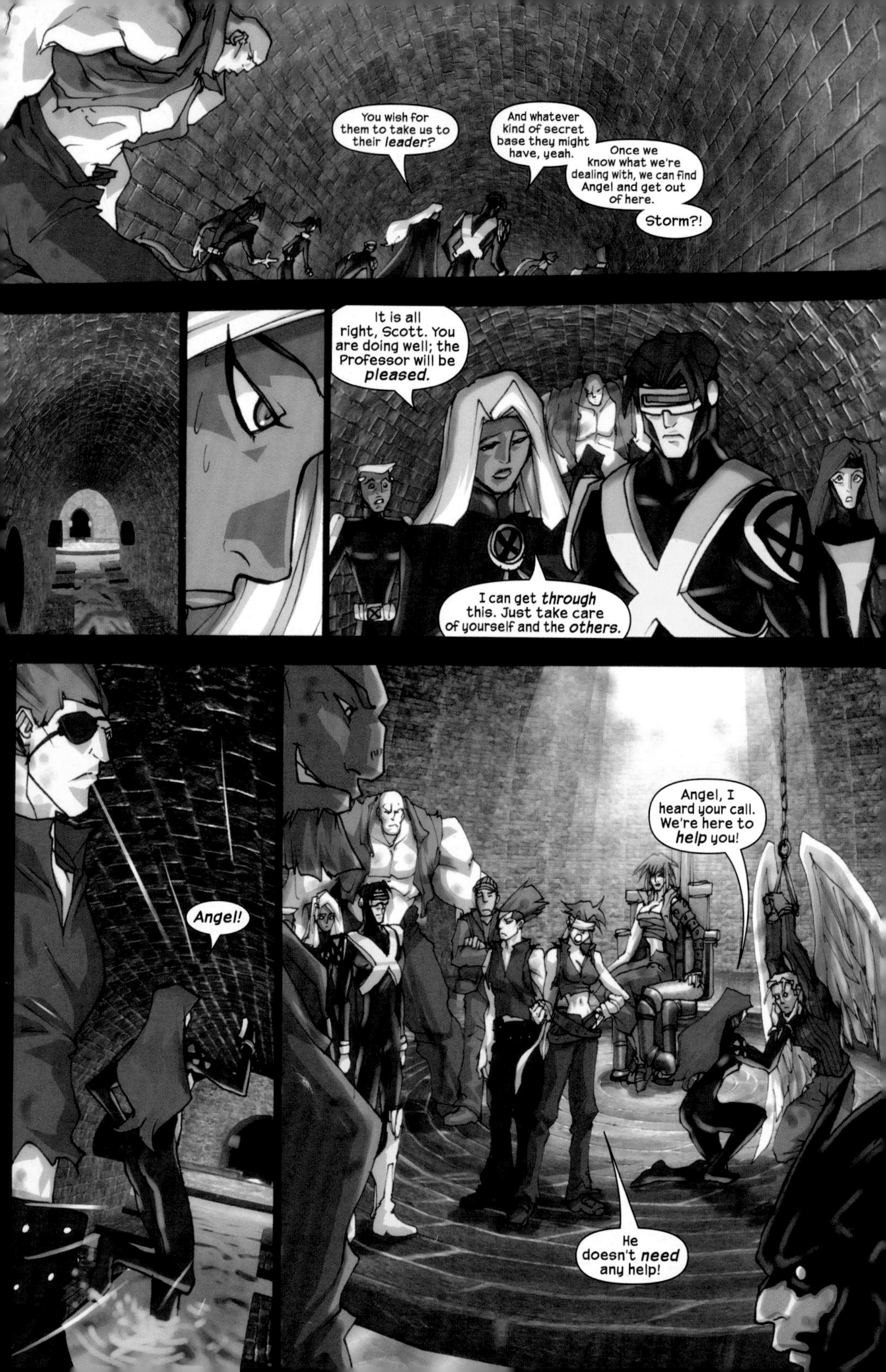
You wish for them to take us to their *leader?*
And whatever kind of secret base they might have, yeah.
Once we know what we're dealing with, we can find Angel and get out of here.
Storm?!
It is all right, Scott. You are doing well; the Professor will be ***pleased.***
I can get *through* this. Just take care of yourself and the *others.*
Angel!
Angel, I heard your call. We're here to ***help*** you!
He doesn't ***need*** any help!

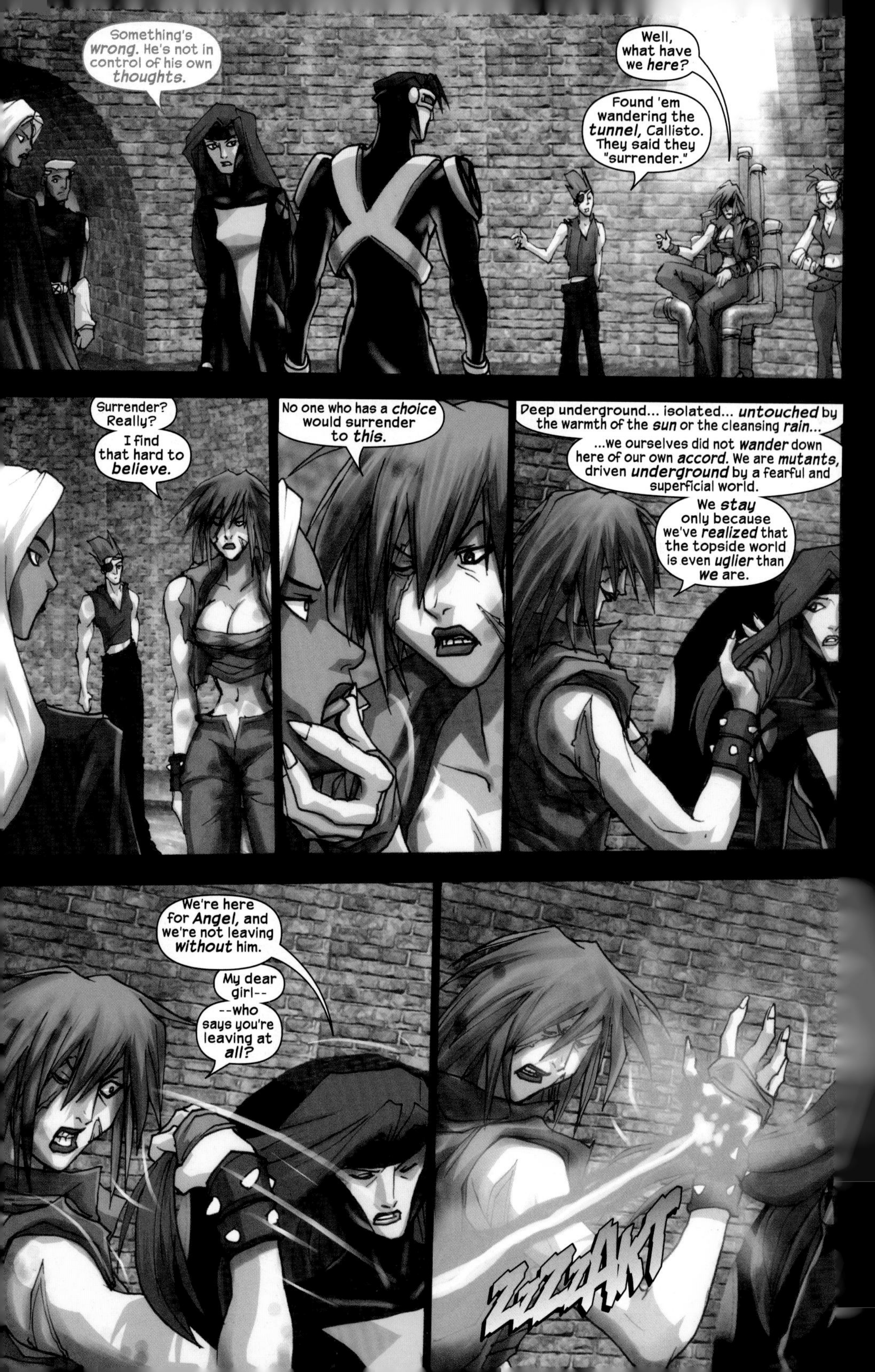

Something's wrong. He's not in control of his own thoughts.
Well, what have we here?
Found 'em wandering the tunnel, Callisto. They said they "surrender."
Surrender? Really? I find that hard to believe.
No one who has a choice would surrender to this.
Deep underground... isolated... untouched by the warmth of the sun or the cleansing rain...
...we ourselves did not wander down here of our own accord. We are mutants, driven underground by a fearful and superficial world.
We stay only because we've realized that the topside world is even uglier than we are.
We're here for Angel, and we're not leaving without him.
My dear girl--
--who says you're leaving at all?
Z-ZZZAKT

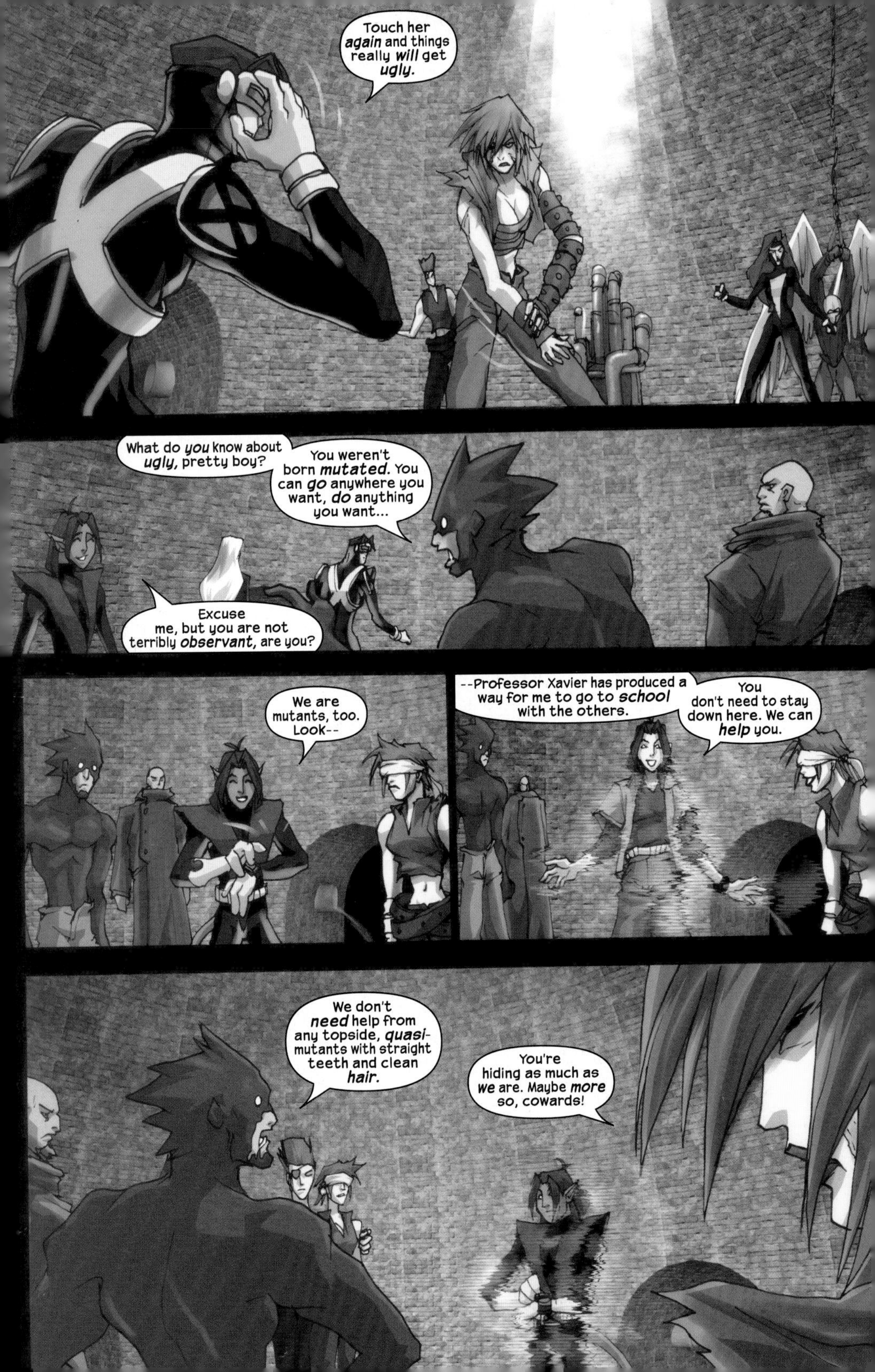
Touch her again and things really will get ugly.
What do you know about ugly, pretty boy?
You weren't born mutated. You can go anywhere you want, do anything you want...
Excuse me, but you are not terribly observant, are you?
We are mutants, too. Look--
--Professor Xavier has produced a way for me to go to school with the others.
You don't need to stay down here. We can help you.
We don't need help from any topside, quasi-mutants with straight teeth and clean hair.
You're hiding as much as we are. Maybe more so, cowards!

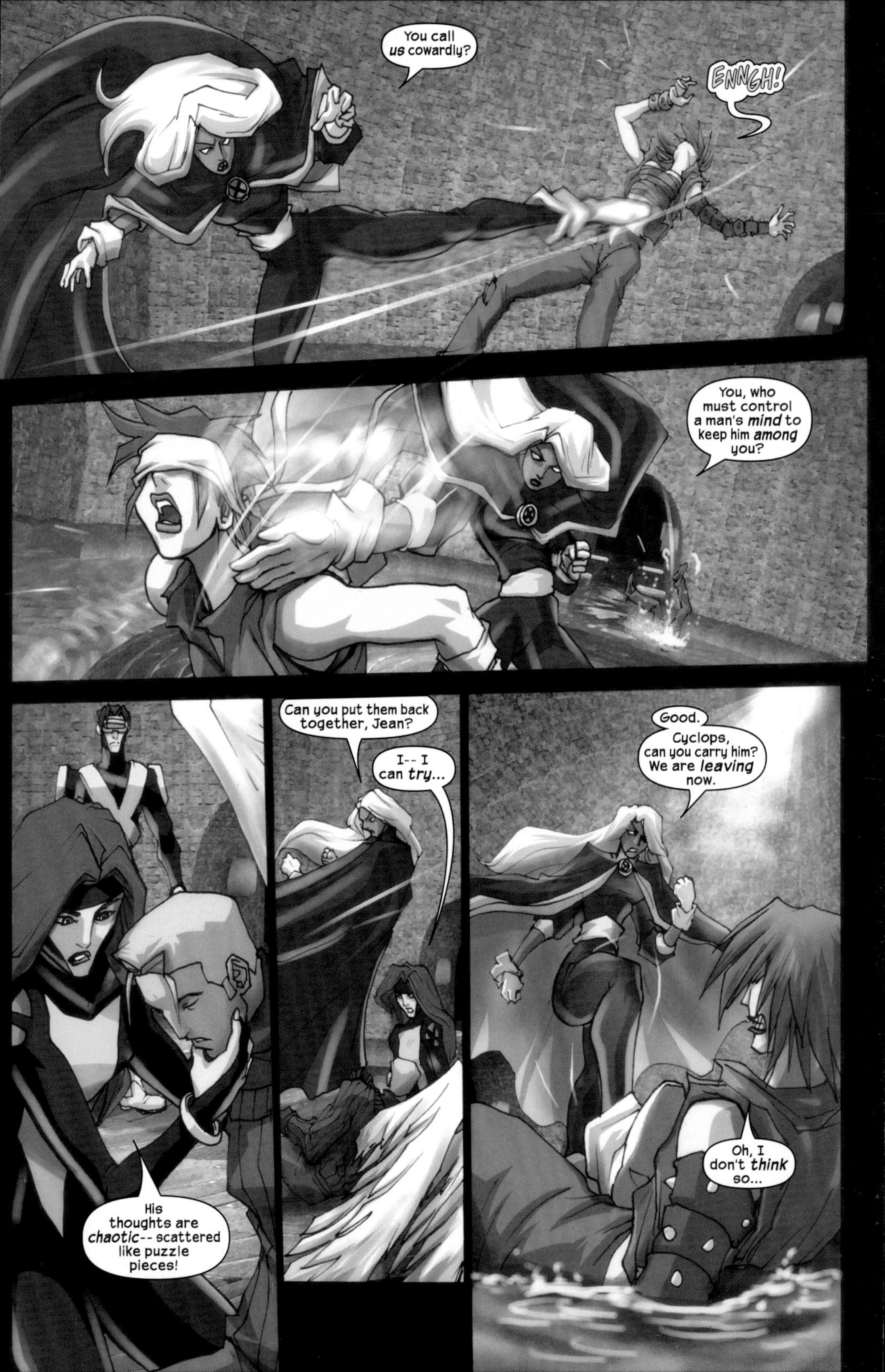
You call *us* cowardly?
ENNGH!
You, who must control a man's *mind* to keep him *among* you?
His thoughts are *chaotic*-- scattered like puzzle pieces!
Can you put them back together, Jean?
I-- I can *try*...
Good.
Cyclops, can you carry him? We are *leaving* now.
Oh, I don't *think* so...

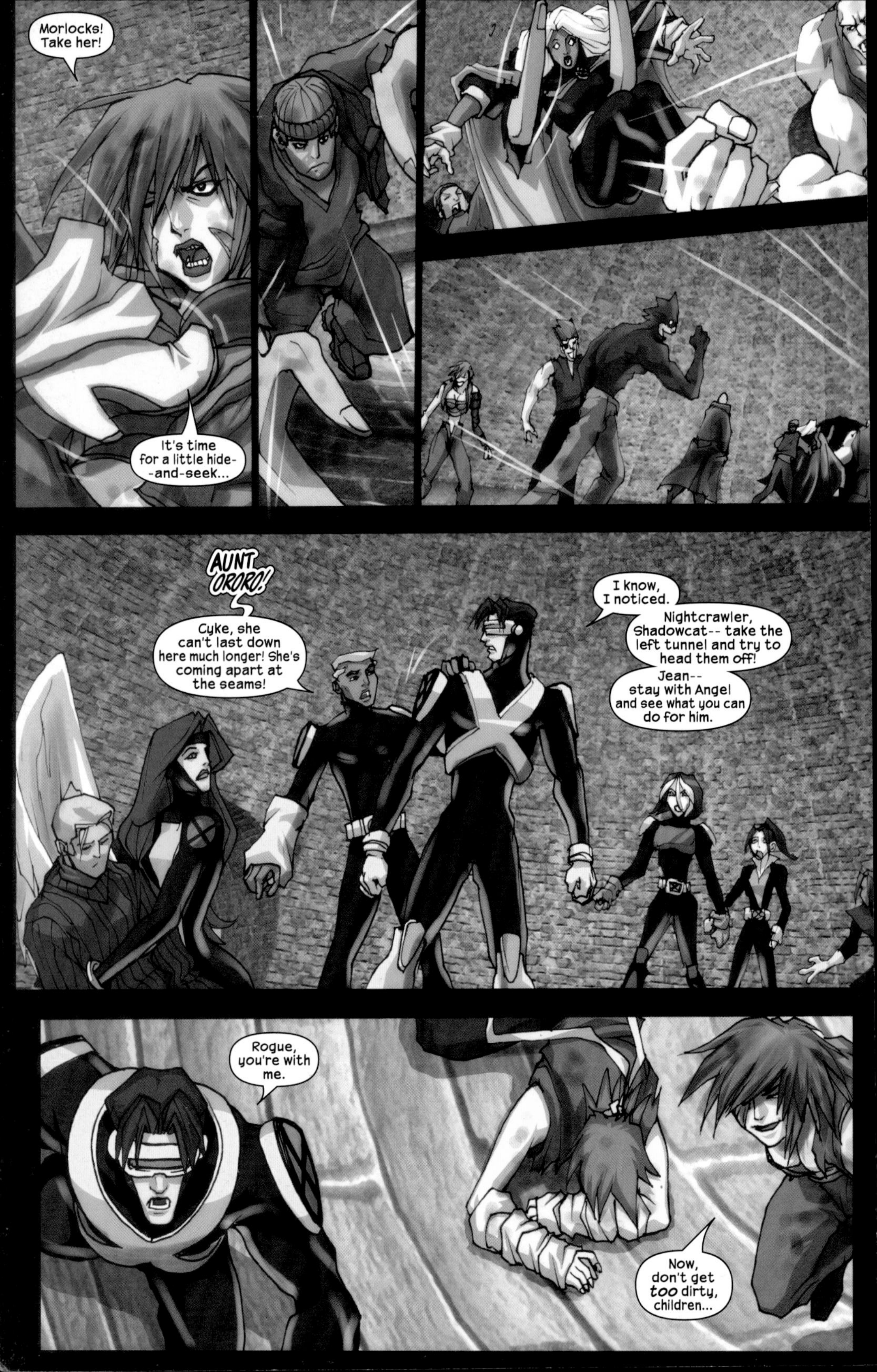
Morlocks! Take her!
It's time for a little hide--and-seek...
AUNT ORORO!
Cyke, she can't last down here much longer! She's coming apart at the seams!
I know, I noticed.
Nightcrawler, Shadowcat-- take the left tunnel and try to head them off!
Jean-- stay with Angel and see what you can do for him.
Rogue, you're with me.
Now, don't get *too* dirty, children...

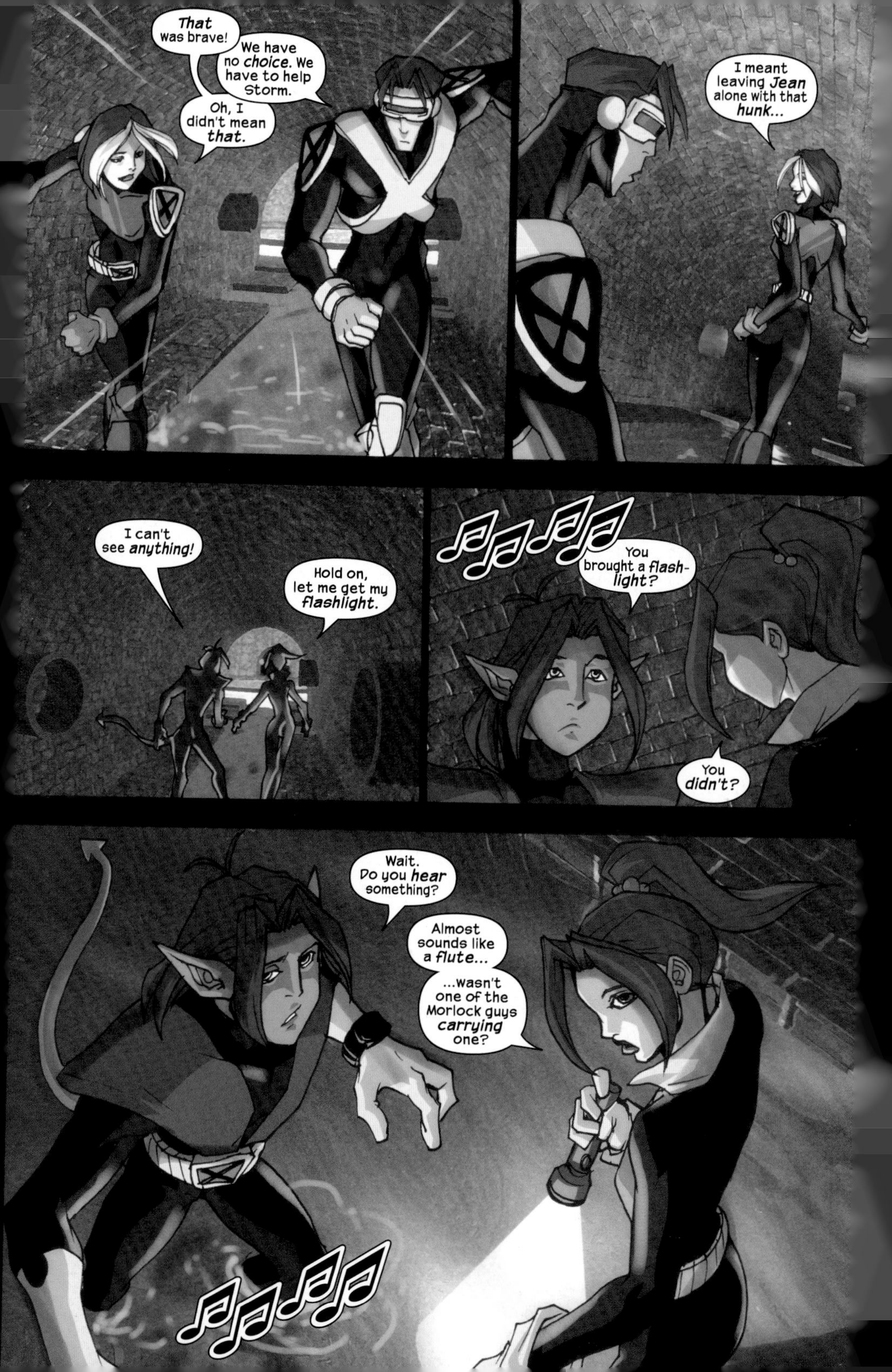
That was brave!
We have no choice. We have to help Storm.
Oh, I didn't mean that.
I meant leaving Jean alone with that hunk...
I can't see anything!
Hold on, let me get my flashlight.
You brought a flashlight?
You didn't?
Wait. Do you hear something?
Almost sounds like a flute...
...wasn't one of the Morlock guys carrying one?

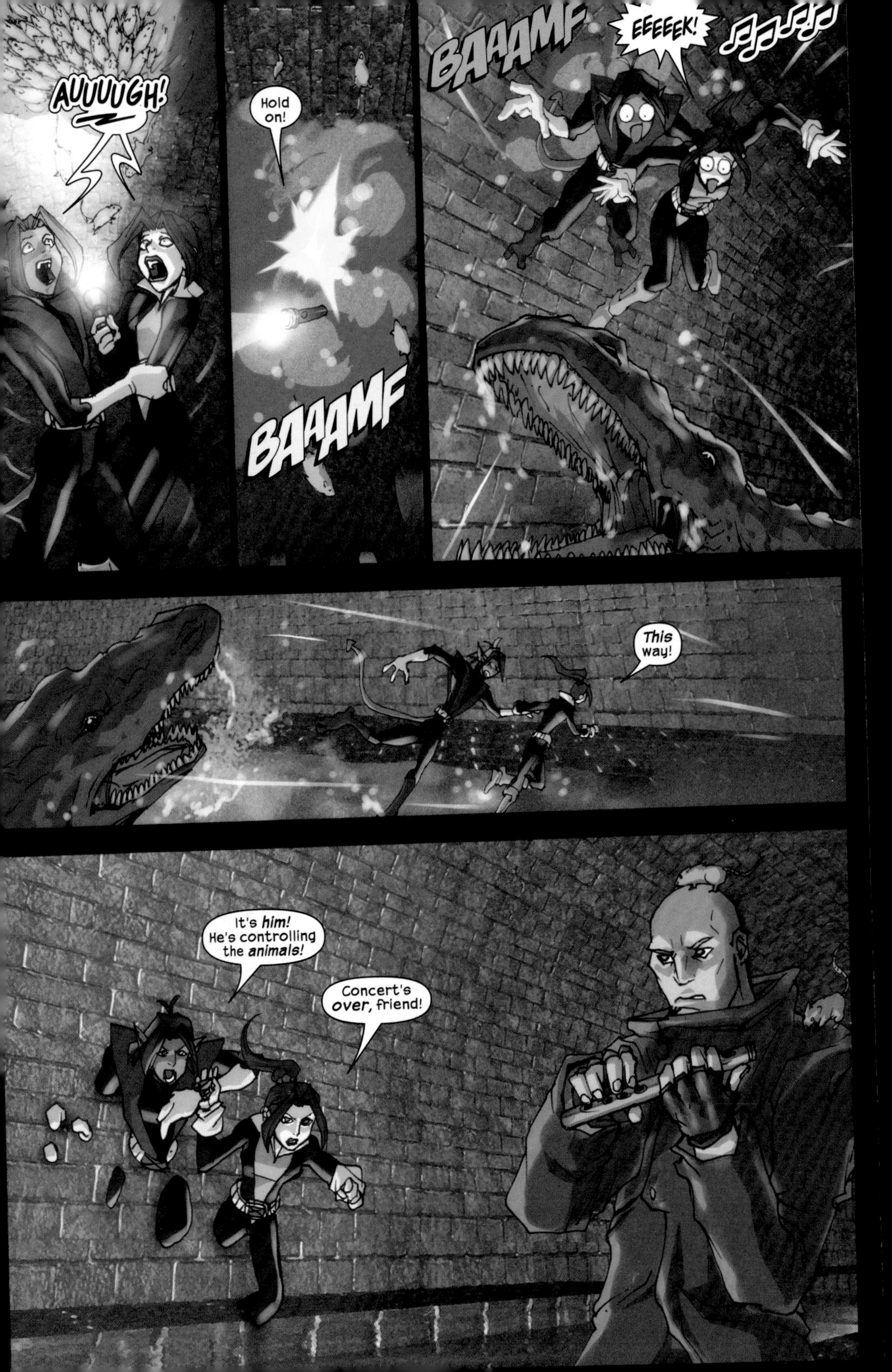
AUUUUGH!
Hold on!
BAAAMF
BAAAMF
EEEEEK!
This way!
It's *him!* He's controlling the *animals!*
Concert's *over,* friend!

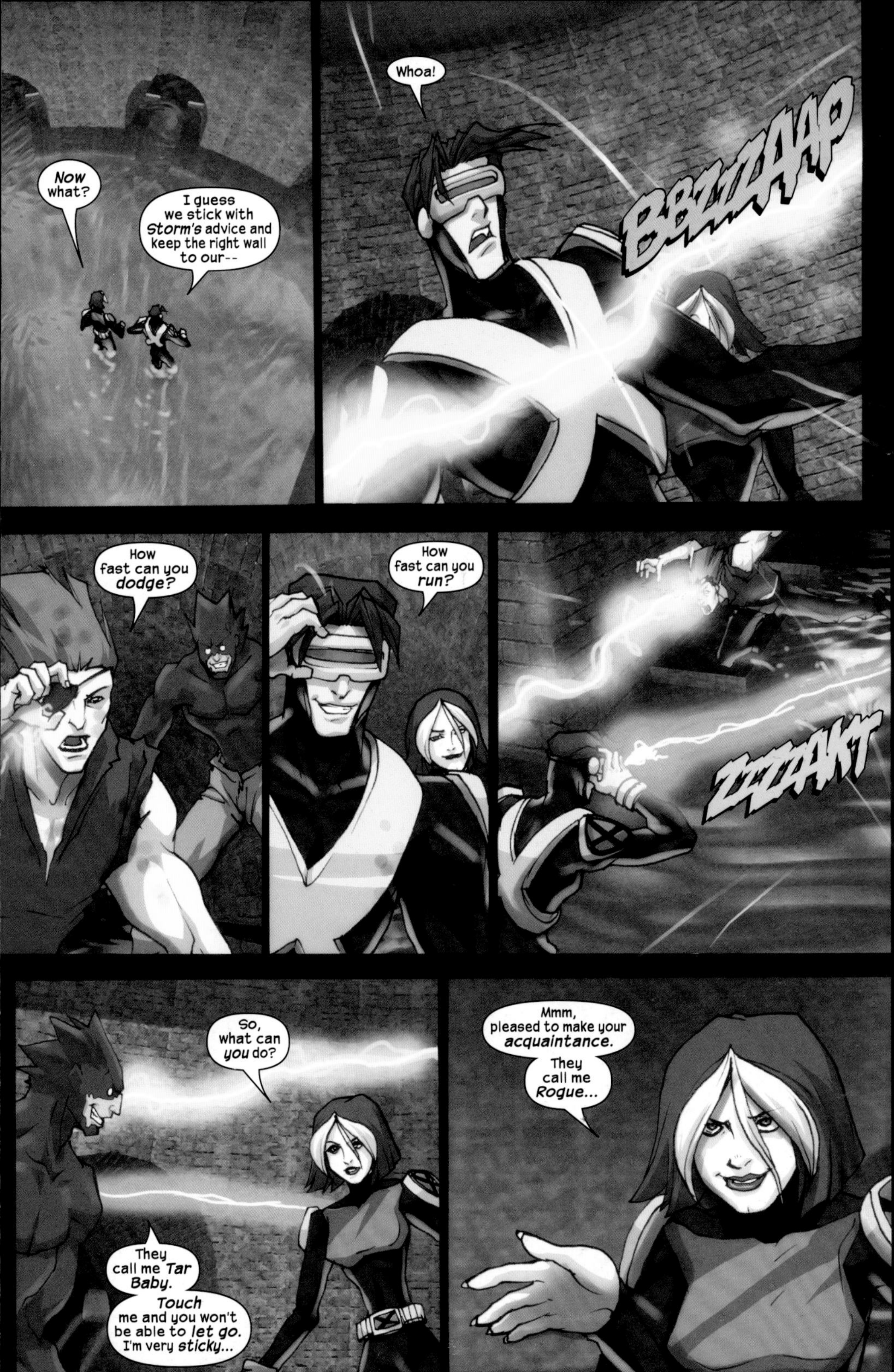
Now what?
I guess we stick with Storm's advice and keep the right wall to our--
Whoa!
BBZZZAAP
How fast can you dodge?
How fast can you run?
ZZZZAKT
So, what can you do?
They call me Tar Baby.
Touch me and you won't be able to let go. I'm very sticky...
Mmm, pleased to make your acquaintance.
They call me Rogue...

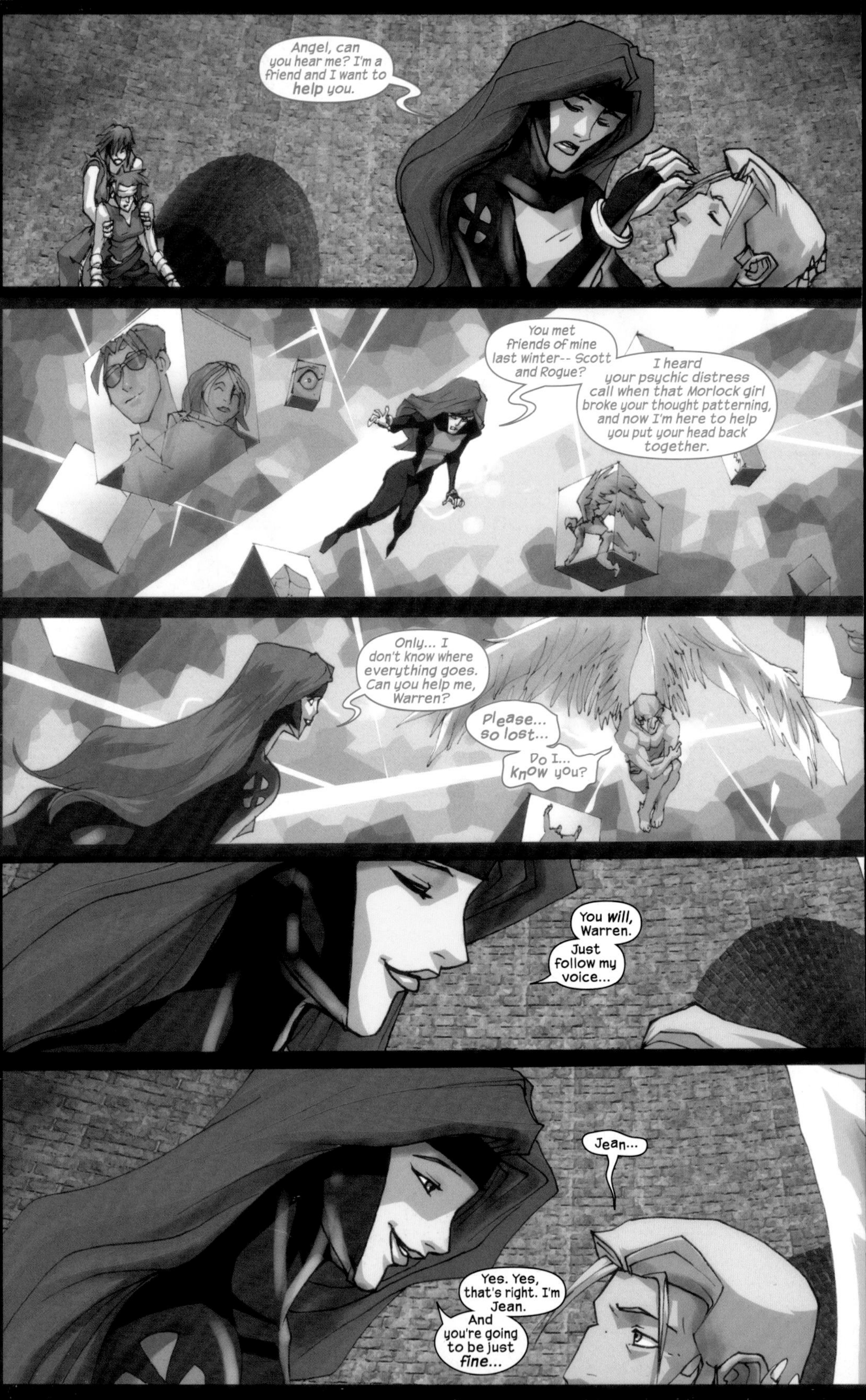
Angel, can you hear me? I'm a friend and I want to help you.
You met friends of mine last winter-- Scott and Rogue?
I heard your psychic distress call when that Morlock girl broke your thought patterning, and now I'm here to help you put your head back together.
Only... I don't know where everything goes. Can you help me, Warren?
Please... so lost...
Do I... know you?
You will, Warren.
Just follow my voice...
Jean...
Yes. Yes, that's right. I'm Jean.
And you're going to be just fine...

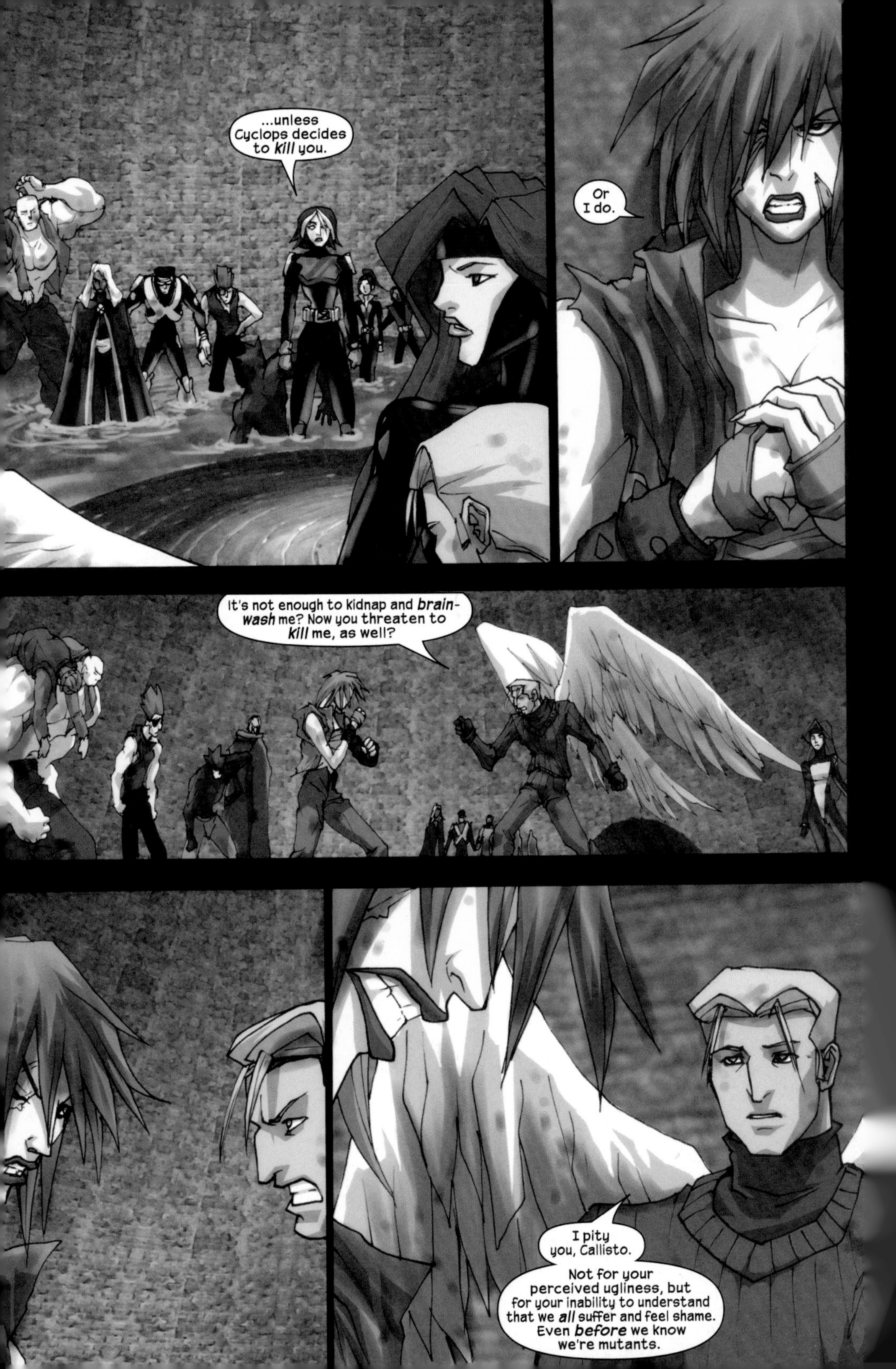
...unless Cyclops decides to *kill* you.
Or I do.
It's not enough to kidnap and *brain-wash* me? Now you threaten to *kill* me, as well?
I pity you, Callisto.
Not for your perceived ugliness, but for your inability to understand that we *all* suffer and feel shame. Even *before* we know we're mutants.

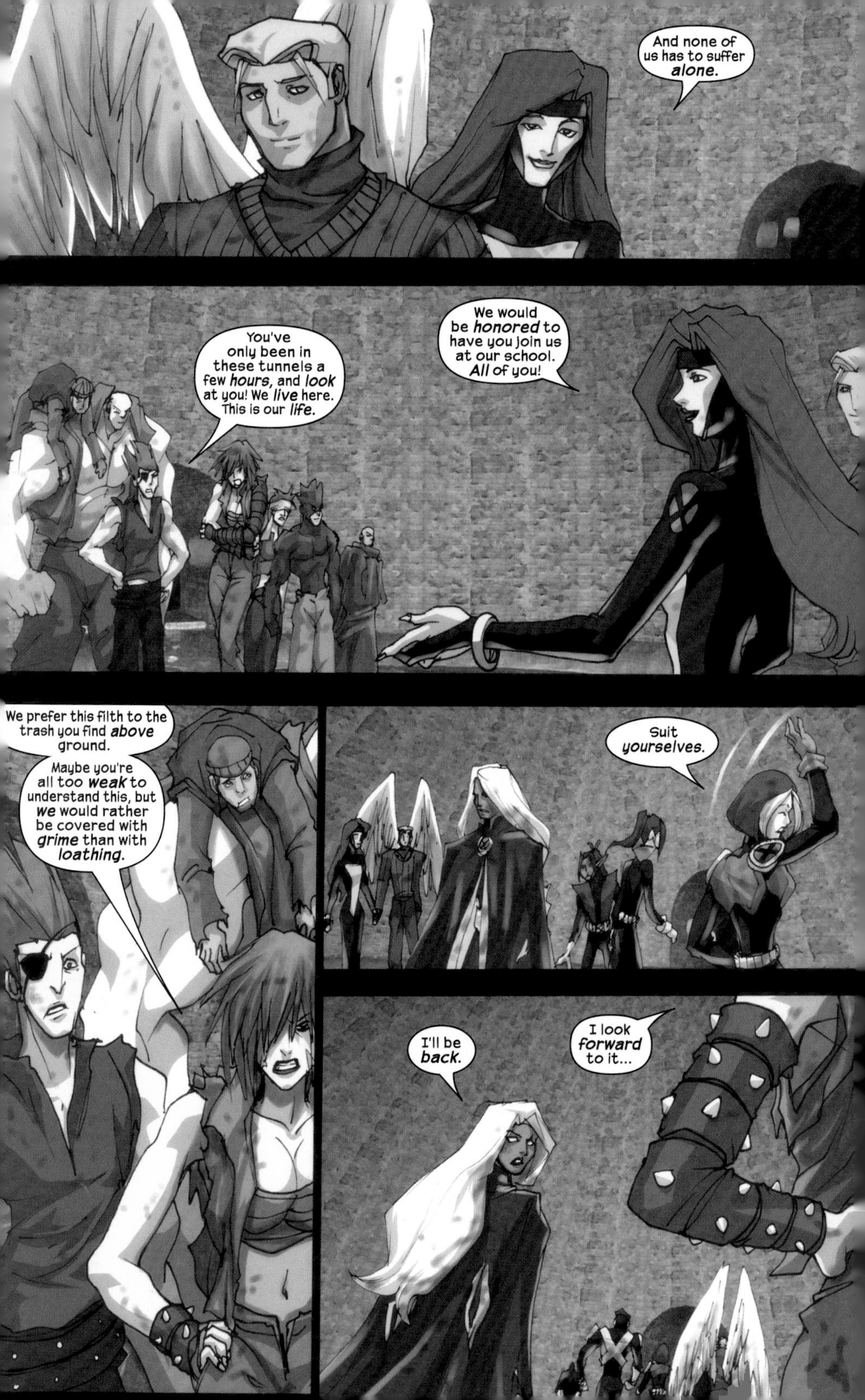

And none of us has to suffer alone.
We would be honored to have you join us at our school. All of you!
You've only been in these tunnels a few hours, and look at you! We live here. This is our life.
We prefer this filth to the trash you find above ground.
Maybe you're all too weak to understand this, but we would rather be covered with grime than with loathing.
Suit yourselves.
I'll be back.
I look forward to it...

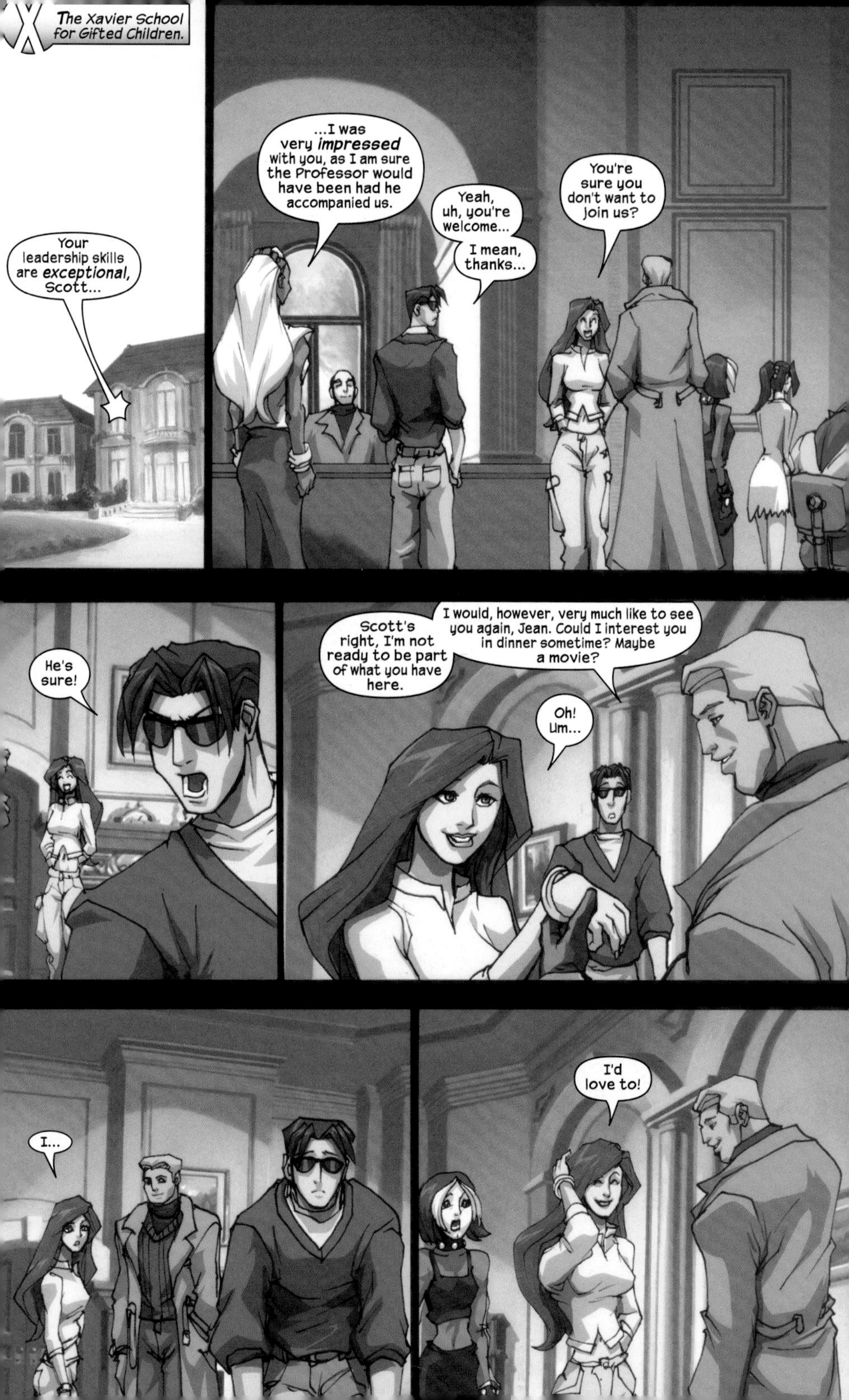
The Xavier School for Gifted Children.
Your leadership skills are *exceptional*, Scott...
...I was very *impressed* with you, as I am sure the Professor would have been had he accompanied us.
Yeah, uh, you're welcome...
I mean, thanks...
You're sure you don't want to join us?
He's sure!
Scott's right, I'm not ready to be part of what you have here.
I would, however, very much like to see you again, Jean. Could I interest you in dinner sometime? Maybe a movie?
Oh! Um...
I...
I'd love to!

I wish you could have come *with* us, Mr. McCoy!

INSTANT MESSAGE FROM Xessen:
I'd really like to meet you in person to discuss this in more detail.

INSTANT MESSAGE FROM HMcCoy:
I'm afraid that's not possible, but thank you again for your generous offer.

Yes, I'm sorry to have *missed* it, Kitty. I hear you were very *brave*.

Who told you that? Kurt? He's probably just hoping I won't tell anyone that we both screamed like kindergarteners!

Oh!

What *is* it?

INSTANT MESSAGE FROM Xess
I'd really like to meet you in person discuss this in more detail.

INSTANT MESSAGE FROM HMcC
I'm afraid that's not possible, but than you again for your generous offer.

INSTANT MESSAGE FROM Xessen:
I hope you're not refusing to meet with me just because you're a MUTANT. I assure you that I know all about that, and it's of no concern to me whatsoever...

Diiing

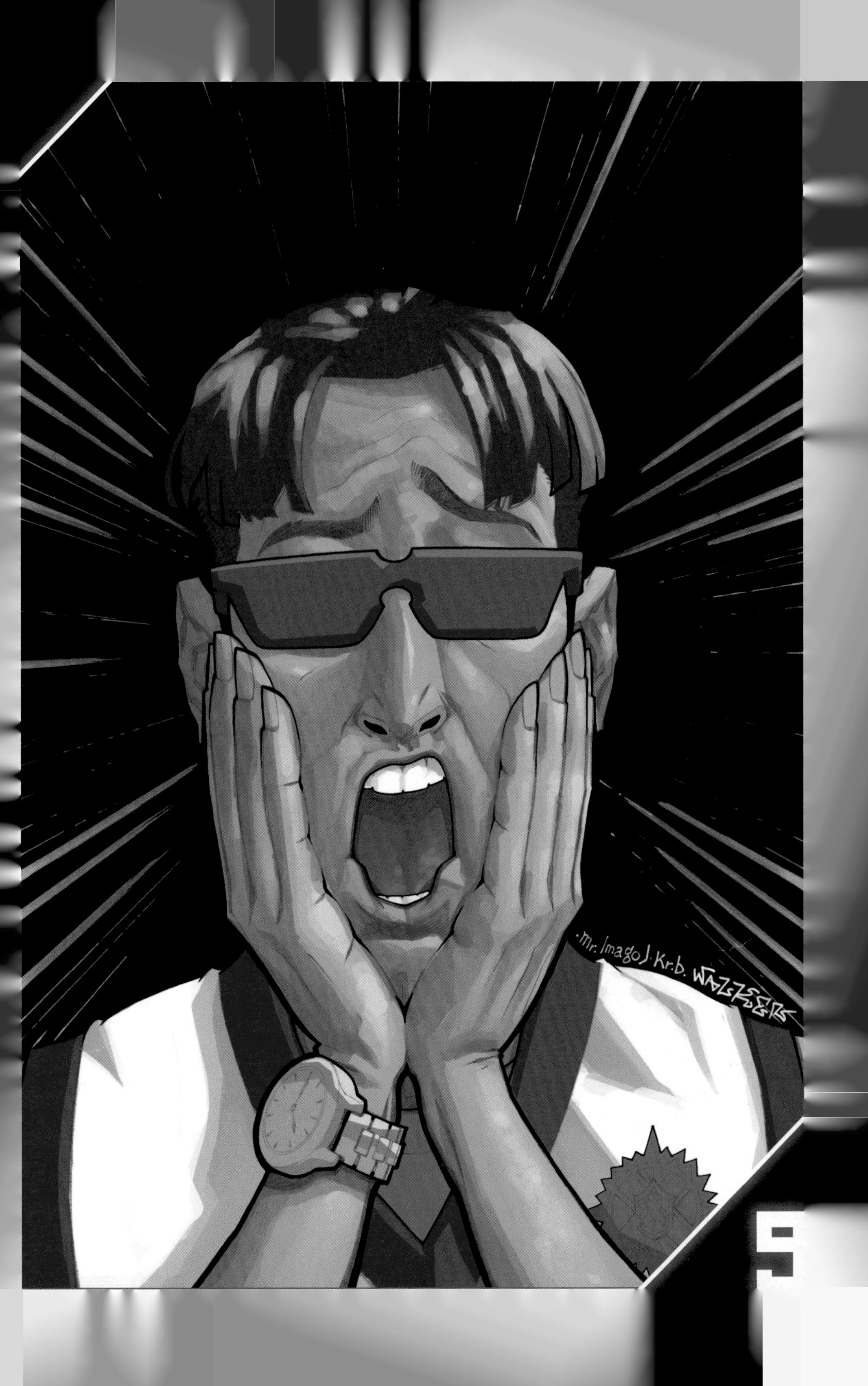

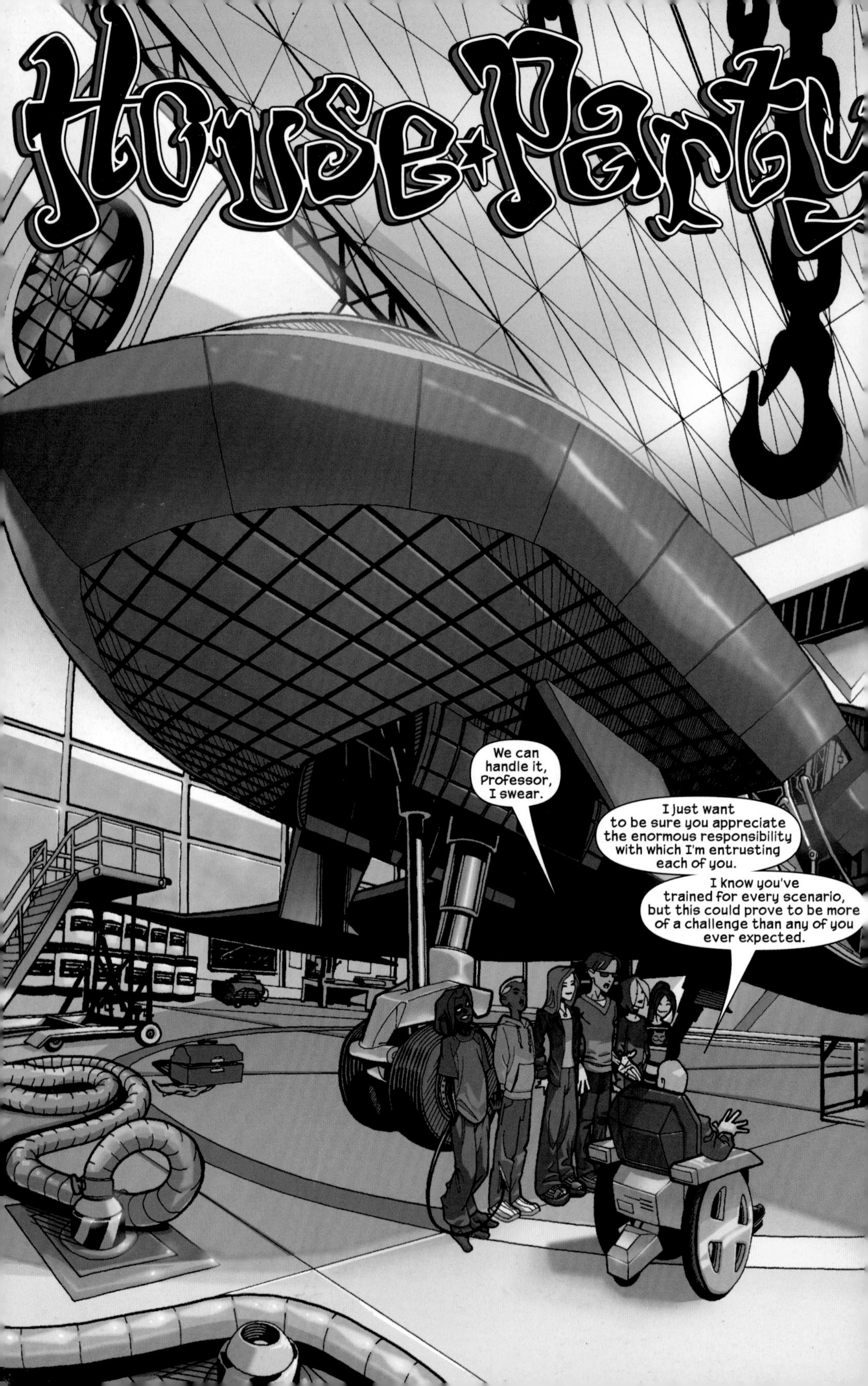
House Party
We can handle it, Professor, I swear.
I just want to be sure you appreciate the enormous responsibility with which I'm entrusting each of you.
I know you've trained for every scenario, but this could prove to be more of a challenge than any of you ever expected.

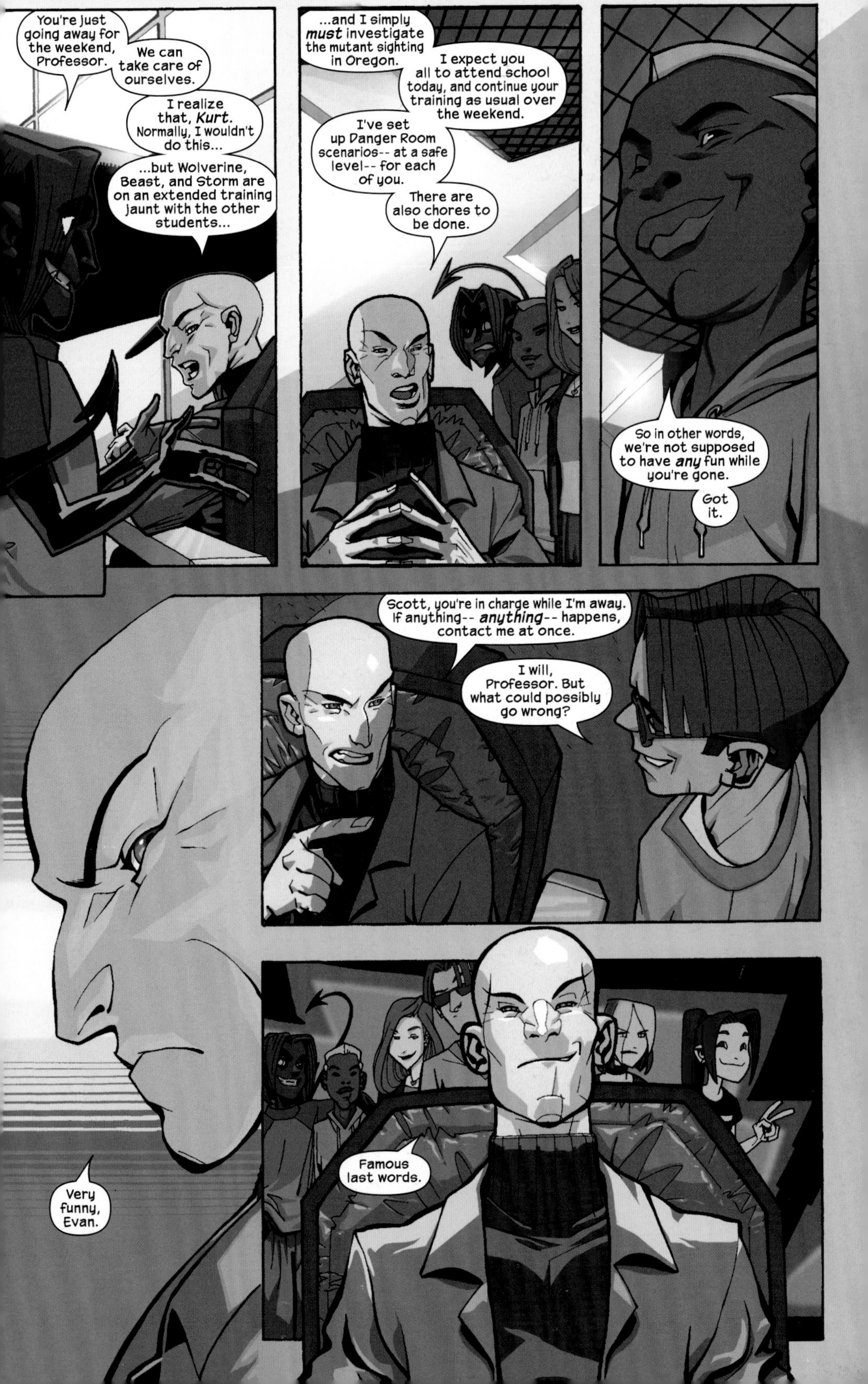
You're just going away for the weekend, Professor.
We can take care of ourselves.
I realize that, Kurt. Normally, I wouldn't do this...
...but Wolverine, Beast, and Storm are on an extended training jaunt with the other students...
...and I simply must investigate the mutant sighting in Oregon.
I expect you all to attend school today, and continue your training as usual over the weekend.
I've set up Danger Room scenarios-- at a safe level-- for each of you.
There are also chores to be done.
So in other words, we're not supposed to have any fun while you're gone.
Got it.
Scott, you're in charge while I'm away. If anything-- anything-- happens, contact me at once.
I will, Professor. But what could possibly go wrong?
Famous last words.
Very funny, Evan.

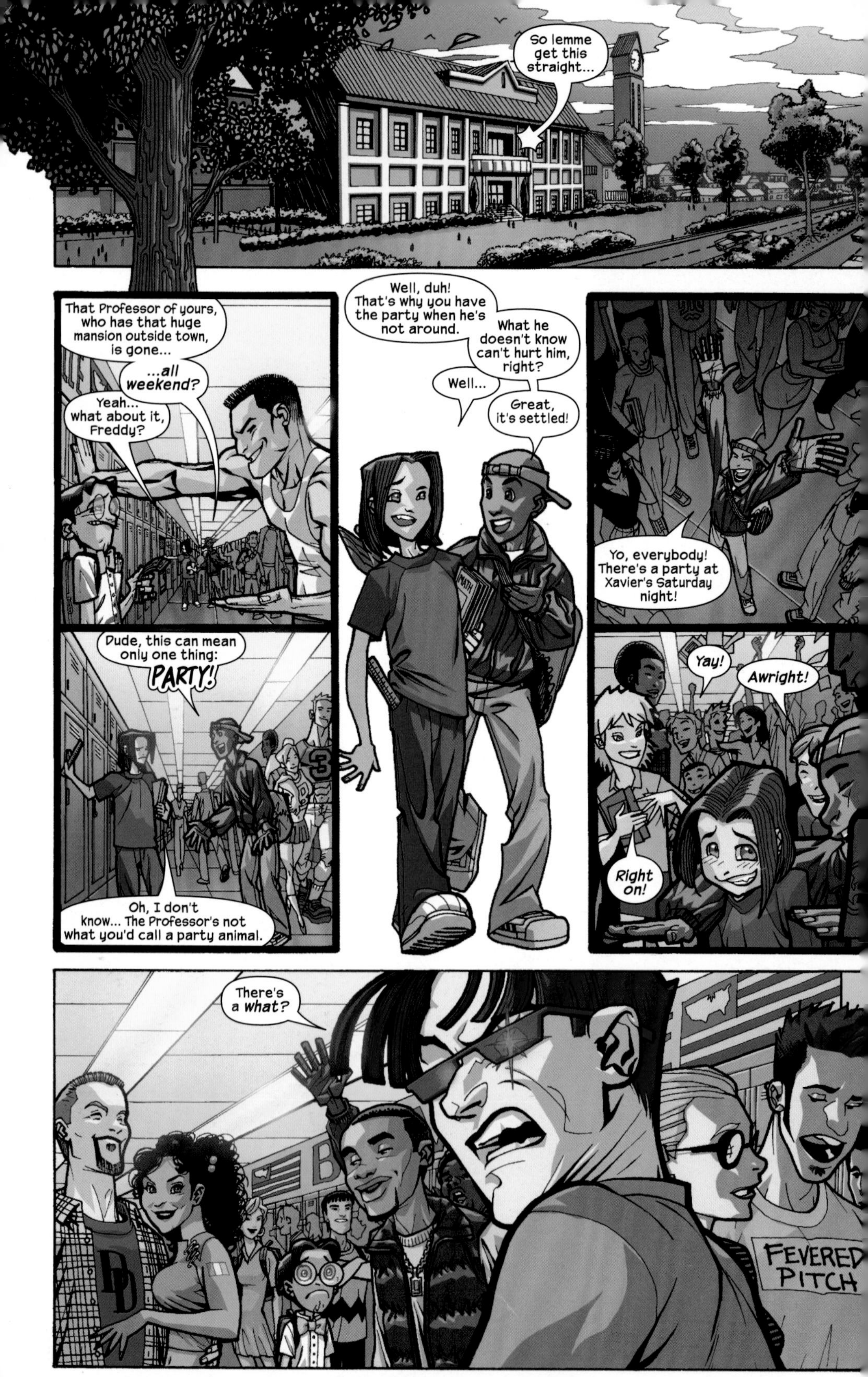
So lemme get this straight...
That Professor of yours, who has that huge mansion outside town, is gone...
...all weekend?
Yeah... what about it, Freddy?
Dude, this can mean only one thing: PARTY!
Oh, I don't know... The Professor's not what you'd call a party animal.
Well, duh! That's why you have the party when he's not around.
What he doesn't know can't hurt him, right?
Well...
Great, it's settled!
MATH
Yo, everybody! There's a party at Xavier's Saturday night!
Yay!
Awright!
Right on!
There's a what?
FEVERED PITCH

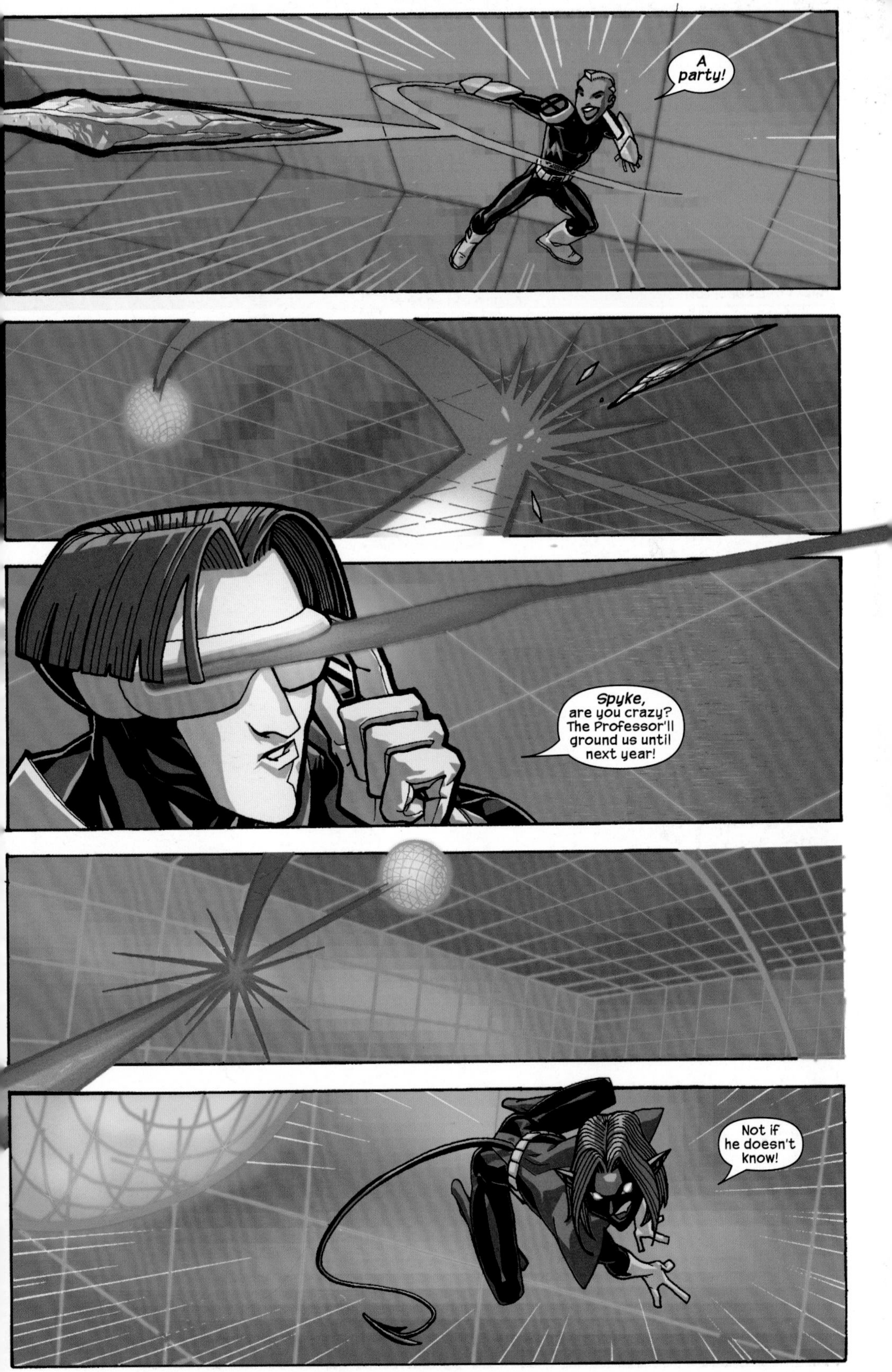
A party!
Spyke, are you crazy? The Professor'll ground us until next year!
Not if he doesn't know!

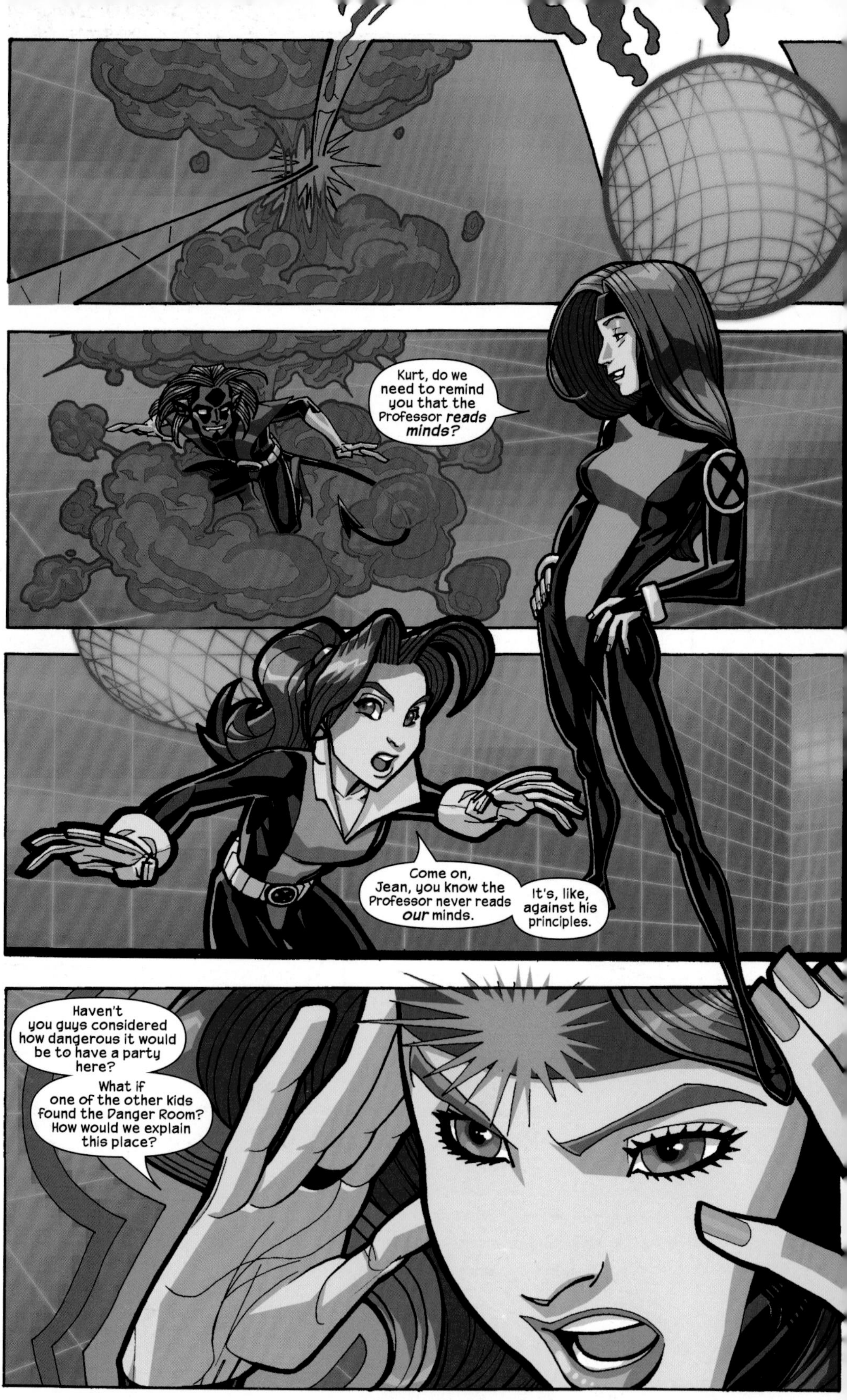

Kurt, do we need to remind you that the Professor *reads minds?*
Come on, Jean, you know the Professor never reads *our* minds.
It's, like, against his principles.
Haven't you guys considered how dangerous it would be to have a party here?
What if one of the other kids found the Danger Room? How would we explain this place?

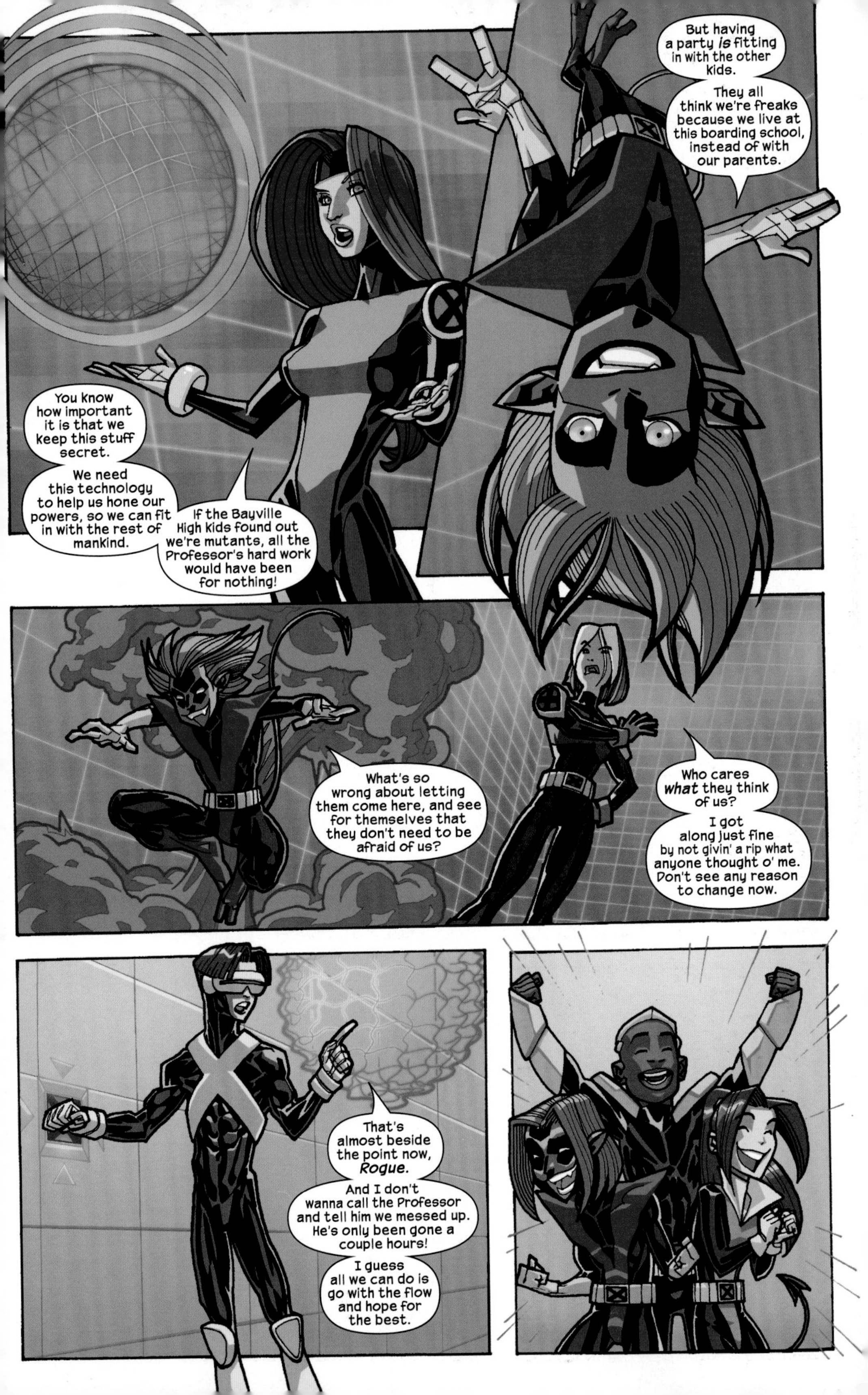
But having a party *is* fitting in with the other kids.
They all think we're freaks because we live at this boarding school, instead of with our parents.
You know how important it is that we keep this stuff secret.
We need this technology to help us hone our powers, so we can fit in with the rest of mankind.
If the Bayville High kids found out we're mutants, all the Professor's hard work would have been for nothing!
What's so wrong about letting them come here, and see for themselves that they don't need to be afraid of us?
Who cares *what* they think of us?
I got along just fine by not givin' a rip what anyone thought o' me. Don't see any reason to change now.
That's almost beside the point now, *Rogue*.
And I don't wanna call the Professor and tell him we messed up. He's only been gone a couple hours!
I guess all we can do is go with the flow and hope for the best.

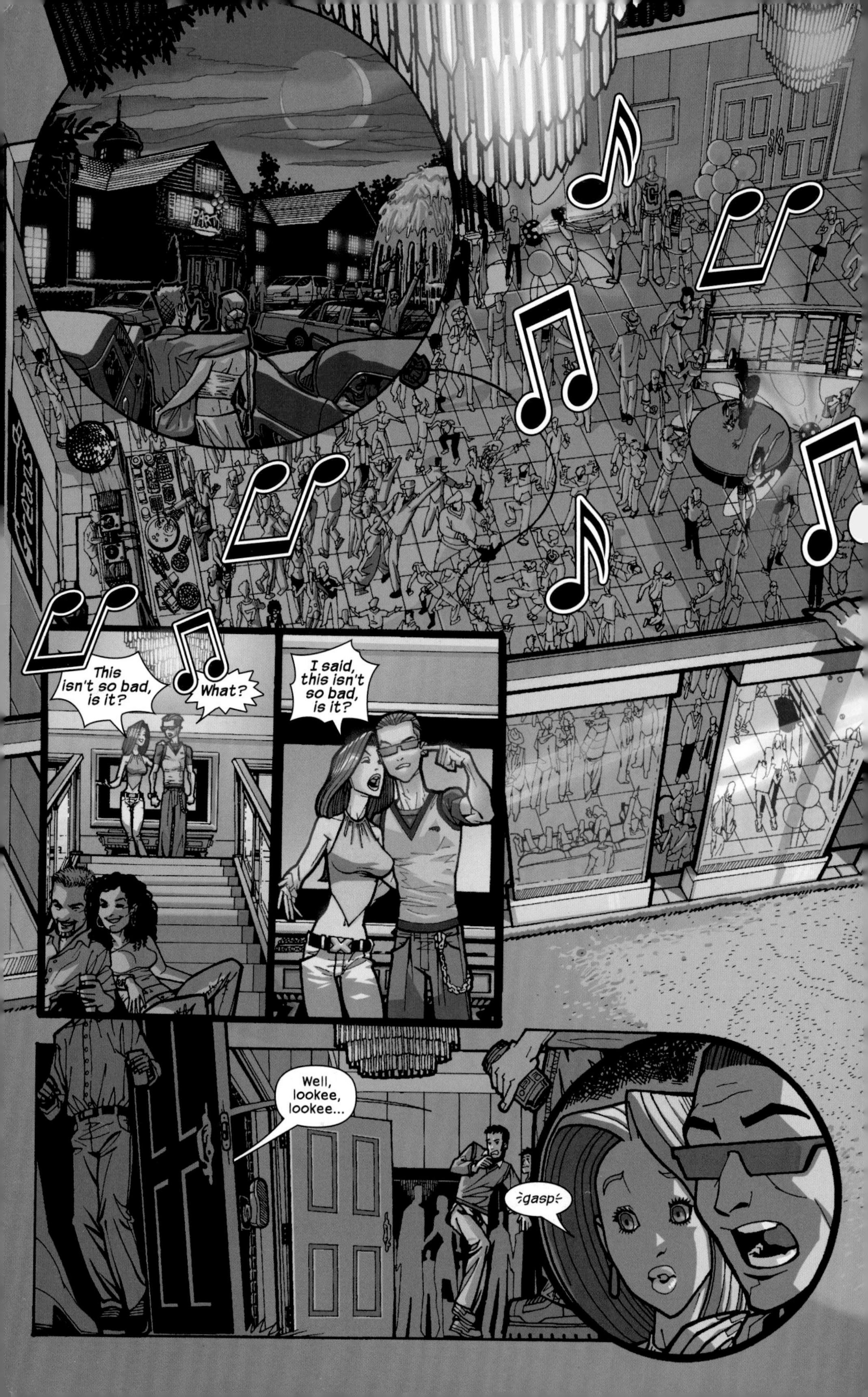

This isn't so bad, is it?
What?
I said, this isn't so bad, is it?
Well, lookee, lookee...
gasp

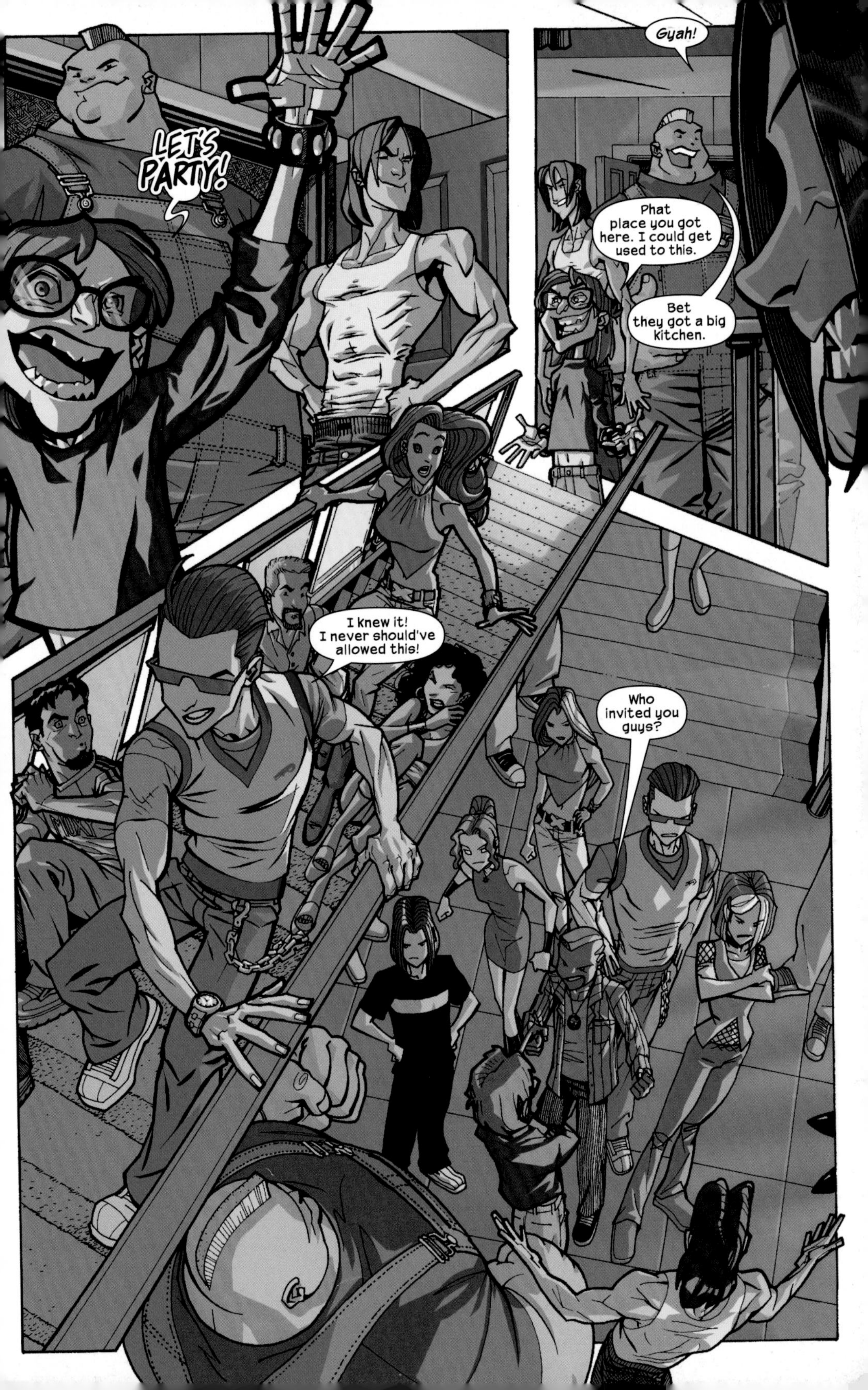
LET'S PARTY!
Gyah!
Phat place you got here. I could get used to this.
Bet they got a big kitchen.
I knew it! I never should've allowed this!
Who invited you guys?

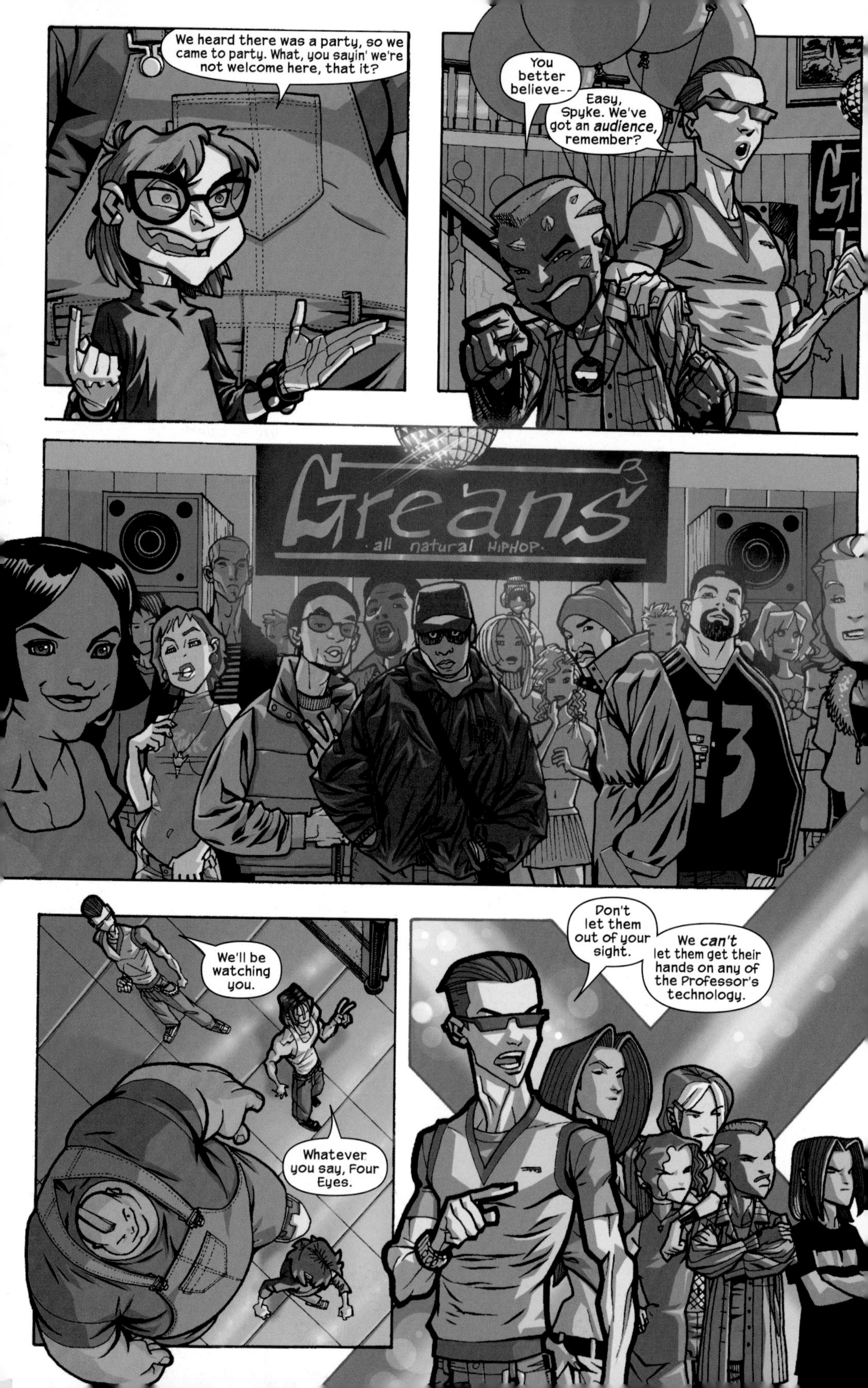

We heard there was a party, so we came to party. What, you sayin' we're not welcome here, that it?
You better believe--
Easy, Spyke. We've got an *audience*, remember?
Greans
all natural HIPHOP
We'll be watching you.
Whatever you say, Four Eyes.
Don't let them out of your sight.
We *can't* let them get their hands on any of the Professor's technology.

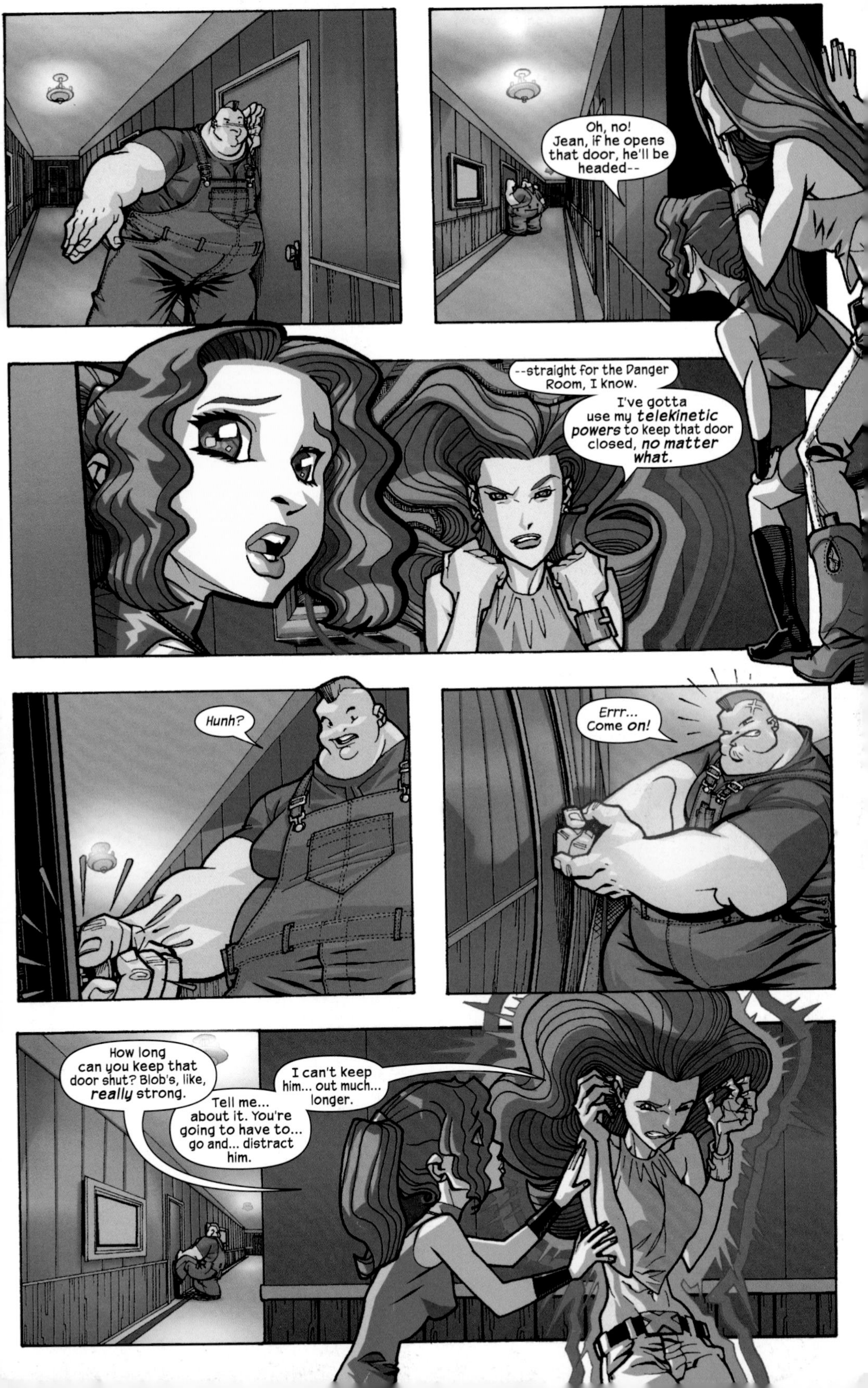
Oh, no!
Jean, if he opens that door, he'll be headed--
--straight for the Danger Room, I know.
I've gotta use my *telekinetic powers* to keep that door closed, ***no matter what.***
Hunh?
Errr...
Come ***on!***
How long can you keep that door shut? Blob's, like, ***really*** strong.
I can't keep him... out much... longer.
Tell me... about it. You're going to have to... go and... distract him.

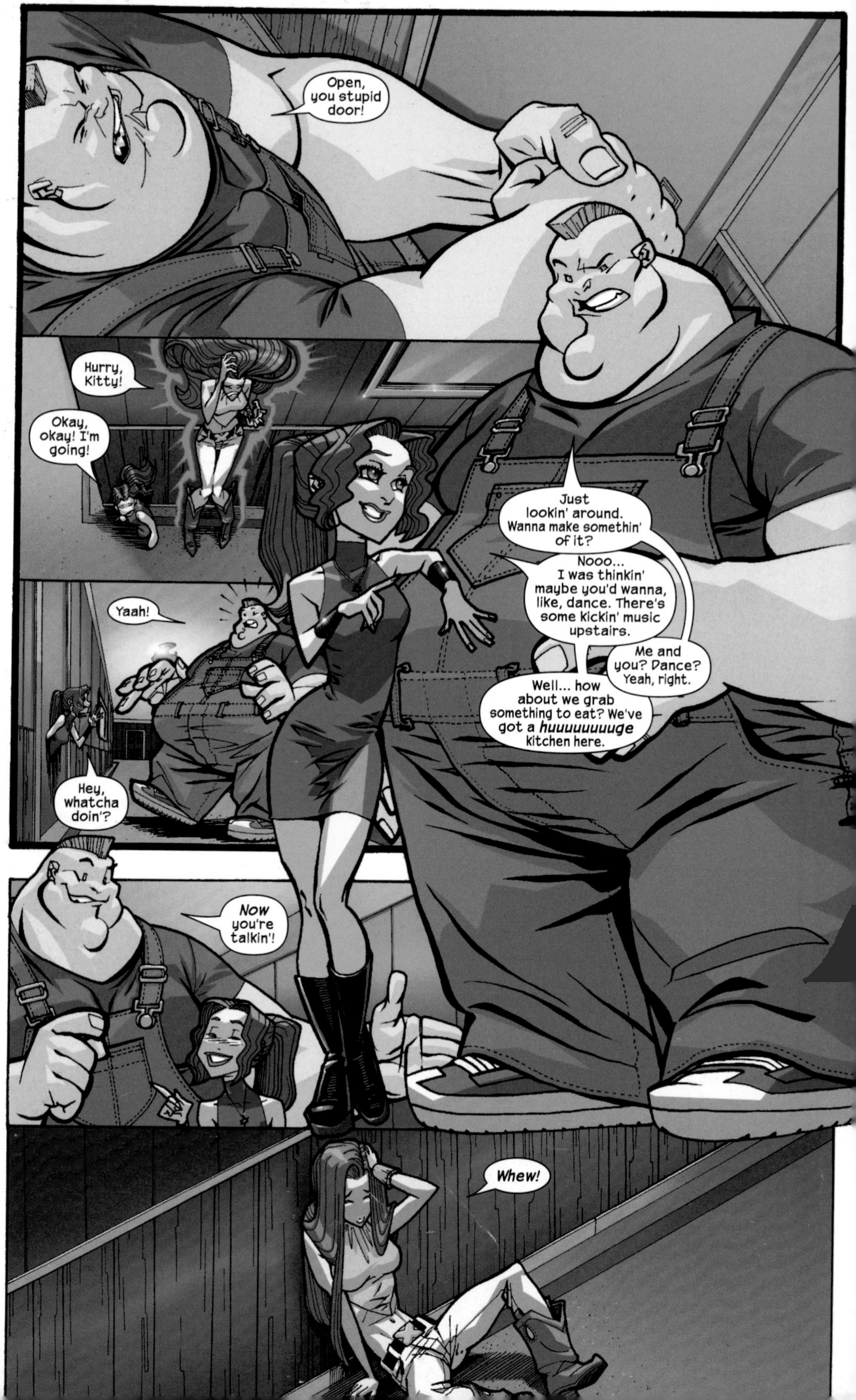

Open, you stupid door!
Hurry, Kitty!
Okay, okay! I'm going!
Yaah!
Hey, whatcha doin'?
Just lookin' around. Wanna make somethin' of it?
Nooo... I was thinkin' maybe you'd wanna, like, dance. There's some kickin' music upstairs.
Me and you? Dance? Yeah, right.
Well... how about we grab something to eat? We've got a ***huuuuuuuuge*** kitchen here.
Now you're talkin'!
Whew!

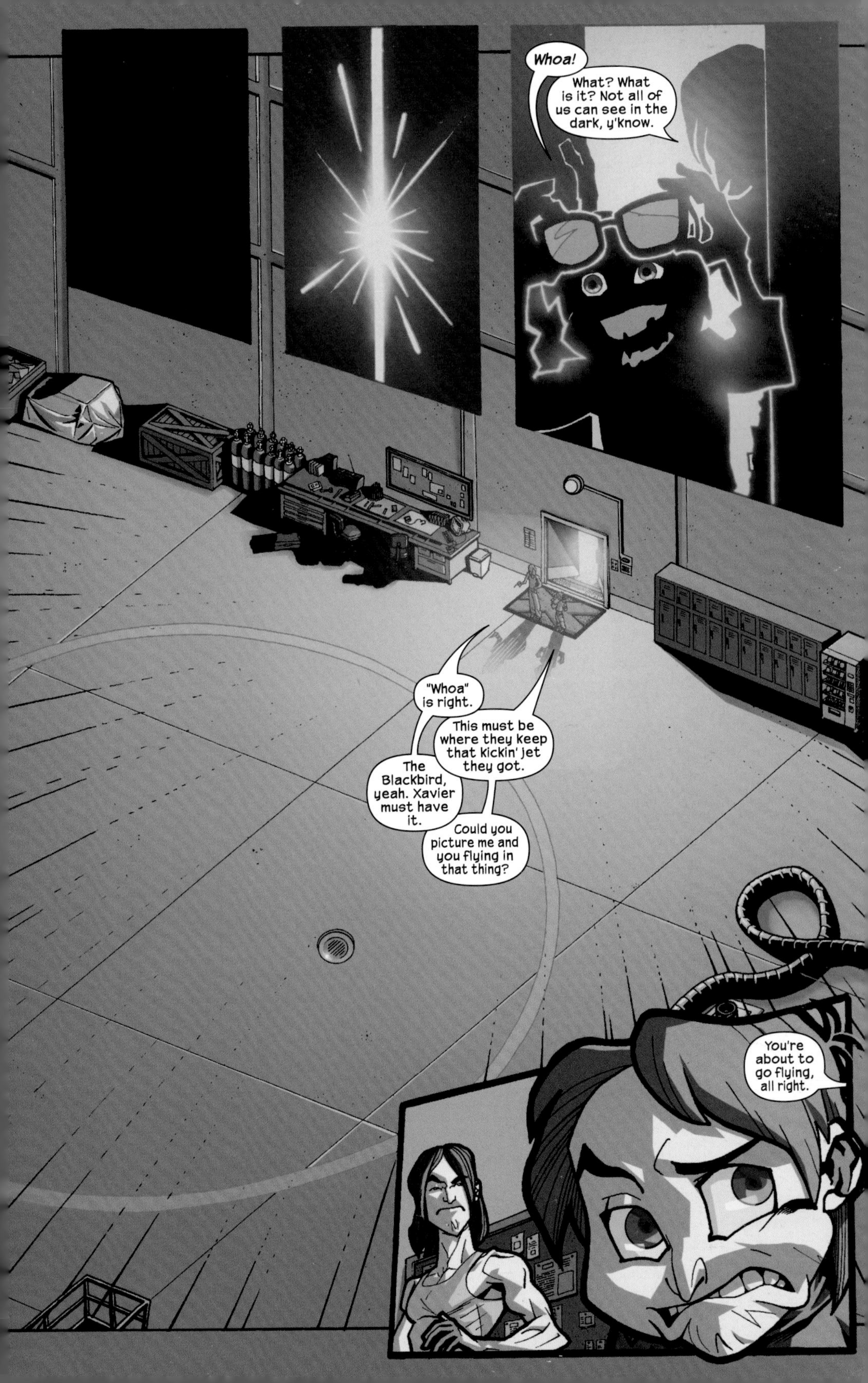
Whoa!
What? What is it? Not all of us can see in the dark, y'know.
"Whoa" is right.
This must be where they keep that kickin' jet they got.
The Blackbird, yeah. Xavier must have it.
Could you picture me and you flying in that thing?
You're about to go flying, all right.

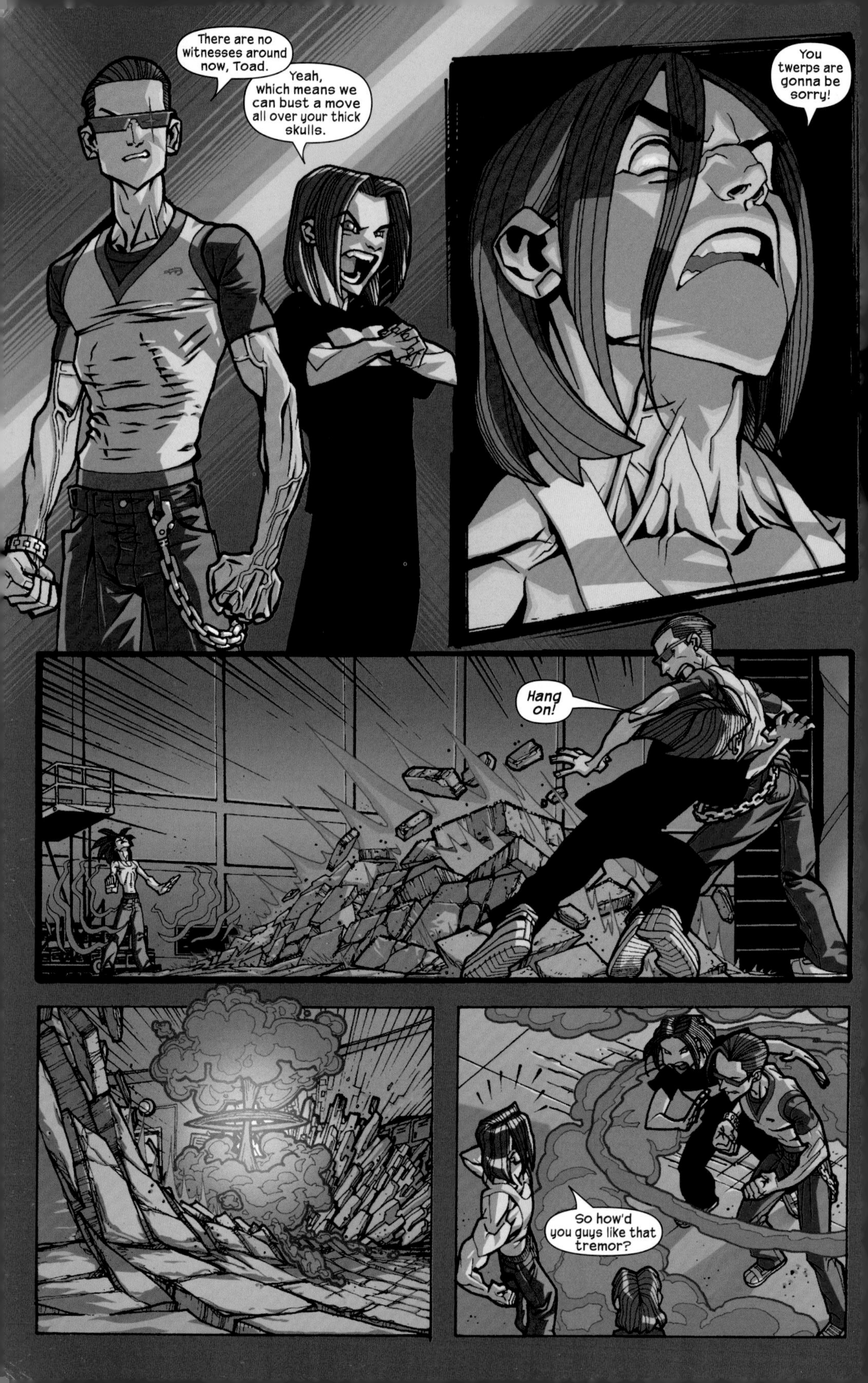
There are no witnesses around now, Toad.
Yeah, which means we can bust a move all over your thick skulls.
You twerps are gonna be sorry!
Hang on!
So how'd you guys like that tremor?

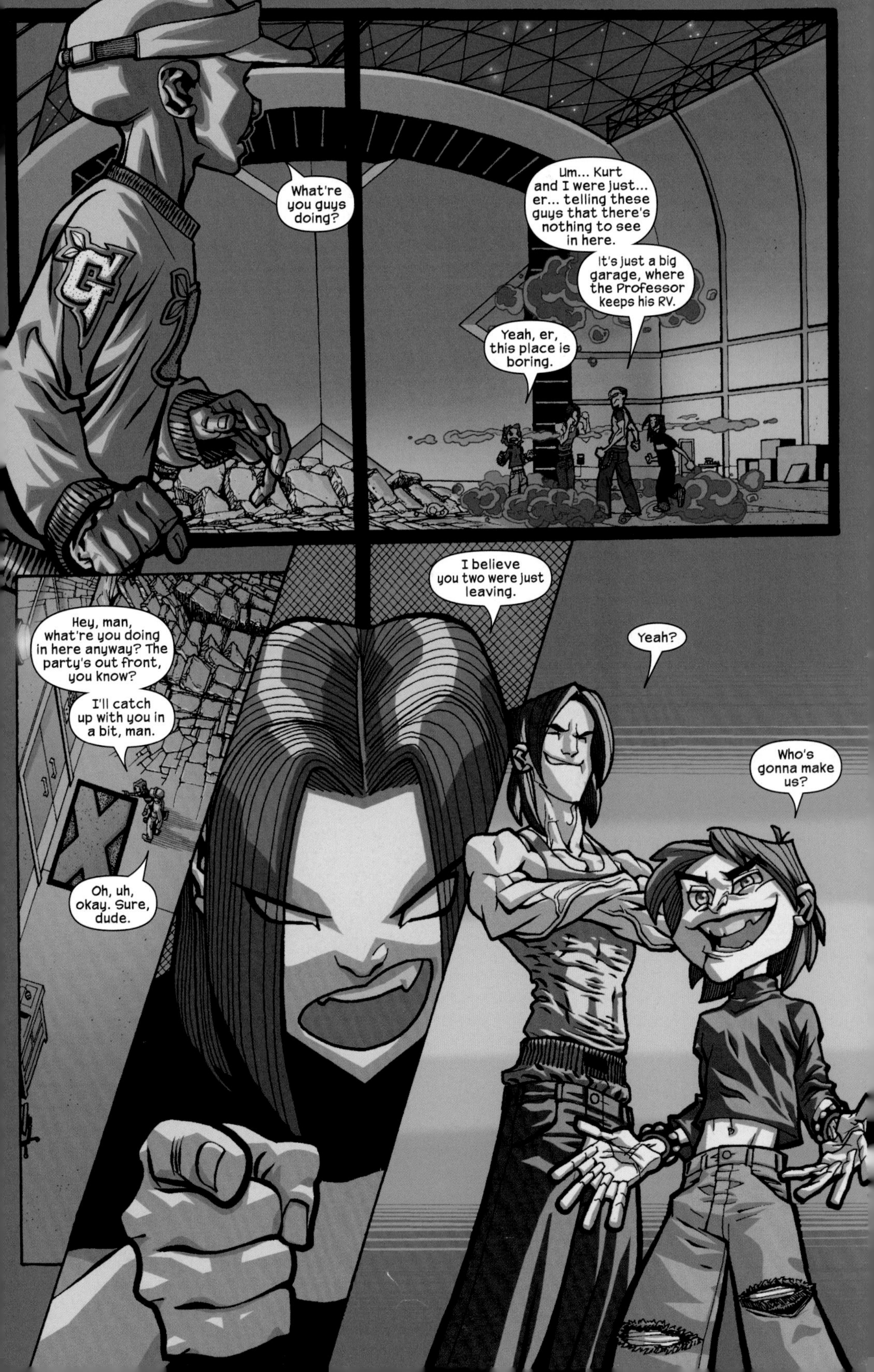
What're you guys doing?
Um... Kurt and I were just... er... telling these guys that there's nothing to see in here.
It's just a big garage, where the Professor keeps his RV.
Yeah, er, this place is boring.
I believe you two were just leaving.
Hey, man, what're you doing in here anyway? The party's out front, you know?
I'll catch up with you in a bit, man.
Oh, uh, okay. Sure, dude.
Yeah?
Who's gonna make us?

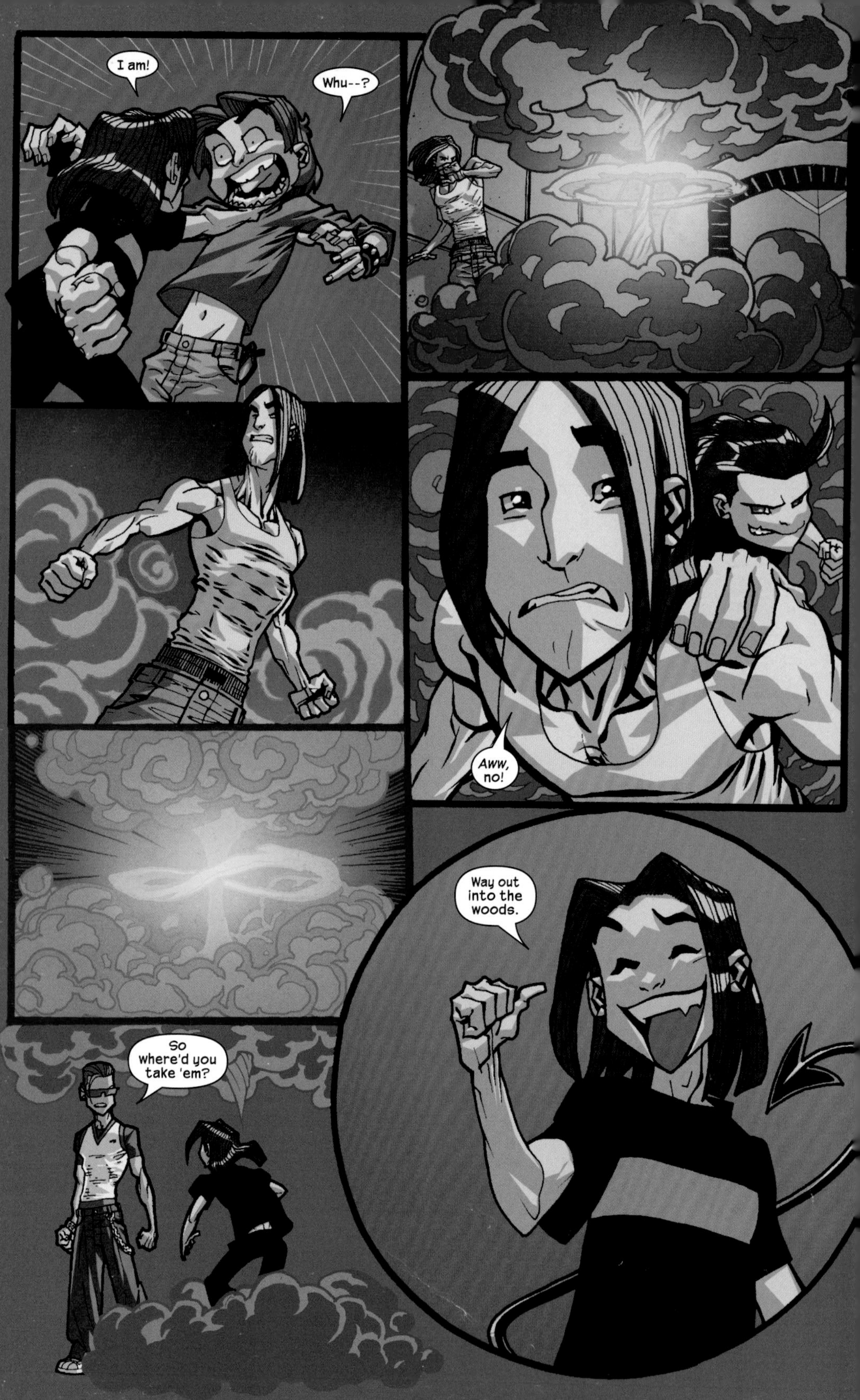
I am!
Whu--?
Aww, no!
So where'd you take 'em?
Way out into the woods.

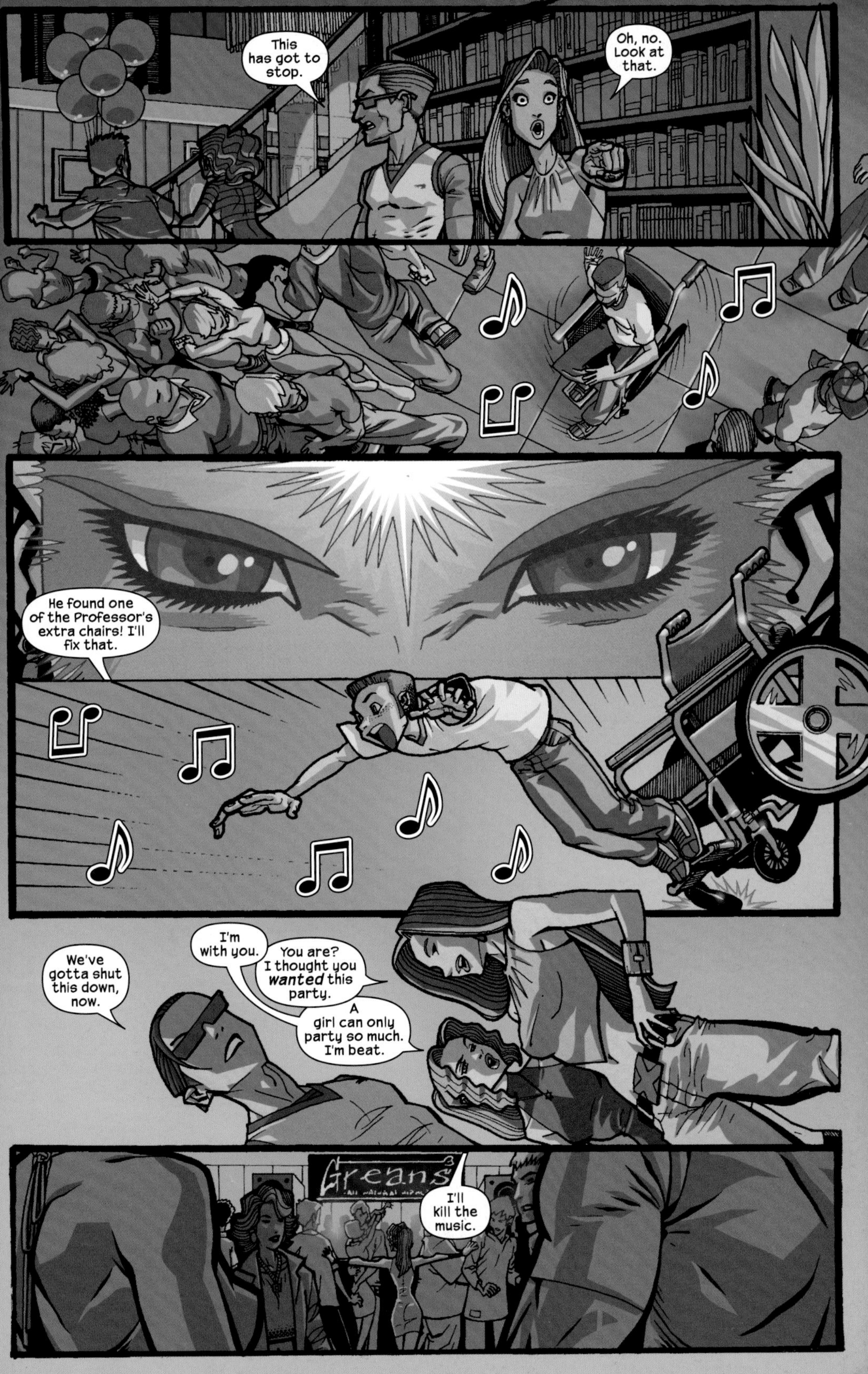

This has got to stop.
Oh, no. Look at that.
He found one of the Professor's extra chairs! I'll fix that.
We've gotta shut this down, now.
I'm with you.
You are? I thought you *wanted* this party.
A girl can only party so much. I'm beat.
Greans
I'll kill the music.

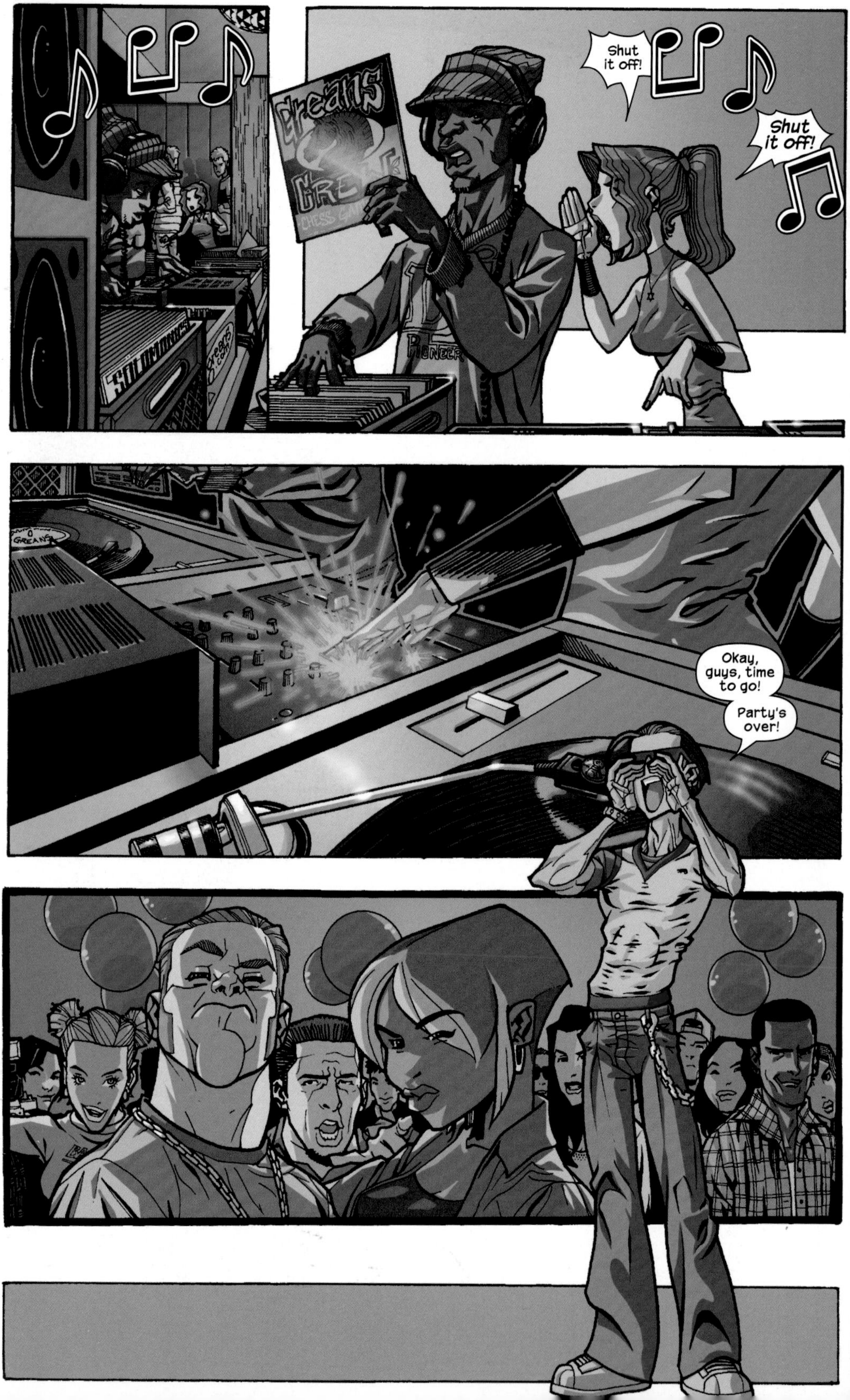
Shut it off!
Shut it off!
Okay, guys, time to go!
Party's over!

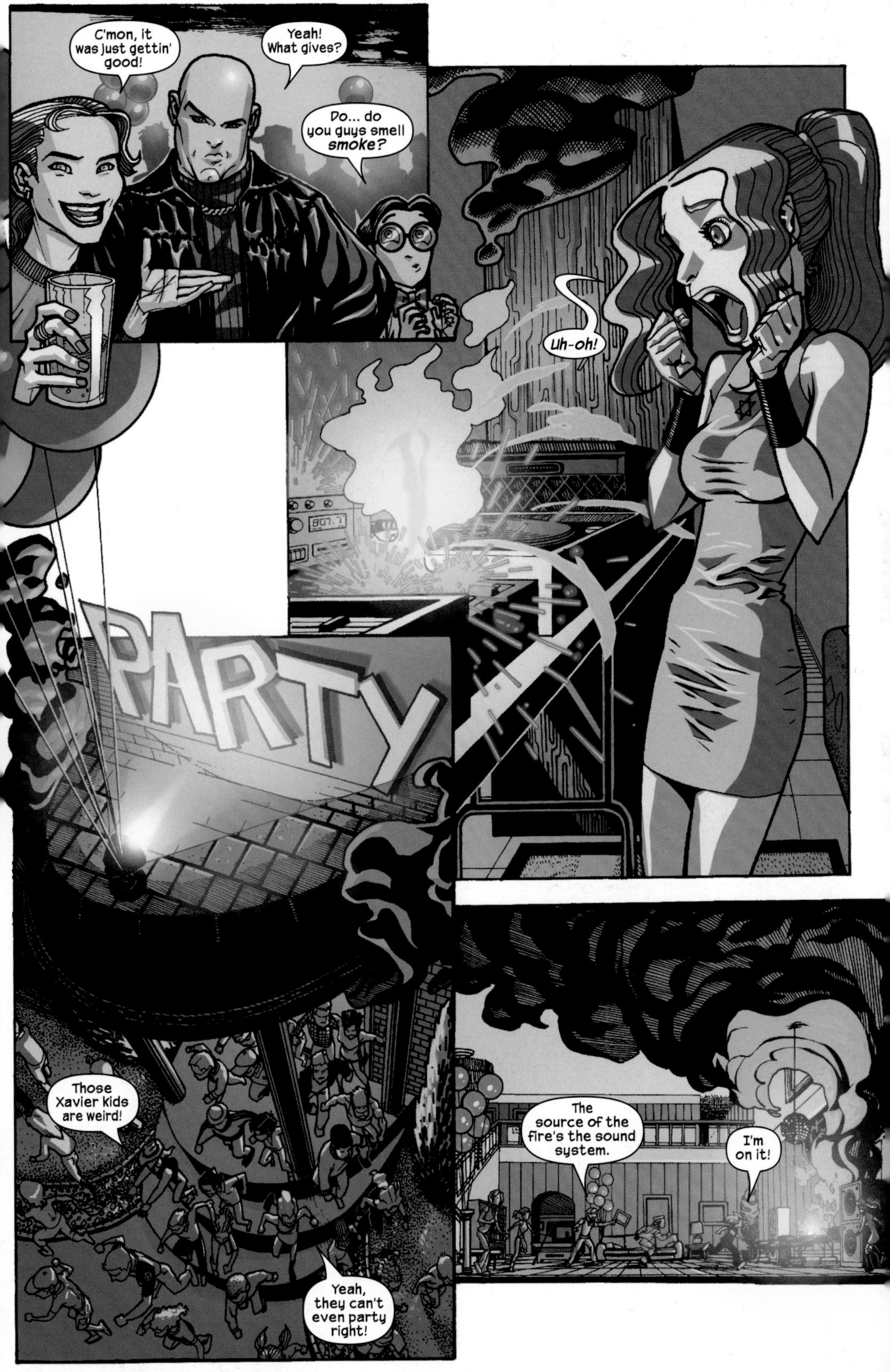
C'mon, it was just gettin' good!
Yeah! What gives?
Do... do you guys smell smoke?
Uh-oh!
PARTY
Those Xavier kids are weird!
Yeah, they can't even party right!
The source of the fire's the sound system.
I'm on it!

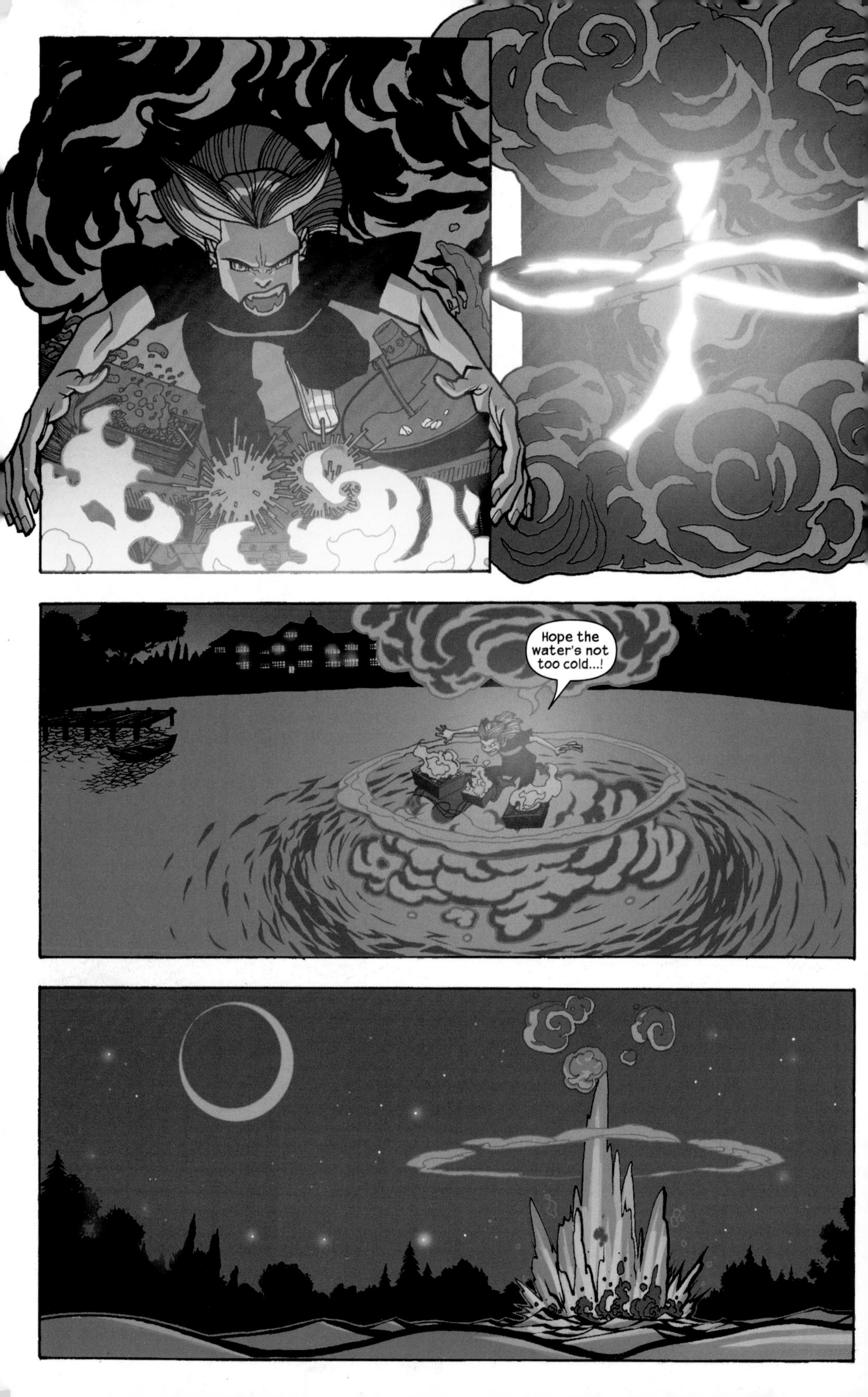
Hope the water's not too cold...!

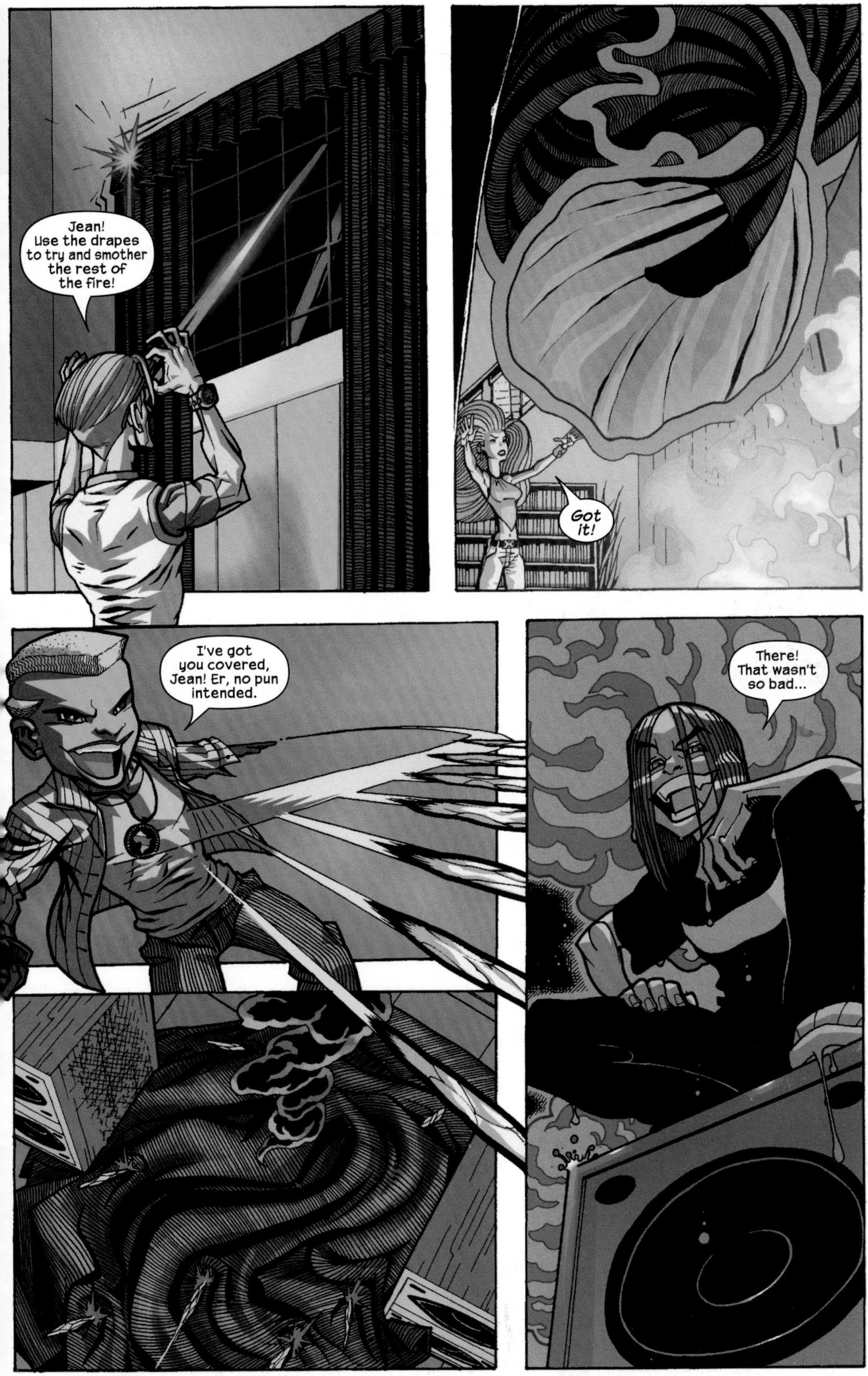
Jean! Use the drapes to try and smother the rest of the fire!
Got it!
I've got you covered, Jean! Er, no pun intended.
There! That wasn't so bad...

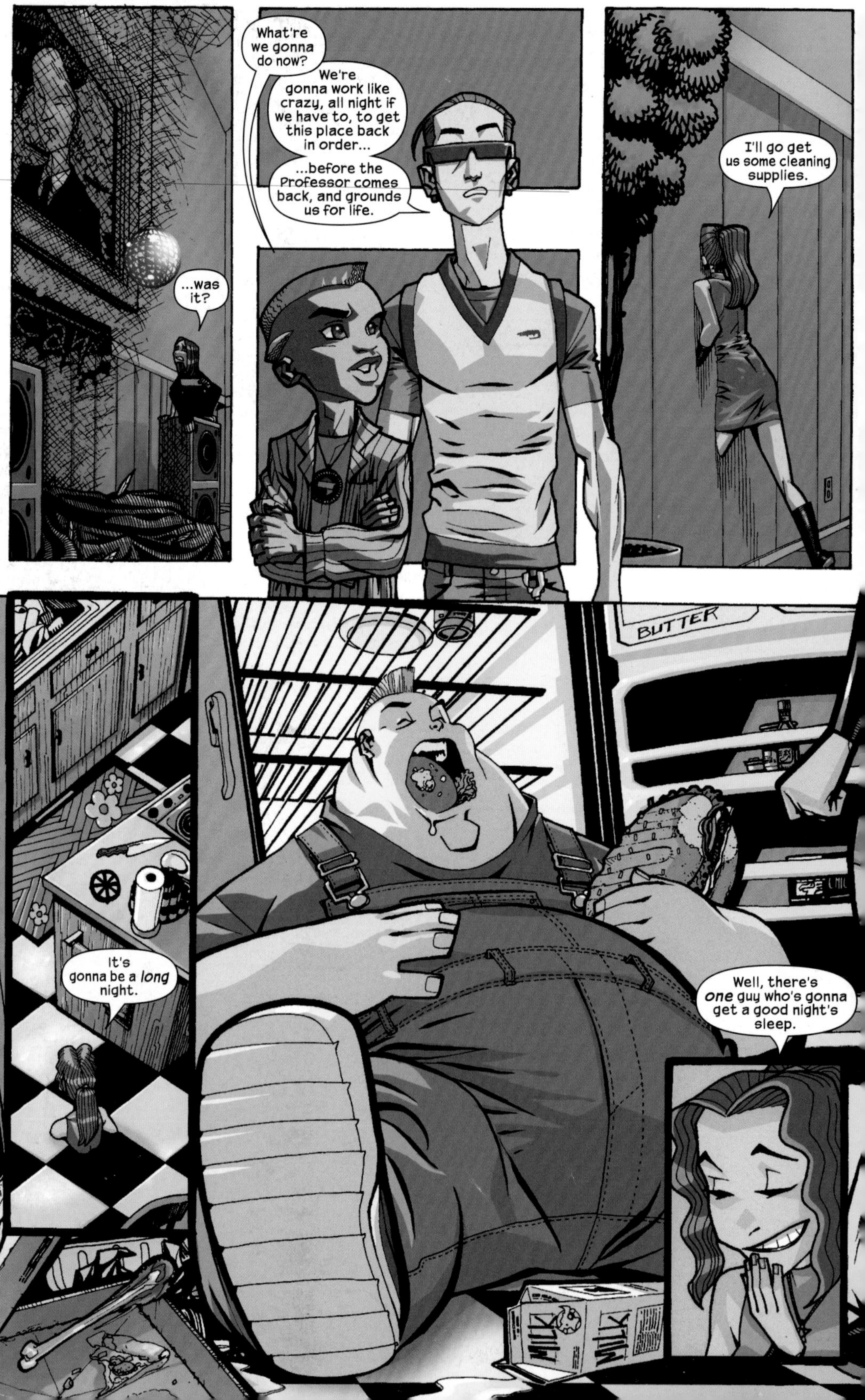
...was it?
What're we gonna do now?
We're gonna work like crazy, all night if we have to, to get this place back in order...
...before the Professor comes back, and grounds us for life.
I'll go get us some cleaning supplies.
BUTTER
It's gonna be a *long* night.
Well, there's *one* guy who's gonna get a good night's sleep.
MILK
MILK

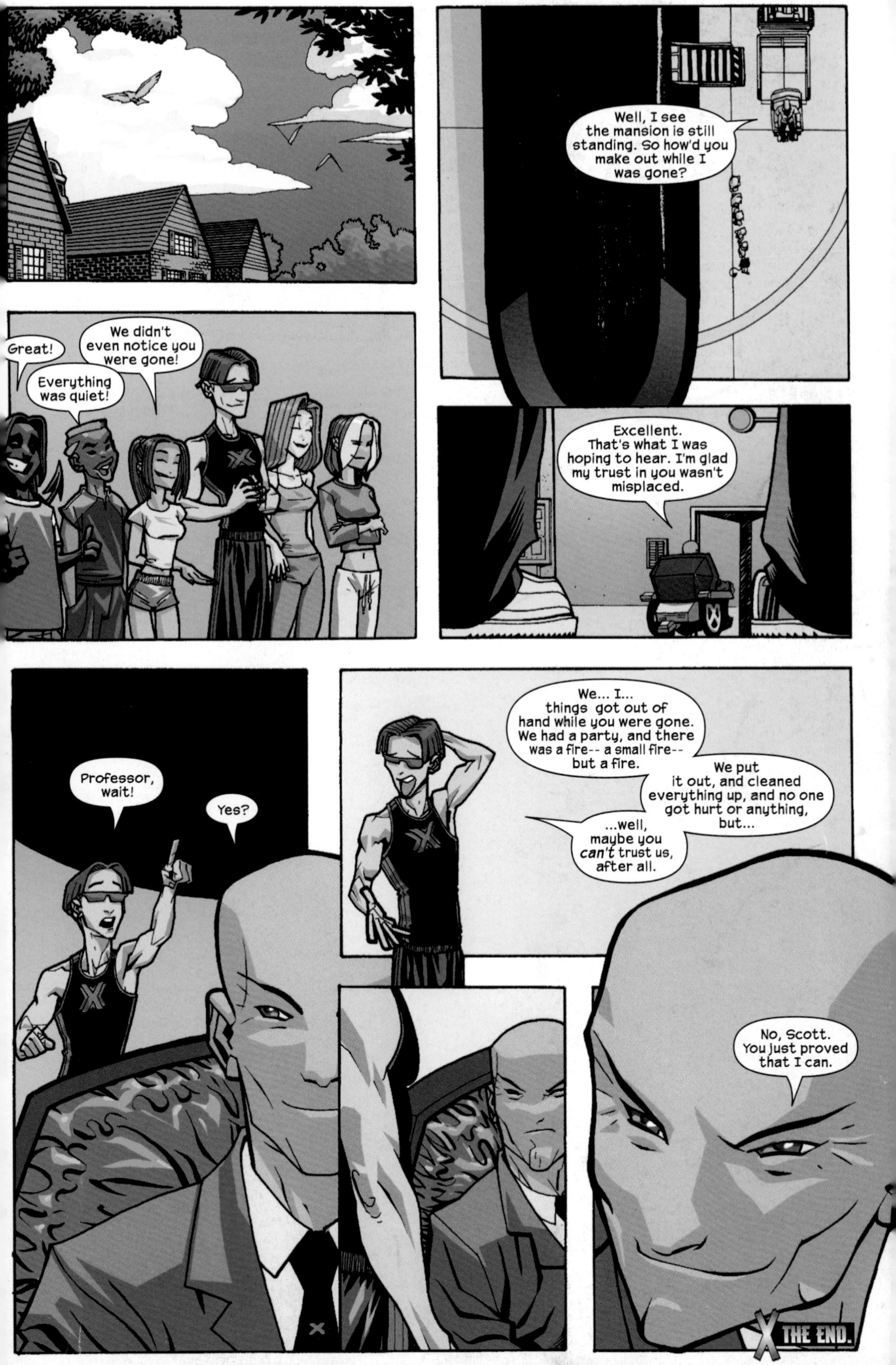
Well, I see the mansion is still standing. So how'd you make out while I was gone?
Great!
We didn't even notice you were gone!
Everything was quiet!
Excellent. That's what I was hoping to hear. I'm glad my trust in you wasn't misplaced.
Professor, wait!
Yes?
We... I... things got out of hand while you were gone. We had a party, and there was a fire-- a small fire-- but a fire.
We put it out, and cleaned everything up, and no one got hurt or anything, but...
...well, maybe you *can't* trust us, after all.
No, Scott. You just proved that I can.
THE END.